The Choir Director

Books by Carl Weber

Torn Between Two Lovers

Big Girls Do Cry

Up to No Good

Something on the Side

The First Lady

So You Call Yourself a Man

The Preacher's Son

Player Haters

Lookin' for Luv

Married Men

Baby Momma Drama

She Ain't the One (with Mary B. Morrison)

The Choir Director

CARL WEBER

KENSINGTON PUBLISHING CORP.

http://www.kensingtonbooks.com

DAFINA BOOKS are published by

Kensington Publishing Corp.
119 West 40th Street
New York, NY 10018

All Kensington titles, imprints and distributed lines are available at special quantity discounts for bulk purchases for sales promotion, premiums, fund-raising, educational or institutional use.

Special book excerpts or customized printings can also be created to fit specific needs. For details, write or phone the office of the Kensington Special Sales Manager: Kensington Publishing Corp., 119 West 40th Street, New York, NY 10018. Attn.: Special Sales Department. Phone: 1-800-221-2647.

Dafina and the Dafina logo Reg. U.S. Pat. & TM Off.

Library of Congress Control Number: 2010939173
ISBN-13: 978-0-7582-3185-7
ISBN-10: 0-7582-3185-7

First Hardcover Printing: February 2011
First Trade Paperback Printing: January 2012
10 9 8 7 6 5 4 3 2 1

Printed in the United States of America

This book is dedicated to my readers: Rebecca Reed, Simone Young, Lynette Robinson, Latonya Townes, Ms. Ruth, Renee Warner, Maxine Thompson, and Joylynn, the people who gave me feedback during the writing process and quite possibly have made this the best book I've ever written.

Prologue

It was Father's Day at First Jamaica Ministries, the largest church in Queens, New York, and the pews were filled to capacity with those honoring the men in their lives. Bishop T. K. Wilson, the pastor of the church, was in top form as he pranced around the pulpit, preaching on what it truly means to be a father and a man in this upside-down world of ours. His sermon was so powerful and his words so inspiring that he brought grown men to tears and had some of the more animated women jumping out of their seats and fainting in the aisles. He touched on the responsibilities of being a husband and a father. What made his sermon so special was that he tied it all into the word of God so well that even the children had no problem understanding it.

When he finished his sermon, everyone in the building felt enlightened, but the celebration was far from over because when the bishop sat down, the choir stood up and the collection plate went around. Halfway through the first song, everyone in the church was on their feet, singing, clapping, and paying tithes.

"Hallelujah!" the bishop said as the choir finished their third selection and sat down. "Wasn't that wonderful? Praise God! Thank you, Jesus. There is nothing like having a good song with the Word. Can the church say amen?"

"Amen!" the congregation shouted back in unison.

"Now, as most of you know from my sermon, today is Father's Day, the day we're supposed to honor our fathers and husbands." He held on to the microphone as he paced from one end of the pulpit to the other. "I know some of you are ready to go home and barbecue with Dad, maybe go to the beach with him, maybe even just sit in front of the TV and watch the game with him, but before you leave, there is one order of business that we have to take care of."

Bishop Wilson returned to the center of the pulpit and placed the microphone back in its holder, then reached under the podium and removed a large plaque. "You see, every year on Father's Day, we give out a Man of the Year Award and a scholarship in the recipient's name. This year, though, I think the committee's outdone themselves with their choice of Man of the Year, and in my opinion, this year's award is way overdue. Not just because I consider the recipient a personal friend, and not just because he's an outstanding father and husband, but also because of all the hours he's spent on making your choir one of the best in the entire country."

As the bishop turned to the choir, the entire congregation rose to their feet in anticipation of his announcement. "Now, ladies and gentlemen, brothers and sisters, it is my absolute honor to announce that the winner of the First Jamaica Ministries Man of the Year Award is our choir director, Mr. Jackie Robinson Moss!"

The crowd erupted in cheers and applause when Jackie, a tall, handsome, olive-skinned man with green eyes, stepped from in front of the choir and approached the pulpit, where the bishop awaited him with the plaque.

Bishop Wilson shook Jackie's hand, then gave him the award. He was about to relinquish the podium to the Man of the Year when he heard a woman shout, "Bishop! Bishop! I'd like to say a few words, if you don't mind."

The bishop smiled his approval when he saw the woman. "Sure. We'd be glad to hear a few words from you, Deaconess Moss. I mean, after all, who knows Jackie better than his wife?"

There was another round of applause as she got up from her seat in the deacon's row and slowly made her way to the pulpit. She was a good-looking, brown-skinned woman in her mid-forties and had been married to Jackie, her college sweetheart, for almost twenty years. Approaching the pulpit, she shook the bishop's hand before stepping up to the podium and adjusting the microphone.

"Hello. As you know, my name is Deaconess Eleanor Moss, and you've bestowed the honor of Man of the Year on my husband." She turned to give Jackie a look of contempt, then turned back to the crowd to deliver totally unexpected words. "I'm sorry to say it, but you have made a grave mistake in giving him this award. Unfortunately, my husband is not the man you think he is. And he is definitely not the man I thought he was. Not anywhere close to it."

Members of the congregation started squirming in their seats. Some were reacting to the uncomfortable awkwardness of the situation, while others were eagerly anticipating some juicy drama getting ready to take place.

Realizing that things weren't going exactly as planned, Bishop Wilson turned to Jackie and mouthed, "What is she talking about?"

Jackie shrugged his shoulders, looking dumbfounded. It was obvious he was as clueless as everyone else about his wife's strange behavior. The two men stood by helplessly as she continued the speech that would destroy all the good feelings Bishop Wilson had created with his Father's Day sermon.

"I know this is going to be hard for many of you to believe, but trust me, it was even harder for me. I've been married to this man for twenty years." She took a breath and straightened her back, as if what she was about to say required all of her strength. Then she delivered the final blow. "But I think you should all know my husband is a homosexual."

It was as if her words sucked all the air out of the room. The entire church went silent, except for one woman who shouted, "Shut up!" sarcastically.

At this time, Eleanor's two best friends, Lisa Mae and Kathy, began handing out quarter-inch–thick xeroxed pamphlets down each row, beginning in the back of the church.

"If you look at the pamphlets the sisters are handing out," Eleanor continued, "you will see copies of my husband's journal, which I found hidden in the ceiling panels of our basement, along with some pretty filthy Polaroids. I'm sorry I could not furnish originals, but I need them for my divorce. The highlighted entries show affairs Jackie has had with different male members of our choir and congregation. You will see names, dates, times, personal comments in some cases, and even pre-ferred activities. I know some of you will be upset by this, but I honestly believe it's better to know now rather than later. I my-self am about to get an AIDS test."

Her business complete, she turned around, walked up to her husband, and slapped him across the face as hard as she could before she walked out of the church.

The congregants, who had now all received copies of the pamphlet, were furiously paging through them. As the sound of rustling pages and confused whispers filled the sanctuary, Bishop Wilson stood, slack-jawed, staring at the man who had been his choir director for seven years. He'd heard rumors over the years about Jackie but he figured those spreading the gossip were just jealous and catering to the stereotype of a gay choir director. Never once did he think the rumors might actually be accurate.

Now he had to ask the question: "My God, man, is this true?"

Jackie didn't answer. He simply turned toward the door by the side of the pulpit. Bishop Wilson followed his gaze and watched four male choir members sneaking out of their seats, headed toward an exit. Two of them were active members of the church, proud family men. If someone had told the bishop that these men were involved in homosexual affairs, he would have placed wagers against it; yet, here they were, their escape practi-cally an admission of guilt.

An abrupt scream startled him, and he turned to the pews to see a physical altercation erupt between a deacon and his wife. He ran to break things up, wondering just how much chaos this incident had introduced into his church.

The Bishop

1

I stepped off the elevator and onto the third-floor oncology unit of Columbia Presbyterian Hospital, holding the hand of my wife, Monique. We were accompanied by my good friend of more than twenty years, Deacon Maxwell Frye. As we walked down the hall, I recognized the pungent odor of medical disinfectant. It didn't matter what hospital I visited; the smell was always the same, and it seemed to embed itself in my nostrils. I hated it because it always reminded me of the imminent deaths of the people in the rooms around me. Oh, I'd learned to tolerate it over the years, especially since visiting people in their last days was part of being the pastor of First Jamaica Ministries, but today's visit wasn't just to any old parishioner on his deathbed. No, today's visit was much closer to home and way more personal for me and Deacon Frye. We were here to see our very dear friend James Black, who was dying of lung cancer.

"T. K., Monique, get your behinds in here," James coughed out when he saw us standing in the entrance to his room. He hadn't seen Deacon Frye yet. Despite his condition, it was obvious he was glad to see us.

As we entered the room, Monique's grip tightened around my hand. I could tell she was struggling to conceal her shock at just how bad James looked. I had tried to prepare my wife before we arrived, but words couldn't describe how much he had deteriorated.

This was the first time Monique had seen him since he'd pled guilty to murder charges a little over a year ago. I still couldn't believe he'd willingly gone to jail for a crime he didn't commit, but I guess some parents will go to any lengths to protect their children. Can't say whether I would have done the same, but I was glad I had never been put into that position. He'd been given a twenty-year sentence, but I pulled some strings after a recent visit when I heard his prognosis, and he was released for medical reasons. Cancer had taken a vibrant, six-foot-tall, two-hundred-pound man and turned him into a talking skeleton. Even more unbelievable was the fact that his hair was completely white. He seemed to have aged twenty years in less than a year's time.

It didn't take my wife long to gather her composure. In a matter of seconds, she leaned in and wrapped her arms around James to give him a kiss on the cheek. She shot me a pointed look when she spotted a picture of his two grown children sitting on the night table beside his bed. Monique hated the idea that his daughter and son were both missing in action and hadn't come to see their father once since his arrest. I didn't fault her for feeling that way, but I knew a little more about the situation than she did. I'd made a promise to James not to share what I knew, even with her.

"James, I've got a surprise visitor for you." I gestured toward the door and watched as a grin broke out across James's face.

"Wait, don't tell me, T. K. You finally pulled it off. You got Holly Robinson-Peete to divorce her husband and become my personal nurse until the Lord takes me home."

"Holly Robinson? Have you lost your mind? Here you are supposedly on your deathbed and the woman you want to spend your last days with is Holly Robinson-Peete? You couldn't set the bar any higher than that? I mean, come on, James. If you're going to fantasize about a woman, you need to go all out and do it with a bang!" Maxwell joked as he appeared in the doorway. He and James had always been like that.

"Well, I'll be damned. Maxwell Frye, how the hell are you?" James smiled from ear to ear. "I'll be honest, brother. I didn't think I'd see you again in this lifetime. How long you back for?"

Deacon Frye had been in Iraq for almost five years. His company, Maxwell Enterprises, was a minority contractor for the government and was doing infrastructure work in Iraq. One of the stipulations in the contract was that he oversee things personally. He'd been back stateside only a few times briefly since.

Maxwell walked around to the far side of James's bed and gave him a hug. "I'm back for good. I was having some heart problems, and they had to fix me up with a pacemaker. Sorry I'm just getting around to seeing you, but I'm only now starting to get readjusted. Things have really changed around here." He glanced over at me and my wife. We had not been married when Maxwell left for Iraq. Like many other church members, Maxwell was surprised by my decision to marry Monique.

"Change . . . don't I know it," James said. "It's good to see you, Maxwell. The Wilsons over there are gonna need your help keeping these church folks in line."

"Well, you know I'll do whatever I can, James."

"I know you will. I feel better about things already."

James turned to my wife as Maxwell took a seat in the chair on the other side of his bed. "So, Monique, how are you? You're looking good as ever." He looked at me and winked. "No offense, old friend, but your wife just gets finer and you just keep getting older."

"I know that's right," Maxwell added.

"None taken." I chuckled. "I think she looks pretty good myself. That's why I married her, remember? And as far as getting old, well, I'm like a bottle of wine: I get better with time."

"Mmph, you sure do, honey." Monique gave me a smile, then turned her attention back to James. "To answer your question, I'm doing fine. What about you? How you doing? You look good."

James laughed. "Girl, I swear, you have fit right into that first lady's role, haven't you?"

I watched my beautiful wife blush.

James spoke gently to her. "Now, I know I look like crap, so you don't have to lie to me, Mo." He sighed. "I know my best days are behind me. I made my peace with that a long time ago. I'm ready to die."

"Who said anything about you dying? You're probably going to outlive us all, you old coot." I was trying to break up the mood in a way only a true friend could do.

"If I do live that long, it's only to be a pain in your ass, T. K." he joked, forcing himself to sit up. My wife helped him by propping a pillow behind his neck. "But seriously, I'm tired and I'm ready to go home. I just hope the Lord's willing to let me in the door."

I hated to hear him say things like that, so I tried to offer him some encouragement. "I don't think you have to worry about that, James. I think you've sacrificed enough, don't you? The Lord—"

James shot me a glance that basically said, "Let's not go there."

I nodded my head out of respect for his condition and his feelings, but that didn't mean I had to like it. That man had sacrificed his entire life for the love of his family, and he had been willing to die in a jail cell because of it.

James quickly changed the subject. "So, Mo, how about him? He taking care of you the way he's supposed to?"

She reached out to take my hand as she answered. "I couldn't have asked for a better man. I couldn't have asked for a better life."

"That's what I like to hear." James nodded his approval. "Are those wenches in the church treating you all right? They're not trying to run over you, are they? 'Cause all you have to do is kick one of them in the ass and the rest will fall right in line," he said with a laugh.

"Oh, you don't have to worry about that. I've got them right where I want them." Monique and I had had a rocky start to our relationship, because certain members of the church—mostly female—thought her rumored past was too dicey for her to be considered a candidate for the role of first lady after my first wife died. She was strong, though, and had withstood the storm. Now she was well respected and loved by most church members. Even those who had been adamantly against our marriage knew enough to treat her cordially now and kept their opinions to themselves.

"Besides," she continued, "we have bigger problems than that at the church. With—" She stopped when I squeezed her hand, signaling for her to shut up, but it was too late. James's body might have been failing him, but his mind was still sharp as ever.

He sat up straight as a board, ignoring the pain. There were three things James loved most in this world: his two children and our church. He knew the ins and outs of church politics like nobody's business. He'd been both a deacon and a member of the board of trustees just as long as I'd been pastor, and we made quite a formidable team. But now, with him being sick, I didn't have the heart to tell him that what we had built together over the years was slowly crumbling.

"What's going on at the church, T. K.?" He was staring directly at me, and his eyes did not budge from my face.

"It's nothing, James, seriously. I can handle it." I glanced over at my wife, who was trying to apologize with her eyes. I loved her to death, but just this once I wished she had kept her big mouth shut.

When I turned back to James, he was still staring at me, waiting for an answer.

"What, do I look stupid? If it was nothing, you would have told me by now. Now spill it. I wanna know what's going on at my church."

My church. He was still claiming ownership in our church, even though most of our members had turned their backs on him when he was arrested for murder. If they only knew how selfless he really was.

He looked at Maxwell. "What do you know about this, Deacon Frye?"

"I've been trying to—"

I cut off Maxwell before he could put himself in a bad position. "He knows what I told him and nothing more."

"So tell me what you know, T. K.," James demanded.

I began to pace back and forth in front of his bed. "James, you've got other things to worry about. You don't need this nonsense. You need to concentrate on your health."

"Dammit, T. K., my health ain't worth a damn right now. Face it—I'm dying. The only thing I got left is that church. Now, are you going to tell me what's going on, or do I have to make some calls and find out myself?"

"Tell him, honey," Monique prodded. "You two have always worked well together. Maybe he can come up with an idea to help."

"Thank you, Mo," James said matter-of-factly.

I continued pacing for a short while before I finally sat down next to my wife and looked at my friend, ready to tell him the truth. "The church is in trouble financially. We're down about thirty-five percent in attendance and almost forty-two percent in revenue. The board's thinking about closing down the school next year if things don't get better, and that's just the beginning."

"What?" His body tensed up angrily. "I built that school. We had plenty of money put aside in the school fund before I went to prison."

"Priorities changed when you were arrested. The country went into recession. People aren't giving as much as they used to. The rates on our adjustable mortgages have reset much higher than anyone expected. I tried to keep things simple, but Simone Wilcox was voted chairwoman of the board of trustees, and last year she pushed to have money directed to the building of new senior housing. We've got a lot of working capital tied up in that project."

I could see James running the numbers through his head. He'd always been good with figures, which was why he'd been elected chairman of the board of trustees despite his reputation as a womanizer.

"You gotta be kidding me. We can't afford to be building at a time like this. What's that heifer Wilcox trying to do, bankrupt the church? Why the hell you let them elect that woman head of my board, I don't know. She's not her father, T. K. Simone Wilcox ain't out for anyone but herself. The woman's a diva with an agenda. Trust me, she's always got something up her sleeve."

"You of all people would know, James," Maxwell joked, taking a jab at the fact that James used to sleep with Simone.

"Don't get smart, Maxwell. That was a long time ago."

"Not to her," my wife commented. "But in her defense, James, she's got an MBA, and she runs one of the largest car dealerships in the area."

"Oh, give me a break. That's only because her daddy retired and didn't have any sons to leave it to. She could never have built a dealership like Wilcox Motors by herself. I bet you half her staff has already left. I'm surprised it's still standing." James shook his head. "I know she's your friend, Mo, but Simone's best asset is between her legs. I could tell you some stories."

"That's chauvinistic, James. You're just hating on her because she's a successful woman," Monique snapped.

"No, that's just realistic. There are plenty of women who could have done a good job as chairwoman. Simone's just not one of them."

"Like who?"

I glanced over at Maxwell, shaking my head. My wife had just opened up a can of worms she might not be able to close.

"Did you guys take Lisa Mae into consideration?"

Monique scrunched her face like there was a bad odor in the room at the mention of Lisa Mae, a one-time rival for my affection. "No, we did not consider *that woman,*" Monique told him. She didn't know I knew it, but she'd secretly campaigned to make sure Lisa Mae never had a shot at the chairmanship. "However, Simone couldn't have been but so incompetent. Things were going pretty well until attendance dropped."

James was clearly frustrated by this news. "Answer me this: Why'd attendance drop? Something must have pissed everybody off. What, did Simone start charging a fee at the door for people to get in? People don't just stop going to church en masse."

"They do when the choir director's trying to sleep with their husbands and sons." Monique was trying to hold back a laugh. The situation definitely wasn't funny, but just like plenty of other people, my wife had a weakness for gossip.

James looked at me with a frown. "Oh Lord, it was Jackie, wasn't it?"

I nodded.

"Well, I guess he wasn't as harmless as you thought. I told you we needed to get rid of that SOB years ago, T. K."

Clearly, James had been much better than I at judging the truth. I'd wanted to dismiss it as rumors. James had always predicted Jackie would cause trouble, and he had been painfully correct.

"Yeah, you did." There was nothing I hated more than listening to one of James's I-told-you-so rants. "I just wish I had listened to you. That man's wife has got the whole congregation in an uproar."

"What's she doing?"

"She found his journal. Turns out all those rumors were true, and he recorded every sordid detail in that diary," I admitted. "She didn't waste any time spreading the news either. Over a third of the men in the choir found themselves in that journal in some capacity or another, and the other two-thirds were considered guilty by association."

I felt badly for Jackie's wife, and part of me could understand why she reacted the way she did. You can imagine how devastating the discovery must have been for her, and, well, misery does love company. Unfortunately, her coping method left me with a huge problem on my hands. Word spread quickly, and within two weeks, the entire choir disbanded, even though Jackie had already been fired and was no longer attending the church. My wife and I had been trying to put it back together to no avail. I never knew how hard a choir director's job was until then.

"Now we've got no choir," I said as I finished summing up the turmoil we'd been struggling with. "Now, I'm a heck of a preacher if I do say so myself, James, but nothing goes better with the Word than music. Our choir has always been a cornerstone of our church. Putting my ego aside, wasn't it you who once told me that half the people in the pews on Sunday were there to hear the choir and not me?"

He chuckled. "Yeah, I guess I did say that, didn't I?"

"Well, from where I'm sitting, you're sounding more and more like a prophet."

"Man, I can't believe something like this could take down the church," Maxwell added.

"Neither can I. Plus, when you add that to the financial troubles we're having, it's like the perfect storm. To be honest, I don't know what we're gonna do. We've got a huge balloon payment on one of the church's mortgages next year."

"You're right. Only thing that's gonna save us is getting people back in the church. What about Savannah Dickens? Maybe we can get her to help," he suggested. At one time, Savannah Dickens's voice could light a fire in the soul of even the greatest heathen. But like so many other things, that had changed too. She left the church to start a career singing pop music. It looked like she was going to make it, too, until she got hooked on drugs. She fell hard and she fell fast, and no one in the church had seen or heard from her since.

"Already thought of that, James, but it looks like Sister Savannah has lost her way to drugs. She's not even a member of our church anymore."

"I know what we have to do, honey," Monique interrupted. "We have to hire a choir director. But not just any old choir director. We need someone young, someone so talented and so charismatic that he can put together a choir that will blow the roof off the church. This choir has to be so good that everyone in the borough of Queens will be fighting for a good seat in the pews just to hear them sing."

"I understand what you're saying, baby, but do you have anyone in mind? 'Cause I don't know anybody like that."

James snapped his fingers. "I do!" His sunken features suddenly looked a little brighter. "T. K., do you remember last year before I got locked up when we went to visit Reverend Simmons's church in Jarratt, Virginia?"

"Mmm-hmm. What about it?"

"Do you remember his choir? There was only about ten of them, but they were some kind of good."

"Yeah," I said with excitement. "I remember. They had that young kid leading them with all the Kirk Franklin moves and the BeBe Winans voice. What was his name?"

We sat quietly for a moment, both of us trying to remember. James finally recalled it. "Aaron," he announced with a smile. "His name was Aaron Mackie. And he's exactly what we need." He folded his arms. "He's the total package, T. K. He's got looks, charisma, and sex appeal in a church kind of way. There's no doubt in my mind the boy could save our church."

"Well, then, I guess I'm gonna have to go down to Virginia and have a talk with Mr. Aaron Mackie."

Aaron

2

"Yes! Yes! That's it, Aaron! Make me sing, baby! Make me sing!" Sandra pleaded, but I paid her no mind. I didn't even understand why she'd brought up singing at a time like this. This wasn't choir practice, and even if it was, singing wasn't her strong suit at all. So, no, I wasn't trying to make her sing. I was trying to make her come, which is why I had her bent over my kitchen table, pumping my Johnson into her like I was drilling for oil. Nope, I didn't want her to sing, but a few loud moans and groans would have been nice, and after a few more healthy thrusts, that's exactly what I got.

"Oooohhhhh, Lord have mercy!" she finally screamed, making my own excitement that much more intense. A few strokes later, I did a little moaning of my own as I exploded and then collapsed on top of her, drained but satisfied. I had to give her credit—she might not have been able to sing, but Sandra sure knew how to please a man. I'd never been with a woman who made me feel that good on the very first time. Then again, she was full of surprises today, the first one being that she broke into my house after church, and the second one being that she was waiting for me on my sofa wearing nothing but her Sunday hat.

I have no idea how long I lay on top of her, but I could have stayed there all afternoon if it weren't for a loud knock on my front door. I reluctantly lifted myself off of her and the table.

Sandra reached back, trying to stop me from exiting her. "You're not going to answer that, are you?" She sounded offended.

"Nah, I'm just gonna peek out the window to see who it is.

Then we can continue our activities in the bedroom. I know I must have been getting a little heavy lying on you like that, and that hard table's got to be uncomfortable."

She gave me a smile as she slid off the table. "No, you and it were just fine. I've never done it on a table before, and I like doing new things. I love how spontaneous you are." She stood up, and I admired her body. Those women in the rap videos didn't have a thing on her.

"You were pretty spontaneous yourself. But if you think that was something, let me see who's at the door and then I'll be back to show you just how spontaneous I can really get."

"I don't know how you're gonna top the kitchen table."

"Oh, really? Have you ever done it on top of a washing machine on the spin cycle?"

Sandra shook her head, blushing. "No, but I'm willing to try anything. Tie me up and spank me if you want to. Baby, it's been a long time since I had lovin' this good, and I'm ready for everything you got."

"My girl. Now, that's what I'm talking about." I grinned, chuckling to myself. It never failed. Most of these churchwomen were nothing but a bunch of undercover freaks. The more sanctified they claimed to be, the freakier they were when you finally got them in the bedroom.

Whoever was at the door knocked again, so I put on my clothes and excused myself. I walked into the living room of my two-bedroom house. My first guess was that the visitor was one of my other lady friends in search of some Sunday afternoon loving. I wasn't married and made it very clear that I didn't have a steady woman, so I wasn't worried about any drama. But what I wasn't prepared for when I peeked out the window were the two men standing outside my front door. One of the men I knew very well; the other seemed vaguely familiar, but I couldn't put my finger on where I knew him from.

"Crap," I said out loud.

"Don't tell me it's one of your women, 'cause I don't do threesomes, and there's only enough whipped cream for two."

I turned to see Sandra standing in the doorway to the kitchen, as naked as the day she was born, with whipped cream smiley faces on each of her breasts. And she had the nerve to call me spontaneous. I don't think she would have been so damn spontaneous if she knew who was standing on the other side of my front door.

"No, but you might want to get rid of the whipped cream and put your clothes back on. Reverend Jenkins is outside, and he's got someone with him."

The color drained from Sandra's honey-brown face as she went into panic mode. "Oh Lord! What's he doing here?"

I shrugged. "I don't know, but they saw me when I looked out the window, so I gotta open the door."

"Don't you open that door," she threatened as she ran frantically back into the kitchen. I could hear her scrambling to gather up her clothes, and a few seconds later, she was standing in front of me wearing only her bra and panties. As awkward as the situation was, I had to giggle, because her panties were on backward and she looked stupid as hell.

"I don't see a damn thing funny," she said with a pout.

I didn't have the heart to tell her about her panties. I just pointed down the hall. "Maybe you should go hide in the bedroom."

I didn't have to tell her twice. She hightailed it down the hall in a flash. Although I was amused by the panties, the last thing either of us wanted was for her to get caught in my house, mainly because there wasn't an excuse in the world we could come up with for why she was there, other than the truth that we were getting our groove on.

When I was sure that Sandra was securely hidden in my bedroom, I took a deep breath to calm my nerves, then opened the front door. I was greeted by Reverend Alfred Jenkins, a short, heavyset, light-skinned man in his early forties. He was the newly appointed pastor of our church, and technically, he was my boss. Reverend Jenkins was accompanied by a tall, stately looking, brown-skinned man with salt-and-pepper hair and a well-maintained beard. I still wasn't sure where, but I was now positive we'd met before.

I halfway blocked the door, because Reverend Jenkins had a way of just entering your house without an invitation. "Hey,

Rev, sorry it took so long for me to answer the door, but I was half dressed. I was just about to jump in the shower and head up to Richmond."

"No, no, Mackie. You don't have to apologize. I tried to give you a heads-up, but you didn't answer the phone, so I just came over. I wanted to introduce you to a good friend of mine from New York. He's got a proposition he wants to run by you. You don't mind if we come in for a moment, do you?"

I should add that Reverend Jenkins wasn't one to take a hint, either, because most people would figure if you don't answer the phone, you're busy.

"Ah, well, sure, come on in. The place is a mess, but you're always welcome in my house, Reverend. I hope you understand we're gonna have to make it quick, though. I really have to get up to Richmond."

"No problem. This should only take about ten, fifteen minutes tops."

"Okay." I gestured for them to come in and have a seat.

Reverend Jenkins's friend sat down in the armchair, while the pastor and I sat across from him on the sofa.

"Aaron Mackie, I'd like you to meet my good friend Bishop T. K. Wilson of Queens, New York."

When he said the name, it all clicked. "Bishop Wilson, I think we met a few years ago when Pastor Simmons was alive." I offered him my hand and he took it. "You got a pretty big church up there in New York, don't you? First Jamaica Ministries?"

The bishop smiled, nodding as we shook hands. "I'm impressed you remember my church."

"Well, I've seen you on TV a few times, and I'm a choir director. Everyone in my field knows First Jamaica Ministries won the national choir championship three years in a row a few years back. It's hard enough to win that championship one time, but three years in a row, that's one heck of an achievement."

"Well, thank you," the bishop said.

"Y'all had Savannah singing for you back then, didn't you?"

"We sure did." He gave me a proud smile. "That young lady really could sing."

"She sure could. You guys would have been unstoppable if she had stuck around. I saw her on TMZ last summer. It's a shame what happened to her career."

"It truly is, but that's what drugs will do to you. I don't know if we'll ever see the old Savannah again. She blew a great opportunity . . . which is kind of why I'm here to see you."

I raised my eyebrows. If this was going where I thought it was . . .

"We have a vacancy at First Jamaica Ministries, and I'd like you to fill it. I'd like you to be my choir director."

I turned toward Reverend Jenkins. "Is he serious?"

He wrapped his large arm around my shoulder. "Yes, Mackie, he's serious. But I've already told Bishop Wilson that you weren't going anywhere, that you and I made a promise to Pastor Simmons before he died that we were going to take our church to the next level together. However, with the kind of money Bishop Wilson put on the table, I had to let you hear the offer for yourself, make your own decision. But I know you're going to do the right thing."

"Offer? What kind of offer are we talking about?" I turned back to the bishop.

"Aaron. Can I call you Aaron?" he asked.

"Call me Mackie. That's what everyone around here does."

"Okay, Mackie it is." The bishop nodded. "Now, I heard your choir today. You guys were fantastic for your size. And, brother, let me tell you, you have one phenomenal voice." The bishop gave me a huge smile of approval that made me proud.

"Thank you. Coming from someone like yourself, that's a real honor."

"How many people do you have in your choir?"

"About twenty today, but it varies. Five of them aren't worth a dime."

The bishop nodded his understanding. "What do you think you could do if you had fifty to a hundred members?"

I sat there for a second, imagining the possibilities as a grin spread across my face. "Man, I'd blow the roof off the church."

He gave me a confident look. "I'm sure you would."

"Bishop, I appreciate your confidence, but I've already got a job. I'm the choir director at Mount Olive."

Pastor Jenkins tightened his grip on my shoulder. "That's what I told him, Mackie."

"I know that, but don't you think it's time you moved up from the minor leagues to the majors?" Bishop Wilson turned to Reverend Jenkins. "No offense, Pastor."

The pastor gave him a sideways look but said nothing. I'm sure he was pissed off.

"I think it would be quite an opportunity for you. Here you only have about twenty choir members. If you come to New York, you would have your pick of two or three hundred voices. A young man like you could become a big star in New York, Mackie. I wouldn't be surprised if you had a national championship of your own next summer."

"I'm just a country boy from Emporia, Bishop. What would I know about being a star in the big city?"

Of course, I was displaying false modesty. I'd always wanted to be a big star. I didn't know a choir director who didn't. I'd studied every choir I could. Heck, Kirk Franklin didn't have nothing on me. To a huge extent, the bishop was right; I was stuck with a bunch of no-talent hicks, and look what I'd done with them. Man, if I had a real choir that I could handpick, there'd be no stopping me.

"You probably didn't know this, but I'm just a country boy, too—from Richmond. So I know what you mean, but some would say I had a gift: a gift that would never have reached its potential here in central Virginia. I believe you have a gift, Mackie. You have a gift to entertain and spread the Word through song. You should be spreading that gift on a bigger stage. I can help you do that."

Wow, this dude was deep, and he made a lot of sense. "Okay, let's just say I was interested—and I'm not saying I am—but if I was, how much money are we talking about?"

The bishop smiled as if he knew he was about to answer my prayers. "How much do you make now?"

"About three hundred sixty a week, not including funerals and weddings when I play the piano."

"We're willing to offer you fifty thousand dollars a year and the same deal. You keep all the wedding and funeral money.

Plus, we'll lease you any Cadillac you like. One of our members owns a dealership."

I sat up on the edge of the sofa. "Any Caddie? That includes the Escalade?"

"It sure does, a 2011, any color you want. I've got one myself, although I'm a Mercedes man. We usually switch up every two years." The bishop kept smiling, and so did I. He really did have the answers to my prayers. It sure would be nice to drive a new car instead of the beat-up 1999 hooptee I had parked outside.

"So, what do you think?" he asked.

I glanced over at Reverend Jenkins, whose arm was no longer around my shoulder. He was looking a little agitated, probably because he was afraid I was going to break my promise to Pastor Simmons and leave him high and dry. The thing is, though, if the roles were reversed and Reverend Jenkins were offered the opportunity to go preach for a megachurch, I wasn't sure that he'd be sticking around to honor a promise to our dead mentor either.

The chances of that kind of offer coming along were pretty slim, though. It wasn't as if Reverend Jenkins gave the type of enlightening sermons that made everyone flock to a church. No, if our little church had a chance of expansion, it would be through the success of the choir, and I'm sure he knew that. So he was undoubtedly concerned that if I left, his chances for growth were over. I thought of my friend, the late Pastor Simmons, and as much as I dreamed of stardom, I couldn't see myself breaking my promise.

"You know, you're right, Bishop. Deep down I really do want to be on that big stage. I think about it all the time." I could see the bishop trying to hold back a satisfied smile, like he knew all along that I would accept his offer. But I delivered the sentence that made his smile disappear. "You've made quite an offer, and I appreciate your consideration, but I'm gonna have to decline."

The look on his face was one of pure disbelief as he sat back in his chair. I'm sure he wasn't used to people turning down fifty thousand dollars a year and brand-new cars. It didn't take him long to compose himself, though.

"Well, ah, what if I sweeten the pot a little more?" He scooted to the edge of the chair. He was looking me directly in the eye, and his face was dead serious. "I'll up my offer by twenty-five thousand dollars, and we'll give you fifteen percent of all prize money you win in competition."

I sat up straight, more than a little surprised by his counter-offer. "You do realize how much the prize money for the national choir championship is, right?"

"I sure do." The bishop wiped his brow. "And that's not including all the other competitions you can enter. You can make a tidy sum for yourself."

"Wow, that I could." I sighed and leaned back casually, hoping to mask my true emotions. My heart was racing with excitement over the opportunity being put before me. I glanced over at the pastor, who looked like he wanted to jump across the coffee table and strangle the bishop.

I thought again of Pastor Simmons. Although he had been almost twenty years my senior, he had been the only real friend I had before his death. He'd literally saved my life and was a big part of the reason I moved to Petersburg and started working at the church in the first place. So, I did owe him something. I just didn't know if he'd want me to forgo such an opportunity. Even he couldn't have predicted this coming.

I said a quick prayer, hoping to receive some kind of sign that would guide me toward the right decision, but all I heard in my heart was silence. I was on my own with this one, I guess, and I didn't think I could do it.

"I appreciate the opportunity, Bishop, I really do, but my answer is still going to be no. I made a promise, and the only thing I've really got left in this world is my word. I'm gonna see that through. Me and Reverend Jenkins here, we've got a good thing. We might not be in the major league yet, but one of these days we're going to meet you on that big stage."

The bishop paused for a brief second before he nodded and then stood, offering me his hand. It was obvious he was disappointed. "I think I understand. And I appreciate your time, Mackie. I'm really sorry we're not going to get a chance to work together. It could have been a lot of fun."

"I'm sure it would have, Bishop, but who knows what the future holds?" I placed my arm around Reverend Jenkins's shoulder. He still seemed a little perturbed as the three of us walked to the front door.

"Here's my card if you change your mind, or even if you just want to chat. My cell phone number's on the back. I'm driving up to Washington to visit my son and daughter, but I'll be back in New York in the morning."

I took his card and watched the two of them get into separate cars and pull away. I was still feeling unsettled about turning down such a great offer. Maybe Sandra could do something to make me feel better, I thought as I headed toward her hiding place in the bedroom.

Monique

3

I pulled into the parking lot of the church a little after twelve, knowing I should have been there at least an hour and a half ago to sit in on the finance committee's meeting while my husband was out of town. I know this sounds irresponsible, and I'm embarrassed that it seemed to be happening more often than not, but I got caught up getting dressed. T. K. was going to lose his mind when I told him why I didn't make the meeting, especially since he was always complaining about how long it took me to get dressed.

What made it even worse was that he'd called that afternoon to remind me about the meeting. But I just couldn't find the right outfit. I must have tried on six or seven different ensembles before settling on the blue skirt suit I was wearing. I'd wanted to wear something a little lower cut, but with everything going on at the church the past few months, the last thing we needed was for people to be whispering about how inappropriate the first lady looked.

Besides, I'd only recently won over the members of the women's Bible study group, many of whom hated that T. K. had chosen me to be his wife. After that hard-won battle, there was no need to rile up the members of the finance committee. So, I went conservative—well, as conservative as I get. The skirt was still snug around my round hips, and my blouse was tight enough to make every man in the building take notice, but for the most part, I'd behaved.

I parked my new Mercedes in my assigned space and frowned at the sight of my husband's empty parking spot beside mine.

He'd been gone only a couple of days, but I missed him so much. I was tempted to call him, but I was afraid of what he might say when I told him I wasn't at the meeting. He was already upset that this choir director he was trying to recruit had rejected his offer, and I did not want him taking that out on me. I hurried out of my car and headed for the building in the hopes of catching the tail end of the meeting.

"Hey there, First Lady!"

I glanced in the direction of the voice and saw my friend Simone Wilcox coming out of the administrative section of the building looking fierce. "You might as well slow down, 'cause if you're trying to catch the finance meeting, you're about ten minutes too late."

"Daggone it." I snapped my fingers in protest. "How the heck am I going to tell T. K. I missed this meeting?"

"Don't worry. I can fill you in if you want me to." Simone walked over and gave me a hug.

"Girl, you just don't know. You're a lifesaver." I hugged her back, then gave her the once-over, up close and personal.

Simone was an extremely beautiful woman in her late thirties. She must have been drinking from the fountain of youth, because she didn't look a day over twenty-five. Quite frankly, she may have missed her calling as a supermodel. She was that attractive, with her flawless features and long, muscular legs. Many people said she looked like Halle Berry, but personally I thought she was prettier.

Born on the right side of the tracks, Simone had been spoiled to death by her father since she was a child, and she had a reputation for being quite a diva. Many men had discovered that she could be ruthless when things didn't go her way. The only way to describe Simone would be to say she was high maintenance all the way. Although she had a good job running her father's car dealership, she didn't mind spending her suitors' money. As a matter of fact, she preferred it. Everything she wore, down to her drawers, was designer. She'd been spoiled her entire life and expected it to continue no matter who the man in her life was. However, with all that being said, she was a very bright woman who ran her family car dealership and was elected chairwoman of the church's board of trustees.

I eyed the yellow-and-black tailored suit she was wearing. I wasn't big on yellow, but I'll be damned if she wasn't rocking it to the point I felt like I needed to find one in my size.

"I'm scared of you, sista. What you wearing and where'd you buy it?"

"Christian Dior. And I got it at Saks."

"Mmm-mmm-mmm, that suit is some kind of bad. Probably set you back a mint, didn't it?"

"Please. It didn't set me back a dime," she said nonchalantly. "I got Lamar to pay for it."

"Oh my goodness. Who is Lamar?" I leaned against my car, folding my arms as I waited to hear about my friend's latest love interest. She seemed to trade them in every other week. I guess that's why I liked talking to Simone, because her life was like a juicy soap opera with all her men and their drama.

"Lamar is just another fool who wants some goodies, but he won't get any until I'm good and damn ready, which, quite frankly, may be never after last night."

I shook my head. "Okay, so what happened last night?"

"We went out to dinner and I asked him to pay my mortgage." She sucked her teeth in disgust. "And you know what his cheap behind had the nerve to tell me?"

"No, what?" I wished I had some popcorn, because this was getting good.

"That fool told me he'll see what he can do! This man makes close to six figures and has the nerve to tell me, 'I'll see what I can do.' I'm about to put it on him like he's never had it before, and he tells me he'll see what he can do? Well, you know I sent him home with a hard dick and told him when he comes up with my mortgage money, I'll see what I can do about his hard dick."

"Oh, no, you didn't!" I stared at her with my mouth half open.

"Oh, yes, I sure as hell did." She looked around, probably hoping no one else had heard her language. Simone knew as well as I did how quickly the people in this church would ostracize you if they deemed you unworthy of their "holiness."

"You are crazy. You know that?"

"Maybe, but I am so glad I didn't give that man any goodies

yet. But it's okay, because at least now I know he's really not my type and probably never will be, with his cheap ass."

I laughed. I always got a kick out of Simone's antics. In some ways, her free-spirited attitude reminded me of myself before I married T. K. "I didn't know you had a type."

"Girl, I have always had a type." She smiled as if she were talking about her favorite subject. "Well, you know I find it hard to resist a really fine man, but to be honest, rich is my type. The richer the man, the more generous he is. The more generous he is, the finer he looks. The finer he looks, the better his chance of getting some of this. Which brings me back to my point: I love rich men. They are so fine."

"Simone, you are a hot mess." I shook my head at the take-no-prisoners attitude of my gold-digging friend. I had to admit, she really was a diva. "Shame on you."

"Oh, please. Men are always getting what they want, Monique. I'm just making sure I get what I want, too, by any means necessary. If they don't like how I do things, they know where the door is. They can give me what I want or keep it moving, 'cause there's another one just like them waiting right outside the door."

She wasn't lying either. Men had been asking her to marry them since she was sixteen, and she'd broken more hearts than any woman had a right to, all in the name of getting what she wanted. Now she was thirty-eight, still single, and living the good life, with no thoughts of settling down. It was too bad, because for the right man, she would actually be a very good catch.

"I hear you, girl." I nodded, ready to end this particular conversation. "Did you know T. K. and I went to see James Black at the hospital the other day?"

"Oh, really? So how's he doing?" She looked down at her fingernails, up at the sky, at her feet . . . everywhere but at me as she spoke. She was trying to come off as uninterested, but I knew better. She was very interested in anything that had to do with James Black. She could act like a diva and talk junk all day about the rules she had for men, but none of that held any weight when it came to my husband's best friend, James Black. You see, Simone had been in love with James since she was twenty-five years old. She would have married him, too, and had a whole house full of babies for the man, but like most women who were turned out by James Black, she ended up with a broken heart.

"He's dying, Simone. The cancer is eating him up. I don't think he's going to be around much longer. You should go and see him."

"I can't," she snapped.

"Can't or won't?" She still hadn't looked at me.

"Both!" She finally looked up at me with her eyes filled with tears. I felt bad for her. "I hate that man more than I hate anyone in this world, but the last thing I want to see or hear is that my beautiful James Black is dying."

Wow! Now that's what I call love. I handed her a tissue and she wiped her eyes.

"You mind if we talk about something else?"

"Not at all. You going to be okay?"

"Eventually, I hope. That man put me through the wringer, but I can't help but to still care for him."

"You should go see him."

"Anyhow, didn't you want to know what happened at the meeting?"

"Yes, I sure did."

"Well, most of the meeting was spent talking about this new choir director your husband wants to hire. A few of the more conservative members are against it. They want to promote someone from within the congregation so they don't have to pay out so much money."

I cut her off. "You don't have to worry about that. Bishop called a few hours ago and told me the director rejected his offer."

"Really? So what's he going to do now?"

"I don't know. He sounded mighty depressed when I spoke to him last. I think he was really shocked the man turned down his offer."

"I'm sure he was. It's not often that someone says no to Bishop T. K. Wilson and First Jamaica Ministries. I'm a little insulted myself."

"I know, right? We've been rejected by a country bumpkin." I shook my head.

"Look, things are going to work out. You'll see." She glanced down at her BlackBerry, shook her head, then quickly typed something in response. "Girl, I got to go."

"Everything all right?"

She gave me a huge grin. "Sure is. Lamar just texted that he's got my mortgage money. I guess he's gonna get some goodies after all."

I laughed. "You go, girl. Don't let me hold you back." I knew that as the first lady, I probably shouldn't have been encouraging her, but the truth was that no matter what I said to her about the sin of fornicating, nothing was going to stop Simone Wilcox from getting her money.

"Listen, about James . . ." She hesitated. It looked like she was trying to keep her emotions in check. "Tell him I said hello next time you see him."

I nodded. "Don't worry. I will do just that."

Aaron

4

As I walked down the hall toward my bedroom to finish what I'd started with Sandra, I studied the business card Bishop Wilson had given me. I slapped the card against my hand three times, biting my lip in frustration. Had I just made the biggest mistake of my life by turning down the bishop's offer? I wasn't quite sure, but I was definitely starting to second-guess myself. It was times like these that I wished Pastor Simmons were around to give me counsel. He always seemed to know the right thing to do. There was no denying I had a good life here in South Virginia: a decent place to live and more women at my disposal than any man had a right to. Hell, I even had a little local fame, but it wasn't anything in comparison to the life I'd dreamed of living—the life the bishop was offering. Just the idea of having a choir with a hundred or so members was intoxicating. When I closed my eyes, I could almost see my name outside the church: AARON MACKIE AND THE FIRST JAMAICA MINISTRIES CHOIR. Man, would that be a dream come true.

I opened the bedroom door and stuck my head in. I was greeted by Sandra's soft lips pressing against mine. Like before, she was completely naked. Instinctively, my arms wrapped around her waist, my hands roaming the bare flesh of her round buttocks as we kissed passionately.

"I took off my clothes again as soon as I heard them leave. Who was that man with the pastor, and what did they want?" She helped unbutton my shirt, kissing my neck and chest as she questioned me.

"His name is Bishop T. K. Wilson, and he's the pastor of one of those megachurches up in New York. He offered me a lot of money to move to New York and be his choir director." I smiled; she didn't. She actually looked upset.

"You didn't take it, did you? New York's a nice place to visit, but you don't want to live there, Aaron."

"You're just saying that because you finally got me to lie down with you and now you don't want me to leave." I laughed.

I was joking, but from her facial expression, I could tell that she didn't feel this was a laughing matter. "You damn right I don't want you leaving. Not after today, after waiting all this time to be with you. Aaron, you have no idea how it felt listening to those choir bitches brag about what you'd done to them in bed, knowing I wanted you too."

She gave me an annoyed look as my shirt came off. I was busy wondering which women from the choir were talking. I had better start choosing my women more carefully to weed out the ones who were prone to gossip about it afterward.

"And you made it even worse because you wouldn't pay me no mind. We probably would have never slept together today if I hadn't taken matters into my own hands," she said as she caressed my abdomen and then reached for my belt.

"Well, yeah, breaking into my house and waiting for me naked definitely got my attention."

She slid to her knees, opening my pants. "I've got something else that's going to get your attention." She reached into my boxers and pulled out my Johnson, slurping it into her mouth before I could respond.

A wave of pleasure quickly took over my body and I moaned. "Great googamooga." Now, if she was trying to give me incentive to stay in town, it was working like a charm, because I was a sucker for a good blow job. Although many tried, not every woman gave good head. Truth of the matter was, most women didn't know what the hell they were doing, but Sandra Jenkins knew how to give a good blow job.

"Like that, don't you?" she asked.

Did I like it? She had me with my back against the door, squirming around like Spider-Man trying to climb a wall, and she wanted to know if I liked it. My only response was an enthusiastic "Uh-huh."

She stopped for a second, smiling as she tied her hair in a bun. "Well, honey, you ain't seen nothing yet. I'm about to give you your wings and take you to heaven."

I liked the thought of that. But before she could get started, my doorbell rang again.

"Damn, this place is busier than Union Station up there in D.C. Who is that?" she bellowed.

"I don't know. It could be Reverend Jenkins or the bishop. Maybe the bishop wants to try and convince me to move to New York without Reverend Jenkins around. Just sit tight and I'll get rid of whoever it is."

She held on to my stuff, refusing to let me go. "Maybe we should have gone to a hotel. At least then I'd get your full attention."

"Just relax. I'll be right back."

She gave my manhood one last kiss, then pulled up my boxers and pants, zipping me up.

"Go, but hurry up and get rid of them." She stood up and kissed me.

I slapped her on the ass playfully and then headed to the front door. I peeked out the window and saw that I was right. It was the pastor again, but this time he was alone. I really didn't want to open the door, but he already knew I was home, so I had no choice. I figured he'd doubled back to thank me for not accepting the bishop's offer. That would have been all right, but Reverend Jenkins was a long-winded son of a gun who could talk to you about nothing all day.

"What's up, Rev? You forget something?" I opened the door, hoping I could hold him at bay right there, but he stepped past me, almost knocking me over as he barged into my house. He didn't say a word until I closed the door.

"No," he growled angrily. "I'm not here for what I forgot. I'm here for what belongs to me, you dirty son of a bitch."

"Huh?" I was taken aback by his attitude.

He looked like he wanted to hit me. What the hell was his problem? It wasn't like I was leaving his ass high and dry to go to New York and follow my dream. Did he somehow not realize that I'd just thrown away seventy-five thousand dollars a year to help his ass?

"What's wrong with you? What, I didn't defend you well enough when the bishop was here or something? What the heck is your problem?" I got right up in his face. I liked him, but sometimes this guy could be so ungrateful.

"My problem is you! You think you pulled the wool over the fat man's eyes, don't you? You think I'm stupid? Well, guess again, pretty boy. I ain't blind, and I ain't stupid. Both of you are going to pay for trying to make a fool outta me. You can bet your pretty ass on that."

"Rev, what are you talking about? I didn't accept his offer. I'm not going to New York. I'm staying, okay?" He was starting to make me angry with his paranoid rambling.

"I don't give a rat's ass about you going to New York. I wanna know where she is."

Things were suddenly clear, and the situation was not good. This man wasn't paranoid or rambling; it appeared he knew exactly what he was talking about, and his next sentence proved it.

"Motherfucker, where's my wife?"

As my stomach clenched into a ball of lead, I tried to play dumb, lying with a straight face. "Your wife? Rev, I have no idea what you're talking about. You haven't been drinking, have you?"

"Oh, you don't know where she is, huh? Well, maybe this will jar your memory."

That's when I saw the black .45 he always carried pointed in my face. I raised my hands in a nonthreatening manner, trying to gauge whether he was serious about shooting me. He may have been a man of God, but he was still a man, and right about then he was a very angry, jealous man. "Don't make me kill you, Mackie. I know she's here."

"What would make you think that, Rev?" Yes, he had a gun in my face, but I was not about to admit anything until I knew exactly how much he knew. That old cliché "The truth will set you free" was a bunch of BS when a man had a gun pointed in your face, accusing you of having an affair with his wife. In the situation I was in, the cliché should have been "The truth will get you dead, so lie your ass off."

"You're a piece of work, you know that, Mackie? Okay, you

wanna know how I know? Sit your ass down and I'll make it very clear." He motioned with his gun for me to sit in the same armchair the bishop had sat in earlier. I did what I was told, making sure the palms of my hands were visible to him. I was careful not to make any sudden moves, because he was starting to breathe heavy and get that crazy, I-don't-give-a-shit look in his eyes.

He looked so intense I was actually surprised when he sat down on the sofa across from me—that is, until he switched the gun from his right hand to his left. He then reached down on the right side of the sofa with his free hand. When his hand reappeared, he was holding a pink-and-white woman's hat. Once again, my stomach did a flip.

"Uh-huh, just what I thought." His knuckles were turning white as he wrenched the hat in his hands. "You know, Mackie, you son of a bitch, I wasn't one hundred percent sure this belonged to my wife until now, but I'd know this brim anywhere," he said in angry certainty.

And he was right; the hat did belong to Sandra. If you haven't already figured it out, she was his wife. It must have been thrown on the side of the sofa during the heat of our passion when I'd first arrived home.

As we sat there in silence for a few seconds, I could see Rev brooding as he studied the hat. It wasn't going to take much at all for him to completely lose it. I had to say something to defuse the situation before he went on a rampage and we all ended up on the six o'clock news.

"Rev, you got it all wrong, man. That's not your wife's hat. That's LaDawn Williams's hat. She left it over here last week." I tried to laugh it off.

For a brief second, his face seemed to soften and he took a long breath. *Man, if he buys this, I'm never messing with another man's wife as long as I live,* I promised myself.

"Oh, really, it's LaDawn's, huh? You know, Mackie, I can't tell you how happy that would make me if it were true. Only, I bought my wife this hat about two weeks ago when I was down in Charlotte. Coincidently, she was wearing hers this afternoon when she went down to Rocky Mount to a woman's retreat."

He scrunched up his face, breathing hard. He looked about as upset as a man could get without breaking down. "Funny thing is, I had it monogrammed with her initials right here." He pointed at the monogram, then threw the hat in my lap for good measure. "Now, tell me again how this ain't my wife's hat and she isn't here, so I can blow your ass away like the piece of shit you are."

He lifted the gun, pointing it directly at my head. Lord help me, I did not want to die, especially not because I slept with Sandra Jenkins, that's for sure.

I sat there in silence, trying to deal with the situation like a man, but inside I felt like a little bitch. If he flinched, I probably would have peed on myself, because I believed every word he said when he threatened to blow me away. Rev had always been a nice man, a big, jolly, happy-go-lucky guy, but everyone close to him knew he was obsessively jealous when it came to his wife. Most people were under the opinion, myself included, that his jealousy was based on his insecurity about his weight and the fact that his wife was a good fifteen years younger than him. She wasn't the finest woman in the face, but she had a body like nothing I'd ever seen before.

Believe me, when he first showed up at the church with her, there was plenty of whispering amongst the congregation about the two of them. Most of it was about what she saw in him, other than his five-bedroom house, fifty-thousand-dollar-a-year job at Phillip Morris, and his preaching salary.

"You know, Mackie, there's only one thing I wanna know." He stared at me with these pitiful, teary eyes. I knew what he was going to ask before he asked it. "Why? I just want to know why. With all these women at your disposal, why you got to go and mess with my wife? You had to know if I ever caught you that I'd end up killing you. I just wanna know why." He really did sound like he wanted to understand.

I couldn't even look him in the eye anymore because I couldn't say what I wanted to say. Telling him the truth would have just made things worse.

I mean, it wasn't as if I'd pursued her. She was the one who pursued me. Hell, for the past three years, I'd avoided Sandra like the plague, while she, on the other hand, had done everything but throw her stuff on a table in front of me. I hadn't wanted to go down that road. I had a hard and fast rule about committing adultery—that is, until today. I mean, I'm only human, and when a man comes home and there's a naked woman sitting on his sofa, and the woman has a body like Sandra's, well, can he honestly be held responsible for his actions? Hell, as much as I liked Reverend Jenkins, if it wasn't me, it damn sure was going to be someone else, so I figured I might as well take what was being offered.

"Answer me, dammit!"

"Rev, I know this may get me shot, but I really don't have any answers for you right now. At least not any that are going to make sense. I messed up. This should have never happened."

"Well, maybe your fuck buddy has some answers. Why don't we call her in here so I can ask her? Go on. Call her, Mackie."

I took a long breath. I really didn't want her out here. The best thing for me and her was that we remained separated. "Look, that's not gonna help anything."

"Did I ask for your opinion? Matter of fact, get up." I didn't move fast enough and he cocked the gun, sliding a bullet in the chamber. I closed my eyes briefly. I honestly felt that this was it; I was about to die. "I said get up," he repeated.

This time, I didn't hesitate. I stood up quickly, and he gestured for me to walk down the hall. I did what I was told, stopping in front of my bedroom door.

"Open it," he whispered. I glanced at him, and he said, "Don't play with me, Mackie," then pressed the gun against the back of my head. I turned the knob and pushed open the door.

A part of me wished she had climbed out the window or something, but when I opened the door, there she lay, as naked as a jaybird. She had her eyes closed, posing like a centerfold girl, her bosoms pushed out and, believe it or not, her beaver propped open for the world to see. By my calculations, I had about ten minutes to live, because there was no way Reverend Jenkins wasn't going to kill me after this.

Don't ask me how, but Sandra didn't even realize her husband was standing at the door. "It's about time. I was getting so horny

I was about to start without—" She opened her eyes and went into panic mode.

"Oh my God, Alfred!" she shouted as she scrambled to cover her nakedness.

"You better call God, because right now He's the only one who's gonna save your ass!" Rev screamed.

Sandra's beautiful almond skin was now a pale tan at best. Her eyes were stretched wide with fear. "Alfred, baby, it's not what it seems," she babbled. "You know how much I love you. I'm just glad you're here to take me home."

The rev glared at her as tears fell from his eyes, but he still kept the gun pointed at my head.

"Get in the room," he barked at me, gesturing with the gun to where he wanted me to sit.

In my mind, there was only one way out now. I was going to have to take the chance of getting shot and go for the gun. The more I thought about it, the better I felt my chances were. Here I was, six foot two, thirty-one years old, in the best shape of my life, while he was short, in his forties, and almost a hundred and fifty pounds overweight. The odds were overwhelmingly in my favor—until you considered the fact that he was an expert marksman and he'd already slid a bullet in the chamber. That, of course, placed the odds in his favor, but if I was going to do anything, I had best do it quick.

"I asked Mackie a question a minute ago, and he couldn't give me an answer. Maybe you can, Sandra." He moved the gun back and forth between her and me. He had no idea I was sizing him up. "I just want to know why. I gave you everything you asked for, took you out of that hick town up in the mountains, made you a respectable lady. Hell, I even married you knowing you had had so many abortions you couldn't have kids. Them niggas up there was passing you around like you was a piece of shit. I saved your fucking life! So, dammit, tell me why you did this to me."

"It wasn't me, Alfred. It was him. He made me do it! He forced me to sleep with him! I swear to God." She pointed at me without an ounce of remorse in her eyes. She was basically signing my death warrant, and she didn't even flinch. Yeah, I really had to start choosing my women more carefully.

My stomach did a backflip and two somersaults. I raised my right hand like I was in a court of law. "Rev, I swear, you can shoot me right now, but I do not want to die with that lie on my head. You know my background. You know I would never do anything like that! Now, I may have slept with her, but I didn't make her do shit. She lied and got my key from Sister Tremont, who cleans my house, and she snuck in here. When I got home, she was sitting on that sofa out there naked, just wearing that hat you bought her. I swear. You gotta believe me!"

"Alfred, he's lyin—" Before she could get all the words out of her mouth, he backhanded her so hard she went flying across the bed. The preacher in him was nowhere to be found. Most people didn't know this, but Rev had spent a lot of time in the streets before, and even after he was saved and became a minister. When Pastor Simmons was alive, Rev was the church's outreach minister, going to the local jails and prisons.

"Bitch, did you forget that's the same shit you did to me when we first met and you begged me to take you outta Winchester?"

He looked back and forth between us. "I can't stand your ass, Mackie, and you're a lot of things, but I know you ain't a rapist." He turned to Sandra. "Once a ho, always a ho."

"Alfred . . ."

He raised a hand and she shut up, scurrying to the far end of the bed.

"Pick up that phone, Mackie," he ordered.

I stared over at the phone on my nightstand. Unsure where he was going with his order, I complied, but I was still thinking about going for his gun.

"She may be a ho, but she's my ho, bought and paid for. Now, we can do this two ways, Mackie. One, I can shoot your ass dead right here along with my wife, or two, you call the bishop, accept his job offer, and then pack your shit and get the hell away from me, my wife, and my church. The choice is yours." He lifted the gun and pointed it at my head. "You have five seconds to make a decision. One . . . two . . ."

I cut him off quick. "Look, I'm outta here. You ain't got to worry about me no more. I swear to God!" Hands trembling, I found the bishop's card and dialed the number.

"Bishop T. K. Wilson."

"Hello, Bishop, this is Aaron Mackie." I tried to sound like everything was fine, but I had one eye on Rev the entire time.

"Mackie, how can I help you, son?" The bishop sounded surprised but happy to hear my voice.

Reverend Jenkins was so mad he looked like he could burst into flames at any moment. "Well, I just called to tell you I've had a change of heart."

"And—?"

"Well, I want to take the job as your choir director, if it's still available." I held my breath. *Please, Lord, don't let this man say no.*

"Yes, of course it's still available. But I have a couple of questions to ask you."

"Sure. Ask away." *Just make it quick before Rev pulls the trigger.*

"Do you have a wife, girlfriend, or children who will be moving with you?"

"No, Bishop. I'm single with no kids."

"Well, then I need to ask you one other question."

"Sure."

"This is a little bit difficult and not exactly politically correct, so I hope you don't take offense. But believe me, with things that have recently gone on at our church, it's important."

"Okay, sure, you can ask me anything."

"All right. Well, I'm glad to hear that, because I just need to know . . . Are you gay?" At first there was silence on both ends of the phone, then suddenly the bishop rushed to offer an explanation for this unexpected question. "It's not that we won't hire you if that's the case, but I just need to know. We've had some incidents in the past that I'd like to avoid."

"There is no need to explain, Bishop," I said in an effort to move the conversation along. "I've been a choir director for a few years now, so I think I understand." I looked over at Sandra cowering on the bed. Less than an hour ago, I was screwing her brains out. I shook my head. "You can rest assured—the last thing you've got to worry about is me being gay, Bishop."

I could hear him sigh thankfully through the phone. "I appreciate your understanding, Mackie, I really do. And with that being said, when can you start?"

"I can be packed up and in New York day after tomorrow."

The bishop laughed. "Now that's what I call anxious to get started, but the end of next week is fine. I'm sure you want to give Reverend Jenkins some notice and get your personal life in order."

I glanced at the gun in Rev's hand. "Like I said, Bishop, I'll be there day after tomorrow. I'm sure Reverend Jenkins won't even want two weeks' notice, and as of right now, I don't have a personal life."

The Bishop

5

I walked into the administrative section of First Jamaica Ministries with a feeling of accomplishment and a sense of optimism for the future. I'd just returned from my trip to Virginia with a quick stop in D.C., and there was no doubt in my mind that Aaron Mackie was the perfect choice to direct our choir and lead our church back to financial stability.

Now all I had to do was convince the board of trustees and deacons' board that I'd made the right decision and that they should pay the man his money. Usually this was just a formality, but when I called my good friend Maxwell Frye yesterday, I was surprised to find out that quite a few of the deacons were up in arms that I'd made any offer without their approval. The salary I'd offered was quite a bit more than what we'd paid the last director, and when they heard the amount, they'd nearly lost their minds.

"Good morning, Bishop. Glad to have you back." The church secretary greeted me with a smile at the door. "How was your trip?"

"It was good, Sister Tia. Very successful. I think we've finally found a new choir director. He's the perfect choice."

"So your wife has told me. I can't wait to meet him." Tia handed me a cup of coffee and my messages. I was about to walk into my office and call my wife when Tia said, "Bishop, Deacon Smith is in the conference room waiting for you, along with a couple members of the deacon and trustee boards."

"Oh, okay. What's Smitty want anyway?"

Jonathan Smith was a good friend and the chairman of the

deacons' board. He and Simone Wilcox, the trustee board's chairwoman, were the first people I planned on contacting about my recent offer to Aaron Mackie. With their support, Mackie's hiring would be in the bag. I'd already had preliminary conversations with both of them about it before I left town, and they were both on board. So, I took a confident step toward the conference room, but Tia stepped in front of me, blocking my path.

"Um, Bishop . . ." She stepped closer to me, looking around before speaking in a hushed voice. "I hate to be the bearer of bad news, but Deacon Smith isn't here as a friend. He's trying to stop you from hiring that young man. And, Bishop, trust me, he means business. He's already organized a campaign against you on this."

"Smitty?" I gave her a perplexed look. "I can't believe Smitty would go behind my back like this. We've always been able to sit down and work things out. He's a reasonable man."

"Believe it, Bishop," Tia said sadly. "He's not trying to be reasonable about this at all. From what I've been hearing, he's out for blood, and for some reason he wants your head on a platter."

"Well, Sister, I like my head just fine right where it is," I replied rather dryly. I just wished I knew where this was all coming from. Jonathan Smith was supposed to be my ally. "So, who has Smitty got lined up against me?"

"Trustee Duncan, Trustee Whitmore, and Deacon Brown are the only ones he has in the conference room, but he's been burning up the phones the past two days while you were gone. He called and spoke to my father three times yesterday. Shoot, I saw him whispering all secretively with Trustee Wilcox just before you got here."

"Simone? Nah, I'm not worried about her. She wouldn't betray me. She's one of my wife's closet friends."

"Humph. Maybe the first lady needs to keep better company. Simone would sell her soul for a ladies' Rolex and a Coach bag. She's so selfish. I still can't believe y'all elected her to the board of trustees, let alone made her chairwoman."

I sighed unhappily. "Anybody in that conference room I can call a friend?"

"Just Deacon Frye for right now." Good old Maxwell, always there when I needed him. "I called a few of the other trustees who usually support you, but most of them are working. I spoke to my father, and he's on the way."

"Okay." I nodded, feeling a headache coming on.

"Bishop, doesn't Deacon Smith know we need a choir director? Why is he doing this?"

I shrugged. "To be honest with you, I don't know why he's acting like this, but I sure plan on asking him that very question."

These were the times I wished James was around. If he were here, I would have never had to go through this with Smitty. He would have put him in his place right away. Well, at least Maxwell was in there pulling for me.

"Sister Tia, I'm going into my office to drink this fine cup of coffee you brought me. In about five minutes, I want you to tell those folks in the conference room that I'm pretty busy and that if they want to see me, they need to come to my office. Those men planned on lulling me into the conference room and ambushing me. Well, let's see how they like walking into the lion's den."

Sister Tia smiled. "You know, Bishop, for a preacher you've got a pretty devious mind."

"Well, then, let's pray God judges us from what's in our hearts and not in our minds." I took a sip of my coffee and then headed into my office, closing the door behind me. I walked around to my plush leather chair and settled into it, sipping my coffee while I thought about how I was going to deal with the situation. It didn't take long before the intercom on my desk snapped me out of my thoughts.

I pushed the TALK button. "Yes?"

"Bishop, Deacon Smith and a few other trustees and deacons would like to see you."

"Sure. Show them in." I picked up a folder that was on my desk and opened it, pretending to be hard at work. My office door opened a few seconds later, and Deacon Jonathan Smith stormed in, followed by his three flunkies and my boy Maxwell.

Smitty made quite an entrance if I do say so myself, stomping into my office and plopping down in front of my desk, folding his arms and staring at me coldly. You would have never thought that my wife and I had dinner at his place last weekend with him and his wife. I was anxious to see what the problem between us was.

The rest of his group found chairs and circled around my desk. When they were all seated, the room went silent. I'd been through this type of thing before, so the first thing I did was eye Trustee Whitmore and Deacon Brown, whom I considered the weak links. Neither one of them would make eye contact, which confirmed my suspicions that they were followers in this little witch hunt.

Surprisingly, I was the one who broke our silence. "So, Smitty, how's Maria? You know, I still can't get over how good that pot roast she made last weekend was. She is quite a cook."

My approach worked; it took him off guard. He sucked in his breath as if I'd punched him in the solar plexus. "Ah, yes, thank you. That was a good pot roast, wasn't it?" He shifted in his chair and adjusted his pant legs. "Bishop, we need—"

"Best I've ever had." I cut him off, turning to Maxwell. "Deacon Frye, have you ever had Maria's pot roast?"

"No, can't say I have. Is it that good?" Maxwell saw what I was trying to do right away.

I rolled my eyes heavenward, smiling like I was in true bliss. "To die for."

"Um, Bishop, I thank you for the kind words about my wife's cooking, but we're not here for that," Smitty stated, regaining some strength in his voice.

"I see. Why exactly are you here, Smitty? Is there a problem I don't know about?" I folded my arms and sat back in my chair.

"Well, some of the trustees and deacons wanted to know—"

"Some of the trustees and deacons, or you, Smitty?" I cut him off again, swiveling my head back and forth between Trustee Whitmore, Trustee Duncan, and Deacon Brown. "Is there a problem, Deacon Brown?" Brown didn't say a word, so I turned to Whitmore, who still couldn't make eye contact with me. "Trustee Whitmore, is there a problem?" I glanced at Trustee Duncan. "Trustee Duncan, you got anything to say?"

He sounded nervous, but at least Trustee Duncan spoke. "Bishop, Deacon Smith has brought some things to our attention, and we have some concerns. Maybe he'd be better explaining it."

I turned back to Deacon Smith. "Okay, Smitty, I take it you're the spokesman for this little gathering, so you tell me, what exactly are your concerns?"

"You hired a choir director without my—I mean *our*—consent."

No, he meant *his,* but what I didn't understand was exactly what he was up to. His attitude was a complete reversal of the way he'd acted when we spoke before my trip, and I had no clue what caused this about-face.

I paused, measuring my words. "I've been hiring choir directors around here for more than twenty years. Why would you or your board take issue with that?"

"It's my job to take issue with anything that might place this church in jeopardy." He raised his voice to talk over me.

I sat up in my chair and spoke very seriously and directly when he was finished. "Smitty, how long have we known each other? Fifteen, twenty years?" Deacon Smith nodded. "And in that time, have I ever put this church in jeopardy?"

"Bishop, it seems there's a first time for everything."

"On that we can agree." I looked purposefully at each one of them and then sat back in my chair. "We're a church without a choir. How could hiring a choir director be putting the church in jeopardy?"

"How do we know that this person is any good?"

"You don't, except for the fact that I told you he is. Is my word no longer good around here? Do you think I'm having a lapse in judgment?"

Smitty folded his arms, shifting around in his chair. "No, but I'd like to know how much you offered this man."

"The man's name is Aaron Mackie. He's one of the most talented choir directors in the country, and I offered him seventy-five thousand a year. In my judgment, he's worth every penny."

"Seventy-five thousand! Have you lost your mind? Our church is in financial trouble and you want us to pay a choir director seventy-five thousand dollars a year? I don't make that much, and I run an entire department for the city."

I said in a calm, even voice, "First off, Deacon, this is not about you; it's about the church. Secondly, the amount of money that Aaron Mackie is going to make us is going to be ten times what we pay him. He's that good. So y'all need to stop with this nonsense and let me do my job."

Smitty gave me a puzzled look, which made me think that he really believed I'd lost my mind. "You know what, Bishop? Maybe you are having a lapse in judgment, because I don't think you know how bad things are around here. We can barely pay our mortgages!" he shouted.

I turned my attention to the two trustees in the room. "You're supposed to be the money people in the room. What do you think?"

Trustee Whitmore spoke up for the first time. "Bishop, that's just too much money to pay a man to direct a choir."

"You've got to spend money to make money, Trustee. Y'all want the glory without the pain."

"Maybe if you can get him to take half of that, we can make this happen," Trustee Duncan added.

"I promised that man seventy-five thousand. I can't go back on my word. That will kill our credibility with him. Besides, I've never seen a man who could perform like he did this past Sunday. He puts Jackie Moss to shame. He was a hair shy of being magnificent. If I ask him to take less money, I might as well tell him to stay home."

Smitty glanced over at the other men in the room. "Maybe that's for the best. None of us feels this is a good idea, Bishop."

"Speak for yourself." Maxwell finally interjected himself into the conversation. "I stand with the bishop on this. The only way we're going to increase revenue is to bring people back into the church. A good choir can do that."

"We don't see it that way, Deacon Frye. What we see is the bishop recklessly spending money we don't have. Now, as I tried to explain to you earlier in the conference room, we've already got the votes needed to reject hiring this Aaron Mackie."

Smitty's eyes never left mine. "You fight us on this, Bishop, and you might be the one looking for a job."

"Are you threatening me?"

"No, Bishop, I'm not threatening you. I'm making you a promise." He sat back in his chair with a smug expression.

"Well, then, I guess we don't have anything else to talk about, do we?" I stood up and gestured toward the door, letting them know I was ending our impromptu meeting.

Tia

6

"Please, listen to me very carefully. I need you to get out of the house. It's not safe. Get out now." Although the words I was saying were very serious, I tried my best to say them calmly. After all, I needed to make sure that I kept the woman on the other end of the phone calm.

Every time the phone rang to the church's rape hotline, my stomach always did flips. I never knew what to expect. Every call was different, but every woman on the line was the same. I knew that no matter what the circumstance or the situation, ultimately, that woman was me. That woman was who I was and where I had once been in my life: a victim.

Not only had I been a victim, but I walked around with a degree of guilt as well. A part of me always felt that what happened to me, my own rape, had somehow been my fault. After all, how many times had my brother warned me about my lifestyle?

No, I wasn't some country girl who went off to college and lost her mind, engaging in drinking, drugs, and sex with any- and everybody. As a matter of fact, I had had a steady boyfriend. Unfortunately, he was the one who did all the drinking and drugging.

Don't get me wrong. He wasn't all out there like that. He drank at the frat parties and smoked a little weed every now and then, but only when he had a major test coming up or something. He said it relaxed him, and he did his best work when he had a buzz. Now, I'm not advocating the use of marijuana on college campuses—or anywhere else, for that matter—but I kid you not, that fool got an A every time. Any other time, he was an average C+ student at best. So there had to be something to it.

My college boyfriend was a sweetheart. I loved him so much. I would have done anything for him. And I did. I lost my virginity to him. And as far as I know, the drinking and the drugging he did with other people, but the sexing, now, that he only did with me.

It didn't matter to my brother, though, that I thought the world of my boyfriend. My brother couldn't stand him. He would always warn me that he wasn't my type, that he wasn't the kind of man I needed. He hated that my boyfriend indulged in college nightlife the way he did. My brother—who never even finished college and worked at Pep Boys—felt that my boyfriend wasn't good enough for his little sister.

"Tia, that ain't even you, going to parties and hanging out and stuff," my brother would complain. "Girl, you didn't even go to homecoming or prom, but now I hear you at parties, backing that thang up. That fool is trying to turn you out. With that clown, you gon' end up someplace you don't want to be."

My brother's words always went in one ear and out the other. I just thought he was being the typical big brother, overprotective and sickened by the thought of his little sister screwing and having a good time.

It wouldn't be long before I wished I had listened to my brother. Maybe then I wouldn't have suffered the heartbreak that I did once the so-called love of my life turned on me. Once I became a victim of rape.

No, I wasn't raped by my boyfriend—not my body anyway. Some other jerk managed to do that. It happened at one of the college parties I went to in order to meet up with my boyfriend. He got so wasted that he threw up all over himself and passed out. When I went upstairs to find something to clean him up with, I was pulled into a room and raped—not by one but by five different men.

After the rape, everything changed between my boyfriend and me. It was like I had the plague, and he didn't want to be seen with me. He didn't want to be near me. I felt as if I had been raped all over again, only this time instead of my body being raped, he raped my heart. The person I always thought would be there for me wasn't.

Dealing with the rape was rough for me for years. There were times when I wanted to take a pill or two to see if it would relax me. But instead of turning to drugs, I turned to God. And I thanked God every day for Bishop Wilson—and my brother, of course, who was now more protective than ever. I could tell that my brother was still walking around with some degree of guilt. I tried convincing him to come to church, take it to the altar and give it to God like I did. To date, that hadn't happened, but I was still working on him. I knew one day he was going to walk through the doors of First Jamaica Ministries and surprise me.

Until then, I had to focus on making sure the women who called into the rape hotline were taken care of. I had to make sure they become the woman who I am now—a survivor—and not the woman I used to be—a victim.

My mission included the woman who was on the other end of the phone.

"Is your husband in the home now?" I asked her.

"No, he stepped out. Probably to get flowers or some lame thank-you card. That's what he always does." The woman began to cry. "I can't take this anymore. One day he's going to kill me. I can't let that happen. I have children to raise. So, it's going to be either him or me."

"Where are the children now?" I asked her.

"At my mother's."

"Good." I pulled out the piece of paper from my desk that outlined an action plan for an escape from an abuser. I proceeded to tell the woman exactly what she needed to do. She kept interrupting me with question after question of what-ifs. I wasn't surprised that by the time I ended the call, she'd decided to give her husband another chance.

"I really believe you should get out now while you can," I reiterated to her, to no avail.

"I don't have anywhere to go. I mean, I have a sister, but then I'd have to tell her my business. Nobody knows what I've been dealing with. Besides that, I don't have any money. And my children love their father. They'll hate me for taking them away from him. I can't do it. I just can't do it. Not this way. Not now. Thank you so much for your help, though. Thank you." And the phone went dead in my ear.

I hung up the phone feeling like a failure, but not even Jesus Himself could get everybody saved. I reminded myself, "You can't save 'em all, Tia. You can't save 'em all."

Aaron

7

I stepped out of Penn Station and onto the corner of Thirty-fourth Street and Eighth Avenue carrying two huge suitcases, a knapsack, and my portable keyboard. I'd given the rest of my stuff away before I left Virginia that morning. Everything I needed to take New York by storm was packed in the bags I had with me.

I looked up at the skyscrapers surrounding me and smiled. God, I loved this city, with its big lights and fast-moving people. You know what they say: If you can make it in New York, you can make it anywhere. I gave myself one year, and I was going to rule this city.

"Hey, taxi!" I yelled thirty minutes later, flailing my arms up and down like one of the sisters doing the holy dance. It was to no avail. The son of a gun drove right past me like I wasn't even there.

Thirty minutes. I'd been standing out there for half an hour trying to flag down a cab. Frustration and anger consumed me. How the hell was I going to take over the city if I couldn't even catch a taxi? Anyhow, I guess it was true what they said about trying to hail a cab in New York City when you're a black man: It's impossible. Whether it was driven by a white man or a black man, a Latino or an Arab, each cab I saw whizzed right by me as if I were waving a 9 mm handgun instead of just my arm, which was beyond tired at this point.

Luckily, about five minutes later, a cab pulled up to the curb right in front of me and let out two passengers. I grabbed the car door so fast when it opened that the people getting out probably thought I was a doorman. I left the door open so the cab wouldn't pull away and then turned to grab my belongings. When I turned back to the cab, this dark-skinned sister around my age with a scarf around her head slid into the backseat.

"Hey, wait a minute! That's my taxi." I was holding a suitcase in each arm, and my keyboard was flung over my shoulder.

"I don't think so," the woman replied curtly. She reached to close the car door, but I stepped in front of it, holding it open with my hip.

"Is there a problem?" she asked, giving me a withering look.

"Yes, there's a problem. You're in my taxi," I snapped. I wasn't usually this rude to women, even when they were wrong, but she was the one who started giving me attitude first.

"If this was your cab, you'd be sitting in it, not me. Now, can you close the door?"

If I hadn't been standing out there for thirty minutes, I might have relented, but I was tired, hungry, and wanted to get where I was going.

I heaved a deep sigh. "Look, it's late. Why don't we compromise? We can share the cab."

"I don't think so," she snapped. "I'm headed to Queens."

"See there, today must be my lucky day. I just happen to be going to Queens too."

"Well, that doesn't mean you're traveling there in this cab. Besides, I don't share cabs with strange men, especially not one dressed like a thug." Her eyes traveled up and down, appraising my outfit, which clearly didn't impress her.

I felt like I'd been taken out at the knees.

"A thug! You think I look like a thug?" I dropped both bags, spreading my arms out to show off my outfit. "Lady, this is a three-hundred-dollar Sean John sweat suit. These sneakers cost almost two hundred dollars. Don't be talking about my clothes, especially if you don't know a damn thing about fashion."

She laughed. "What would make a grown-ass man spend that kind of money on a sweat suit and sneakers? I bet you don't even own a suit. You know, for someone so cute, you should really grow up."

"Who the hell do you think you're talking to? You don't know me!" I guess my tone kind of scared her, because I saw her flinch. But that didn't mean she was going to back down. As soon as I moved my hip slightly, she managed to pull the door closed. With that, the cab sped off.

"Dammit!" I made a fist and shook it in the air. I wanted to call the strange woman the word that rhymes with *itch,* but I said I would never call a black woman out of her name. Instead, I stomped my feet to release some of my pent-up frustration.

Man, if that's how the sisters up here acted, I was going to have to import a few from down South. I'd heard rumors about how cold-blooded New Yorkers were, and I'd just witnessed my first example.

At the rate I was going, I was never going to get a cab out of Manhattan. Who could I call? I thought of the bishop. His number was already in my mobile phone, so I punched it in.

He answered on the second ring. "Bishop T. K. Wilson speaking."

"Hey, Bishop, this is Aaron Mackie."

"Mackie, how you doing? My wife and I were just talking about you. You make it into town all right?"

"Yeah, I'm here in town, but I can't get a cab for the life of me. Can you tell me what subway I should take to reach that apartment you got for me in Queens?"

"You don't need to take the subway, Mackie. My wife and I just left Columbia Presbyterian Hospital uptown. Give me fifteen minutes and we'll be there to pick you up."

Monique

8

I turned to my husband, taking hold of his hand as we pulled out of the hospital parking lot. We were headed home after visiting James. I snuggled up next to him, resting my head on his shoulder. He'd been gone the past few days on his mission to entice Aaron Mackie to come work for us. Now that he was back, I was hoping for a little attention of my own when we got home. I wasn't sure about him, but this sister was about due.

"You okay?" I asked.

He'd been pretty quiet ever since I left him and James alone to go to the ladies' room. Whatever they were talking about sure had him preoccupied, because he hadn't said much since. As a matter of fact, now that I thought about it, he really hadn't been himself since he picked me up earlier that afternoon to drive us over to the hospital. His little talk with James just seemed to make his mood that much worse.

When he didn't respond to my question, I probed further. "You been mighty quiet since you came back. Is everything all right? I thought you'd be happy now that you've hired a new choir director."

"I am happy about it, sweetheart. I've just got a lot on my mind. I'll be fine." He never even looked at me as he drove down 125th Street toward the RFK Bridge. I decided to back off, hoping he'd work through whatever was on his mind before we made it back to Queens.

After a few more minutes of silence, he announced, "I just don't understand black folks. They always have to do things the hard way."

"What are you talking about, T. K.? I want to know what's going on."

"Who said anything was going on?"

I sat up, turning my head to look directly at his stone-faced profile. "Don't patronize me, T. K. I'm not some stupid woman who doesn't notice the things around her. I've got ears and eyes, and I can see and hear things with them. You didn't have James looking at all that paperwork for his health; I know that. Oh, and don't think I didn't notice you left a copy of the church by-laws with him."

He glanced over at me. "You saw that, huh?"

"I sure did, and I wanna know what's going on."

"Monique Wilson, always the perceptive one, aren't you?" He sighed. "All right, I'll tell you what's going on."

I waited expectantly, but all he did was let out an angry sigh. I finally said, "Come on, T. K., just tell me."

"Smitty is what's going on. I think the man has lost his mind. He's totally unstable."

"Jonathan Smith, Maria Smith's husband?" He had to be talking about someone else. Jonathan and Maria Smith were our friends. They'd been the first two to support our marriage from the start.

T. K. cut his eyes at me and said, "Yep. Hard to believe, isn't it?"

It sure was, and if it had come from anyone other than my husband, I wouldn't have believed it. "So, what's his malfunction?"

"He's trying to get the board of trustees to vote down Aaron Mackie's hiring as choir director."

I whipped my head around. "Huh? Why would he do that? Didn't you explain to him why this is so important to the church?"

"I explained everything to him before I left for Virginia, and he didn't have any objections. I was under the impression he was one hundred percent behind me—that is, until I got back today and he and a few of the deacons and trustees came into my office acting like a lynch mob. Thank goodness Maxwell was there."

"I don't understand this. Jonathan and Maria are supposed to be our friends."

"That's right. They're supposed to be, but he wasn't no friend of mine today, Monique. Smitty was out for blood. And if he can't get Mackie's blood, he's made it clear he'll settle for mine."

"What do you mean?" I was still having trouble understanding how the attitude he was describing could belong to the Jonathan Smith I knew.

"What I'm saying is that my *good friend* Jonathan Smith doesn't want Aaron Mackie as the choir director of our church, and he's willing to do whatever it takes to secure his objective. And that includes having me removed as pastor of our church if he doesn't get his way. He's already got half the board of trustees and the deacons lined up against me."

I couldn't believe what I was hearing. "Why would he want to do that? He knows you're a good pastor. What is wrong with him? What did you do?"

I didn't mean to sound accusatory, but this didn't make sense.

"I'm not really sure, honey, but this whole thing feels personal. Smitty wouldn't turn on me like this without cause. I guess somehow without knowing it I offended him, but for the life of me, I don't know what I did." He was gripping the steering wheel so tightly I was sure the circulation was cut off to his fingertips.

"Well, maybe it's time I spoke with Maria. I'm sure she can talk some sense into him."

He shook his head. "No, I wouldn't do that. Maria has enough problems of her own." He turned to me and attempted a reassuring smile. "Listen, don't worry about this. I've got it."

As usual, my strong husband was ready to take the world on his shoulders. He was always worried about taking care of others before himself. That's what made him a great pastor, but he was still a man—my man—and I was going to support him no matter what he said.

"Don't worry? How can I not worry about you? You're my husband, and Jonathan and his cronies are lining up the heavy hitters against you. It's bad enough we've always got people who don't even really know us trying to take us down, but now we've got our friends doing the same thing." I wanted to slam my fist into the dashboard I was so angry. I didn't care if they went after me. People had been going after me my entire life, and I could take it. But when they went after T. K., it pissed me off.

"Honey, is he even worth all this?"

"Is who worth it?" he asked.

"This man, Aaron Mackie. Is he even worth all of this drama and aggravation? I mean, they're going after your job over this, T. K. You could lose the church." Just the thought ticked me off more. "Maybe we should back off. You don't owe him any-thing—"

"Yes, I do." He cut me off, tilting his head so that he could see me and the road. "I gave that man my word and asked him to leave his life behind."

"I'm not trying to second-guess you, baby, but, again, are you sure he's worth the trouble?"

"Monique, this past Sunday, I sat in that hot church, with horrible acoustics, and watched something very special. Not only did he put on a show, but he also shocked the hell out of me when he started to sing. The man has a gift when it comes to music, and he can save our church. So, yes, I'm sure he's worth it. He's worth the trouble, and he's worth the money. What Smitty doesn't understand is that Aaron Mackie is quite possibly the only one who can save First Jamaica Ministries."

I hadn't heard that much passion in his voice since he said "I do" at our wedding.

I kissed him on the cheek. "Well, husband, if you feel that strongly about him, then so do I."

His cell phone started ringing and he laughed. "Speak of the devil." He hit the Bluetooth button on the car.

"Bishop T. K. Wilson speaking."

"Hey, Bishop, this is Aaron Mackie."

His voice had a sexy baritone sound to it that made me fanta-size about what he might look like.

"Mackie, how you doing? My wife and I were just talking about you. You make it into town all right?"

"Yeah, I'm here in town, but I can't get a cab for the life of me. Can you tell me what subway I should take to reach that apartment you got for me in Queens?"

"You don't need to take the subway, Mackie. My wife and I

just left Columbia Presbyterian Hospital uptown. Give me fifteen minutes and we'll be there to pick you up."

"Okay, Bishop. Thanks. I'm down here by the Hotel Pennsylvania."

T. K. glanced at me and I gave him a nod, letting him know everything he had said was fine with me. Shoot, now I wanted to see the face behind that sexy voice even if I knew that fantasy rarely ever lived up to reality.

Not long after, we were on FDR Drive headed toward midtown Manhattan, and then we were driving up Thirty-fourth Street to pick up Aaron Mackie. We had just stopped at a traffic light, and I was about to suggest we call and find out exactly where he was when my husband said, "There he is."

"Where?"

"Over there, standing on the corner next to those suitcases."

I looked in the direction he was pointing. "That's Aaron Mackie?" I almost gasped.

"That's him," T. K. replied.

I could not believe my eyes. I was hoping he'd be good-looking, but the man I was looking at was straight-up fine. So fine, in fact, that I had to turn my head to keep my husband from seeing my initial reaction.

Wow! Now, he definitely lived up to the fantasy. He was the kind of man who, if I were still single, I'd jump on with a quickness. Too bad for him I loved my husband. I will say this, though: Life around First Jamaica Ministries was about to get much more entertaining, because when word got around about how fine our new choir director was, the sisters were going to lose their minds. I couldn't wait to get home and get on the phone.

"So, what do you think?"

I glanced over at my husband, who was staring at me with a devilish smirk, like he knew exactly what was going through my mind.

I took a breath, trying to act casual as I turned back to the handsome man across the street. "Well, there's no question he is definitely easy on the eyes. If he sings and conducts a choir half as good as he looks, our church is going to be on its way back to prosperity."

T. K. smiled as he slapped his hand down on his thigh. "Now, that's what I'm talking about."

"You know what I was just thinking? A guy that good-looking is going to have to fight off the single sisters at the church. Is he married or dating anyone?"

"Nope. Far as I know, he's a single man."

I raised an eyebrow as I turned back toward my husband. All of a sudden, Aaron Mackie's good looks and mannerisms made sense.

"He isn't gay, is he?" Just the thought of this fine man being with other men made my stomach hurt.

"No, he's not."

"You sure? How do you know?" I pushed.

"I asked him, honey. We don't need any more scandal around here, so I went out on a limb and asked him. He says he's not gay."

"And you think he told you the truth?" I asked as the light turned green.

"I have no choice but to believe him." And on that note, he pulled up to the curb next to Aaron Mackie. T. K. stepped out of the car and shook Aaron's hand. I got out of the car as they were putting his bags in the trunk. Lord have mercy, he was even more handsome up close.

"Aaron Mackie, this is my wife, First Lady Monique Wilson." T. K. smiled as he introduced us.

"Pleased to meet you, Mr. Mackie," I said, politely offering him my hand.

"The pleasure's all mine, ma'am." He took my hand and kissed it. "And, please, call me Mackie. All my friends do."

"Okay, Mackie." I know T. K. must have wanted to kill me, because I turned all kinds of red, but when I glanced over at him, he had a neutral expression on his face. When he looked toward Aaron, his face took on an expression that I can only describe as prideful, like on the day his son graduated from law school. It was clear that he believed he'd found the best choir director— the only choir director—who could rescue our struggling church.

"My, you really have a beautiful wife, Bishop," Mackie commented. He turned to me. "You're a beautiful woman."

Was he trying to embarrass me? Couldn't he see I couldn't stop blushing? This man certainly knew how to work with what he had.

"Why, thank you, Mackie," T. K. replied, walking around to the driver's side. "I think she's a pretty fine-looking woman myself."

When I finally got myself under control, I said, "Mackie, why don't you sit up front with the bishop?"

"Only if you don't mind." He flashed those pearly whites at me.

"Don't be silly. Could you open the door?" He opened the rear passenger door so I could get in.

As I squeezed past him and bent over to get into the backseat, a shock went through my entire body.

No, he didn't, I thought. *No, he didn't just squeeze my ass.*

I stood up straight and turned to him. I couldn't believe what he'd just done. Thank God T. K. hadn't seen my reaction.

"Oops, sorry about that," he said sheepishly. "I tripped on the curb."

I gave him a skeptical glance. "Mmm-hmm. Lucky for you, you had something soft to break your fall."

"Yeah, well, it was an accident."

"What's going on?" the bishop asked from the driver's seat.

I glanced at Mackie, who was giving me a look that begged me not to tell T. K. what he'd just done. If my husband weren't so gung ho on this guy, I would have told, but I couldn't burst T. K.'s bubble.

"Nothing, honey. Mackie just tripped. I was making sure he was okay." I scowled at Mackie and got into the backseat, promising myself that I would keep a close eye on him. He might not present the same problems that Jackie had, but it didn't mean this new choir director didn't come with his own set of challenges.

Aaron

9

It was my first day of work, and I have to admit I was pretty excited as I walked from my new apartment to Merrick Boulevard. I still had a few more blocks to go before I reached First Jamaica Ministries, but I didn't mind the twenty-minute walk since it was such a nice day. I wanted to get to know my surroundings on foot before I started driving around town. Besides, if everything went as planned, I wouldn't be walking anywhere for too much longer. One of the first things I had on my agenda when I saw the bishop was to ask him when I was getting the car he'd promised me. The Escalade had been my dream car for as long as I could remember. I'd always loved SUVs, and the Cadillac Escalade was the top of the line, the ultimate in American car engineering.

I had to laugh, because despite all the craziness with Reverend Jenkins pulling a gun on me the other day, it looked like my life was actually going in the right direction for a change. Here I was with a great new job, a fantastic new apartment, and about to get a new car. It all seemed so surreal. There was only one thing standing in my way, and I'd have to deal with that sometime next week. In the meantime, I was going to enjoy every moment of my recent turn of good fortune.

When I arrived at the corner of 108th and Merrick Boulevard, I was awestruck by the sight of the church. As the choir director for Mount Olive in Virginia, I'd traveled around the country quite a bit, visiting and performing at different churches. I'd been to my share of megachurches, but I don't know if you could call the structure before me a church. It looked more like one of those European cathedrals you see on TV. It was absolutely magnificent. I don't think any black church I'd ever seen could compare to it. I couldn't wait to take a tour inside.

"Mr. Mackie! Aaron Mackie?" A female voice snapped me out of my astonished admiration of the building.

I looked up the stone stairs that led to the church's entrance and saw a woman dressed very conservatively in a white blouse and navy blue skirt. Being an avid observer of beautiful women, it was obvious to me that her conservative look was an attempt to hide a stunning figure. I mean, it's not every day you see a woman with D-cup breasts, a tiny little waist, and oversized round hips. I instinctively checked her left hand for a wedding or engagement ring, smiling as I filed away the observation that she didn't have either. I loved a woman with a nice figure, so she was my kind of woman. The fact that she had baby-smooth charcoal skin with dimples on both sides of her face didn't hurt matters either. A lot of brothers tended to ignore the real dark-skinned women, but I preferred them. I found them extremely attractive and, for the most part, dynamite in the bedroom. My motto was "the blacker the better," and this sexy-behind woman put the *B* in "black."

"Are you Aaron Mackie?" She smiled, showing me the whitest teeth I'd ever seen.

"Yes, I'm Aaron."

She walked down the stairs and I met her halfway. I don't know what type of perfume she was wearing, but it made her smell like heaven.

"Hi, Aaron. I'm Tia Gregory, the church's administrative secretary." She offered me her hand and gave me a firm shake. The only thing I could think was how soft her hands were. If her hands were that soft, how soft was the rest of her?

"Nice to meet you, Tia. You look very familiar. Have we met before?" She tried to pull her hand back, and I held on to it a second or two longer than I should have. The look she gave me was far from pleasant. *Okay,* I told myself, *pull your mind out of the gutter.* I had work to do, and this wasn't the first pretty sister I'd ever met.

I let go of her hand. "Sorry about that. I was just admiring how soft your hands were."

"Uh-huh." She took a step back, putting some space between us. "Bishop Wilson asked me to bring you to the choir practice room. We're having a meet and greet there."

"Practice room? The choir has a practice room?" This was too good to be true.

She gave me a condescending smirk but then put her professional face back on. "Oh, my bad. I forgot the bishop said you were from a small church down South. But yes, to answer your question, we do have a practice room for our choir."

She turned around and gestured for me to follow. I followed all right: followed those swinging hips of hers right up the stairs, around the side of the building, and to a pair of double doors in the back.

"This is the street entrance to the practice room. There is also an entrance from inside the building. I'm sure they will give you keys to both after the vote tomorrow afternoon."

"What vote is this?"

"Uh, nothing. I'm sorry. I misspoke," she replied, looking flustered. She might as well have had *liar* written all over her face.

"Tia, is there something I should know?"

"Mr. Mackie, I'm sure the bishop has told you everything you need to know. Now, are you ready to meet your new choir?"

"I've been ready for this moment my entire life." Then under my breath, I said, "It's showtime." Sure, I talked a good game, but my heart was palpitating, and my hands were sweaty. I was nervous as hell. After Tia's cryptic comment about some kind of vote, I had no idea what to expect.

I inhaled deeply before pushing open the double doors and walking into what looked like a mini auditorium. I raised my right eyebrow and gave everyone in the room the patented Aaron Mackie smile.

My eyes did a quick sweep around the room, and I was shocked to see that the large area was occupied by only a small number of people. There were about fifteen people present, all women except for two men in their fifties. I thought the megachurch would have been packed to meet the new choir director. I know my face probably mirrored my first reaction—big letdown—so I forced a smile.

"Well, hello, Mr. Mackie," the first lady called out. "We've been waiting for you."

I know you have, I thought. *I know you have.* Confidence was one thing I was never lacking when it came to me and the opposite sex.

Monique

10

I watched Aaron Mackie stroll through the double doors of the practice room like he owned the place. There was no question in my mind that T. K. had made the right decision to bring him on board when I heard the collective sigh of the women who'd been patiently waiting to meet him. I hadn't seen Aaron since T. K. and I dropped him off at his apartment two days ago. Lord forgive me for thinking it, but he sure did clean up nice. I mean, that man really was easy on the eyes, even more so now that he was dressed in a designer suit. The way he strutted into the room, I could tell he knew how good he looked. I wasn't even sure he recognized me as he scanned the room, because his eyes were focused on hot-behind Porsche Moore, but I quickly made my presence known.

"Well, hello, Mr. Mackie," I called out. "We've been waiting for you."

He looked a little surprised to see me when I walked toward him, but he still smiled, offering me his hand. "Hello there, First Lady. I wasn't expecting to see you again until Sunday service. Are you going to be joining our choir?"

I smiled back and took his hand. The thought flashed through my mind that this was the hand that had rubbed up against my backside and squeezed my ass just two days before. Sure, he'd said it was an accident, and I had accepted his apology, but I didn't believe him. The problem was that when I reflected on the incident now, I felt my heart rate increase a little bit. Certainly not the way a first lady was supposed to be reacting.

"Um, no." I shook my head. "Singing really isn't my thing."

"So, what exactly is your thing?" He winked, giving me this devilish smirk that I really didn't know how to interpret. Was he flirting with me?

As wrong as it was, I could feel the blood rushing to my face as he held on to my hand, which was starting to perspire. I should have been upset, but a small part of me was flattered. Men never flirted with me like that anymore, at least not since I'd become first lady. In a way it made me feel good. Make no mistake—I loved my husband. It was just nice to have a little attention thrown my way by a handsome younger man.

"My husband," I replied. "My husband is my thing."

"I'm sure he is." Aaron chuckled as if it were a game.

Afraid that someone might misinterpret—or even worse, properly interpret—my blushing, I pulled my hand back, glancing away so that no one other than Tia could see my red face. Thankfully, Tia's eyes were too preoccupied looking at Aaron's ass to be concerned with me. Knowing her background, I didn't think she was that type of girl, but her eyes were all up in his Kool-Aid. She wasn't the only one either. You should have seen the reaction of the other women in the room. The way some of them were looking at him, you would have thought it was a bachelorette party and he was about to do a striptease.

I cleared my throat. "Ah, Tia, everything check out down there?"

"Mmm-hmm, everything checks out just—Oh my goodness." Tia looked up from Aaron's behind to see me peering over my glasses at her. At the same time, Aaron was glancing over his shoulder with a big grin on his face. Poor girl was so embarrassed she dropped her clipboard.

"Oh, excuse me. I thought he had something on his pants."

I couldn't help but laugh. It was time to get this meet and greet under way before anyone else got themselves into trouble behind this fine man. "Well, Mr. Mackie, why don't we introduce you to your new choir?"

"That sounds like a plan."

I led him toward the group that had assembled in seats near the front. "Good morning, everyone. I have to admit I'm a little disappointed in the crowd, but I'm sure that with our new director in charge, we'll have members flocking back to the choir in no time. With that being said, I want everyone to give Mr. Aaron Mackie, our new choir director, a warm welcome."

"Welcome, Aaron," the women said in unison.

Aaron stepped forward to shake each woman's hand one by one. He seemed to be winning them over, too, but among the group were two dissidents from Jonathan Smith's camp of Judases. One of them, Trustee Duncan, said, "I want to know what qualifies you to be the choir director here. Other than that suit."

A few of the women chuckled, but most turned to hear what the trustee had to say.

"Yeah, I'd like to know that myself," Trustee Whitmore, who was seated next to him, added. "Did you ladies know they wanna pay this man seventy-five thousand dollars a year to lead our choir? How many of you make that much in two years, let alone one? I guess the bishop forgot we're still in a recession when he decided to throw away your hard-earned money on this supposed choir director. We don't even know if he can sing, let alone play an organ or piano."

A few of the women sat back in their chairs, suddenly looking less interested in Aaron, no matter how gorgeous he was. Personally, I wanted to smack the trustee for talking bad about my husband.

Aaron stood there in front of these people, fidgeting with the lapels on his jacket—until he heard Trustee Whitmore express doubts about his singing ability. That's when Aaron flexed his long, graceful fingers and went over to the piano. He sat down with a flourish and began to play "Stand" by Ron Winans.

Oh, he could play the heck out of the piano, but the truly special moment was when he opened his mouth and began to sing. It was as if angels had flown into the room. He had a voice that ranged from bass all the way up to tenor. Some of the women in attendance actually gasped when his voice really started to soar. Now, I'd heard good singing before, but listening to him was like nothing I'd ever heard inside the walls of First Jamaica Ministries. Once again my husband turned out to be right. Aaron Mackie definitely had skills.

When he was finished, each and every woman present jumped to her feet to give him a standing ovation. Both trustees stayed put, scowling in their seats.

One of the older, more prominent sisters turned toward Trustee Whitmore and said, "I don't care if he wants a million dollars. I want that man to be our choir director, you hear?"

Aaron stood up from the piano and walked to the front of the crowd. "We're going to be doing some new things here at First Jamaica Ministries. I really think you're going to like it. I, for one, plan on winning a few of those national choir championship trophies y'all have displayed in that case over there. But I can't do it by myself. I'm going to need all of your help in doing it and more. So, please, tell all your friends."

"You don't have to worry about that," one sister around Aaron's age said, then took out her phone and took his picture. "You about to be all over Facebook."

While Aaron was charming the skirts off the women present, I watched with amusement as the two trustees scurried out of the practice room. They were probably itching to report back to Deacon Smith before the vote this afternoon. I would have loved to hear what they planned on telling him. Not that it mattered. T. K. had something for Jonathan Smith and his cronies. Something that would put his old buddy Smitty right back where we wanted him.

I turned to Tia. "So, what do you think of our new choir director?"

She nodded. "He can sing, that's for sure."

"I know he can sing. Everybody in the room knows he can sing. I wasn't talking about his musical ability. What do you think of him as a man?" I raised both eyebrows twice, giving her a look I knew she would understand.

She turned her head, trying to hide a smile. "He's cute, I guess. Not really my style."

"Cute, you guess?" I rolled my eyes. "Tia, I know we're in the church, but aren't you taking this whole Goody-Two-shoes-church-girl thing a little far? I mean, less than ten minutes ago, I had to darn near scrape your eyes off the man's behind."

If you didn't think real-dark-skinned women could blush, well, news flash: they can. That's exactly what Tia was doing.

"I wasn't looking at his behind. It looked like he had something on his pants."

"Well, whatever it was must have been right on his butt, because that's where your eyes were."

"First Lady, I swear—"

I lifted my hand to stop her. Because of her past history with men, I knew Tia was uncomfortable with talk that was even remotely sexual. As a fairly new first lady, I was still learning to control my mouth. I tried to put the brakes on this conversation before it got out of control. "Tia, it's okay. Ain't nothing wrong with looking at a handsome man. It's just looking."

She nodded, still looking a little annoyed. "And I can appreciate that he's a good-looking man—a very good-looking man—but he's just not my type. And I definitely don't want to end up with a reputation like Porsche Moore over there."

I turned and saw Porsche Moore, one of the church's more "active" women, all up in Aaron's face. She had what every man wanted and what every woman envied: a huge, perfectly round butt and long, flowing hair that hung below her waist. She wrote something on the back of a business card and boldly handed it to him. I was pretty sure it had nothing to do with music or the choir.

"Uh-huh, I see what you mean." I gestured for Tia to come a little closer, lowering my voice. "Tia, the church has a lot riding on Mr. Mackie over there, and we don't need him falling into the wrong situation, if you know what I mean."

"I think I do," she replied.

"Why don't you show Aaron around? Keep him occupied and out of trouble. He doesn't know the area, and I would hate for someone like Porsche to be his guide."

"I don't know, First Lady. I don't want to give him the wrong impression."

"You won't, because we're going to make it very clear to everyone that you're the choir's new administrator, along with being the administrative secretary. Plus, I would consider it a personal favor. I don't have to tell you, but we don't need any more controversy, and you know how these churchwomen can be. All you're going to be is a chaperone."

She still looked a little uncomfortable with the whole idea, but if Tia was anything, it was loyal to the church. "Okay, if you put it like that, I'll do it, but you can deal with *her.*" She gestured toward the door as my friend Simone strutted into the room. At first I thought she was headed toward Tia and me, but instead she headed directly toward Aaron.

"So, you're the new choir director everyone is talking about?" Simone said.

I watched as she blatantly eyed him from head to toe before offering her hand. I knew that look; I'd seen her give it to men in the past. Simone was on the prowl, and Aaron Mackie was her prey. Aaron was a little less conspicuous, but it was pretty obvious from where I stood that he liked what he saw. Poor guy didn't know what he was getting into. He didn't have a chance.

The thought crossed my mind to pull her off to the side and ask her to back off, but I was sure I'd be accused of wanting him for myself.

"Yes, I'm Aaron Mackie." He took her hand. "But everyone calls me Mackie."

"I'm Simone Wilcox, the chairwoman of the board of trustees. And if everyone calls you Mackie, then I'm gonna call you Aaron." She winked at him. "A girl's gotta have something to herself."

Mackie smiled. "Miss Simone, as pretty as you are, you can have whatever you want."

"Be careful what you ask for. You might just get it." She released a throaty chuckle, then turned to wave at Tia and me. No doubt she wanted to make sure we were witnessing her in action. "Well, anyway, I just wanted to meet you before the vote this afternoon."

Aaron looked frustrated. "Why do people keep talking about a vote?"

Simone looked over at me and shook her head accusingly. "I take it no one told you that the board of trustees and deacons have to vote on whether to accept you as our choir director before you officially have the position."

"Excuse me?" Aaron raised his voice. "You mean to tell me I moved all the way up here and I don't even have the job yet?"

"Sweetie, all I can tell you is that you've got my vote." The look she gave him made it clear that he could have a lot more than just her vote.

Thank goodness most of the people had started to leave, because Aaron did not look happy as he approached me. He was followed by Simone, who was tilting her head to get a better look at his ass.

We were all silent for an uncomfortable nanosecond until he spoke. "Is this true? I don't officially have the job yet?"

"Aaron, calm down. I think you should talk to the bishop. He'll explain everything to you."

"Damn right he will. Where can I find him?"

"He's in his office." I sighed, wishing I could text my hubby a heads-up, but he barely ever looked at his text messages. "Tia, why don't you show Mackie to the administrative offices while I wrap this up?"

"No problem, First Lady." She gestured toward the door. "You ready, Aaron?"

"Um, Aaron, before you go . . ." Simone reached into her purse and handed him a business card. "Call me after the vote. I'm the one who's in charge of getting you that Escalade you were promised." With that, she spun on her heels and sashayed toward the doors with Aaron watching every step she made.

Well, with Simone around, I don't think we have to worry about Porsche Moore anymore.

The Bishop

11

I was enjoying what was left of the pork-chop sandwich my wife had prepared for my lunch when the intercom on my desk came to life. "Bishop Wilson!"

I jumped up out of my chair when I heard my secretary's voice. She scared the heck out of me, because I thought she was with my wife at the choir reception for Aaron Mackie. Truth is, I should have been there myself, but I'd been sidetracked waiting for that fool Smitty to show up. I'd asked him earlier in the day to stop by my office around noon so we could talk. I was hoping to talk some reason into him and settle our differences before the joint meeting of the deacons' board and the board of trustees, but he'd had me waiting for almost an hour and a half.

"Yes, Tia?" I was half expecting her to tell me that Smitty had finally arrived. I didn't know what kind of game he was playing, or why my supposed friend suddenly had such a vendetta, but there was no doubt in my mind that Smitty was determined to prevent Aaron's hiring. And from what I'd been hearing behind the scenes, it went even further than that. If he had his way, there would be a second vote, where he'd have me thrown out on my ass.

"Aaron Mackie is here to see you."

Hmm, now that was interesting. It looked like Smitty was going to stand me up. It also looked like the reception for Mackie was over earlier than I would have expected.

"Oh, okay. You can send him in."

I quickly wrapped up my lunch and placed it in an empty drawer just as Mackie entered the room. I stood to greet him.

"Mackie, how'd your reception with the choir go?" I took his hand and pulled him in close. I was starting to like this kid a lot. I released my embrace only to see a frown on his face.

"Well, Bishop, to be honest, it was a little disappointing."

"Really? I'm sorry to hear that. There wasn't a very big crowd down there, was there?"

He shook his head as he spoke. "No, there really wasn't."

"Have a seat and let's discuss it. There are a few things I think you should know." I was feeling a little embarrassed that I hadn't spoken to him about the church's troubles earlier. I guess I was hoping that things would work themselves out before he had to get wind of any of the strife. "I probably should have told you this earlier. The reason we're having such low attendance is—"

He raised his hand to interrupt me. "Hold on for a second, Bishop. You don't have to worry about that. I can deal with the low-attendance issue. I just have to build the choir up. And building a choir is what you brought me here for, if I'm not mistaken."

I nodded. "Yes, Mackie, it is. If anyone can turn our choir around, I believe it's you. From day one, I felt you were the man for the job."

"Bishop, I'm humbled by your praise, but what I need to know is why you had me quit my job and come all the way up here only to find out you didn't have the authority to hire me. Why'd you do that to me?" He folded his arms angrily.

Clearly, he was not a happy camper. I wouldn't have been either if I were in his situation.

I walked around to the front of my desk and sat down next to him. "Aaron, I don't know what you were told, but I didn't lie to you—at least not intentionally. You see, I do have the authority to hire you. I've hired every choir director this church has had for the past twenty years."

Now he was really looking confused. "Then what's all this about a vote? If you've hired me, why are all these people telling me my job is up in the air until after the vote? And why are they upset about my salary?"

"Who told you that your job was up in the air?" I felt a sudden urge to strangle whoever it was. On top of all the troubles our church was already facing, this whole thing was a headache I did not need.

He didn't reveal his source. "All I want to know is do I have a job or not?"

"Relax, Mackie. I've got everything under control." I placed what I hoped was a reassuring hand on his shoulder. "You have a job. The vote is just a formality. All that talk is just a few deacons and trustees who are riled up because you're going to be making more money than them, that's all. Don't worry. It won't be long before you and your choir have everyone convinced that you're worth every penny."

Aaron did not look convinced. His brow was furrowed in anxiety. "Doesn't sound like it's just a formality to me. You know, I'm here to help the church. I don't want any drama."

"Don't worry. There won't be any." I looked him straight in the eye to make sure he understood my sincerity. "And if by chance there is, I'll make you one promise: If you don't pass that vote, they're not only going to lose a great choir director, but they're going to lose a great pastor too."

"Are you serious?" His eyes were wide with disbelief. I almost couldn't believe I'd said it myself. "You'd do that for me, Bishop?"

"Mackie, a man is only as good as his word. I gave you my word. And if the church won't back up my word after all these years, then there is no reason for me to be its pastor." I got up from my chair and straightened out my suit jacket. "But with that being said, I don't have any intention of going anywhere, so neither one of us is in jeopardy of losing our jobs."

He smiled. "I hope you're right. I need this job. I don't think I can get my old one back."

"I need mine too," I said with a laugh. "I haven't seen any help-wanted ads in the newspaper for pastors of megachurches."

Aaron stood up, reached over the desk, and shook my hand. "Thank you, Bishop. I feel a whole lot better now."

I walked him to the door, and when I opened it, lo and behold, there was Smitty. He was pacing in front of Tia's desk, as if he were the one who'd been kept waiting two hours for our appointment.

I wrapped my arm around Mackie's shoulder and plastered a big grin on my face. "Deacon Smith, this is Aaron Mackie, our new choir director." I could see Tia trying to hide her snickering behind her desk.

"Pleased to meet you, Deacon." Aaron offered him his hand, but Smitty only gave him a cold glare, ignoring the gesture.

"You wanted to talk?" Smitty growled at me.

"Sure did," I replied matter-of-factly.

He walked past Mackie and me and into my office.

Mackie lifted an eyebrow and glanced at me.

"Don't mind him. He's a legend in his own mind."

Mackie let out a sigh and nodded good-bye. Clearly he understood that Smitty was one of the people potentially standing in the way of his new job. He walked past Tia to leave.

"Hey, Mackie," I called after him. "Listen, I'll catch up with you later. Maybe we'll have dinner to celebrate your official instatement." I said it loud enough that Smitty could hear me.

Back in my office, Smitty was sitting in the seat Aaron had just vacated. I walked over to my desk and sat in my leather chair, rocking a few times and staring pointedly at Smitty before I spoke.

"So, how's Maria, Smitty? Everything going all right between you two? Is your marriage on firm spiritual footing?" I steepled my fingers, putting on my "concerned preacher" pose to keep my true feelings in check.

Smitty gave me the most confused look I'd ever seen. It was so easy to take him off his game. "Um, yes, my marriage is fine, but is that why you asked me here, to find out about my marriage?" He grabbed the arms of his chair as if he were about to push himself up. " 'Cause if it is, I don't have time for this. I came here to talk church business."

"Sit down, Smitty!" I ordered. My hands were out of their nonconfrontational steeple pose and now balled into fists on my desk. "What kind of church business do you wanna talk about?"

"Look, I don't wanna beat around the bush anymore, Bishop. We both know why I'm here."

"Oh, and why is that, Smitty?"

"You want me to cut your little choir director friend a break, but it's not happening. I want you to understand that we are not going to stand for you hiring this young man. We don't have the funds."

"Do you really want to fight me on this, Smitty? I've beaten better men than you in that boardroom." Suddenly I realized that if we continued our conversation in this manner, things were going to turn ugly. As mad as I was, I still had to remember that I was a spiritual leader—and that not too long ago, I considered this man a friend.

I took my tone down a notch and said, "Heck, let's be real about it: Most of those times it was you fighting alongside me. I don't want to fight you, Smitty. Why don't you go hear the kid sing? I think it will convince you we're making the right choice."

My peacemaking attempt got me nowhere. He would not back down. "No, thanks. I'll pass. And yes, I was fighting alongside you, but you're not thinking rationally, so someone has to take you down a few pegs."

I cleared my throat. "What has gotten into you? We're supposed to be friends."

"We are friends, T. K., but I have to do what's best for the church—and having you as pastor and him as choir director is not in the church's best interest."

So, the rumors were true. Smitty, for whatever reason, was trying to take me out. Well, so much for handling this with diplomacy. If my enemies were going to come gunning for me, I would have to use some ammunition of my own.

"I'm not quite sure what that's supposed to mean, Smitty, but I've got to do what I think is best for the church also." I reached into my lower desk drawer and pulled out a folder. "After you read this, I think you will agree that I'm not going anywhere, and neither is he."

Smitty opened the folder and examined the contents, which caused him to gasp. Expressions of shock, recognition, and then fear rippled across his face.

"Oh dear Lord, where did you get this?"

"James Black knows the dirt on everybody in this church, Smitty. You know that. You do recall how close we are, don't you? Well, I now have possession of all his files." I leveled a steely gaze on him. "It sure would be a shame if this information leaked out, wouldn't it?"

"You wouldn't," he challenged.

I smirked. "I wouldn't hesitate."

"But . . . but you're a pastor, a man of God. You wouldn't stoop this low. This is blackmail. It's goes against your moral code."

"Who are you to decide what my moral code is? And for the record, I'm still a man of God, just one with something hanging over your head. You didn't really think I'd let you railroad me out of my job or push out a man after I gave him my word, did you? You should know me better than that. And a lesson for future reference: Before you come after any man, you should always be sure your own skeletons are in check."

"T. K. . . ." Smitty was backing down in a hurry. "Bishop, you don't understand. If this gets out, my life as I know it is over."

"You've been keeping secrets for so long you don't even realize that life as you knew it has been over for a long time now. But I'm gonna give you a chance to keep the status quo."

"And how are you going to do that?"

"I want you to go into that meeting and let them know you want to keep Aaron Mackie as the choir director. You do that and I'll see to it that your secret stays with me."

Suddenly, it was as if all the fight had gone out of him, like his body was shrinking before my eyes. He was clearly a defeated man. What I didn't know was that the pressure he was feeling wasn't coming solely from me.

"You don't understand. They have the same information that you do, T. K. This is way bigger than just some simple hiring of a choir director. This is about you. They want you out, and they are not going to stop until you're gone."

"Who, Smitty? Who could want me gone that bad?"

He didn't give me an answer. With fear in his eyes, he got up and headed for the door, his head hung low. "I can't go into that meeting and say what you want me to say, old friend. They'll ruin me if I do. But I'll give you a fighting chance by not showing up at all. You think that will be good enough?" For the first time since I returned from hiring Aaron, I saw the real Smitty again. I saw my friend—and he looked deeply troubled.

"If you're not there to push them, it just might be. But, Smitty, please, I need to know who's doing this."

"I can't do that. You're a man of God, so I'm going to trust that you'll do the right thing, the godly thing, and keep my secret. Them, on the other hand . . . there's no telling what they'd do if I revealed their identities. I have a family to consider. All I can do is warn you. Resign before this thing gets ugly. This whole thing is way bigger than you or me."

Simone

12

Aaron Mackie and Simone Wilcox. I wrote it on my day planner and surrounded it with a heart. Silly, right? Well, I had been doodling silly stuff like that all day long. I'd met the man only two days ago, but I just couldn't get him out of my head. Sure, I'd had my share of crushes over the years on some of the finest men you'd ever want to meet, but this was different. It was like he was a missing piece of me I didn't know existed. I truly felt like he could complete me. Lord knows it had been a long time since a man had taken over my mind like this. A very long time.

"Simone, your father's on line four." Anita Lowery, my secretary, popped her head into my office, snapping me out of my fantasy world and back to the reality of running a car dealership.

Oh, great. Just what I didn't need today, a call from dear old Dad.

"How'd he sound, Anita?" I held my breath as I waited for her reply.

"He sounded agitated. He snapped at me twice."

That wasn't a good sign because Daddy liked Anita.

"He didn't ask to speak with Willie, did he?" I asked hopefully.

"No, he just wanted to speak to you. I told him you were on the floor with a customer, and he said he didn't care, that I should go get you."

"Oh Lord, what the hell does he want?" I wondered out loud. Anita shrugged, probably glad that it wasn't her he was upset with. "Okay, Anita, thanks. I'll take it from here."

Anita pulled her head back and disappeared into the hallway, shutting my door. I, on the other hand, stared at the phone, willing it to spontaneously disconnect the call. I took a deep breath and finally picked it up, pressing the flashing red button.

"Hey, Daddy," I said in an upbeat, almost teenage-sounding voice. I was in my late thirties, but I knew the best way to keep my father calm was to butter him up and keep him thinking that I was still his little girl, helpless and always in need of his help. "How's the greatest father in the world? Still handsome as ever, I'm sure."

It wasn't a lie. My father was a great-looking man for sixty-six. He was still trim and fit. Since he and my stepmom retired to a Sarasota, Florida, senior community, he walked and exercised every day. He even lifted weights. He pranced around like a male peacock, so I treated him like one.

"Don't you BS me, girl. I'm not in the mood."

His voice sounded brusque. This was a problem. It was evident that he wasn't buying what I was selling, which could only mean he'd found out something that I didn't want him to know. The real question was what did he know, and just how damaging was it?

"What do you mean, Daddy? I wouldn't BS you." I stuck with the girlie voice in case it might still soften him up.

"Did you fire Michael Nixon?"

Damn! How'd he find out about that? My palms got sweaty, and my heart started pounding. I knew what was up, and I wasn't in the mood for a confrontation. I sure wished the nosy-behind folks around here would mind their own damn business. They were always diming on me. Just jealous, that's what they were.

"Yes, Daddy, I fired him." I sighed loudly as I pulled the phone away from my ear in anticipation of the yelling I was sure to hear. My father didn't disappoint.

"What the hell is wrong with you? That man is our best damn salesman!"

The phone was three feet away from my ear, and I could hear every word he said as clear as a bell.

"Daddy! Daddy! Please . . . please hear me out before you start screaming again. Please."

"You got two minutes!" he huffed.

Michael Nixon had been working at Wilcox Motors for almost fifteen years, and my father was right; he had been our top salesman since the day he started. With that being said, I still fired his ass last week when I found out he was getting married. No, it wasn't the brightest move I'd ever made, but it sure as hell made me feel better. You see, on top of being the best salesman, Mike Nixon was by far the most handsome man in the company. I'd started sleeping with him about two years ago when my father retired and turned the business over to me. It wasn't anything serious, at least not for me, and after a few months, I got bored and gave him the boot. I did, however, let him keep his job. I figured it was the right thing to do. Like I said, he was our top salesman.

Everything was fine until he started strutting around the dealership last week talking about getting married. Now, I didn't even know the woman he was marrying, but there was no way I was gonna let him support some floozy with company funds when he was clearly just on the rebound from me. So, I fired his ass and hired two cuter, noncommissioned guys for half of what he made.

"Daddy, I didn't want to fire him, but I had no choice when I found out he was planning on opening his own dealership down the block next year. No way was I going to let him finance our demise and tear down what you built with money we paid him. I'm sorry, Daddy. Maybe I should have spoken to you first, but I felt I had to act fast." I knew I shouldn't be lying to my father, but a girl's gotta do what a girl's gotta do. Besides, I'd been lying to him for as long as I could remember. It was practically second nature at this point.

There was silence on the line when I finished speaking. Then my father exploded. "That sneaky son of a bitch!" he shouted. "Don't worry about it, baby. You did the right thing."

"Thank you, Daddy." I held the phone away from my mouth and exhaled.

"But don't think you're off the hook yet. Weren't you supposed to get me a check out last week?"

"We didn't send you that check?" I tried to sound surprised. "I'll have to check with accounting on that." I was stalling for time and trying to placate him. Unfortunately, he wasn't buying it. As often as I lied to him, there were still times I couldn't fool him.

"Don't play games with me, Simone. You know that check didn't go out. I already called Lisa in accounting."

"Daddy, I'll be sending it at the end of the week. I promise."

"I don't want your promises, Simone. I just want my check. And it better not bounce," he warned. "You do not want me to catch a plane to New York and make some changes. You may run the company, but technically I still own it."

"I know, Daddy. You've made that pretty clear the past two years."

"Don't you dare patronize me! You missed last month's payment, and when you finally sent it, it bounced. I didn't put you in charge of my company so I could worry about my retirement."

"You don't have to worry, Daddy. I got this, okay? And you don't have to come to New York. I'll get you a cashier's check and text you the tracking number tonight, all right? Look, I gotta run. Love you."

"I love you too . . . sometimes."

"Sometimes?" I repeated, not believing my ears.

With that, Daddy hung up. I closed my eyes and rubbed them, thankful to get out of that conversation with just a mild tongue-lashing and a demand for a check. Daddy could be so cold-blooded when it came to his money. I was going to have to get him that check. Last thing I needed was for him to be taking a trip to New York and snooping around with all the things I had going on.

Anita stepped into my office and closed the door behind her, looking flushed. She leaned against the door frame and fanned herself with her hand.

"Anita, what is wrong with you?"

"Simone, there is a customer out there waiting to see you, and he is so fiiiine!"

"He asked for me?" I had an inkling I knew who the gorgeous man was. "Is his name Aaron Mackie?"

"Mmm-hmm." She nodded.

"Oh my God. He's here?" I lifted my head, primping my hair

with my hand. "He wasn't supposed to come by until around six." I glanced at the clock. It was six, all right. Where did the time go?

"Gurrl, who is he?"

"He's the new choir director at my church." I smiled proudly.

"Well, then consider me a new member of your church." It was clear from the look on her face that she was dead serious.

"Anita, you are a trip."

"I didn't see a ring. Is he available?"

"No, he's not available." I cut my eyes at her as I brushed off my suit. "And if you value your job, I better not catch you flirting with him."

She raised both eyebrows. "Oh, my bad. I'm so sorry. I didn't realize he was one of yours. I mean, he's just so damn fine. I wasn't thinking."

"Well, now you know." I gave her a pointed look to make sure she understood that the conversation was over.

I liked Anita, and she was a good secretary, but there were reasons I didn't have very many women working here. Number one: I don't like competition, despite the fact that there usually isn't any. Number two: Bitches are sneaky when it comes to men. I knew I was, and if I would do something, I damn sure knew another bitch would too. However, it did feel good to watch another woman go crazy over a man who was mine—or at least who was going to be mine.

"You want me to show him in?" Anita asked with a hint of an attitude. Obviously she was pissed about the way I spoke to her, but I didn't give a damn. All's fair in love and war.

"No, wait. Just a minute." I picked up my compact, freshened up my lipstick, swiped my makeup sponge over my face, and ran my hand through my hair. I sat up straight in my chair and crossed my legs. "All right, you can send him in now."

She nodded, then stepped out of my office, no doubt rolling her eyes once her back was turned. Three minutes later, I was standing up to greet my future husband and the father of my unborn children.

"Trustee Wilcox, so nice to see you again. You're looking well."

You're looking better than well, I thought as we shook hands. "Nice to see you, too, Aaron. I'm glad to see you made it through the vote unscathed."

"Thanks to you and the bishop. I heard you were instrumental in swinging the vote my way. Thank you, Trustee."

"No thanks needed. Besides, you had nothing to worry about with the bishop in the room. Now, on another note, would you please stop calling me Trustee? I thought I told you when we first met that my name is Simone, at least when it comes to my friends. And I hope we're going to be friends."

"I hope so, too, Simone," he said, letting the sexy back into his tone. "I was just trying to be professional."

I'd like to give you a professional.

"I appreciate that, but I'm not like the rest of those stuffed shirts at the church. I'm pretty laid-back." I paused for a moment to let him imagine me "laid back," preferably naked in his bed. "Well, with that being said, I take it you're here for the car that was promised to you."

"Yes, ma'am. I thought I'd come down and pick up my ride." He was smiling like an excited little kid.

I picked up my phone and dialed an extension.

A man answered. "Wilcox Motors, Willie speaking."

"Willie, this is Simone. Do you have that burgundy Escalade ready?"

"Yep. It's all prepped and ready to go."

"Okay, I'll be out with the owner in a minute." I hung up and looked over at Mackie, who was still grinning. He looked so cute. "Well, your car's ready. How'd you like to take a sister out for a ride and some dinner as payment?"

"I'd like that a lot." He gestured toward the door. "Lead the way, fair lady."

I got my purse and guided Aaron to the new-car prepping lot and our very first date.

Aaron

13

I was on cloud nine as I drove down the Wantagh Parkway in Long Island toward Jones Beach. I still couldn't believe I'd finally gotten the Escalade I'd been dreaming about for the past five years, and without one dime coming out of my pocket. I didn't think life could get any better—until I glanced over at fine-ass Simone. She was sitting in the passenger seat beside me, rocking her head contently as John Legend played on the satellite radio. Out of the corner of my eye, I sneaked a glimpse of her long legs. They seemed to pour out of her red miniskirt, right into a pair of sexy red stilettos. Talk about the perfect accessory to a luxury vehicle. She was so beautiful I was almost afraid to approach her, but she'd been giving me that unmistakable vibe ever since we sat down to dinner a few hours ago. My instincts never seemed to fail me when it came to women, so there was no doubt in my mind that she was just as interested in me as I was in her.

The only problem was that I had to approach her carefully. Simone wasn't one of those slam-bam-thank-you-ma'am church sisters I'd run into down in Virginia. No, she was in a class by herself, and putting aside the fact that she was the chairwoman of the board of trustees at my job and technically one of my bosses, she was closer to being girlfriend material than anyone I'd met in a long time.

"So, what did you think of the food at Costa de Espana?"

"It was good. I've had Mexican and Cuban food, but I've never had authentic food from Spain before. Same flair, but a different taste."

"Uh-huh. I found that place about two years ago. I only take people I'm trying to impress." She smiled, showing off the huge dimple in her left cheek.

"I'm honored, but you wanna know what really impressed me?" Even as I spoke, I was thinking about how I couldn't wait to get her into bed so I could impress her.

She nodded. "Yeah, I do. What?"

"The fact that you speak Spanish so fluently. I know a few words, but you were having a full-fledged conversation with that hostess when we were leaving. It looked kind of intense. What were you talking about?"

"You."

"Me?" I was used to women talking about me, but the fact that it was one as beautiful as Simone was flattering. "What about me?"

"She was asking me if I could get your autograph for her and her friends. Didn't you notice there were a lot of people staring at us?" I shook my head. "Well, evidently, Mr. Mackie, you look like some Spanish soap opera star."

"Get out. Really?" I was getting a kick out of this. "They say we've all got a twin. I guess mine is a Latin TV star." I laughed. "You should have told me. I would have given them all an autograph."

"That's exactly why I didn't tell you. You've got enough going on with being First Jamaica Ministries' choir director. I didn't want you to get a big head."

"I heard that, but the truth is I didn't notice anyone looking at me because I was staring at you." I lifted one eyebrow, giving her the patented Aaron Mackie smile.

She smirked. Clearly she was used to admiration from the opposite sex too. Still, she tried to stay humble. "It wasn't because I had something stuck in my teeth, was it?"

"No," I said with a laugh. "It's because you're a beautiful woman, Simone Wilcox."

She blushed. "Thank you."

"You are most welcome." I took her hand and kissed the back of it. "And I really am impressed that you speak fluent Spanish."

Coyly, she said, "If you think that's impressive, you should hear my French."

I hoped she was telling the truth. Two foreign languages? There was nothing more attractive than a fine-looking woman with brains to match. This woman was sophisticated. She might be more than girlfriend material; I was starting to think she could end up being wife material.

"You speak French too?"

She leaned in close, placing a hand on my leg as she whispered in my ear, "Only when I make love, *mon amour.*"

"Oh my, my, my," I sighed. Needless to say, all the blood in my body rushed to my groin. Thank goodness we'd just pulled into the parking lot of Jones Beach, because any more talk like that and I might have had an accident and killed both of us.

"So, where'd you learn to speak all these languages?" I asked as we got out of the truck.

"My best friend in grade school is from the Dominican Republic, so I learned Spanish from her. If you didn't know how to ask for it in Spanish, you didn't get anything to eat in her house. And I took French in high school and lived in Paris for a year when I was a college student, so I learned the language firsthand."

"Amazing." We began to walk down the beach.

"So, enough about me. Tell me about you. Who is Aaron Mackie?" Simone asked.

"That's a good question," I replied. "I guess deep down I'm just a country boy trying to fulfill his dreams."

"What kind of dreams?"

"My major goal right now is to win a national choir championship and put First Jamaica back on the map; then I'd like to get a recording contract. Don't take this as bragging, but I think I'm as good as Kirk Franklin and them."

"After what I heard in the rehearsal room, I don't think there's any doubt about that. You really can blow."

"Thanks." We stopped walking, and she took off her shoes.

"So, have you always wanted to be a singer and choir director?"

"No, I never sang anywhere other than my shower until I was

a senior in college. Heck, I wouldn't have even done that if I hadn't been trying to run behind a girl who was in the choir." I picked up a rock and threw it in the water.

"Wow, now that's a pretty remarkable story. Where'd you go to school?"

"I went to the University of Virginia."

"You went to UVA?"

"Yeah." I nodded.

"No wonder I like you. My father went to UVA. That's a hard school to get into. They rejected me, even with a legacy." She stopped walking and turned to face me. "Boy, my daddy is gonna love you."

"You think so?"

"I know so." Simone slipped her hand into mine, and we trudged through the sand, just holding hands.

"So, is that why you're still single?" I asked after awhile. "Your daddy hasn't approved of your men?"

I was playing with her, but she got a little attitude with me. "I'm a grown woman, and my daddy doesn't have to approve of anything I do."

I pulled her close and kissed her, gently yet passionately. Not a whole lot of tongue, but enough to let us both know the road we were going down.

"So, do you approve of that?"

"Mmm, I sure do, but let me see something." She wrapped her arms around me and pulled me closer. This time she instigated the kiss. "Wow. You're a really good kisser."

"Why do you say that?"

"Because most men don't know how to kiss—at least not how to properly kiss a woman. You've obviously had some practice over the years."

I grinned, but skillfully avoided her attempt to get me to spill about past relationships. "Well, if you thought that was nice, what do you think of this?" I pressed against her and kissed her as deeply and as passionately as I could. She offered no resistance. We were locked together as tight as Siamese twins, oblivious to any other people on the beach.

"I don't think I've ever been kissed like that before," Simone said with a sigh when we finally separated.

She looked dreamy-eyed. I knew the look; I think I had it my-self.

"I like you, Aaron. I like you a lot. And I might be making the biggest mistake of my life by inviting you over, but would you like to come over to my place for a drink?"

As a man, I'd learned that most women decide whether they're going to sleep with a man in the first fifteen minutes. Likewise, I'd made up my mind I was going to sleep with Simone thirty seconds after she walked into the choir practice room and I saw her for the first time.

"Why are you afraid of inviting me over for a drink?"

"It's not the drink that I'm afraid of. It's what comes after the drink."

"Nothing's going to happen after we have a drink if you don't want it to," I reassured her, though I was pretty certain she wouldn't try to stop me if I made a move. "No means no to me. I won't do anything that you're not ready for. Matter of fact, we don't have to go back to your house. I'd be just as happy to go to a bar and have a drink with you."

She shook her head and took my hand. "I want you to come to my house, and whatever happens, happens."

Bingo! I knew how to read between the lines, and I eagerly followed her as she led me back to the car.

Monique

14

I was in my private bathroom, primping in front of the mirror in the sheer Victoria's Secret peignoir set my husband had bought for me. He did that type of thing when he was in a good mood, and there had been a sense of elation in our house the past two days. T. K. had gone in front of the joint boards of our church and successfully secured the installment of Aaron Mackie as choir director for the next three years. It turned out that without Jonathan Smith leading them, the bishop's detractors slid right back into the holes they crawled out of, just as James Black had predicted from his hospital bed. The vote ended up being over-whelmingly in Aaron's favor, and a testament to the bishop's control of the church. From the way he'd been humming and whistling around the house, T. K. was quite pleased with him-self. He didn't have a clue, but in a few minutes, I was going to show him just how pleased I was, too, if you know what I mean.

I sprayed my shoulder blades and my wrists with one of the most seductive perfumes I owned. Then, after one last glance in the mirror, I stepped out of my bathroom, striking a pose to model my outfit for my husband. He was sitting up in the bed with his laptop, working on his new book. He wouldn't be working for long, though. I planned to seriously put it on him. We both had a way of communicating without words when we were in the mood, so when he looked up from his computer and spotted me, I was sure he heard me loud and clear.

He smiled when I spun around so he could see all that he was about to get. T. K. loved when I did my little stripteases. I'd wanted to take one of those pole-dancing courses they advertise in the local newspaper, but I was afraid someone might find out about it and start some crazy gossip. I could hear all the rumors now about the first lady being a stripper and working in some club in Queens behind my husband's back. Can you imagine the drama that would crop up behind that? I didn't even want to think about it.

I strutted over to the bed. T. K. moved his laptop and I straddled him. He kissed me passionately, moving his lips down to the sensitive spot on my neck before lightly blowing in my ear. I purred as his hands cupped my breasts, kneading them through the silk nightgown. I let out a low moan as he moved his lips back to mine.

"I love you so much, Bishop T. K. Wilson," I murmured, pushing him back gently. "I wouldn't give you up for anybody in the world."

"I love you, too, my wife. I couldn't have asked for a better woman to spend the rest of my life with."

I kissed his neck and began to slowly work my way down.

"Mmm," he murmured, sniffing my shoulders. I knew this was his favorite scent. "You always smell so good, and you look so beautiful in this nightgown. Is it new?"

I looked up, shaking my head at him. Men can really be a trip sometimes. "You know, it really is a good thing I love you, because the average woman would slap you upside your head, T. K."

"Slap me upside the head for what?"

"Because this is the negligee you just bought for me and left in my office, that's why. Did you even pick it out?" The thought of him sending Tia or another member of our congregation to pick out a gift infuriated me.

"I didn't pick anything out, because I didn't buy anything. I don't know what you're talking about, honey. I didn't leave any negligee in your office."

"Stop playing, T. K. This isn't funny. You mean to tell me you didn't buy this for me?" I sat up. "You know what? I'm starting to lose the mood." Maybe that would make him tell me the truth so we could get back to business.

He gave me a stern look. "No, Monique, I didn't. I wish I had, but I didn't. Maybe one of the sisters left it for you. Did you do something nice for someone recently?"

"I always try to do something nice for people, but nothing

that sticks out in my mind. And not for anyone who would buy me Victoria's Secret lingerie."

"Hmm . . . maybe you have a secret admirer."

He was trying to lighten the mood, but he wasn't funny. Not knowing who had purchased me something so intimate made me want to rip it off my body.

Then a thought struck me. There had been only one person who'd shown me any interest as of late, and that was our new choir director, and I knew he wouldn't . . . well, I hoped he wouldn't do anything like . . . but then again, he did squeeze my ass that one time.

Before I could ponder it further, the phone rang, interrupting our little chat. T. K. reached over to the nightstand. As a minister, he believed in answering the phone no matter what time of day or night it was, or even when we were getting romantic. He always liked to be available for the parishioners. While he answered the phone, I took the opportunity to quickly slip out of the nightgown of mysterious origins.

T. K. greeted the caller.

"Bishop?"

Whoever was on the other end of the call must have been speaking very loudly, because I could hear everything. He sounded agitated.

I climbed back into bed and laid my head on T. K.'s chest to wait for the phone call to be over—and to listen to what was said. I knew I was eavesdropping, but as far as I was concerned, this came with the territory of being the first lady. Often T. K. told me things in confidence, but a lot of things he held inside, so it was my job to get it out of him before it ate him up.

"Bishop, it's Smitty. You got a minute?"

My husband looked down, noticing my nakedness for the first time. I smiled, licking my lips hungrily to let him know what I had in mind. "Um, Smitty, I'm kind of in the middle of something. Is it possible for us to talk in the morning?"

"Well, no, not exactly, but this will only take a second, I promise. I just wanted to say I was sorry about everything that happened between us. You're a good friend, and you've been a good pastor to me and Maria."

"Thank you, Smitty. What's the matter? You sound a little distraught. Are you okay?"

"Yes. No . . . no, I'm not all right. They told her, T. K. They told Maria everything. My life as I know it is over. I might as well just put a gun to my head and end it all right now."

"What?" T. K. couldn't hide the shock in his voice. "Smitty, I don't think I heard you right. Did you say—"

"Yes, you heard me right. I can't take this anymore."

T. K. hesitated, his face softening with sympathy. "Relax, Smitty. It's gonna be all right—"

He cut the bishop off again. "No, it's not. Stop fooling yourself. They're mad that I didn't show up to the vote. They're extra mad that you're still the pastor of the church and that that boy is the new choir director. But they had more on me than what you had. They're still threatening to tell the rest."

"Who, Smitty? Who are 'they'?" T. K.'s voice revealed his rising level of frustration.

"The people who are blackmailing me. The very same people who are out to get you."

I felt my body stiffen with anger at the thought of someone out to get my husband, but I had to remain calm so T. K. wouldn't know I was listening. I didn't want him to get out of bed and finish his conversation elsewhere.

"Who are these people, Smitty? Please tell me who is blackmailing you. And what else do they still have on you? I may be able to help you if you just tell me who they are and what they have."

"You wouldn't believe me if I told you without proof. So don't worry about me. They've already beaten me." He sighed loudly and there was a pause before he spoke again. "Listen, if anything happens to me, take care of my family. And take care of yourself and that beautiful wife of yours. There is still a lot of danger out there."

"Danger? What kind of danger? Smitty, you're not making any sense. What's going to happen to you? Look, maybe we should call the police."

"Man, are you crazy? The police are already involved. T. K., don't trust anybody. Do you hear me? Don't trust anyone."

"Smitty—"

"Look, I've gotta go. Please promise me if anything happens to me you'll take care of my family. Please, T. K."

"Okay, Smitty, I promise, but nothing's gonna happen to you. Listen, why don't you come over here so we can talk?"

After that, all I heard was "Thanks," and the line went dead.

T. K. quickly dialed the number back several times, but Jonathan never answered.

"What happened?" I asked. My simple eavesdropping had turned into concern. T. K. was obviously shaken by the call, because he didn't even bother to hide the details the way he might have if it had been another church member calling to talk.

"It's Smitty. Someone is blackmailing him and he won't tell me who. He's acting like there's some great conspiracy out there to take over the church and destroy me and anyone close to me."

I sat up and searched my husband's face for some clue as to how real he felt this threat was. Some of the things Smitty said made me think that not all of this was news to T. K. Like they had discussed this before. "Do you believe him?"

He placed his arm around me, pulling me in close. "I'm not sure, honey, but from the sound of his voice, Smitty believes it, and that's enough to make me concerned."

Simone

15

I laid my head on Aaron's shoulder as we exited the Grand Central Parkway and made our way up Francis Lewis Boulevard toward my Jamaica Estates home. The ride home was pretty quiet, yet filled with the sexual tension of what was soon to come. I still couldn't believe I'd broken my own cardinal rule and invited him home on the first date. Then again, I'd never had anyone kiss me the way he did. His kisses did things to me that no man had done since James Black broke my heart years ago. I was like putty in his hands, and he had carte blanche to do whatever his heart desired with me.

I looked over at him grinning and humming to himself happily. I was sure he was under the expectation that once we crossed my threshold we'd wind up in bed. Hell, who was I fooling? He was probably right.

I wanted him so badly my entire body was trembling with anticipation. The last thing I wanted to do was disappoint him or myself. At the same time, I didn't want to appear easy or loose, either, because I was nobody's slut. I kept telling myself that we'd just have to see how things progressed once we arrived at the house and had a few drinks. My money was on us having a passionate night that neither of us would forget.

"Hey, sweetie, we're at 136th Avenue. You said you live on 138th, right?"

He called me sweetie. How cute was that? I blushed like a little girl.

"Oh, that was quick." I lifted my head from his shoulder to give him some directions. "Make a left at the next corner. I'm the fourth house on the right, the brick colonial. Just pull into the driveway."

Aaron turned the corner and I sat up, searching my purse for my house keys.

"Sweetie, I can't park in your driveway."

"Why not?" I stopped searching through my purse and looked up.

"Because." He pointed to direct my attention to what was blocking him.

My heart leaped in a slight panic when I saw the Range Rover parked in my driveway with the lights on. I knew only one person with a Range Rover, and he was the last person I wanted to see right now. "What the hell is he doing here?"

"What the hell is who doing here?" He eased up on the gas.

"Don't stop, Aaron. Keep driving!" I demanded.

I tried to scrunch down in the seat so I wouldn't be seen. Instead of moving forward, though, we stopped. Aaron's expression was a mixture of confusion and frustration. Obviously he'd been expecting to have fun with me, but this wasn't the type of game he thought he'd be playing.

"You gotta be kidding me. This is ridiculous." Aaron paused for a second and then his eyebrows furrowed. "You aren't married, are you? Please don't tell me you're married," he barked.

"No, no, I'm not married," I said as if I were the only one who had the right to be agitated. "Now, will you keep driving before he sees us?" I didn't mean to snap at him, but he was moving entirely too slow.

He gave me a doubtful look; then, thankfully, he stepped on the accelerator, moving us down the block and past my house. I eased back up in my seat, looking in my side-view mirror. I didn't see any sign of the Range Rover backing out of the driveway or anyone following us, so I heaved a sigh of relief. I was still trying to process what was going on and why that man was parked outside my house. Coming by unannounced was the ultimate no-no in my book.

About two blocks later, Aaron turned the corner and pulled into a parking space. He did not look like a happy camper, and I felt a migraine coming on. I tried to speak to him with my eyes, because I didn't have the words to explain. Besides, he'd never understand.

"What's going on, Simone? That your man or something?"

Ordinarily I would have checked any man who tried to question me, but Aaron was different. I really liked him, so I didn't mind him asking questions, but I wasn't sure he was going to like my answer.

"No, I swear it's not like that, but I can't really explain it right now." I looked out the window once again for any sign of the Range Rover. "You just have to trust me." I glanced at him sadly, then reached for the door handle.

"Whoa, where you going?" He gripped my arm tightly. "Look, don't you think you owe me an explanation?"

"Aaron, I'm sorry things turned out this way, but something's come up. I'm gonna have to give you a rain check on that drink, okay? I swear I'll make it up to you."

"That's your explanation?" All the sexual tension that had been building between us was now fuel for his frustration, and he was pretty close to shouting.

"That's about as good an explanation as you're gonna get from me right now." I glanced at my arm, which he was still holding on to. "Can I have my arm back?"

At first his eyes flashed with anger like he was about to explode, but then he loosened his grip on my arm and exhaled, placing both hands on the steering wheel. "Sure, no problem. Thanks for a wonderful evening," he said without an ounce of sincerity in his tone.

I leaned over to kiss him, but he just sat there stoned-faced, looking forward. I kissed him on the cheek. "Aaron, I'm sorry. I'll call you tomorrow, okay?" When he didn't answer, I opened the door with a sigh and stepped out of the truck.

I looked back at him, and we shared a fleeting glance as I stood on the curb. I wanted to get back into his truck. I wanted to apologize and say, "Take me back to your place," but instead I stood still and watched him drive down the block.

I shook my head in anger as I looked in the direction of my house. *This had better be fucking worth it.*

As I stood there contemplating my next move, my phone

chirped a text. I know it was wishful thinking, but I was hoping it was from Aaron. It wasn't. It was from that fool in the Range Rover. I flipped open my phone and read the text:

I KNOW IT WAS YOU THAT JUST PASSED ME IN THAT TRUCK WITH ONE OF YOUR MAN WHORES. I'M STILL AT YOUR HOUSE AND WE NEED TO TALK. I'M NOT THE ONLY ONE WITH SECRETS. REMEMBER THAT.

Yeah, but yours are a lot more damaging than mine, I thought as I began to walk the two blocks toward my house. Suddenly my mind was focused again, and I had my eye on the prize. This idiot really didn't know who he was fucking with, did he?

Aaron

16

I'd been lying in bed for about fifteen minutes, wondering what time it was and listening to the blaring sirens of fire engines in the distance. I didn't know if I would ever get used to that sound, but I was starting to like New York. It had its good and its bad points, but so far mostly good. Even though Simone had kicked me to the curb for that guy in the Range Rover, I was enjoying my new home, my new life, and my status as choir director of First Jamaica Ministries. Now that all the drama surrounding the vote was over, I knew it was only a matter of time before I built up the choir membership and took them to a championship win.

My cell phone started vibrating on my nightstand. It was probably Simone again. She had been texting and calling me since about an hour after I dropped her off a few blocks from her home. Don't get me wrong; I liked Simone. I originally thought she was the type of woman a man could take home to his mother, but now I wasn't so sure. You let a woman like her punk you once and she'll end up punking you for the rest of your life, so I hadn't returned any of her calls or texts. Not yet, at least.

Besides, there were way too many women at First Jamaica Ministries to be worried about just one. Sure, maybe they weren't all as pretty as Simone, but I was sure I could find quite a few who didn't play her type of games. That was one thing I didn't do: put up with a shady woman. I always let a chick know from the get-go what was up. Had she given me the same re-spect, then maybe I'd be answering her call right about now. Instead, I let it go to voice mail as I glanced down at Porsche Moore, who was positioned between my legs, going down on me like she was expecting to get paid. Sure, my ego was bruised after the way Simone treated me, but I wasn't gonna let her steal my joy. Not with women like Porsche waiting around to fill the void.

How did Porsche end up over at my place? Well, after the incident with Simone, I loathed the idea of going home alone to my empty apartment. You see, I firmly believe that the best way to get over one woman is to get on top of another. I was actually thinking about hitting T.G.I. Friday's or a local bar and seeing what type of action I could find there, but then I remembered that Porsche had slipped me her number the day I was introduced to the choir. It stuck out in my mind that she'd distinctly written underneath her number that I could call anytime. So, I figured I'd give it a try and see what was up. True enough, anytime meant anytime. Not only could I call her any time, but I could hit that anytime as well. I had no idea it would be so easy to get her into bed. All it took was a phone call, some BS about how I'd been thinking about her lately, and forty-five minutes later, we were rolling around in the sheets.

After an hour or two of getting busy, Porsche had me sleeping like a baby—that was, until about twenty minutes ago, when her warm tongue woke me up. I'm not gonna lie; I could get used to being woken up like that. Old girl really knew what she was doing with that tongue of hers. She sure proved she could do something with it besides hit the high notes in "Amazing Grace." Actually, she had me about to hit a high note or two myself when my doorbell rang and broke my concentration.

Of course, the first person who came to my mind was Simone.

"You expecting company?" Porsche managed between slurps.

I didn't answer her. I just pushed her gently aside, slipped on my boxers and robe, then stomped to the door. I was fuming. This Simone had a lot of nerve.

Without looking through the peephole, I flung open the door. "What do you want?" I snapped.

"Uh, I thought we were going to go to breakfast before we went to Long Island City to look at new choir robes." It was Tia, the church secretary and choir administrator. I was relieved it wasn't Simone, but embarrassed by how I had opened the door and greeted her. "I called you before I came up," Tia said, looking confused.

"Oh, my bad, Tia. I thought you were someone else." I quickly closed my robe. Not a very professional way to greet the bishop and first lady's right-hand woman. However, I had to play this off as though I were unfazed by her being there, catching me with my pants down . . . or, rather, off. "I thought we were supposed to meet at eight thirty." I glanced outside and suddenly felt a little stupid. It was evident from the bright sun and the chirping birds that it wasn't evening anymore. Porsche was so good she had me losing all track of time.

"It's already quarter to nine," Tia informed me.

"Jeez, is it that late? Where did the time go?"

"Yep." She nodded, shrugging her shoulders. "I tried calling to give you a heads-up when I left my house, but you didn't answer then either. I thought you might have been in the shower or something." She looked me up and down, then smirked. "I guess you were still sleeping."

"Yeah, I was knocked out. I had a late night." I added a yawn and stretch for further confirmation.

She glanced around me. "Nice place you have there. Can I come in? I feel a little weird standing out here in the hall talking to you in your underwear and robe. We have a lot of church members in this building. People might get the wrong idea."

"Sure, I'd love to invite you in," I said without moving out of the way to let her pass. I turned toward my living room to do a quick check and spotted Porsche's bra hanging over a chair. I turned back to face Tia. "But to be honest, I have company, and she's not exactly decent right now. Is it possible for you to wait downstairs? I'll be out in ten, fifteen minutes tops. I just have to take a shower. I'm a little funky." I told you I was honest about these types of things from the get-go, but the way Tia wrinkled her nose at me, I realized I may have taken my honesty policy a bit too far.

God, I hope this woman isn't one of the church gossips.

"Oh, I see." She couldn't even look me in the eye anymore.

Perhaps she was more embarrassed for me than I was for myself. "Take your time. I'll see you downstairs."

She turned toward the staircase, and I watched her hips swaying naturally as she walked down the hall. Once again, she was wearing a conservative skirt suit, trying to hide the phenomenal body God had given her, and once again the suit had failed her. I'd mentally put her on my "Women to Do" list when we first met, but now I was going to have to cross her off. No way would she give me any after this debacle. Had it been Simone, my chances with her still would have been good, because obviously she knew the game. After all, she tried to run it on me last night.

When Tia disappeared down the hallway, I headed back to my bedroom. Porsche was laid out across my bed as naked as the day she was born. The thought of jumping on her to finish what we'd started came to mind, but I quickly changed my mind. "Sweetie, I had a great time last night, but I'm late for work and you've gotta get on out of here."

She looked offended as she started to gather up her clothes, but still she asked, "So, you gonna call me tonight?"

"We'll see. Like I told you last night, I'm really not looking for anything serious. Only thing I can commit to right now is the choir. But I had a great time, and I'm sure we're going to be doing it again." I got a smile out of her, but I knew that was not what she wanted to hear. Telling her what she wanted to hear was what had gotten her here in the first place. Now I just needed her to leave.

I walked over and kissed her cheek. "Look, I've gotta take a shower so I can get outta here. You don't mind letting yourself out, do you?"

Without waiting for an answer, I went into the bathroom and closed the door. I thought for a second that maybe I should let Porsche leave after me so she wouldn't have to do the walk of shame past Tia outside. Then I realized that Porsche's "friendly nature" was probably no secret to anyone in the church anyway.

Tia

17

I walked out the door of Aaron's apartment building, shaking my head. It wasn't any of my business, but my curiosity got the best of me, and I wanted to know if the person in his apartment was anyone I knew from church. Maybe, just maybe, he was pulling a stunt like our old choir director and had a man in there. I shook that thought off quickly. He'd specifically referred to his company as "she." Besides, he'd been way too cool, calm, and collected to have been hiding a man in his place.

I couldn't believe I was outside waiting for him to finish up his business. I didn't feel like I needed to be there in the first place—at least I hadn't thought so. When the first lady asked me to keep an eye on Aaron, I was skeptical about the entire chaperone thing, but I guess she was right: Aaron really did need a babysitter . . . or maybe more like a bodyguard. But why did it have to be me? Sure, I loved the choir, but wasn't I doing enough charity work running the church's rape hotline? I mean, that was my real passion, although no one else seemed to care. No one ever asked, "Hey, Tia, how's your ministry coming along?" Nope, to them it was no more important than a 1-900 dating line.

But enough of my complaining. I did understand that the first lady felt it was important to keep Aaron focused on the task at hand. And even though this morning had been awkward, I liked Mr. Mackie. He was intelligent, very funny, and a genuinely nice man, along with being a phenomenal singer. Oh, and as the first lady seemed to remind me on a daily basis, he was easy on the eyes. I just never felt comfortable around pretty boys like him, which was probably the real reason I wished I could hand this chaperoning job off to someone else.

As I looked around, I had to smile. I hadn't seen it on my way in, but there was Aaron's new SUV. He'd told me how much he wanted an Escalade, and now he'd gotten it. I had to admit it was cute, and I'd never seen one in burgundy before, so it was different. It was a little big for my taste, but it suited him well.

I walked over to get a better look. Simone had really hooked him up.

Simone, I thought. *Could it be? Maybe* . . . Perhaps she was the woman up in Aaron's apartment.

I heard footsteps approaching me quickly. They couldn't have belonged to Aaron, because even Superman couldn't have taken a shower and gotten dressed that quickly. Instinctively, my hand slid into my handbag. I wrapped my fingers around the pepper spray I carried with me and turned toward the possible assailant.

"Hi, Tia."

I released my hold on the pepper spray when I realized it was Porsche Moore making her way toward me with a nasty sneer on her face. I should have known it was Porsche up there—the girl that every man has ridden. The angry glare she was shooting at me spoke volumes. She was angry that I had broken up her little love fest this morning.

I shook my head. As fast as Porsche had gotten down those stairs from his apartment, she probably hadn't even washed her behind. The least she could have done was fix herself up. Her makeup was smeared, her clothes looked wrinkled, and her hair was all over her head. Pitiful.

"Hi, Porsche," I said sweetly, trying to hide my distaste for her actions. She was a straight-up whore as far as I was concerned. First Lady Monique was going to lose her mind when she found out, and there was no doubt she would, whether I told her or not. Along with being a whore, Porsche had a big damn mouth and had no problem telling everyone her personal business. Both her mouth and her legs were always wide open.

"You waiting for Aaron?"

Well, even if there had been a question in my mind about who was up in Aaron's apartment, Porsche had just cleared that up.

I'm sure that was exactly her intent too. Like a cat, she was spraying her territory. I almost laughed out loud when I realized she was looking at me as her competition.

"Yes, we're going to look at choir robes this morning," I told her, making it very clear we weren't there for the same thing. I could not have her thinking I was there for her sloppy seconds.

"Okay, well, it was nice seeing you, but I have to get to work."

Without washing your ass? Oh, that is so nasty, I thought as I watched her get into her Honda Civic. I had to laugh as I watched her pull out and spotted her license plate: I-PORSCHE. Why the hell would someone put *Porsche* on a Civic? Then again, why would someone name their child after a sports car they couldn't afford?

About ten minutes later, Aaron came out of his building. I could tell from his damp hair and the fresh scent of soap that he'd taken a shower. More than I could say for that nasty-behind Porsche.

"Hey, why don't we take my car?" he asked, approaching me.

I hesitated. After what I'd lived through and what I'd heard from other rape victims, I was slow to trust any man. What if he mistook me for one of these other skanks he was used to?

I think he could detect my hesitation. "I'll bring you back and get your car." He grinned good-naturedly.

I thought about it. He'd never made a pass at me. As much time as we spent together, he'd always been a gentleman. I probably didn't have anything to worry about. Besides that, there was always my pepper spray. "Okay," I relented.

It only took about five minutes to drive to the IHOP on Hillside Avenue per my suggestion that we have breakfast first. As we got settled in a booth, I looked over at Aaron and said, "So, I see you're getting to know the sisters in the church."

Aaron gave me this do-we-really-have-to-talk-about-that face. "Why is the conversation always about me? I'd like to know more about you."

He managed to dodge that bullet.

"There's not that much to tell." I shrugged, staring out the window.

"Everyone has some type of story to tell," he pressed. "Are you seeing anybody?"

"I'm kind of a private person. I don't like to discuss my personal business," I said.

"You seem really involved in the church."

"I guess that is my life. Otherwise, my life's kind of boring. I'm thirty-two and living with my brother, of all people. I used to be the church's office assistant, but now I've been promoted to administrative assistant since the other office assistant was involved in that scandal they had at Jamaica."

"Yeah, I heard about it."

Obviously Porsche had had a chance to let some good old gossip fly out of her mouth before she put something unmentionable in it.

"I'm also a rape counselor at the church," I added.

"Really? Tell me about it."

I was surprised that he even wanted to hear about it. This was a first, and I was glad to share.

After we ordered our breakfasts of pancakes, sausages, and eggs, we were talking like old friends. Aaron was a great listener, and because of that, I didn't mind talking.

"I'm not trying to get in your business," I said, poking my fork at the remaining food on my plate. "That's not the way I want what I'm about to say to come off."

"What are you talking about?" Aaron asked innocently.

"I just hope you used protection . . . you know, with Porsche."

"Why? You saying she might have a disease?" Aaron looked frightened.

"That, too, but did you ever think she might want to get pregnant? Everyone knows about your salary."

"Why would she want to get pregnant? She's not married."

I didn't know if I should believe his question was genuine. No one could be that naïve, could they? "Plenty of women nowadays don't care about having babies and not having a husband."

"True." Aaron wiped his mouth, then washed his breakfast down with a last gulp of coffee. "But no worries. I've always used condoms."

"That's good. You do realize that abstinence is the best policy?" I didn't want to seem self-righteous, but I'd been abstinent since my rape. I would be lying if I said I didn't miss men, but I wanted God to pick the next man for me instead of me picking one for myself. My last choice didn't turn out to be such a good one. As a result, I was determined not to have sex outside of marriage ever again. I can't say I missed the pregnancy scares, and nowadays, there were so many diseases a woman could catch it was downright scary. Women like Porsche were really playing Russian roulette with their lives. Heck, even condoms didn't offer foolproof protection from HIV. I remember quite a few of them breaking back in the day with my boyfriend. No, I didn't feel like I was missing out on much, besides danger, by remaining abstinent.

Aaron clearly didn't agree, because he ignored my last comment and started eating in silence for a while. For the remainder of the meal, we stuck to less controversial topics.

We finished our meals and had just climbed into Aaron's SUV in the parking lot when I felt my phone vibrate on my waist. I glanced down, and right away I knew it was trouble.

The text message read: MS. TIA 911 BRANDI. HELP!

Brandi was one of my rape-hotline victims. Just a few months ago, I'd moved her out of the line of fire from her boyfriend's drunken tirades. She, like most date-rape victims, wouldn't press charges because she didn't have anywhere to go. I got her some help and into a domestic violence shelter. Recently she'd found a job and her own place. Things had been going pretty well for her—until now, I suppose.

I texted back: BRANDI, WHERE ARE YOU? WHAT'S WRONG?

She replied: I'M AT THE GAS STATION NEAR MY HOUSE. I CAN'T GO HOME. HE'S DRUNK AND WAITING FOR ME.

I didn't text back this time. I dialed her number. "What happened? And how did Reggie find you?"

"I called him to see what he was doing."

I wanted to smash my hand through Aaron's windshield. "Why did you do that? Didn't I tell you not to give him your number or tell him where you lived?" I scolded. And why on earth did she care about what he was doing?

"Yeah . . ." Brandi sniffed. "But I got so lonely. And he was talking so nice on the phone—"

"Shoot, Brandi! I can't believe you did that!"

She broke down blubbering, and I started rubbing my temple. I knew it was time to pull back my emotions. This wasn't personal. I had to be there for her. She was already in a bad way. She'd called me for help, so who was I to be judgmental and make her feel even worse?

"Look, that's water under the bridge. What happened after that?"

"He came over, just to talk, and we had a few drinks. But when things got romantic, I told him I wouldn't give him any. He said he was going to take it whether I liked it or not. Then he jumped on me and beat me up . . . before he raped me again." By then, Brandi was crying so loudly into the phone it darn near pierced my eardrum. "Ms. Tia, I'm sorry. I know I fucked up, but I was lonely."

"Okay, okay, calm down, sweetie. You stay where you are until I get there. Which gas station are you at? Give me the exact address." After she told me where she was, I turned to Aaron, who was just finishing up a call of his own. "I'm sorry, but I need you to take me back to my car. I've got somewhere I have to go."

"Everything all right? I thought we were going to look at choir robes."

"We were, but something's come up. They're going to have to wait. This is an emergency. So, can you please take me to my car?" I was agitated. I didn't have time to explain all the details to Aaron right now. I had to get to Brandi.

"Tia, relax! What happened?" Aaron took hold of my hand.

"I can't relax. One of my rape victims is in trouble. Her life may even be in danger," I said frantically, pulling my hand free. "Now, can you take me to my car, please? I've got to go."

"Why don't I just drive you? It'll be quicker. Where is she at?"

I was a little hesitant at first. I didn't know how Brandi would react to me bringing a man, but time was of the essence. Anything could happen from the time Aaron took me all the way back to my car and I drove to Brandi. Going on instinct and discerning that Brandi was in grave danger, I opted to accept Aaron's offer.

"She's in Rego Park. Get on the Grand Central Parkway."

Aaron headed toward the highway, and within minutes we arrived at the gas station, where we found Brandi hiding behind a parked car. She didn't recognize the car I was in, so she remained crouched down until I approached her. I felt my knees go weak when I saw how badly she'd been hurt. Her eye was swollen shut, and her face was bruised. This beating looked even worse than the one she suffered when I first met her. It looked as if Reggie had tried to kill her.

"Oh, Brandi," was all I could say. I put my arms around her and tried to will my strength into her body.

"I'm sorry, Miss Tia. I know I told you I was going to stay away from him, but—"

"We have to take you to the police," Aaron interrupted.

Brandi tensed when she heard the male voice.

"It's okay, Brandi. This is Aaron. He's with the church. He brought me here to help you," I told her, relaxing her somewhat. "He's right, though. We need to get you some help."

"I don't want to go to the police," Brandi protested. "You've got to get me out of here before Reggie finds me."

"We will get you out of here, but you need some help, Brandi." I looked over my shoulder at Aaron. "Let's take her to the hospital," I said. "This woman's been raped. The police can meet us there."

After getting Brandi into the back of the SUV, I climbed in with her, and Aaron drove to the hospital. When we arrived at Jamaica Hospital, we informed the check-in nurse what had taken place.

She plugged some information into the computer and then took Brandi aside. "Come with me."

Brandi looked like a frightened little girl.

"It's okay, Brandi," I assured her. "She's going to do a rape kit on you." I held her hand for support. "This way you can prosecute and Reggie won't be able to do this to you again."

Brandi nodded and went with the nurse.

A woman with dreadlocks walked up to me. "Hey, Tia," she said. "I see you've got another one."

"Hey, Paige." I waved my hand listlessly. This work took its toll on me. Even so, I took the time to introduce Aaron. "Paige, this is Aaron Mackie, choir director at Jamaica Ministries. Aaron, meet Paige Hunt, NYPD. Paige is the head detective over at the Rape Unit." I turned back to Paige. "This is the third time he's raped her," I offered. "She knows her perp."

"I take it we're talking about a boyfriend who can't take no for an answer." Paige shook her head.

"She had moved away but made the mistake of giving him her phone number."

"Okay, I'll go interview her. Hopefully she'll press charges this time." Paige spun on her heels and strode purposefully down the corridor to find Brandi.

"We'll be here waiting for Brandi," I called out to her.

After Paige left, I caught Aaron staring at me.

"What's the matter?" I asked.

"You know what?"

"What?"

"You're a very special woman."

"There's nothing special about me. I'm not doing this to make me feel special. I'm doing this because it's the call I have on my life." I didn't want to tell him I'd been raped before and had stood in Brandi's shoes.

"Hey, Tia, do you think . . ." Aaron hesitated as we sat down in the waiting room.

"Do I think what?"

"Do you think I could help with your rape hotline?"

"You serious?"

"Yeah. You do important work. Of course I'm serious."

"Really? Well, I guess that makes you pretty special your-self."

Monique

18

I was walking down the corridor toward the administrative wing of the church when Simone literally bumped into me, spilling coffee all over my blouse. She was coming out of the choir rehearsal room looking distraught. Whatever was bothering her must have been pretty serious, because she had her panties all tied up in a bunch.

"Oh, excuse me," I said.

"Watch where the hell you're going!" she hissed, looking down at her fine apparel. "This is a three-hundred-dollar suit I'm wearing. And I know you didn't get coffee on it!" She examined her suit for any sign of a stain. "What have you got, two left feet?"

"I said excuse me, Simone. Daggone it! And I don't care how much your suit cost, 'cause you're not the one with coffee spilled all over you. I am!" I barked back. I could give as good as I got when I had to.

Looking up from her suit at me, she finally took the time to notice who it was she had bumped into. "Oh, Monique, I'm sorry. It was an accident. Are you okay?"

"Yeah, I'm all right." I looked down to examine my own clothing. "But I don't think my blouse is. Good thing I keep a change of clothes in my office."

"I am so sorry. I've just got a lot on my mind."

"I can see that. Is everything all right?"

"Yeah, I'm all right." She sighed, trying to help me wipe off my clothes.

"You don't look all right." I stopped her from helping because she was making things worse. "You look like you missed a seventy-five-percent-off sale at Bloomingdale's." I was trying to put a lighthearted spin on things. Simone usually laughed at my jokes, but the way she cut her eyes at me and pursed her lips, I knew she wasn't in the mood for my jokes. "Girl, what's wrong with you?"

"Have you seen Aaron?" She pulled her bag tightly over her shoulder. Given the tone of her voice, I'm not sure I would have wanted to be Mackie when she found him.

I shook my head. "He and Tia were supposed to go out to New Jersey today."

"What's he going to Jersey with Tia for? He went to Long Island City with her a couple of days ago," she snapped.

I could see a flash of jealousy in her eyes before she quickly regained her composure. She waved her hand, trying to act like we were just sharing church gossip, but I could clearly read between the lines. She was worried that Tia and Aaron had gotten together. I guess she hadn't heard the rumor that Porsche Moore was spreading around about herself.

"I mean, what's going on with him and Tia anyway? They have been spending a lot of time together." She must have realized how jealous she was sounding, because she toned down her attitude this time.

"Girl, you know there's nothing between him and Tia. She's been appointed the choir's administrator. They just work together. They're friends. Why? You got some interest in our choir director? What's really going on, Simone?"

"Nothin'." Simone blushed, something I was not used to seeing in her. For a fleeting second, this dreamy look passed over her face and her beautiful features softened.

Then, just as quickly, she gathered her senses. She waved her hand in dismissal. "We went out the other night when he got his car. I had a really good time. It just didn't end well."

Oh Lord, I did not like the sound of that.

Curiosity piqued, I looked Simone directly in the face. "Girl, what do you mean it didn't end well?"

"I messed up, Monique. I messed up bad and I don't know what to do. He won't even talk to me." She was back to looking distraught again. "He won't take my calls or anything. I'm not used to that. I'm usually the one sitting there watching my phone ring and hitting the ignore button."

"Messed up how? You act like you're pregnant or . . ." I paused, worried by just the thought. "You're not pregnant, are you? No, you couldn't be—"

She finally cut me off. "No, I'm not pregnant. The man's only been in town a week. I haven't even had a chance to feel his sweetness inside me."

I had to hold back a grin. "You haven't had a chance to feel his *sweetness* inside you?" I couldn't help it. I started laughing. Who says stuff like that? What was wrong with her?

"It's not funny. You know what I mean." She folded her arms defiantly.

"I know, I know. I'm sorry, but I just can't believe you said that." I was still laughing. "So, you really like him, don't you?"

She nodded eagerly. "I'll tell you something, Monique. He's different from any of the guys I usually date. We went out only that one time, but we actually talked."

"Isn't that what you're supposed to do when you go on a date with someone?"

"Yes, but I'm usually matching wits with players who are trying to get over on me while I'm trying to get over on them." That starry light in her eyes now shone even brighter. "But Aaron's different. He could be the one, Mo—that is, if I can ever get him to speak to me again."

I almost dropped what was left of my coffee. I couldn't believe my ears. Was Simone talking about settling down? I was truly surprised. I'd never known her to like a man for himself. She generally only went for his bank account. I'd always known her to be as cold-blooded as any man could be when it came to her feelings.

"The one? You like him that much?" She nodded her head to my query. "So, how is he that different than any of these other men you go out with? I mean, you just met the man."

"I thought he was a country bumpkin at first, someone I could use as an arm ornament, but he's actually very intelligent. Do you know he went to the University of Virginia? My father went to the University of Virginia."

"That's not exactly a reason to buy a wedding dress, Simone." We began to walk down the corridor as we talked.

"It's a reason to think about it."

Okay, I was convinced this woman had lost her mind. And for what, some conversation? She said it herself that she hadn't even slept with him yet, so it wasn't like the girl was sexually whipped. I was still slightly confused as to why Aaron had my friend tripping like this. I mean, he was definitely a cut above the rest in the looks department, but a woman as beautiful as Simone had plenty of handsome men at her disposal.

"Monique, I really like this guy," Simone whined.

"I can see that. How much do you like him?"

"A lot."

"James Black a lot?" I studied her face to gauge her reaction to my question. She shocked me by nodding her head.

"Mmm-hmm."

I took a step back. I couldn't believe it. I'd never seen Simone put a man in James's league.

"Wow, you really do like this guy."

She nodded again. "I do, and I can't believe I screwed it up."

I glanced around to make sure there were no eavesdroppers nearby. I didn't need any rumors starting now that the choir was finally starting to regain its footing. "So, what happened? How did you mess up?"

"Oh, I'm sorry." She sighed. "I still haven't told you, have I? Well, we went on this perfect date. We talked, had dinner, went on a romantic walk on the beach. When we got back to my place, there was someone parked in my driveway."

"Who was it?" I was hanging on to her words as we entered my office.

"That's not really important. Let's just say it wasn't someone I wanted Aaron to meet."

"Oh my goodness. I told you about having all these different men come to your house. They didn't fight, did they?"

"No. I made Aaron drop me off a couple blocks away."

"You did what? No wonder he's mad. I'd be mad too."

"I know, but it wasn't like that."

I opened my office door and was surprised to see a gift bag

tied with a ribbon on my desk. I didn't want to be rude to Simone and cut her off; otherwise I would have rushed over to examine it. The unexplained lingerie gift still had me on edge.

"Speaking of men, it looks like your husband has bought you something. Since you're all in my business, what's up with this?" Simone demanded.

Now that she'd given me the green light to exit her topic of conversation, I rushed over to the bag. Simone was right behind me, looking over my shoulder as I removed a jewelry box from the bag.

"Hmm, Bloomingdale's. I see the bishop has good taste," Simone commented. "I would have never thought him to be a Bloomingdale's shopper."

He isn't. I felt my heart beating a little faster as I lifted the lid off the box. There was no card with the gift, and I felt it was safe to assume this one came from the same mystery person who'd left the Victoria's Secret package.

I was surprised to see a set of shiny gold bangles studded with diamonds. As I fingered the jewelry, I didn't know what to think. I was relieved that it wasn't as personal and intimate as the lingerie, but it was disturbing in its own way. It had to have cost a few thousand dollars. Who would spend that kind of money and not even reveal their identity?

"Bishop is a more interesting man than I thought he was," Simone remarked. "Oh, look at you." Lifting her eyebrow, she gave me a teasing look.

My stomach was in knots. "Wait right here, Simone. I'll be right back." I stepped out of my office and into the reception area. I was thankful that Tia, who hadn't been at her desk just a moment before, had returned.

"Tia, who's been in my office?" I asked.

"The only one who came by was Aaron, looking for the bishop or you."

"Did he go into my office?"

"I don't think so. I don't know. No one's been in this area since Aaron and I got back from the mall."

"What were you and Aaron doing at the mall?" I asked. "I thought you two were going over to Jersey."

"Yeah, we did, but somehow when we got back to the city, I ended up at the mall. Even though I was the one who talked him into running in real quick with me, Aaron is the one who ended up with a lot of bags." She chuckled.

"Hmmm." I turned and went back into my office, where Simone was waiting.

She stood up, smoothing her skirt. "Well, I've got to go to work." She gave me a conspiratorial grin. "And, uh, just for the record, everything I told you about Mr. Choir Director . . . uh, it's just between me and you."

Half paying attention to Simone, I replied, "Oh, yeah, you don't have to worry about that." And she didn't. The last thing on my mind was why she was so sprung on Aaron. What I had to figure out, as I stared down at the gift on my desk, was if he was sprung on me.

Tia

19

The pews were only half full and the balcony was completely empty, but it had still been the best Sunday turnout we'd had in weeks. It was obvious that word had gotten around about our handsome new choir director, because in the pews I saw plenty of women who hadn't visited our church in quite a while. Women always brought men back to the church.

I had to give a lot of credit to the first lady, because she'd been in her office all week, burning up the phone lines bragging about Mr. Aaron Mackie's debut performance today. I can't lie; I'd made a few calls myself to let my girlfriends know about our new choir director, too, although I was a lot more subtle. And I was glad I did, because even though there were still only a small number of us performing in the choir that Sunday morning, we turned First Jamaica Ministries out.

You could hear "Oohs," and "Aahs" all over the congregation. We were all having a holy good time and the atmosphere was contagious. It was like a nonstop church party, and I for one was just happy I was there to attend.

People can say whatever they want about Aaron Mackie, but in my opinion, he was worth every penny they were paying him. He was a crowd pleaser, along with being a musical genius and a fantastic choreographer. He had everyone in the church on their feet, clapping, stomping, and singing to our songs. Things got so emotionally charged that several women fainted, and the ushers had to revive them with smelling salts. Despite the small size of our choir, Aaron had us sounding like we were fifty members strong. He'd hidden all our flaws perfectly by choosing the right songs, using movement and colorful robes to distract the eye and alternating soloists to give our sound depth. I'd never seen anything like it before, and regardless of my previous complaints about working with him, I was proud to be both a member and the administrator of the choir.

When we finished our last song and sat down, the congregation was in a frenzy. To bring them back down to earth, Aaron walked over to the piano and started to play a slower song. He held the audience's attention as if he were a rock star. If he were in a nightclub, the women would have been throwing their panties up on the stage. Well, today he'd just have to settle for Bibles and church hats.

"Sing it, brother!" someone bellowed out. "Sing it."

I noticed old phony Simone standing in the aisle of the church, front and center so everyone could see her "holiness." She was waving her hands in the air from side to side.

I had to stop myself from rolling my eyes. Now, I can't read a person's heart, but it was pretty clear that Simone was doing this just to get noticed. I'd never seen any indication that she had a personal relationship with God, and no matter how good the choir sounded, I doubted that she was truly feeling the Spirit.

I realized how judgmental I was being, so I said a quick prayer to ask for forgiveness, then turned my attention back to Aaron's performance. I tried to ignore Simone.

When Aaron finished the song, everyone was sweating profusely. Many of the women had tears streaming down their faces. The men were even pumping their fists in signs of approval.

"That brother can really blow!" someone yelled out as Aaron wound things up and stood from the piano.

"Thank you, thank you. Ladies and gentlemen, my name is Aaron Mackie, and this is your First Jamaica Ministries choir." He took a deep bow and made a semicircle backhand wave of introduction toward the choir. We stood and bowed at the waist. Then, as we rose to a standing position, we pointed at Aaron with our right hands. That was our way of acknowledging the job he'd done in preparing us for that moment.

I glanced over at Bishop Wilson as we sat down, and he was

beaming like a proud poppa. I could tell that he, like so many others, was amazed by what Aaron had done with the choir in such a short time.

"Praise the Lord! Praise Him!" Bishop shouted, holding his hands up to the ceiling as he stood. "This is incredible! Good Lord, please give these young people a hand!" The congregation erupted in praise. "Have you ever heard a first performance like that before? I just paid fifty-five dollars to see Shirley Caesar last week, and I feel like I need a refund."

The congregation erupted in laughter.

I'd never been more proud of our choir, and I felt so proud of Aaron too. I don't think I've ever seen a musician work as passionately as he did. We'd become quite close in the short time he'd been here. He felt like a brother to me, so I was happy for him. I was happy for us as a choir.

"I've really got to hand it to you," I whispered to Aaron when he sat down next to me in the choir box. "I haven't seen the church react that positively to anything in quite awhile. You really killed them. I'm so proud of you." I reached over and pumped his hand.

Aaron nodded back appreciatively. "Yeah, but we still have a lot of work to do. This place isn't close to being filled." We both scanned the pews.

"Don't sell yourself short. You weren't here when this place was a ghost town. You did a great job, and as far as I'm concerned, you are the man."

"Thanks." Aaron sounded humble, but I could see the beam of satisfaction on his face.

The congregation was still on its feet, and Bishop Wilson turned to us and said, "Why don't we see if we can get these folks to give us another song? Lord have mercy, nothing goes better with the Word than song!"

I smiled, encouraging Aaron to get back up. He stood and turned toward the choir and got us to join him in the latest rendition of Jennifer Hudson's song "You Pulled Me Through." Once again, the entire congregation was singing, clapping, and stomping their feet.

Before the church could calm down and stop clapping, a loud

commotion sprang from the back of the church. Everyone turned around to see the disturbance and where it was coming from. There were so many people standing up I couldn't see a thing.

"Outside! Outside!" a woman screamed.

Voices rang out, filled with questions, and then the whole place erupted in commotion.

"Lord have mercy, what is it?" I watched as the bishop and others ran to the back of the church. From my spot in the choir, I still couldn't see the source of the screams, but it was definitely a woman's voice.

"Bishop! Outside!" she called out again. "Outside! He's dead! Oh my God, Bishop, he's dead!"

Simone

20

I was standing in the church aisle, swaying from side to side with my hands in the air, giving everyone in the church the impression that the Holy Ghost had struck me. I know it may have appeared I was playing games with God, but I wasn't. I was just showing emotion. I couldn't help how other people took it. Besides, I wasn't the only one expressing my emotions. Everyone around me, young and old alike, was clapping, dancing, and singing along with Aaron's choir. I felt like a teenager at a concert and my favorite singer was onstage. I almost melted every time Aaron sang his solo before the choir joined in with him. I still couldn't believe he'd pulled off such an excellent performance with so few members and so little time to prepare.

"That's gonna be my man!" I wanted to proudly proclaim to the world. But who was I kidding? I still hadn't even gotten him to talk to me or take any of my calls since our date fiasco.

I caught the first lady's eye, and she smiled knowingly. Monique knew I was feeling me some Aaron. Oh my goodness, he was just so sexy. I knew I was in church, but watching Aaron do his thing up there on that pulpit had my insides dripping. He was something else, a man's man if there ever was one, and I wasn't the only one mesmerized by him. As I looked around, it seemed that every woman in the place was gawking at him.

My cell phone vibrated at my waist. A few seconds later it happened again, and when I glanced down, I noticed I had missed two text messages. I was too caught up in the moment to read the words. It buzzed two more times before I decided to read them.

Oh Lord, what does he want? I thought as I read the sender's name.

MEET ME IN THE PARKING LOT.

Was he kidding? Didn't he know I was watching my baby sing? I started back swaying, eyes closed tightly. I took myself back to Jones Beach and the time Aaron kissed me. If I could bottle those kisses and sell them to women all over the world, I'd make a billion dollars. I visualized myself lying in Aaron's arms and fantasized about how we'd both find ecstasy. I'd never been this caught up with any man, not even James. I was tingling with excitement from head to toe. I would give that man anything in the world—if I could ever get him to talk to me again.

Five minutes later, another text came through. This time the message was marked "urgent" with a red exclamation point.

MEET ME IN THE PARKING LOT NOW!

I let out a sigh. Obviously he wasn't going to stop until I responded to him. I texted him back.

WE'RE IN THE MIDDLE OF SERVICE. WHAT DO YOU WANT?

Within seconds, he replied: I HAVE THE MONEY YOU ASKED ME FOR. IF YOU WANT IT COME OUTSIDE AND GET IT NOW.

I texted back: I'LL GET IT AFTER CHURCH SERVICE.

He sent: IF YOU DON'T COME OUTSIDE AND GET IT NOW IT'S OVER. I'M DONE WITH YOU.

I shook my head. Forget him! He wasn't running this show; I was. Who the hell was he to tell me what I was or wasn't going to do?

I tried to concentrate on Aaron and the choir, but the thought of all that money was too enticing, so I finally gave in and went outside to get it. I eased out the side exit, stepping into the bright morning sun.

"Where the hell is he?" I muttered, shading my eyes as I searched the rows of cars in the parking lot. I would have thought after all those damn texts he'd be right out front.

I sent him a text. WHERE THE HELL ARE YOU?

I got no response. Now I was pissed. Had I just left possibly the finest performance by the hottest man ever to come out and be stood up in the parking lot? Finally I spotted his truck parked in the northeast corner of the parking lot.

I stalked in that direction, hurrying the best I could in my stilettos. I wanted to get back and catch the last of the choir's performance. I also wanted to do something else I hadn't been able to do: catch Aaron's eye. I wanted to give him a personal thumbs-up when he finished his song and turned to face the audience. Getting this money shouldn't take more than a minute or two if this fool didn't try to play games.

As I approached the SUV, something seemed strange. Why hadn't he gotten out of his truck? He knew I wasn't going to get inside his car. Then I noticed there was a dark red smudge on the driver's side window. At first I wasn't sure what I was seeing, but the closer I got, the clearer it was. It was blood.

What the hell was going on? My brain slowly registered what I was seeing, and panic coursed through my body. I should have run. I should have run as fast as I could back to the church to get help, but instead I leaned in and peered through the windshield. He was slumped over the steering wheel. For a moment, I froze, unsure of what to do next.

And then, as if on autopilot, I sprinted back to the church, my stilettos flying off as I went. I burst through the double doors at the back of the church and let out a scream that shattered the joyous atmosphere inside the building.

I was so discombobulated I could only manage one word: "Outside! Outside!"

Bishop dashed in long strides from the pulpit. "What's the matter?"

"Bishop! Outside! Outside! He's dead! Oh my God, Bishop, he's dead!"

He grabbed me by the shoulders and then everything went black.

The Bishop
21

The Spirit had moved me in a way it hadn't in a long time, and for the first time since Jackie had been outted by his wife last Father's Day, I felt comfortable about the direction the church was going. Yes, I knew we still had some hurdles to clear financially, but listening to Aaron and the choir gave me hope that our church was on its way to recovery. Once again I was reminded that God only places upon your shoulders what you can handle, and through that we grow stronger.

I stood up to applaud as Aaron finished a wonderful solo performance. I was about to praise him and the choir to the congregation once again, but suddenly the doors to the church burst open and all hell broke loose.

"Outside! Outside!" I heard a woman shriek. When she came into view, I realized that it was Simone Wilcox and dashed from the pulpit to the back of the church. I was followed by Aaron, Maxwell Frye, and several others. When I reached her, I scooped Simone up in my arms, telling Aaron and Maxwell to keep the crowd back.

"What's the matter, Simone? What happened?" I pleaded.

"Bishop! Outside! Outside!" she shrieked. "He's dead! Oh my God, Bishop, he's dead!"

I couldn't make sense of the whole scene, going from the beauty of the choir's performance to this chaos. Was it possible? Was there really a dead man outside my church? "Who, Simone? Who's dead?"

Simone drew a deep breath and managed to get out the words as I leaned in close. "Jonathan Smith. He's dead."

There was a long pause before I could speak. "Smitty?" I muttered under my breath. "Smitty's dead?"

My eyes began to well up with tears. The knot that had developed in my stomach was tightening more as each second passed. I glanced at my wife, who was standing in the front of the crowd about three feet away. It was as if time had stopped. Smitty couldn't be dead. Why? How? Where?

Suddenly, Simone felt heavier in my arms. I looked down to see that she was completely unconscious. The stress must have been too much for her. I wished I could have joined her. Maybe then I wouldn't have had to cope with this turn of events. But as it was, I was the pastor of this church, and I had to gather my senses and take charge of this chaos.

I gestured for my wife to help me.

"Monique, you and Aaron watch Simone. Maxwell, come with me." By now it had really sunk in that Smitty was dead—outside the church. I jetted through the atrium into the church's parking lot. Maxwell was on my heels. I filled him in on who we were looking for as we exited the building.

"Where?" Maxwell asked. "Where is he?"

"I don't know."

We searched the parking lot until I spotted his SUV. "There! Over there!" I pointed to the back of the parking lot. *Dear God, please don't let my friend be dead.*

We approached the car cautiously, stopping in our tracks about twenty feet away.

"Is that blood?" I asked Maxwell solemnly.

"Yeah, looks like it."

"You think he's . . ." I couldn't even say the word.

"Dead?" Maxwell finished my sentence. "I don't know, but I'll be honest with you. It doesn't look good."

"Lord, this can't be happening." I leaned against a nearby car. I could feel my hands throbbing, so I knew my blood pressure must be through the roof.

"You okay, Bishop?" Maxwell inquired.

I had to give him credit. He was the one with the bad heart, but he was hanging in there like a trouper.

"No, I'm not. I can't believe this. This is all my fault. If I hadn't put so much pressure on him, he'd be here right now."

"No, he wouldn't. That man had more issues than *Jet* magazine." Maxwell took a step toward the SUV. "Look, I've seen this type of thing before when I was over in Iraq. You hang back and call the police while I take a look."

"Okay." I was grateful that he was taking the lead. I pulled out my cell phone from under my robe.

As I placed the 911 call, I watched Maxwell walk up to the car and peek in. From the look on his face and the way he shook his head, I knew it wasn't good.

"It's Smitty all right. Simone was right. He's dead," Maxwell proclaimed after I ended my call.

I didn't want to believe what Maxwell was telling me. "You sure? Maybe we should take him out. We might be able to revive him."

"Nah." Maxwell shook his head. "Ain't no reviving him, Bishop. He's gone home."

"How do you know?" I took a step toward the car, and Maxwell stepped in front of me.

"T. K., please. This is really not something you want to see."

But I was in so much disbelief that I had to see it for myself—and for Smitty, as his minister. I braced myself and walked around to the passenger side of the vehicle. "Stand back," I told the members who'd begun to approach the area. I knew they wouldn't be able to be held at bay inside the church for too long.

Looking inside the truck, I saw a sight I would remember for as long as I live. Smitty was slumped over the steering wheel. Half of his head was missing, and the blood had begun to clot. His right eye was bulging out, hanging by a thread from the socket. "Oh my Lord, Smitty, no!" I turned away, steeling my stomach to keep from vomiting.

From the large crowd that had gathered nearby, I could hear cries of, "What's going on? What happened? Did somebody die?"

It took me a few moments, but I finally regained my composure, remembering that I was the one they were supposed to lean on.

I held up both hands. "Please step away until the ambulance and the police get here. We don't know what happened, but we don't want to contaminate the scene if there's been a crime committed here."

They milled around a while longer, but once they realized they were not going to be able to see anything, many people moved back toward the church.

Every few seconds I glanced over at the car. Was this all my fault? My mind played over our last encounter. I thought about how upset Smitty had looked when I pulled out the folder, which revealed his thirty-year-old secret. Maybe I shouldn't have played my trump card on him, but when he backed me into a corner about hiring Aaron, I had to do what I had to do. Now I had to wonder—did I push him into killing himself? I shuddered with guilt.

This looked like a suicide, but Smitty's warning still echoed in my mind. What if Smitty had not been overreacting when he said there was danger out there? I scanned the crowd, wondering if his tormentors were in the midst of us at that very moment. Were Smitty's blackmailers in the crowd?

I looked over my shoulder at the SUV in frustration. *Dammit, Smitty, why didn't you tell me what was going on?*

Monique

22

As I held Simone in my arms, a part of me wanted to drop her right there in the middle of the aisle and go outside to see about my husband. Judging from the panic on T. K.'s face when Simone whispered to him, it looked like she nearly gave him a heart attack. I needed to see how he was doing. But who was I kidding? I also wanted to see what was going on outside. Who was dead outside of the church? I knew the longer I was inside the church with Simone unconscious in my arms, the longer it would take for me to find out.

"Give her some smelling salts, fast!" I ordered one of the ushers, who rushed over and did just that.

With a couple waves of the salt under her nose, Simone's eyes fluttered open. "What the hell? Do you know how many noses y'all done stuck that thing in?" She pushed the usher's hand out of the way.

"Simone, are you all right?" I asked.

"Yeah, I'm all right. What happened? What's going on?" She sat up and looked around with a scowl on her face—until her eyes landed on Aaron. Then a smile appeared. "Am I in heaven? Because there's an angel standing in front of me."

"She doesn't look all right to me. She seems to be hallucinating. Maybe we should get her to a hospital," one of the church elders stated. "They called an ambulance outside. Perhaps she needs one as well."

At the sound of the elder's voice, Simone looked as though a light went on in her head, reminding her of exactly what was going on. "Oh my God, you have to get help. He's outside," she mumbled. "He's outside . . . dead," and then she passed out again.

"I think you're right," I agreed with the elder. "She does need a paramedic. Go and see if you can find some help for my friend. Hurry. She's passed out again."

Aaron stood next to me rather unemotionally the entire time, but when the EMTs rushed in and carried an unconscious Simone out to the ambulance, I think I noticed a hint of concern.

"Aaron, can you drive me to the hospital? Simone doesn't have any family in the area, and someone from the church should be there when she comes to."

"Sure, First Lady." Aaron didn't hesitate. "You wait here and I'll drive around."

I was glad he agreed. T. K. and I had driven to church together that morning. I didn't want to take the vehicle, not knowing what his situation was. Not able to spot him among the swarming crowd, I didn't have time to waste.

I looked to Tia. "Tell my husband that I'm going to the hospital and to call me on my cell when he gets a chance."

As Aaron headed for his vehicle, I watched Simone being loaded into the ambulance. By the time I found out which hospital they planned on taking her to, Aaron had pulled his Escalade in front of me. He got out, then raced around and opened the door for me. I climbed in as he waited behind me to close the door.

I couldn't help but think, *No free ass feels this time.*

Aaron followed the ambulance as best he could, but after we got caught at a red light, I had to give him the remaining directions to the hospital. By the time we arrived in the ER, Simone had already been taken back and we were asked to wait in the lobby for the doctor to come talk with us.

Aaron kindly escorted me over to a chair. I sat down while he remained standing.

"Well, now that we got her here safe and sound, I think I'm going to go ahead and leave," Aaron said to me. "Will you be all right calling Bishop for a ride home?"

"No!" I shouted, standing back up at the same time. Realizing how loud I was, I sank back down into my seat. "I mean, no, don't leave. Don't leave Simone here like this."

If I wasn't mistaken, Aaron let out a slight chuckle before he repeated my statement. "Don't leave Simone here? But you're here."

"Yes, but you're the one who needs to be here more than anyone else."

Aaron put his hands up in defense. "Look, First Lady, I don't know what Simone is running around telling folks, but it's not like that between the two of us—"

I cut him off right there. "But she wants it to be."

Aaron shook his head. "Nah, I don't think so. Not after she kicked me to the curb for some dude who was parked in her—"

"Yeah, yeah." I waved my hand to show how insignificant I thought that was. "She told me all about that, and she's really sorry. You'd know that if you'd just take her calls." I think what I was saying was starting to sink in for Aaron. "Aaron, don't get me wrong. I know my friend is a handful."

"That she is," he agreed.

"But I imagine you can be quite a handful yourself."

He shrugged, indicating there was some truth in what I was saying.

"See there? Perfect match. Or maybe you two have simply met your match in each other. Maybe finding someone like yourself, seeing yourself in someone else, is exactly what the two of you need to reevaluate who you are in life."

Aaron nodded. I could tell I was making sense to him. I would have loved to sit there with him and really drive it home, but that's when I saw T. K. enter the lobby.

"Just think about that," I said to Aaron. "Think about it while you wait here for Simone, okay? My husband just walked in, and I need to go see about him. So, can I trust you to be here for Simone?"

After a pause, Aaron nodded his confirmation.

Feeling comfortable that he was a man of his word, I went over and threw my arms around my husband.

I could feel a slight tremble. Pulling away from him, I asked, "What's going on? Who was it that Simone was talking about?"

Looking right past me in a state of shock, T. K. replied, "It's Smitty. Smitty is dead."

I stepped back from him, and my hands flew instinctively to my mouth. "Someone killed Smitty?"

T. K. looked me in the eye, shaking his head. "No . . . I mean, yes, Smitty is dead, but the police think it was suicide. Although they can't rule out foul play right now."

There was silence between us. I was trying to comprehend what he'd told me and how Smitty's death was related to his recent phone call with T. K. This whole thing was frightening.

"What about Maria?" I asked when I could finally speak. "Does she know? Did anyone talk to her?"

"Maxwell and I just left her. She's in pretty bad shape. You might want to go over there when you leave."

"I can't. I rode over here with Aaron, and I think he's gonna stay and be with Simone."

T. K. looked over my shoulder at Aaron. "Taken a liking to her, has he? He could do worse. She's a beautiful woman when she doesn't have an attitude."

"Maybe when this is all over, you can tell him that. I know Simone will appreciate it."

"I might just do that." He looked grateful for the brief opportunity to discuss something other than the nightmare at hand. "But anyway, why don't you use my car to go see about Maria?" T. K. took out his keys and handed them to me. "I'm sure Maxwell will be here any minute. I'll catch a ride with him."

I took the keys from my husband. For now, I'd go see about Maria, but later, I was going to make sure I got a chance to corner my husband and find out exactly what was going on. Whether Smitty killed himself or someone else had been involved, there had to be a reason, and I wanted to know what it was.

The Bishop

23

I walked into James's hospital room and was greeted with a smile. " 'Bout time you showed up," he cracked. He was wearing an oxygen tube and had IVs in both arms, but his voice still had a lighthearted tone to it. Although he looked thinner since my last visit a few days ago, he was in good spirits. He seemed determined to live his last few days fully. The doctor had said he probably had less than a month to live with the way the cancer had metastasized. Then again, they had said that last month too. Good ol' James was a fighter. There was no doubt about that.

I wished I could have returned the smile James gave me, but instead I could barely look him in the eye.

"Okay, what's wrong?" he asked. "You look like you're the one who's been given a death sentence, not me."

I sighed, tears welling up in my eyes at the image of Smitty with his head half blown off. "Man, James, I don't even know how to tell you this." I sat down in the hospital chair beside his bed. I didn't want to upset him since he was so frail, but I also knew I had to tell him or he'd drive me crazy.

"What is it?" James leaned forward. "Did Aaron make a fool out of himself? Did the choir flop?"

"I wish it was something that simple." I glanced out the window.

"Then what the hell is it, T. K.?" James was getting more frustrated with me by the second.

There was no other way to say it than to just come right out with it. "Smitty," I said his name as if that was all James needed to hear. I'd had an easier time telling my wife the bad news than spitting it out to my old friend. Maybe because I knew James and Smitty were close, damn close, despite the way James had felt about him lately.

"What about that Judas?" James snapped. "I can't stand that two-faced MF!"

"James, Smitty's dead." I shook my head ruefully.

James pulled the oxygen tube out of his nose, sitting up with a grimace. "What did you say?" He looked like he wanted to slap the words back into my mouth.

I lowered my head again, exhaling before I spoke. "I said Smitty's dead."

James just stared at me for a moment in disbelief. "How the fuck did that happen?" he cursed.

Maxwell walked into the room as James asked his question. "From what the cops told me, it looks like a suicide, but they can't rule out foul play until they get gun powder residue and ballistic reports."

"Damn, here I am talkin' bad about the guy and he's dead," James said. "Poor guy. I hope he's got some peace now."

"Yeah," Maxwell replied sadly. "I hope so too."

"We all do," I said.

While we were all hoping that Smitty had found peace, I wondered if I would ever feel peace about this situation. I still felt some guilt about my involvement. How much did my interactions with Smitty have to do with his death? I was starting to think I would carry this guilt with me until Judgment Day.

"You know, this is all my fault. He'd be alive if I hadn't pushed him so hard."

"Man, don't do that to yourself. I loved Smitty like a brother, but the Smitty who'd been rolling around lately was a snake for what he was trying to do to you and the church," James said. "Besides, you had no idea what the truth was about Smitty. Me, on the other hand, I'd known this about him for years. I had proof of his little secret, but I just never used it until he came after you." He shook his head. "Mmm-mmm-mmm. The secrets some of our members keep."

"But he was being blackmailed," I said in Smitty's defense. "I think his back was up against the wall. Besides, before he died,

Smitty told me that I needed to watch my back. That this was all bigger than him."

"He did?" Maxwell raised an eyebrow.

"Yeah, I'm still not sure what he meant."

I was deep in thought, and then something dropped into my spirit. "Hey, I have a question for you, Maxwell, since you're so close to the police and the military."

"What is it?"

"Can you get me a gun and a concealment permit?"

Maxwell stared at me for a second. "For what?" He folded his arms.

"For protection. I'm worried about my family, man. You do realize a man showed up dead in my church's parking lot today, don't you?"

"Yeah, and it was most likely the suicide of a troubled man," Maxwell replied.

I tried to protest, but he said, "Listen, you don't need a gun. Let me make a few calls. I can have some of my friends from Blackrock provide you and the first lady with security. You're the bishop of a church, not a corner thug. You wouldn't know what to do with a gun if the situation arose."

"Okay, then you look into getting my wife security. I don't need any," I agreed without a fight.

"Look into it for them both, Maxwell," James chimed in, and I rolled my eyes. "I don't wanna hear it, T. K. We've been talking about getting you a bodyguard for years, ever since you ran for borough president. You can't be rolling up in the hood like you do without someone to watch your back. We don't even have to call him a bodyguard. We can call him your driver, just as long as he's packing heat."

"Whatever. It's not the people in the hood I'm worried about," I grunted. "But if we really wanna get to the bottom of this, you need to put your heads together and tell me who my enemies are in the church."

"Who your enemies are?" Maxwell said. "Do you even have any enemies?"

"There was a time when I thought the word *enemy* stood only for the devil, but Smitty said that whoever is behind this is out to get me. That sounds like an enemy to me." I turned to James. "So, Mr. Know-It-All, who are my enemies?"

"Well, Maxwell's kind of right. You are generally well liked. You've ruffled some feathers over the years, but I can't exactly say you've made staunch enemies," James offered.

"Well, how about Deacon Brown and Trustees Duncan and Whitmore?" Maxwell said. "They all seemed to be hell-bent on blocking us from hiring the new choir director. They sounded like they wanted to destroy you, Bishop."

"Followers, that's all they were. What we need to do is get control of those boards and the women's groups," James said pointedly. As weakened as his body had become, James continued to show that his mind was still sharp. "We control them, then we pretty much control the entire church. Then can't nobody hurt you in the church."

"Well, I know from the way she spoke at the last meeting before the vote that Simone is on our side," I offered.

James gave a little snort of disgust. "Keep your eye on that woman, T. K. She may be acting all nice now, but a tiger don't change her stripes. She's only cool as long as she gets what she wants. Let's hope that the choir director of yours she's been chasing keeps her occupied." I wondered how James knew about Simone's interest in Aaron, but now wasn't the time to ask him about his sources.

"Maxwell, I know you have a lot on your plate, but with Smitty dead, I think it's time you took over as chairman of the deacons' board," I said confidently.

Maxwell tried to conceal a grin. I knew he relished the idea of taking a position of leadership at a church he loved as much as James and I did. Still, he didn't reveal his enthusiasm. "Bishop, you know I'll do whatever it takes to help you and the church, but I've been gone a while. I'm not sure folks won't like me trying to bully my way in. Some might even see it as me taking advantage of Smitty's death."

James scratched his skinny chin. "Bishop, when I was in the church, I had more enemies than you—many of them female. I can't remember anyone particularly disliking you. Sure, we all have haters, but not enough to do this."

My phone rang, signaling a call from my wife. Although it could be quite embarrassing for me at times, she liked me to have Aretha Franklin's "Natural Woman" as her ringtone. She figured with that song playing on a grown man's phone, I'd be quick to take all her calls. I reached down to my waistband to pull out my mobile phone.

"Wait just a minute." I held up a finger to James and Maxwell, and then excused myself by turning away. "Hey, baby," I said, talking into my cell phone.

"How's James?" Monique asked.

"He's doing okay."

Monique paused. "I have to ask you a question."

"What is it?"

"Did you by any chance buy me three dozen roses and those Godiva chocolate truffles I love?"

"No. Why? Was I supposed to?" I searched my mind to see if I'd forgotten anything important like a birthday, holiday, or anniversary.

"It would have been nice, but someone beat you to it."

"What?" I said it so loud that both Maxwell and James turned toward me.

"Yep, someone left a huge box of truffles and roses on my car seat. I found it once I got home. And that's not all. Whoever this somebody is left a card that was typewritten. It reads . . ." I heard Monique rustling a piece of paper. " 'I just wanted you to know that I live and breathe for you.' "

"Monique, I'll be right home. Somebody's playing games," I said, then hung up the phone. I usually remained calm under pressure, but this thing was getting sinister. Who could be giving my wife gifts? Were they actually giving *me* a sign? I worried that somehow her secret admirer was connected to this thing that Smitty warned me about.

I turned to James and Maxwell. "Y'all think about what I asked you. I have to go home. I have an emergency."

Simone

24

"Everything checked out okay, but I'd still like to keep you overnight for observation," the doctor said as I sat on the examination table in a paper hospital gown.

"Oh, please," I replied, jumping down off the table and heading over to the chair that held my clothes. "I know what that means. It's code for 'you're in perfect health, but we'd like you to stay so we can bill your insurance company a few thousand dollars for a sleepless night.'" I snatched up the outfit I'd chosen specially that morning to catch Aaron's eye. "No, thanks. I think I'll go home to my own bed."

"In all honesty, Mrs.—"

I cut him off. "It's Ms., and I don't need honesty right now. I need to get out of here."

"If you insist on leaving, you're going to have to sign a waiver."

"Well, then give me the form, because I insist," I replied sharply. There was no way I was going to be cooped up in this place any longer than I had to be. I was still trying to piece together the incidents that led me here, and I couldn't do that if I was stuck in a hospital bed. Images of Jonathan Smith's bloody body in his car kept flashing in my mind. I needed to get back to the church, or at least talk to someone to find out what the hell was going on.

"Okay, then," the doctor said as he wrote something on my chart, "it will be noted as a discharge against doctor's order."

"Fine." My nerves were on edge, and at this point, I didn't give a damn what this young doctor thought of me. "Write whatever you want. I just wanna get out of here."

With a look of exasperation, the doctor exited the room, hopefully to go fill out my discharge papers. I finished dressing, then sat on the bed until a female orderly entered the room with a wheelchair.

"Hi. I'm here to take you out."

I looked down at the wheelchair. "Really? I mean, is all this necessary? All I did was faint, for Pete's sake."

I could tell I intimidated the poor girl. She didn't know what to say. And as a matter of fact, I didn't want her to say anything. I just wanted to get out of there. Hospitals gave me the creeps. That was probably one of the reasons why I refused to visit James—that and I hated his guts.

"It's . . . it's . . . hospital procedure," the girl stammered.

A nurse came in with a clipboard in hand. "I know you're anxious to get out of here," she said. "I just need you to sign off on these discharge papers, and then Sara here will escort you out." The nurse looked down at the wheelchair. "Oh, and you must be special. I see Sara brought the ten-passenger stretch."

Okay, obviously the doctor had filled this nurse in on my attitude, and she was giving it right back to me. Her little comment was cute, but I wasn't in a joking mood. I took the clipboard, scribbled my John Hancock, and handed it back to the nurse.

"Your friend is in the waiting room. Sara will wheel you out now."

I was glad to hear that Monique was waiting for me. Now, that was a true friend, spending her afternoon in the hospital when there was so much drama to be tended to back at the church. I couldn't wait to see her so she could fill me in.

I plopped down in the wheelchair and said, "Okay, Sara, let's go."

Sara wheeled me down the hall toward the double doors that led to the waiting room. Rather than enter that room in a wheelchair and look even more pitiful in front of Monique, I stopped her at the doors and announced, "It's okay, Sara. I can take it from here."

She didn't bother to inform me of hospital policy this time. She stopped the chair and offered a weak, "Hope you feel better."

I stood up from the wheelchair and turned around to give her a slight nod of thanks. She disappeared quickly, probably glad to be away from me.

I turned around and entered the waiting room, where I got a surprise I never could have predicted. Aaron was waiting for me.

"You ready to go home?" he asked.

"Wha-what are you doing here?" After the events of this day, Aaron's appearance was almost more than my already-confused mind could handle. "Where's Monique? They said my friend was out here waiting for me."

He shook his head. "I know things have been a little weird between us, but now I'm not even considered your friend?"

"I, uh, didn't mean it that way. I just . . ." I struggled to get myself together. I had been trying too hard to get Aaron to talk to me. Now that he was here, I couldn't let the drama at the church render me stupid.

"Never mind. I'm just here because I promised First Lady I would make sure you were okay. What happened out there in the parking lot anyway?"

"I was hoping you could tell me," I answered. "I have no idea what happened after I passed out."

"All I know is you came into the church screaming about someone being dead. I have no idea what was going on in the parking lot, because I stayed with you until the EMTs came, and then I followed the ambulance to the hospital." He shook his head. "It was chaos up in that church. Bishop came to the hospital later and told me and the first lady that it was Deacon Smith in the car."

"I know," I said quietly.

He cocked his head to the side. "What were you doing out there in the middle of the service anyway? Seems like right before that you were in the aisle feeling the Holy Spirit."

Oh, so he did notice me! I thought hopefully. I was flattered, but at the same time, I was concerned by his question. I couldn't admit my reason for being outside. I tried to stop him before he tried to probe further.

"Look, Aaron, I really don't want to talk about it, okay?"

I must have put a little too much attitude in my tone, because a look crossed over his face that let me know I'd just lost any sympathy points I might have been gaining. Maybe I should have let Sara bring me out in the wheelchair after all.

"Whatever, Simone," he snapped. "Let's just go."

Aaron turned and stalked toward the exit without another word. I let out a little huff. I'd heard of giving someone the cold shoulder, but damn!

I followed behind him to the parking lot. Surprisingly, he opened the car door for me, though he didn't wait for me to get in. He simply walked over to the driver's side, got in, put on his seat belt, and started the engine. Not wanting to be left behind, I climbed into the truck and closed the door. He wouldn't look at me, and it was driving me crazy.

"You going home?" Aaron asked, sounding more cold than concerned.

"Uh-huh." *Where else would I be going?*

Like he was reading my mind, he said, "I didn't know if you were going back to the church to get your car or what."

I'd forgotten about that. "No, I'll worry about that later. You can take me home. You remember how to get there?"

"How could I forget?" He rolled his eyes as we pulled out of the parking lot.

After ten minutes of silence between us, I tried to ease the tension, though I failed miserably.

"So, Aaron, what's this I hear about you and Porsche Moore?"

He gave me such a hard look you would have thought I just told him he had no talent for singing.

"First of all, it's none of your business what I do in my private life. Second of all, I can't believe you're talking about my dating habits at a time like this."

That was enough to shut me up. Silence returned to the car.

"Am I dropping you off here, or should I drive up a couple of blocks and let you out?" he asked when we approached my block.

Oh, so he's still hung up on that. Damn, he sure can hold a grudge!

No matter how angry he was, I still couldn't help myself. Even his slick-ass tongue turned me on. I decided not to sass him back, because once things calmed down with all this drama at the church, I planned on having that slick tongue all over me.

"You can pull into the driveway if you don't mind."

When he parked his car, I hoped he might show some chivalry and walk around to let me out. No such luck. He just sat there silently. Our failed date really was a thorn in this man's side, but enough was enough.

"Look, Aaron, I'm sorry. I shouldn't have asked—"

"Never mind," he snapped.

"But I really want to—"

"You have a good night, now, Trustee Wilcox."

He wouldn't even make eye contact with me. I decided it was time to get right to the heart of the matter.

"Do you hate me?"

Finally, he turned to look at me. "Hate you? Nope. I was pissed off for a while, but *hate* is a strong word. I don't hate anyone."

Okay, so he didn't hate me, but I still had to break down that wall he'd built up after our first date. Time to lay all my cards on the table. "Look, Aaron, I know you're upset with me. I know it probably bruised your male ego or something, thinking that I kicked you to the curb for another man. But here's the truth: I'm not interested in anyone but you."

"Tell that to Mr. Range Rover," he said with a sneer.

My breath caught in my throat for a painful second, but I forged ahead. "I can't." I paused momentarily to try to slow my racing heart. "Look, I don't know if it matters to you, but I really like you, Aaron. You're the only man I have a romantic interest in, and it's killing me that you haven't talked to me."

I could not believe I'd just said that. It was so unlike me to admit these kinds of feelings for any man, because it always puts a woman at a disadvantage. But I truly liked this guy enough to take that risk.

Still feeling a little shell-shocked, I wasn't able to look him in the eye. I stared straight ahead as I waited for his response—which never came. I'd just put everything out there on the line and for what? A big, fat nothing.

If he couldn't appreciate what I was offering him, then fuck it! I was through chasing his ass around. I reached for the handle to open the door and get the hell away from this guy.

"I really like you too."

He was practically whispering when he said it, but it was loud enough for me to hear, and his words stopped me in my tracks.

I turned to face him. "You do?"

"Hell yeah! Why you think I'm tripping like this?" He suddenly looked as relieved as I felt.

"Then why didn't you say something? Why'd you walk around avoiding me and not taking my calls? That's not how you treat somebody you like."

"Oh, yeah? Then why didn't you just tell me the real about you and ol' boy?"

I sighed, relaxing my shoulders. "Because my business is my business. I don't tell everybody everything in the beginning. I mean, it was just all too much. And now with this . . . what happened at the church today . . . you don't know the half of it. It's a long story, and it's really complicated."

He glanced at his watch. "I've got time. Start talking."

"Aaron, you've got to understand something about me. I'm an independent woman who does what she wants, when she wants to. Shoot, you're lucky you got me to admit how bad I've been sweating you ever since that first date. But that's all you're going to get right now. I'm not going to explain myself to you until I'm good and ready. Take it or leave it." In spite of suddenly regaining my backbone, I was seconds away from begging him to take it.

I practically shrieked with relief when he nodded and said, "Okay, Simone. I'll give you time, but that goes both ways. Don't expect a commitment if you can't give one."

"What are you trying to say? If we start fooling around, you're going to see other people?" I wanted to laugh. Once he got some of this, he wasn't going to want to see anyone, guaranteed.

"Do you have a problem with that? I like to be up front."

I both hated and loved his arrogant authority. He was a take-charge kind of man, same as James used to be.

"No, I don't have a problem with it. I know how good this is. Maybe you need to come inside and find out for yourself."

"Be careful what you ask for, because I'm pretty damn good myself."

Now that the ice had finally been broken, I knew it was only a matter of time before we ignited a fire between us.

Within minutes, Aaron had thrown his truck into park and was pressed up against me, placing kisses on the back of my neck as we tripped into my house. I could barely close and lock the door behind us.

"Hold on for a second." I put my hands up against his chest. I could feel his heart beating through his shirt. "Let me go get cleaned up. I've been sitting up in that hospital all afternoon."

"Unh-uh. That might spoil the mood," Aaron said as he placed kisses all around my neck.

"Okay." Once again, I tried to push him off of me, but he was giving me these sweet, succulent kisses that I couldn't get enough of. "How about you shower with me?"

"That'll work," he said, scooping me up in his arms. "Where's the shower?"

I pointed toward the staircase as I locked my lips on his and let my tongue loose in his mouth. He stumbled and bumped his way up the stairs, somehow managing to carry me all the way.

In the bathroom, he eased me down and I hit the light switch and then fumbled over to the shower, all without breaking our kiss. I turned on the water with one hand while I cupped his package in the other. It wasn't an easy feat, but I was feeling rather inspired.

Aaron stopped long enough to take off his shoes. When he went for his shirt, I stopped him.

"Unh-uh, baby, you're going to take all the fun out of it."

Taking off my stilettos, I pulled him into the shower, letting the water drench us both. I'd regret getting my hair wet later, but right now, I was on a mission. We undressed each other in the shower, peeling off wet clothing as if we were peeling bananas. Oh, and speaking of bananas, he was packing an extra-large plantain!

When we were finally naked, he kissed my lips and then went exploring. He kissed my chin and then trailed down to my breasts, sucking them with an expertise I'd never experienced before. Then, to my surprise, he slid his hands between my legs and lifted me up in the air until my kitty cat was right in front of his face. He was a lot stronger than I would have imagined, but I still wasn't taking any chances. I held on to the shower head as his face eased between my legs.

Now, I've had more than my share of men go down on me, but Mr. Aaron Mackie was by far the best. The way he worked his snakelike tongue had me coming so hard that I literally had to push him away because I couldn't take anymore—though I planned to make sure he would be doing that little trick over and over and over again.

He might have played harder to get than most men did with me, but Aaron Mackie was definitely worth the wait.

Aaron

25

I pulled into the church parking lot energized and ready for work after spending the past two days at Simone's place. I was glad to get up and go to work that morning. Don't get me wrong, I really liked Simone, but the woman was a beast in the bedroom. I'd never met someone with such a ravenous sexual appetite in my entire life. All I had to do was look at her, and she was stripping off her clothes, kissing and pawing on me like she was in heat. Hey, I was flattered like hell, but she didn't give a brother a minute's rest. I was so sexually drained that it was actually nice to get away from her for a spell.

As I pulled up to the church, I saw Bishop Wilson and Deacon Frye talking in the parking lot. I rolled down my window to greet them. "Good morning, gentlemen. How're you doing?"

"Doing okay," the bishop replied warmly, although he didn't look so happy. Finding a dead man in your church parking lot could do that to you, I guess. "How about you? That was a great performance you put on Sunday. Sorry I didn't get a chance to tell you, but with everything going on . . ." His words trailed off in sadness.

Deacon Frye quickly made an attempt to pick up the mood. "Sure was a nice performance." He smiled, but his eyes were not on me. Neither were the bishop's, for that matter. Both of them were focused on the far corner of the parking lot. I assumed that was where the body had been found.

My eyes followed theirs, and sure enough, I saw a tow truck parked over there. The driver was out of the truck, pulling down some yellow crime scene tape that had blocked the area. He then loaded a vehicle onto the flatbed.

"So, what exactly happened here Sunday? Did they find out who murdered Deacon Smith?" I questioned.

"It wasn't murder. It was a suicide," Deacon Frye corrected as he finally turned his attention to me. "Did you meet Deacon Smith?"

"Yeah, I met him. That's the dude who was trying to get me fired before I even started working for First Jamaica Ministries. Wow, he killed himself?" I wondered if he had a family. I mean, I disliked the guy because of what he tried to do to me and the bishop, but that didn't mean I wished him dead.

"Don't judge him too hard," Bishop said diplomatically. "He was a very troubled man."

"Yeah, a very troubled man with a whole lot of issues," Deacon Frye added. "Did you know—"

The bishop gave Deacon Frye a stern look as he interrupted him. "Yes, issues that we'd rather not get into at this time."

"Oh, yes, of course. The bishop's right." Deacon Frye shook his head remorsefully.

We all watched as the driver got back into the police tow truck and started it up. As he drove through the parking lot and passed us, I got a look at the SUV's driver's side window. It was splattered with dried blood—lots of it. Poor guy must have shot himself in the head. Frye wasn't lying; he must have really been a troubled man to go that route.

The tow truck passed and we all watched it exit the lot. That's when I got a glimpse of the back of the SUV, and suddenly I felt like someone had knocked the wind out of me. I'd seen that car before. It was a Range Rover, the same kind I'd seen in Simone's driveway that night. Jesus Christ, was her other dude Deacon Smith?

I pointed at the Range Rover. "Is that Deacon Smith's car?"

"Uh-huh, a little flashy for a deacon with those rims, but he sure loved that truck," the bishop replied.

"It almost seems fitting that he died in it," Deacon Frye added.

The flashy rims confirmed my suspicion. This had to be the same car that I'd seen parked in Simone's driveway.

"Will you gentlemen excuse me?" I said hastily, suddenly feeling a need to be alone to get my head together. "I'm gonna go find me a place to park so I can get to work. We've got choir practice tonight, and I have to add about three or four new songs for our competition up in Connecticut in two weeks."

"We'll see you inside, son," the bishop said.

I found a parking space, but I didn't get out right away. I couldn't get my mind around the fact that Deacon Smith had been the one in Simone's driveway that night. Were they having an affair? Was that why she was so paranoid? I guess if I was the chairwoman of the board of trustees and was having an affair with the married chairman of the deacons' board, I'd want to keep things on the low too.

But that wasn't what really bothered me. What bothered me was that he was dead now, and nobody wanted to talk about it—especially not Simone. No wonder she kept fainting after she burst into the church. She'd just found the body of her ex-lover—at least I hoped he was an ex—and from the looks of the car, his brains were half blown out.

Was Simone the reason he killed himself? Maybe they'd had it out that night. Maybe she'd kicked him to the curb for me and he couldn't take it. I had to admit, if Simone had put it on him like she'd put it on me, living without her was probably something he couldn't face. Especially for an old guy like him, who probably wasn't getting much at home.

I thought about calling Simone, then changed my mind. She probably wouldn't tell me the truth anyway. But there was one person who just might. I stepped out of my car to head inside but didn't get far before I heard the bishop calling my name.

"Mackie?"

I looked up, and suddenly all thoughts of Simone disappeared from my mind. I had much bigger things to worry about when I saw the man who was now standing with the bishop.

What the fuck is he doing here? I slowed my pace as I walked toward them. Deacon Frye, fortunately, had gone back into the church. The "he" I was referring to was a short, sloppy, greaseball-looking white man by the name of Andrew Gotti. To say I hated this guy was an understatement.

"Mackie, this gentleman is looking for you," Bishop stated as the man approached me.

I nodded. "Thanks, Bishop. I got it from here. I'll catch up to you in the church." I turned to my unexpected visitor. "Let's talk over here."

Bishop Wilson was standing there as if he expected a formal introduction to this pain in the ass. Well, no disrespect to him, but he wasn't getting one. I placed my hand behind Gotti's back and guided him away from the bishop.

"What the fuck are you doing coming around here?" I demanded in a low tone so I wouldn't be overheard.

He smirked at me. "Hey, aren't you supposed to be some kind of man of God? Why the hell are you cursing, and on church grounds, no less?"

He was trying to bait me, but I wouldn't give him the satisfaction. "What do you want, Gotti?"

"I'm just checking on you. I heard someone offed themselves around here. I wanted to make sure it wasn't you."

"Well, I'm fine."

"That's good. You're gonna have everything we asked for by Friday, of course?"

"Yeah, when have I not? There's no need for you to come here."

He got up in my face. "You don't get it, do you, Mackie? I'll go wherever I damn well please when it comes to you. As far as I'm concerned, I'm your cock. Where you go, I go. So unless you want problems with us, you might want to remember that."

I didn't say anything. I just stared at him.

"I'll see you Friday. And make sure you have everything we asked for."

"I told you I'll have your stuff."

"Good. I'll see you soon," he said.

"Not if I can help it," I said under my breath as I walked toward the church.

"Hey, Mackie!" I turned to see what else he wanted. "Me and my wife have been looking for a new church. You never know. Maybe I'll see you on Sunday too." He laughed, and I walked into the church wanting to flip him the finger so bad I could taste it.

Tia

26

It was a slow night on my rape hotline, but that didn't necessarily mean that it was a good thing. Somewhere out there was a woman in need. Maybe she'd been raped tonight, maybe she'd been raped a month ago, but she was hurting inside from the trauma some bastard had given her. I just wished she would call so I could help.

I glanced over at Aaron, who was sitting next to my desk at a table, waiting to take his first call. I was pleased that he volunteered to help out, but still, I worried that having a man answer a rape hotline might do more damage than good. That's why I had taken both of the calls that had come in tonight. I explained to him that it would be best if he just observed for a while, to get a feel for the types of conversations he might be engaged in.

"Thank you for helping me out with the hotline this evening." I gave him a smile and a thank-you nod. His moral support was truly appreciated.

"Like I said, watching you in action the other day, man, made me feel like what I'm doing here at the church is little kid's stuff. You should really be proud of yourself, Tia."

"Are you kidding me?" Really, was he kidding me? This man was a musical genius. He had to know that. Or perhaps he was just fishing for a compliment. Either way, he deserved all the compliments he could get. "Aaron, please. What you've done for this church? The way you let God use you in song, and then spill that anointing over into us? You have to realize how many souls must get saved because of you."

Aaron gave a modest shrug. "I just do what comes natural.

Making a woman feel good about herself after she's been raped, that's a godsend, a true gift and blessing from the Almighty Himself."

If he knew what I'd been through, he'd understand why I was so good at putting myself in these women's shoes.

The incoming call line lit up on the phone.

"Hold on, let me take this call." I reached for the phone, but Aaron stopped me.

"Wait, let me take this one."

I shifted my eyes in his direction. "You sure?" I asked with uncertainty.

"Yeah, I think so."

I hoped so, because if not, it was too late, as Aaron had already picked up the phone.

"First Jamaica Ministries rape counseling. How can I help you?"

Well, he'd gotten that part down anyway.

Aaron paused and listened intensely. Whatever the caller was saying must have been serious. Aaron's eyes darted back and forth from the phone to me.

"Hit the speaker button," I whispered. Just in case I had to take over the call, I wanted to be knowledgeable of what was being said.

"And I swear to God, I know it's all my fault." I could hear the fragile and shaken voice of a woman on the line. "That's why I'm going to kill myself."

Dear Lord, what was in the water in this city? What was with folks killing themselves?

Obviously, Aaron must have been thinking something similar. He said to the woman, "Trust me, you don't want to do that. Someone who belongs to First Jamaica Ministries just killed himself, and you should see the devastation and destruction it left behind. Yeah, he may not be hurting anymore, but now every one of his loved ones is hurting." Aaron paused for a minute. "You love your family and friends, right?"

"Yes." The woman sniffled.

"Then you wouldn't want them hurting like you are hurting now . . . would you?"

"No," she answered meekly. "But how can I go on? He raped me and it's all my fault. I had no business leaving the club with a complete stranger. I asked for it. I deserved it. I have no one to blame but myself."

"You have that jerk who raped you to blame," Aaron shot back. "You're probably not the first girl he's done this to. And unless you report the rape to the police, and this guy gets caught and you testify against him, there's no telling how many other women he may do this to. But if you're dead, who's going to be in that courtroom to stand up and speak for all those other women?"

Aaron continued as if he'd been doing this all his life. I sat back, listening, and took mental notes. He was saying some things that I'd never even thought to say before.

"Look, the guy who did this to you already feels as though he's won. He doesn't even think what he did is wrong. Sometimes people don't realize what they're doing is wrong and that they're hurting somebody unless they're told. You have to tell him. You have to tell him by reporting him to the police. And then you have to show him that he didn't win, that you are the winner, by moving on with your life."

We both waited with bated breath. I said a quick prayer that his words had touched this woman and saved her life. There was a brief pause, where it sounded like she was drying her tears and regaining her composure, and then my prayer was answered.

"You're right. I can't even believe I was so stupid to think that killing myself would be the answer. That would only make things worse. I'm going to get off the phone and go talk to my mom now."

"Yes, that's a great idea. You're a very brave and smart girl."

"Thank you. Thank you so much."

"You're welcome."

"Hey, what's your name?" she asked.

"Uh . . ." Aaron looked to me to see if it was okay for him to give out his name. I nodded. "It's Aaron."

"Well, thanks, Aaron. You may not realize it, but you just saved my life."

When the call ended, both Aaron and I exhaled—loudly.

"Oh my God. That was crazy," Aaron said, slumping back in his chair like he'd just run a marathon.

I just sat there shaking my head.

"What, did I do something wrong?" He looked worried.

"For heaven's sake, no. You were wonderful, Aaron."

And he was wonderful—not only a wonderful choir director, but also an altogether wonderful human being. He'd just displayed that in the call. I felt so indebted to him.

"Thanks. I can't describe how good it feels to help someone like that. But, man, am I exhausted now!"

I looked over at the clock. "Well, it's about time we get going anyway. As a matter of fact, we should have been out of here a half hour ago." I stood up to get ready to leave. "Hey, have you had dinner yet?"

"Of course not. I've been here with you." Aaron chuckled.

"Okay, then how about I treat you to a meal at Carmichael's Diner? You know, a small token of my appreciation for helping me out."

"I don't have any plans. That sounds great."

"You sure? I mean, what about Simone?" I wished I could take back the words as soon as I said them. It wasn't like me to pry into someone's personal business, and besides, it wasn't like I was asking Aaron out on a date.

"What about Simone?"

"I don't know. You tell me." Shoot! Why was I so interested in this man's private life, and why couldn't I control my dang mouth?

"Well, I would if there was anything to tell. Now, do you want to go eat, or do you want to sit here and starve while we talk about Simone?"

"Okay, okay, point taken." I put my hands up in defeat. We locked up and then headed out to the church parking lot.

"Since it's your treat, the least I can do is drive," Aaron suggested.

"Oh, no, it's fine. I don't mind driving."

"No, I insist. Besides, there's this new song I'm thinking about us doing for the national competition that I want you to listen to."

I gave in. "Sure."

I climbed into Aaron's SUV and was scared half to death by a loud rapping on the passenger's side window.

"What the hell?" A familiar tattooed face was pressed up against the window.

"What the—" Aaron's head swiveled around. "Who is that?"

"Oh my goodness, what is he doing here?" I was so embarrassed I felt like dying.

The young man continued banging on the window. "What the hell you doing in this nigga's car?" he demanded. "Get your ass out here. You think I'm gonna put up with this shit?"

I watched Aaron reach for something on the side of his seat. "Don't worry. I got this."

"No, Aaron, relax. I know him," I said, blowing air through my teeth. "Look, please take a rain check on dinner tonight." I reached for the door handle.

"I can't let you go with him."

"It's okay. I promise."

"Who is that, Tia? Is that your boyfriend or something?"

I could hear the doubt in Aaron's voice. He didn't think this guy would be my type, since I was such a loyal church member in good standing, and I really didn't have time to explain.

"It's complicated, very complicated," I said, exiting the truck and closing the door.

I was pulled away from Aaron's car and dragged toward another one.

Now I was irate. "Kareem, how could you embarrass me like this?"

Aaron

27

After discovering that the Range Rover parked in Simone's driveway had belonged to Deacon Smith, I threw myself into my work and avoided her for several days. I wasn't sure how I felt about the whole thing. I mean, we had a great time together—especially in the bedroom—and I really liked her, so maybe I was afraid to know the truth. If it turned out that he really had been her lover, I didn't know what I would do with that information.

When I did finally confront her with what I knew, she offered me only a brief explanation.

"Look, Aaron, I know it looks bad, but I swear he was only at my house for church business. I just panicked because I didn't want him to see me with you and get the wrong idea. I have a reputation to uphold as a trustee, and I couldn't be seen bringing the new choir director home to my house at that time of night, could I? I mean you've only been at the church a short time. What would that make me look like?"

I wanted to comment that the same could be said about a married deacon being parked in her driveway at that hour to discuss "church business," but she didn't let me get that far.

"That's all I'm going to say about this matter. The man is dead. We should let him rest in peace, don't you think?"

And that's when I knew that Simone and I would never be more than casual sex partners. Obviously there was more to the story than she was admitting. She probably was having an affair with the guy, but I decided that the true details weren't all that important to me. As long as I understood the level of truth I could expect out of her, then I knew where I stood. I wouldn't trust her enough to let her be someone special in my life, but hell, I wouldn't kick her fine ass out of my bed either.

So, I spent a little time with her, enjoying repeat performances of that first night in her shower, but I was always careful not to let things get too serious. Like always, I was up front about not wanting a commitment. She just laughed it off and told me that sooner or later I'd change my mind. If nothing else, she was confident.

Just to remind myself to stick to my guns and not get too serious with Simone, I was still seeing Porsche Moore from time to time. Oh, her ghetto ass couldn't hold a candle to Simone, but she was always available, and the girl gave a helluva blow job.

In the meantime, I was busy with my choir at the church, which was growing larger by the day. We were now forty members strong, thanks to the great performances we'd been putting on every Sunday. Because everyone wanted to be a gospel star, the new choir members were eager to join. They were also excited about going to the New England gospel sing-off in Connecticut, where the top prize was a hundred thousand dollars. More importantly, attendance at the church had increased exponentially. Things were looking up for me, the choir, and First Jamaica Ministries, and that was a good thing.

This evening's rehearsal had ended after we wrapped up a run-through of Kirk Franklin's song "The Fight of My Life."

"Choir members, I thank most of you for being on time, and not on CP time." I heard a few titters, the culprits knowing who they were. I placed my baton on the pulpit. "Practice is over. You're dismissed."

Most people grabbed their song sheets and started for the door. A few members stood around chitchatting.

Tia walked up to me and gave me the fist bump Michelle Obama made famous after President Obama's winning of the primary. I hadn't seen her since her boyfriend ripped her out of the car the other night. It was kind of an awkward moment, as I really didn't know whether we should speak about the situation.

"Aaron, you the bomb," Tia said with a smile.

"Thanks, Tia. Uh, listen, I hope I'm not overstepping my

boundaries, but, uh . . ." I leaned in so that no one could hear our business. "Is everything all right? I really didn't like the way things went down the other night with your boyfriend. That wasn't cool how dude was manhandling you. If you want me to talk to him, I will. I mean, we're just friends, and you should be able to have friends without him tripping on you like that."

"Yeah, I know, but it wasn't what it looked like. He's not my boyfriend. I'd explain it to you now, but I have to go meet a woman for counseling."

"This late?" I asked. It was already after eight o'clock in the evening.

"Yeah, well, she works late, and on top of that, she has to catch the bus to get here." Tia looked up at the clock on the wall. "And I'm already late."

"Well, perhaps if you could have a talk with some of your fellow choir members who insist on being tardy, I could start on time and get out of here on time."

"I know, right? But anyway, I owe you a rain check on that dinner. How about we try it again Sunday after church? Dinner at my place? I'll explain everything then. That way I can kill two birds with one stone."

I was a little hesitant at first. I wasn't feeling her boyfriend's behavior. The last thing I needed was to put myself in a position where I'd have another gun pointed at my head.

Tia could sense my hesitation. "Come on. Don't be *scurred*," she joked. "I promise I'll protect you." She smiled and winked.

Everything about Tia was just so pleasant and carefree. How could I pass up dinner with her? Besides, her filling me in on her boyfriend, I'm sure, was going to make good dinner conversation. "It's a date. I mean, you know what I mean," I said with a smile.

"Yeah, I do." Tia waved good-bye as she rushed off to her meeting.

I watched her leave, thinking about how much I'd been enjoying her company lately. Unlike the complicated drama that came along with someone like Simone or Porsche, Tia was sweet and simple. I liked that about her.

"Man, things are really coming together." The bishop's voice interrupted my thoughts. "I knew you were going to do big things, Mackie. Congratulations. Job well done."

I was surprised to see him. I guess he was doing an impromptu visit to see how the choir was progressing.

"Thank you, Bishop. I really appreciate that. But my job is far from over. I still have to bring home the top prize at the nationals."

"Stop being so modest, son. With the way the choir ministered the past few Sundays, I've already had Tia clear off a space to put the trophy."

He laughed as he held out his hand and I shook it.

"So, uh," Bishop continued, "I hear people are calling on you for friendship and including you in our church's singles group social events. It would be nice if you found a nice woman to settle down with."

I was starting to learn that Bishop Wilson never held back what was on his mind. That was good, because I didn't either—although in this case, I wasn't about to admit to him how many illicit offers I'd already received from members of his congregation.

"I don't know about all that," I said with false modesty.

"Well, I'm not trying to play matchmaker for you. I leave that to my wife. Don't be surprised if she's trying to set you up on dates."

"Bishop, your wife can set me up anytime she likes," I said, and I meant it. Why limit my options?

"I'll let her know that. But anyhow, you are really whipping this choir into shape. I see your membership has doubled in size. How many members you looking to have?"

"I'm hoping to have around seventy-five to a hundred and travel to forty or fifty competitions. That would be ideal."

"Well, you're well on your way." The bishop seemed to be distracted as he looked over my shouder. "Hey, isn't that your friend over there?"

"What friend?" I turned to see who he was referring to.

"Over there." He pointed to the back of the room, where I spotted two men lurking in the last pews. One of them was unmistakably Andrew Gotti.

Uh-oh. Trouble with a capital T.

"Uh, yeah, that's him. Let me go see what he's up to," I said, hoping to sound casual.

Bishop Wilson cast a suspicious glance at my two sinister-looking visitors at the back of the church, but he chose to leave the subject alone.

"All right, Aaron. I'll talk to you later." On his way out of the church, Bishop Wilson walked by the men and gave them both a questioning stare. That scared me to death, because I thought he was going to stop and speak to them, but luckily he kept on going.

I walked over and stood in front of Gotti as he and his companion stood up. "What are you doing here?" I hissed. I looked over my shoulder to make sure the other members who were still hanging around were out of earshot.

"How many times I gotta tell you we can go anywhere we damn well please?" Gotti spat.

"Yeah, don't worry about what we're doing here," the other guy growled. He was big and burly and had a razor scar on his right cheek, which looked almost like a split in a watermelon. His ugly face resembled a bulldog. His name was Vinnie something, and he was Gotti's yes-man. He was also the muscle of the pair.

"Well, we don't have any business until next week," I reminded Gotti.

"Yeah, that's for us to say. I'm coming by your house later tonight around ten."

"Be there," the burly one snarled in a threatening tone.

"What for?" I questioned.

"Because I said so. You got a problem with that? Should I go have a talk with the nice bishop?" Gotti threatened.

There was no way I wanted Gotti and his goon talking with Bishop Wilson about anything, not even the weather outside. So, without hesitation, I replied, "I'll be there at ten."

Gotti smiled victoriously. "We'll see you tonight, then. You still live at one-eighty-nine 138th Avenue, don't you?"

He'd just spit out Simone's address, his way of letting me know he'd been following me. Damn. I couldn't get her involved in this situation. Hell, I didn't even want to be involved in it my-self.

"Well, don't you?" he asked as Vinnie stood next to him chuck-ling like an idiot.

"You know I don't live there."

"Well, you spend enough time there, don't you?" he ques-tioned.

"You don't scare me." In truth, they did scare me, but I wasn't about to let them know that.

"Well, you should be scared. Maybe we'll have a talk with her too."

"Oh, I'm trembling in my shoes," I said sarcastically as I walked away, ready to pound my fist into something.

Simone

28

I walked into the church with my gym bag over my shoulder and three oversized Brooks Brothers bags filled with suits, shirts, and ties for Aaron. Although we weren't advertising that we were dating, we were a couple—as far as I was concerned anyway—and if he was going to be my man, I wanted him to look his absolute best. He needed to complement me as much as possible. Don't get me wrong, the boy was fine. Damn fine! It wasn't that he looked bad in the suits that he wore now, but none of them could compare to the distinction of a Brooks Brothers suit.

I couldn't wait to see his face when I handed him his gifts. I knew he was going to be surprised. Hell, I surprised myself. Simone Wilcox buying a gift for a man instead of the other way around—who would have thought?

"Hey there, Miss Thing." I glanced over to my right, and there was the first lady in spandex, walking up the corridor toward me. "You going to step class tonight?"

About two years ago, the women of the church started an aerobics night every Thursday in the church's smaller gym. To be honest, it started out as just an excuse for a few of the married sisters to check up on their husbands during basketball night, but after a while, it really caught on. It became more popular than anyone could have anticipated. We even had our own locker room with showers and assigned lockers.

"Yeah, I'm going, but I have to find someone first."

"All right, then."

Monique and I gave each other the "girlfriend hug," which included the fake kisses on the cheek so that we didn't smudge our makeup. That was when she took notice of the bags I was carrying. She leaned over in an attempt to get a glimpse of what was inside the bags.

"Mmph, Brooks Brothers. I know that's not for you." Monique shot me an inquisitive look. I could tell she wanted me to elaborate on my purchases.

"Nope, they're not for me. Let's just say that I did a little shopping for a friend."

"A friend named Aaron?" She gave me a knowing smile.

"Maybe, but that's for me to know and you to find out." Her grin was contagious, as my lips, too, spread into one. She knew darn well those gifts were for Aaron, and I knew darn well that she knew, but there was no way in hell I was going to actually say it. I had a reputation to uphold. "Speaking of Aaron, have you seen him?"

Monique hesitated a little before she answered. "Yeah, he's in the choir practice room."

"Okay, then, I'll see you at step class. I'm gonna go see what he's up to." I took a step in the direction of the practice room, but Monique grabbed my arm.

"Uh, Simone, you, uh . . ." The first lady, who was happy-go-lucky just a moment ago, was stammering all of a sudden. What in the world was that about? "You might not want to go down there." She lifted an eyebrow while tightening her jaw.

"Why? What's going on?"

"Oh, Lord, I know T. K. is gonna kill me for getting into other people's business, but you're my friend." Monique looked torn, and now she really had me curious.

"Monique, I swear on everything, if you don't tell me what's going on . . ." I was on the verge of blowing a gasket. If she knew something, then I needed her to tell me, especially if it meant that I was about to make a complete fool out of myself.

"Girl, Aaron is down there with Porsche Moore."

"The whore?" I took a step back and leaned on the wall. I'd heard rumors about them, but I'd dismissed them just as quickly as I heard them. Sure, Porsche had some of the prettiest natural hair I'd ever seen on a black woman, and she had a big old butt that the men seemed to love, but how could Aaron be taken in by that? He was much deeper than that. She was nothing more than trash from over there in Forty Projects. She wasn't even in my league—and she definitely wasn't wife material. I had no idea why Monique was making it out to be so serious and secretive. Porsche Moore might have been a threat to some, but not to me.

"Yep. Although they were only singing when I passed by, Porsche walked over and closed the door. I'm not trying to say anything was going on, but you know how she is. She's hard for any man to resist, and she gives it up quick."

I wanted to say, "Oh yeah? Even the bishop?" But I didn't. I knew that would be pushing it. First lady or not, Monique knew how to kick off her shoes like Fantasia and take off her earrings and pull out the Vaseline like Jill Scott. I did not need a fight with Monique anyway. Porsche was the one I was itching to get to. If I walked into that room and there was anything going on between them, I was going to hurt that ho.

"Listen, Monique, I'll catch up with you later at step class."

Monique didn't want to let me leave. She grabbed hold of my arm again. "Oh, Lord, Simone, where are you going?"

I lifted the bags in the air. "I've got a lot invested in that man, and not just with my credit cards. I'm not going to just let him slip away. I'm gonna go break up that little whore's party."

"Girl, whatever you do, do not put your hands on that woman." Monique pointed a stern finger at me like she was my mother instead of the church's first lady.

I'd rarely ever seen her this serious. Even so, I couldn't keep a laugh from slipping out. "I'll take that under advisement."

Monique released my arm, but not before giving me a questioning look.

"I promise I'll try to keep my hands to myself."

I pushed through the double doors of the choir rehearsal room without knocking. Just like Monique had said, they were there together. Porsche was playing the piano, while Aaron stood behind her, running his fingers through her hair and singing. With my pulse pounding in my ears, I was too angry to even focus on the words of the song, but I didn't have to hear it to know that he wasn't singing for the Lord. It looked more like he was serenading her.

She tossed her hair to one side when she saw me. I guess she was trying to send me a message. I got it loud and clear—so loud and clear that I wanted to pull every strand of that bitch's hair out of her head. I am by no means an insecure woman, but Porsche's hair was the one area where I felt I couldn't compete. That shit was so long and silky, any woman, black or white, would be envious.

I was beyond jealous now, especially since I knew Aaron loved a woman with long hair. On more than one occasion, he'd almost pulled out my weave during our lovemaking. I guess Aaron wasn't as deep as I wanted to believe he was. Apparently he was taken in by Porsche's hoochie-mama looks just like any other man.

Aaron had yet to notice me, so Porsche kept playing the entire scene up with all her squirming and smiling. I was about two seconds from whipping her ass, but then I remembered I was in the church. That ghetto bitch knew just what she was doing, trying to get me to show out in public. Well, she wouldn't get her way. She might have better hair, but I certainly had more class.

"Hey, babe," I said, walking up to Aaron and kissing him on the cheek. Then I waved at Porsche, smiling very politely. "Hey, Porsche."

"Hey, Simone. What's up?" Aaron smiled like he didn't have a care in the world. Porsche just rolled her eyes at me.

"I just bought you a few things, and I thought I'd drop them off before I went to step class. You still taking me out for Italian tonight, right?" I handed him the bags.

Aaron's face lit up, and he walked over to a table to check out his gifts. I turned and smiled deviously at Porsche. She didn't see me, though, because she was too busy watching Aaron pull out the expensive clothing she could never have afforded. The look on her face told me I'd scored a point against her.

"Yeah, I'll meet you in the large gym after basketball," Aaron replied to my query.

"Sounds like a plan." I looked at Porsche. "You going to step class, Porsche?"

"Yeah, I'm going." She sounded defeated.

"Good, I'll walk down with you." That was my subtle way of letting her know that her butt needed to rise up out of there.

Though I'm sure he didn't realize he was doing it, Aaron helped me to twist the knife a little deeper in Porsche's wound. "Simone, I can't believe you bought me all of this stuff. It must have cost a small fortune." He came over and wrapped his arms around me in a bear hug. He didn't kiss me, but there was no doubt from where Porsche was sitting who was number one in his eyes.

"Don't worry about the cost. I just want you to look good, okay?"

Aaron nodded, going back to the bags. "You are an amazing woman. How'd you even know my size?"

"I checked your suit and shirt size after you fell asleep last night." Oh, if looks could kill, Porsche would have had my head on a platter after I said that.

He came striding back over to me and hugged me even tighter than before. "I don't know what to say. No one has ever done anything like this for me before."

"I'm sure you'll find something to say tonight." He let me go and I patted him on the behind.

"I'm sure you're right."

"You ready to go?" I asked Porsche in the sweetest of tones.

"Yeah, I'm coming." Talk about a broken-up face.

I stood there long enough that she got the message and got up and left the room without even saying good-bye to Aaron.

I'd won the battle with Porsche in the rehearsal room, but I still couldn't dismiss the image of Aaron's fingers playing in her hair. As a matter of fact, I couldn't even focus on the exercise routine, so I left step class early.

I was in the locker room, having already showered and put on my makeup by the time the room filled up with about twenty of the sisters who'd been in the exercise class, including Porsche and the first lady, who sat down next to me.

I watched as Porsche slipped off her gym clothes and put a towel around her body. I wanted to go in there and kick her ass for messing with my man, but she'd soon be getting the message loud and clear that I wasn't playing around.

I sat there fuming as I listened to Porsche talking to one of the sisters. "I really got my workout on today. I feel like I lost five pounds of pure sweat!"

"Yeah, girl, I know what you mean," the other girl replied.

The first lady turned to me, and I could see her studying my face in the mirror. "How come you left step class so early?" she asked.

"I got a hot date and didn't wanna be late," I said for the entire locker room to hear.

"Well, just don't make it too hot. Remember we're Christians," Monique joked.

"Don't worry. I'll be here first thing in the morning to ask for forgiveness," I joked back, and quite a few of the sisters laughed, including the first lady. I loved that Monique was still real. She didn't try to change and become all judgmental, even if she had been elevated to the position of first lady after she married T. K.

"How'd things go with her?" Monique whispered, gesturing in the direction of Porsche. "Glad to see neither of you has any scratches or bruises."

I waved my hand like it was nothing. "Oh, please. That woman is not even in my league. You see who's going on a date tonight and who isn't?"

"I know that's right. Let me go ahead and take me a shower so I can see if I can get my husband to take me on a date." She went to her locker and grabbed her body wash and shampoo. I watched as Porsche finished up her conversation and did the same before heading into the shower room. I waited for the fireworks that I knew were about to begin.

About five or six minutes later, a bloodcurdling screech came from the showers. I followed all the other women who rushed in the direction of the cries.

The women who made it there first started in right away with a chorus of "Oh my God! What happened?" and "This is awful!"

I slowly made my way through the crowd to view the cause of the commotion. Boy, oh boy, was it a sight for these sore eyes. There was Porsche, naked as the day she was born, screaming at the top of her lungs. She was dripping wet, with tears rolling down her face. In both hands, she clenched gobs of her long, curly black hair. With all the bare patches on her head and her eyeliner running down her face, she looked like something out of a creature-feature magazine.

Good. Maybe now she'll think twice before she has my man's hands all up in her hair.

"My hair! My hair! What the hell happened to my hair?" Porsche screamed.

"Oh, no. And that girl had some beautiful hair," Sister Teresa yelled, making Porsche even more hysterical.

"See now, that's why I stopped messin' with them perms," a sister commented. "More sisters need to look into the natural thing." She patted her own natural fro with pride.

"That wasn't no perm, girl. That was all her natural hair," another sister replied, putting more flame on the fire.

"Get outta here! Now I know why she's crying," the first sister cracked.

"Yep, I heard she has Indian in her family . . . for real."

I turned away and walked back to my locker with a satisfied smirk on my face.

"What did you do?" Monique asked when she appeared behind me. She was wrapped in a towel and dripping wet.

"Who, me? What are you talking about?" I went to continue my strut, but Monique grabbed my arm, pulling me to the side.

"Don't you 'who, me,' Simone. What did you do to that girl's hair? I know you did something. I can see it in your eyes. You're still smirking." She was shaking her head in disbelief.

"I didn't do a thing, but it couldn't have happened to a better person."

"Simone, there are some things you just don't do because God don't like ugly. One day this is all gonna fall on your shoulders."

"Oh, please, Monique. I didn't do anything, okay? And even if I did, if someone made a move on the bishop, you'd do worse. Besides, whose side are you on anyway?"

"I'm not on anybody's side—not when it comes to hurting someone. And need I remind you that me and the bishop are married?"

"So? Me and Aaron are going to get married one day. Only difference is you got a piece of paper."

"Get out of here, Simone, because I think you've lost your

mind." Monique made her way back over to try to comfort Porsche. I didn't take it personally, though. I knew that was part of her duties as first lady.

I closed my locker and picked up my bag, heading out the door to meet Aaron. Monique could say whatever she wanted, but if she were in my shoes, she would have done the same damn thing. Besides, Porsche's hair would grow back eventually. Hell, I'd only put a little Neet in her conditioner. Truth is, I didn't even know if she'd put it in her hair, as bad as it smelled. Turned out it couldn't have worked more perfectly.

As I exited the locker room, I almost wanted to reach around and pat myself on the back. I wondered, *When are people going to realize that you don't fuck with Simone Wilcox?*

The Bishop

29

I was sitting in my office, working on my sermon for Sunday's church service as I savored the taste of Sister Andrea Cottman's peach cobbler. I'd titled the sermon "Having God's Favor in These Critical Times," and that was just how I was feeling—like God had blessed our church during a very difficult period. We'd fought through a recession, the Jackie scandal, and Smitty's death, all to land on our feet with our heads held high. I was really proud of the church and loved the direction things were going in, especially the choir.

And what could I say about Aaron? He'd turned out to be a godsend who had gone way past my expectations in such a short period of time. He was prompt, diligent, enthusiastic, and had grown the choir to fifty members. They'd already won a couple of competitions, and the church's attendance was almost back to the pre-Jackie days, although revenue was still down significantly with the recession and all.

To top that off, Maxwell was doing a good job tightening up the deacons' board. Things were really looking up.

"Thank you, Lord," I prayed out loud.

I heard a light tap at my door and invited the visitor to enter.

Tia poked her head into my office. "Excuse me, Bishop. I'm sorry to interrupt you, but can I talk to you for a few minutes?"

I waved her in. "Sure, come on in. I wanted to talk to you anyway. The first lady has told me what a help you've been with Aaron and the choir. I just wanted to let you know that I really love the job you and Aaron are doing. You should be proud of yourself."

She walked in, standing in front of my desk humbly. "Thank you. I really appreciate that."

"I should be thanking you. Have a seat. How are you doing?"

She sat down in the chair in front of my desk. "I'm doing okay."

"So, how can I help you?"

"Well, it's just that I have a little problem."

"What is it?" I became concerned by the look of unease on her face. I knew that Tia's rape had left her emotionally fragile, and though she was doing well now, I worried that any bad experience could lead to a setback for her. My train of thought ended up being way off track. I never could have imagined what she was about to tell me.

"I just came from the bank. When I went to cash my check, they said there were not enough funds to cover my check."

"What?" I sat back in my chair. Things just didn't add up. "I don't think that's possible, Tia. Are you sure it wasn't an error on the bank's behalf?"

"I know the church has money, but I've been having a few problems with Trustee Wilcox, and I was wondering if that had something to do with my check."

I rubbed the crown of my head and contemplated the possibility that Simone was playing some type of game with Tia's check. My wife had told me about what happened to poor Porsche Moore's hair and that she believed Simone had something to do with it. It looked like Simone was playing for keeps when it came to Aaron. I'd seen her act this same way back when she was interested in James. I could also see why she might have considered Tia a threat, considering how closely she and Aaron worked together and the tight relationship that everyone could see they had been developing. As far as I could tell, Aaron and Tia were only friends, but Simone wasn't the type to accept any woman, friend or not, around a man she'd laid claim to.

"I hope it's just a bank error, but I'll look into it." My cell phone rang and I excused myself to answer it when I saw the church janitor's number on my caller ID. Harley never called my cell unless it was an emergency.

"Bishop, this is Harley. The bank won't let me cash my check. What the heck is going on over there?"

Another bad check. My stomach became a ball of tension because now I knew this wasn't an isolated incident.

"I don't know, Harley. Something must be going on with our account. Sit tight. Let me find out what's going on, and I'll call you right back."

"Call me back, please, Bishop. I need my money. I gotta pay my rent."

"I understand, Harley. I'll call you right back." I hung up the phone.

Tia took a deep breath, almost sounding relieved. "It wasn't just me, was it?"

"It appears not." I shook my head. "Listen, Tia, give me five minutes to make a couple of calls. I promise I'll get to the bottom of this before you leave work today."

As soon as Tia left the room, I picked up the phone and punched in Simone's number at the dealership. If anyone was going to have the answers I needed, she would.

"Wilcox Motors, Simone Wilcox," she answered.

"Hello, Simone. Bishop Wilson here."

"Oh, Bishop. How are you doing?" The way she paused before she said it didn't do much to ease the feeling in the pit of my stomach.

"I'm not doing well at all, Simone. People are having problems cashing their payroll checks. The bank says there are insufficient funds in our account. I can't see that being possible, can you?"

I heard a catch in Simone's voice. "Oh my, not to worry, Bishop. I've just got to transfer the money over to the payroll account." She hesitated again, and my heartbeat kicked up a notch. "Tell them I'll have everything taken care of by the morning."

"By the morning? Simone, this is over a hundred peoples' livelihoods we're talking about. You should be able to do a transfer in fifteen minutes online." My voice rose. I knew I sounded like I didn't believe Simone, and in all honesty, a part of me didn't. Something was wrong with this picture. We'd been taking in more money in the past two months than we had in the last six months combined. We should not have had this kind of problem.

"Okay, Bishop. I'll take care of it as soon as possible," she snapped back with a little more attitude than was befitting a trustee talking to her bishop.

"Take care of it now, Simone!"

I hung up the phone without saying good-bye. Before I could get up and go talk to Tia and assure her everything would be taken care of, Maxwell walked into my office and took his usual seat to the left of my desk. He looked perturbed.

"What's the matter with you, Maxwell? Run out of Viagra?" I laughed, trying to lighten my own mood.

"You got a lot of angry people out there in reception. They've all gone to the bank and can't get their money. They didn't expect to have payless paydays at the church, and I can't say I blame them. What the heck is going on?"

"Simone Wilcox is what happened." I shook my head. "She said she forgot to transfer money into the payroll account."

Maxwell shot me a funny look. "You believe that?"

"Not a word," I replied.

I got up and closed my office door. I turned to Maxwell and spoke seriously. "I want you to do something on the Q.T."

Maxwell nodded. "Sure. What do you need?"

"I want you to do an internal audit on the church's books. I wanna know where every dime of our money has been spent. Turn over every stone. Nobody is beyond suspicion, including me."

"Sure, I can do that. No sweat. I've done audits on my company's books a hundred times, so this should be a cinch. Matter of fact, I'll bring in my accountant, Sherman. He'll get to the bottom of this."

"Great. Thanks," I said. "Oh, and, Maxwell, be discreet. I don't want this getting around the church. We don't need another scandal on our hands."

Simone

30

I was sitting in my office, drinking a glass of Moët, talking to Aaron on the phone and missing him like crazy. He'd been out of town at a choir competition for the past two days, and of course you know my baby won first prize. He'd just called to tell me he wouldn't be in until late, so I probably wouldn't see him tonight.

"I miss you," I purred into the phone.

"Yeah, me too," Aaron replied.

I knew it wasn't the most ladylike thing to do, but I sought Aaron's verbal affection every chance I got. I'm sorry, but my ego loved to be touched by him just as much as my body did. "What do you miss about me? Is it the way I look, or the way I wrap my legs around your neck when you're on—"

"Simone." His voice suddenly fell to a whisper. "Do we have to do this now? You do know that I'm on a bus with thirty people, don't you?"

"So what? I want them to know you miss me and my kitty." I took a sip of Mo, rolling the flavor of it on my tongue and around my mouth, then across my teeth. "You do miss us, don't you?"

"Yeah," he whispered.

"Yeah what?" I wanted him to say it. I needed him to say it. I had to be reminded in any way necessary that I still had some kind of control in this relationship—even if it meant acting out Destiny's Child's "Say My Name."

"Yeah, I miss you . . . the both of you." I pictured him biting his lip and wanting not to whisper when he said his next words: "Especially your kitty. All right?"

"Is that so?" One point for me. Let's see if I could go for two. "So, tell me, Mr. Mackie, exactly what do you miss about my—"

I was interrupted by my secretary calling me on the intercom. "Simone, you have a visitor and—"

"Tell them to have a seat, Anita. I'll be right out when I finish this call." About five more seconds on the phone with Aaron and my hands would be down my panties. "As a matter of fact, Anita, see if someone else can help them."

"But, Simone—"

Click. I hit the MUTE button on the intercom and returned to more pressing business.

"Now, where were we, Aaron?"

My hand was at the rim of my skirt when I heard, "At work, although it's hard to tell from where I'm standing."

I looked up, horrified. "Daddy!"

My father had taken it upon himself to walk right into my office without knocking. I closed my cell phone quickly and dropped it on my desk. I tried to hide the bottle of Moët, but it was too late. He had seen me slip it into my desk drawer.

"Don't *Daddy* me," he spat in that stern-father tone. "Since when did you start drinking on company time? And get your feet off my desk."

I cleared my throat and straightened up. I had a little buzz, but I wasn't drunk. I spoke in proper English. "Daddy, what are you doing here? I'm so happy to see you. What a surprise."

"Surprise? Yeah, I'll buy that. I don't know how happy you'll be when I get finished. Anyway, I want my check." He eyeballed me fiercely. "Where is my check?"

I bumped myself upside the head with the edge of my palm, hoping it wasn't too dramatic a touch. "Oh, Daddy, I'm so sorry. I really did forget. You wouldn't believe all that's been going on. But I'll cut you that check right this minute." I held up my index finger and went inside my purse like I was trying to find something. He took a seat on the small sofa. "Daddy, hold on one minute."

With arms folded, he watched my every move. His mouth twisted to the side as I pulled out my pen and wrote a check.

"Here you go, Daddy."

He took the check and studied it. "It's two months now, not one."

"Oh yeah, right." I wrote him another check. "Okay, Daddy, all paid up."

He took the second check. "It's not paid up until these checks clear my bank." Examining the checks again, he asked, "And why are you writing it out of your personal account instead of having accounting cut it?"

"Oh, um, just for convenience. Just don't put them in until the end of the week, all right, Daddy?" I threw him the same smile that used to get me out of trouble when I was a little girl. Too bad it didn't work the same way anymore.

"Don't try to play games with me, young lady. I'm not stupid. I know you're up to something. I want to see the quarterly reports."

Damn it! Why did everybody suddenly want to see the books I was keeping? "Well, um, I'm not really sure if they're complete. I had to get rid of Lisa Blackwell in accounting, and—"

"You got rid of Lisa?" He glared at me like I'd just fired my own mother.

"Yeah, I got rid of her. Her fat behind was making too much money, and she wasn't doing her job." *Translation, she was talking to you too damn much.* That suck-up bitch was telling my father everything that was going on around this place, like my father was the one cutting the paychecks. Her loyalty should have been to me. I was the one writing the checks, not to mention the time I allowed her to take off without even docking her vacation days. I didn't give a damn if her husband did have cancer; I had to teach her and the rest of these ungrateful fools once and for all that you don't bite the hand that feeds you, nor do you bite the hand that pointed your ass to the food!

"Simone . . ."

I could see him getting ready to explode like he had that time I smashed up his new Benz, or the time I went over the limit on my credit cards when I was a teenager. My heart was racing, and I could feel sweat starting to soak my silk blouse.

"Look, Daddy, let me explain the benefits of not having—"

"Surprise!"

My first thought was, *Like I really need another damn surprise today!* But then I looked toward the door to see who was there, and suddenly my mood brightened.

"Aha! You thought I was still in New Haven, didn't you?" Aaron's voice was more than just a welcome surprise. It was a breath of fresh air. It offered me much-needed relief from the situation at hand with my father. I could feel the walls closing in on me before I heard Aaron's voice.

"Aaron, sweetheart!"

"Hey . . ." His words trailed off as he looked to my father. "Oh, am I interrupting something?" Aaron raised an eyebrow when my father frowned at him.

"No, no, perfect timing." I walked over and grabbed Aaron by the arm. "Daddy, this is Aaron Mackie." I pulled him a couple steps closer to my father. "Aaron, I want you to meet my father, Brian Wilcox. Daddy, Aaron went to the University of Virginia too."

"So, you're a UVA man."

The frown that had been on my father's face just seconds earlier disappeared. He jumped up and clasped Aaron's hand in his. I'd never seen him do this to any other guy I'd ever introduced him to.

"Yes, sir, I'm a Cavalier through and through," Aaron stated proudly.

"What year did you graduate?"

"Ninety-eight."

"I left there in seventy-three." Daddy beamed. "Simone, seems like a nice young man you have here." He spoke to me but kept smiling at Aaron the entire time.

"Yes, he's our new choir director at First Jamaica Ministries." It was my turn to be proud about something.

"So, you're the one I've heard so much about." My father smiled broadly, showing some of his bridge work. "Bishop Wilson speaks highly of you."

Aaron nodded. He was cocky when it came to women, but Aaron knew how to be humble when the situation called for it.

"Hey, instead of sitting here, let's all go out to dinner—my treat," Daddy offered. He turned to me. "I'll look at those quarterly reports later." He grabbed Aaron by the shoulder as the two exited my office.

I looked up to the ceiling and offered a quick, "Thank you, God," before trailing behind them.

Aaron

31

We were at a Mexican restaurant somewhere in Long Island over by the Green Acres Mall. Simone, her father, and I had just enjoyed a great meal. Mr. Wilcox and I swapped some great stories about UVA, along with some laughs about Simone and her childhood. I was really starting to like the guy, and I think he was starting to like me.

"I can't thank you enough for dinner, Mr. Wilcox," I said, pushing away my plate. "I must admit that was the best Mexican food I've ever eaten. Probably couldn't get any better if I was over in Mexico."

"Not a problem, son. It was my pleasure. We UVA men have to stick together, you know." Mr. Wilcox placed his napkin on his plate.

"Daddy used to bring me here all the time when I was younger for special occasions," Simone added. "Like that time I was voted into student council, and when I got the lead in the school play."

"That must have been nice." I was impressed. From what I'd gathered from Simone, her father had spent most of his time building his company. I never pegged him as one to engage in daddy-daughter time. He was a true family man.

"Yep," Mr. Wilcox confirmed. "There's nothing more important than family. No matter how busy you are, you have to make time for the wife and kids."

"It's been awhile, though." Simone glanced at her father, then took a bite of what was left of her food. "I mean, with you living in Florida and all."

Wow, I could tell Simone missed spending time with her father.

"Well, that means you haven't done anything worthy of me bringing you here, then, doesn't it?" Mr. Wilcox shot back, surprising me. Simone wriggled in her chair uncomfortably, stuffing another forkful of food in her mouth. "That is, until now."

He turned his head toward me and beamed a huge smile in my direction. I had no idea what was going on, but it appeared the two of them were talking in some type of code and I was the subject. I had to look over my shoulder to see if there was something amazing behind me, because there certainly wasn't anything special about me. I hadn't done anything other than just show up at Simone's office and surprise her. Only reason I'd done that was because I was excited about our choir competition win and was looking for a little hot action under the sheets.

"Yeah, he is pretty special, isn't he?" Simone said happily.

"Who, me?" I pointed at myself.

"Oh, don't be shy about it, young man," Mr. Wilcox said to me. "My daughter finally being with someone I approve of is a good thing. A nice churchgoing fella, not to mention a UVA man. If this isn't special, I don't know what is." Mr. Wilcox picked up his iced tea and held it up. "Now, that's something to toast about."

Simone, excited, lifted her glass and tapped it against her father's. When my glass didn't meet theirs, Simone cleared her throat and hurriedly sipped from her glass, leaving her father's to hang in the air while it waited on mine to join it.

"Daddy, go ahead and drink up. Your ice is melting," Simone told him.

I felt it was time to nip in the bud this little misconception that was brewing.

"Mr. Wilcox, I think you might have the wrong idea about things," I said.

"Oh? About what?"

"About Simone and me. You see, we're not really the couple that you think we are."

Simone wasted no time jumping in. "Oh, Aaron, you don't have to explain everything about our relationship to Daddy."

It was a failed attempt to shut me up.

"And see, that's just the thing. We don't have a relationship, not really." I turned to Simone's father. "Not the kind you think we have, Mr. Wilcox. You have a beautiful, intelligent, business-savvy, God-fearing daughter. You've raised her well, Mr. Wilcox, and any man would be blessed to have her as his woman, but Simone and I just aren't at that stage. Not yet, at least."

"Yet," Simone interjected hopefully. "But we're working on it. Right, Aaron?" She looked at me desperately, begging with her eyes for me to say what she wanted to hear. What both she and her father wanted to hear, evidently. Unfortunately, I couldn't, though I also didn't want to embarrass her in front of her father.

"Only time will tell, Simone."

I guess my answer was good enough, because she didn't push it any further. "Excuse me." She stood, placing her napkin on the table. "I'm going to the ladies' room."

I took a drink of my soda, looking around and admiring the place as if I'd just gotten there. The tension between me and Mr. Wilcox was almost palpable.

"So, she's just a lay to you is all," he said.

I dang near spit the drink out of my mouth. "Excuse me?" I wiped my mouth with the back of my hand.

"You heard me. All that you said about Simone. Basically you're just getting your rocks off on my daughter."

"No, Mr. Wilcox, it's nothing like that." I held up my hands in defense. "I like Simone. I really do. It's just I'm not looking for anything serious."

"Who are you kidding? Don't forget we're both UVA men, son," he stated. "Anyway, I know Simone is a handful, but once she's ready to settle down—you know, really ready—she'll be okay. And from what I can see, she appears to be ready. I have never seen her this excited about a man."

"Mr. Wilcox, I appreciate everything you're saying, and I like Simone, but I'm trying to build a career. I don't have time for anyone serious."

"If I were you, I'd make a decision, son. Either you're going to be with my daughter or you're not. There is no in between when she sets her sights on something. You don't know Simone.

She's like her old man: We both play for keeps. With you feeling the way you do, I'd hate to have to come back up here to New York and find out someone got hurt."

"I promise I'm not trying to hurt Simone, sir. I'm being up front with her on everything."

"I wasn't talking about Simone getting hurt, son. It's you I'm worried about."

"Huh? What's that supposed to mean?" I asked as Simone returned to the table.

"What's what supposed to mean?" she asked.

Her father looked up rather innocently. "Oh, nothing. I was just giving your friend here a little advice on how to handle you."

"Well, is he going to take it?"

"I'm not sure yet." Mr. Wilcox gave me a concerned glance.

Just then our waiter approached the table. "May I take your plates?" Everyone nodded. "Can I get anyone dessert?"

"As a matter of fact, I'll have a slice of that chocolate cake to take back to my hotel room," Mr. Wilcox stated, then looked over at Simone and me. "Those two won't be having any dessert, at least not here. Theirs will be served in bed."

I think both Simone and I almost peed our pants when Mr. Wilcox looked at me and winked.

Simone

32

I thought I was going to go through my seat belt when Aaron's truck screeched to a halt in front of my house. From the scowl on his face, I knew that's exactly what he wanted me to do. I didn't have a clue why until I glanced up from where I was nestled under his arm and saw the plain brown car sitting in my driveway with its lights on.

It was like déjà vu.

"Um, whose car is *that*?" Aaron barked.

This time, I had no clue who the driver was or what they could possibly want.

We'd just returned from dinner with my father, and despite a few awkward moments, he was very, very impressed by Aaron. We'd had one hell of a meal, and I was all ready for "dessert," if you know what I mean. I was still a little pissed about Aaron's lack of commitment, but I was more horny than pissed. Besides, I felt that I could best win him over under the sheets.

"I don't know whose car it is."

"Like you didn't know the Range Rover before, huh?" Aaron slipped his arm from around my shoulder and glared at me.

"Don't start, baby, okay?" I held my hand up to halt him.

"I won't start." Aaron kept his eyes riveted on the two men who were stepping out of the car. I opened my car door without waiting for him to let me out like he usually did.

I hadn't gotten ten feet from the car when one of the two men accosted me in an authoritative manner. "Simone Wilcox?"

"Yes?" I tried to make out his face to see if I recognized him. I didn't. I didn't even recognize his voice. "Who's asking?"

"I'm Detective McGraw, and this is my partner, Detective Phillips. We're from the Queens Homicide Unit." They flashed their badges.

My heart started pounding and my mouth went dry. What the heck were homicide detectives doing at my house? I glanced over at Aaron, who was getting out of the truck.

I tried to keep my voice from shaking as I answered. "Yes, I'm Simone Wilcox. Can I help you?"

"We just want to ask you a few questions," Detective Mc-Graw stated.

"Questions about what?"

"We just have a few questions, ma'am. That's all."

"You mind if we step inside your house? We don't want to alarm your neighbors," Detective Phillips requested.

Like a knight in shining armor, Aaron appeared at my side. "Is everything all right?"

Aaron's question kind of snapped me out of a fog, and suddenly it struck me that these men were homicide detectives and could be bringing bad news. Tears flooded my eyes. My first thought was that something had happened to my father between the time we'd left him until now. "Please don't tell me my daddy is dead."

"What's this all about, Officer?" Aaron put his arm around me. He could see I was quite worried.

"Please, allow us to step inside," said Detective McGraw. "We just have a couple of questions. This won't take long, I promise."

My hands were shaking so badly that Aaron had to take my key and open the front door for me.

Inside, Detective McGraw wasted no time starting his interrogation. "Do you know Jonathan Smith?"

I involuntarily gasped. I was relieved that this wasn't about Daddy but didn't fare any better knowing that it was about Jonathan. "Yes, I know him—or at least I did know him. He was a good man."

The detective nodded. "So, exactly how well did you know him?"

Both officers had pen and paper in hand, ready to notate any and everything that I said. I kept glancing over at Aaron, who was standing to the side, observing the exchange between the detectives and me with more than a keen interest.

"I knew him pretty well. We were both officers in our church," I answered honestly.

"Did you know that you were the last person to speak to him?"

I glanced at Aaron again before answering. Aaron's eyes told me he didn't like what he was hearing.

"I didn't talk to him the day he died. He was dead when I found him."

"So, you were the one who found him?"

"Yes." Both officers were scribbling in their notepads like crazy.

"You said you weren't the last person to speak to him, but just before his death, he was texting back and forth with you. What was that all about?"

"Well, we were texting about some money he'd promised me," I admitted. Once again, I was telling the truth; he had promised me money. The two men eyed each other. What made it even worse was that Aaron was leaning in closer to make sure he heard every word that came out of my mouth.

"Why would he promise you money?"

I hesitated. Now I regretted that I'd allowed this questioning to go on in front of Aaron, but initially I'd had no idea this would be the subject. "Well, he promised me money because I was . . . I was a little short."

Aaron's neck turned as he frowned at me.

"You say you were a little short. How much is a little short?"

"I don't know. It was a few weeks ago. I don't remember."

"Does thirty grand sound about right?" Detective Phillips barked.

How did he know the specifics? I know damn well Jonathan and I never once texted the actual dollar amount. Who the hell had been talking?

I couldn't look at Aaron anymore. Things were getting too intense. "I don't know, maybe around that much. Like I said, it was a few weeks ago." I squirmed in my seat. There was absolutely no getting comfortable.

"Ms. Wilcox, were you and Mr. Smith lovers?" Detective Phillips shot at me.

"No!" I denied emphatically. Now I looked directly into Aaron's eyes. "I swear to God we weren't."

"Then why would he have promised you all that money?" Detective McGraw charged. Detective McGraw and Detective Phillips spoke to each other with their eyes, and they were both coming to the conclusion that I was lying about something.

"He didn't give me any money," I replied.

"No, but he had thirty thousand dollars in cash in his car when we arrived at the scene, so I'm gonna need an answer to my question."

"What question?" I wasn't paying attention now. I was thinking about the money. Damn, if only I had had the wherewithal to really look in his car, I could have gotten my money and then called 911. That would have solved a lot of the problems I was having now.

"Stop playing games, Simone, and answer the man's damn question," Aaron snapped at me.

His outburst caused the detectives to look at him, and then at each other with eyebrows raised.

"Ms. Wilcox, would you feel more comfortable if this gentleman left the room?" Detective Phillips interceded.

I shook my head. Why couldn't he have asked me that five minutes ago? Now it was too late. Aaron had heard enough that I would have to give him an explanation. Something told me this entire scene was screwing up my chances of getting laid big-time.

"No, he can stay."

"Once again, why did you ask Mr. Smith for money?" Detective Phillips repeated.

"He owed it to me," I said flat out, with a hint of venom that I pray to God went undetected.

"The last thing that he texted you was . . ." Detective Phillips looked down at his pad and flipped back a couple of pages. " 'If you want this money, come out to the parking lot and get it.' "

He looked back up at me. "From what we can determine, when you came out to get the money, he wound up shot."

Wait a minute. Were they saying what I think they were? "Are you saying he was murdered? I thought it was a suicide."

"We're not so sure of that. There are a lot of unanswered questions." Detective Phillips stared at me, trying to read my reaction.

Well, he didn't have to try to read it. I was going to make it clear. "Are you trying to say I killed him?" My voice cracked in disbelief.

This was obviously Aaron's breaking point. "Hold up. Is she under arrest?"

"Why? You her lawyer?" Detective Phillips shot back.

"No, but I know enough of them to know she should get herself one." Aaron stepped in between the detectives and me. "Baby, don't say anything else unless your lawyer is present."

"Is that what you want, Ms. Wilcox? You want a lawyer? You guilty of something?"

"No, I'm not guilty of anything," I replied, then turned my attention to Aaron, whose interference was starting to make me look bad. Hell, I could do that on my own. "Aaron, move, baby. I don't need a lawyer." *Not yet anyway.*

Aaron frowned, shaking his head. I could tell he didn't agree with my choice to proceed. "Baby, that's not wise—"

"You heard the lady. Now, move out of the way before I arrest you for obstruction." Detective Phillips leaned in, pressing the issue and ignoring the advice Aaron had just given me. "Did you kill Jonathan Smith?"

"No, I would never do anything like that." I was appalled. I mean, it could be said that Simone Wilcox was a lot of things, but damn it, a murderer I was not!

"Why should we believe you wouldn't?"

"Because Jonathan Smith was my biological father, for God's sake!"

I didn't pay any attention to the look on the detectives' faces. All I could see was the shock written on Aaron's face. Ironically enough, he'd just met my father, the man who was married to my mother when I was born and the only father I'd ever known.

"Jonathan Smith was just trying to pay me back for being a shitty-ass father and not being there for me as a child. I guess you could call it back child support."

The detectives gave each other a long look, and then they started writing in their notepads again. They'd wanted an answer to the texts; now they had one. I just hoped they, along with Aaron, would keep their mouths shut.

Tia

33

When I heard the knock on my front door at seven o'clock sharp, I removed my apron and smoothed my hands down the hot-pink silk blouse that I wore to complement my dark-wash skinny jeans.

"Prompt, aren't we?" I teased when I opened the door.

"You know I'm the king of promptness," Aaron reminded me.

How could I forget? I was late to choir rehearsal one time because I'd been on a call at the hotline, and he didn't even give me time to explain before he nearly bit my head off. I know I had a small solo, and they couldn't practice the song without me, but dang!

"Well, King, I'm sorry I don't have any red carpet to lay out, but would you honor me by entering my humble abode anyway?" I bowed and extended my arm for him to enter.

"You're too much, you know that?" Aaron said as he entered.

"Why don't you have a seat on the couch? The main course is ready. I'm just going to get the garlic bread out of the oven. I hope you like spaghetti," I called over my shoulder as I headed for the kitchen.

"I love it."

"Dinner is served," I announced a few minutes later as I returned carrying a bowl of pasta and a basket of garlic bread to the table.

"Great, because I'm starved." The male voice that replied to my announcement didn't belong to Aaron.

"Kareem, what are you doing here? I thought you were out playing basketball."

"I bet you did," Kareem replied. "The game got canceled, though, so it looks like I'll be able to join you and your boy for dinner." He shot me a knowing look. "That is, if it's okay with you, sis."

"Ah, mystery solved. You're her brother." Aaron sounded relieved. He extended his hand to Kareem. "Sorry we didn't get a chance to talk that night in the parking lot," he said. I thought it was a diplomatic way of bringing up the subject without actually mentioning my brother's bad behavior.

"Yeah, man. You know how it is," Kareem replied. "I just gotta watch out for my little sister here." He looked at me. "She's all I got, you know."

"I feel you. I don't have any sisters myself," Aaron admitted, "but I imagine I'd be the same way if I did."

"Yeah, there's too many brothers out there looking to take advantage of a woman, you know?"

Oh, no! I had to stop Kareem, because he sounded like he might actually start discussing my rape if I didn't.

"Okay, well, enough of this," I said, trying to sound lighthearted. "I didn't slave over the stove for two hours for nothing. Let's eat."

We all headed to the table. After I blessed the food, we dug in, enjoying a good meal and good conversation. Well, Aaron and I talked. Kareem just stuffed his face and listened to us go back and forth.

By shortly after nine, Aaron was on his way out the door. "Thanks again for the meal, Tia. Dinner was delicious." He held up the plastic container full of spaghetti. "And thanks for tomorrow's lunch."

"Anytime. You be safe out there."

"I will," Aaron assured me. He looked over my shoulder at Kareem, who was sitting on the couch flicking through television channels. "And it was nice meeting you, Kareem. Later."

Kareem waved, and I closed the door behind Aaron.

"Aaahh," I exhaled. "I guess I better go hit those dishes."

"Nah, nah, I'll get it. You've done enough."

"You sure?" Kareem never cleaned up.

"Yeah. Why don't you go on back there and do what you

women do after a date or something . . . call each other on the phone and all that mess," Kareem teased.

"Boy, please." I waved my hand to brush off his statement. "That was not a date. Aaron is our choir director. I owed him a dinner for the one you so rudely kept us from having the other night."

"Okay, so it might not have been a date, but you and ol' boy definitely got some chemistry going on, the way y'all sat across from each other at the table talking and eyeballing one another."

I gave him a skeptical frown. "What dinner were you at? Because it surely wasn't the one that just took place at that table right there." I pointed. "Aaron's a good listener. We have good conversations. That's it."

"Yeah, well, I know a couple in the making when I see one, and you and that choir director, well, you two would make a good couple. And if it means anything to you, he seems pretty cool. Your big brother approves."

I shrugged off Kareem's nonsense and headed to my bedroom, not giving what he'd said another thought—at least not while my eyes were open. When I closed them that night after slipping into my pajamas and climbing into bed, it was an entirely different story.

Simone

34

Ever since Aaron and I started dating, I'd been in my own fantasy world. This had to be what heaven felt like. Oh, our lovemaking was as rapturous as I could have ever imagined it would be. We were perfectly suited for each other. Sexually, no man had ever taken me to the places that Aaron had.

I couldn't wait for us to get together again, but I was trying to play it cool, and I think he was too. He kept insisting on staying at my place only two or three times a week, and every once in a while, he'd ask if I thought things were moving a bit fast. Fast? In my opinion, things couldn't have been moving any slower. I mean, when you know the person you are with is the one you want to be with forever, why prolong the thing? And I knew Aaron was the one for me. I mean, I was letting him sleep over at my place, for heaven's sake. No man other than James had ever gotten that far before.

I could already imagine us marching down the aisle hand in hand after Bishop pronounced us man and wife. Unfortunately, there was still one person standing between us even now that Porsche was out of the picture: that phony, holier-than-thou bitch Tia.

Every time I looked, she was all up in my man's face, cheesing and shit. They'd go to the mall together; they'd go to breakfast on Sunday before church. She even got him involved with this rape hotline thing, which I didn't approve of one bit. Then, of course, as if she didn't spend enough time with him already, she went and invited him to her house for a home-cooked meal. Now, cooking might not be my favorite thing to do, but I could hold my own in the kitchen if I had to, so I didn't know who she thought she was trying to impress.

With that being said, today was the day I was going to put Miss Thing in her place and end this shit. I planned to marry Aaron one day, so she could just take her ugly mug and go sit down someplace, because Aaron Mackie was mine. His name was written all over my kitty cat, and if I had to go as far as to show her, then I would.

I entered the church and went straight to the administrative offices, where I found her at her desk, working on her computer.

"Hey, Trustee Wilcox, can I help you?" she asked.

I could tell by the look on her face that the bitch didn't like me—most women didn't—but I didn't really care. I wasn't there for their approval. Besides, anyone who didn't know by now that I was not to be played with better go ask Porsche Moore with her bald-headed ass.

"Is the first lady or the bishop here?" I asked innocently. My eyes scanned the back office, and they were nowhere in sight. Thank goodness, because what I had to say was not for anyone's ears but Tia's.

"No, they're not here. They're at an off-site meeting."

"Oh, that's good, because I came here to see you."

"Oh, really?" Her tone made it clear that she couldn't have cared less about what I had to say, but she would entertain me anyway. Good. At least the bitch knew her place when it came to church hierarchy. "What did you need to see me about?"

I felt like strangling her ass, sitting there like she was all innocent. "I came to speak to you woman to woman." I eyed her with a firmness to let her know this was no joke.

"Okay, go ahead. Shoot." She fell back against her chair like she didn't have a care in the world.

"What would you do if you had a man and there was another woman all up in his face?"

She looked confused for a second, and then slowly I watched her expression change as she realized what I was saying. She still tried to play dumb, though. "Are you asking for advice, or are you making an accusation?"

"You know what I'm talking about!" I shouted. "Don't act

like you all innocent. Everyone can see how you're always up in Aaron's face." I paused for dramatic effect. "Well, you really need to stop!"

She crossed her arms over her chest and leaned forward in a defiant posture. "First of all, why are you shouting? Second of all, what are you talking about?"

"I'm not shouting! And I'm talking about Aaron! I want you to stay away from my fiancé."

Tia looked surprised for a second, but then this condescending smirk appeared, like she didn't believe me. "Wait a minute. Are you trying to tell me that Aaron is your fiancé?"

I was prepared for her doubting ass. "I'm not trying to *say* anything." I showed her the back of my left hand, flashing an old ring some fool had given me years ago. I'd pulled it out of my jewelry box and dusted it off just for this purpose. "He *is* my fiancé, and I want you to stay the hell away from him!"

"I think you're talking to the wrong person. Shouldn't you be talking to him? Besides, if he's really your fiancé, you should trust him."

"It's not him I don't trust." I stared her down.

"What are you trying to say, Simone?" She stood up, surprising the heck out of me. The little wench was a lot more ghetto than I gave her credit for.

"I'm trying to say that chastity belt you be pretending to wear can be opened just as easy as any zipper, so stay away from my man!"

"You know what? I'm a woman of God, but if you don't get away from my desk with this nonsense, you are gonna have a problem! Now, try me if you want to." She snatched off her earrings, balling her hands into fists like she was about to come around her desk. I took a step back just in case I had to head for the exit. I was too pretty to let this chick mess up my face.

She continued her rant. "And for the record, if you try that crap you pulled on Porsche in the locker room with me, I'll whip your ass so bad you'll be hiding the bruises for the next six months. Now, get the hell out of my office." She pointed toward the exit.

At that very moment, Aaron walked into the office. Obviously he'd heard us fighting, because he was glaring at us like we'd both lost our minds.

"Hey, what's all the shouting about?" he demanded.

"This woman is crazy, Aaron. She just threatened me. Did you hear her?" I turned to him. I was hoping he would wrap his arms around me and kiss me to prove to Tia that he was my man, but he was holding me at a cordial distance.

"Tia, is that true?" Aaron looked confused.

"I only threatened her after she came in here harassing me about you." Tia shook her head. "Now, will you tell your fiancée here that there's nothing going on between us, please? That we're just friends? I don't like being harassed at work."

Dammit, that dirty bitch just dimed on me.

The shocked look on Aaron's face told me I had crossed a boundary I shouldn't have.

"Fiancée?" Aaron exploded.

I tried to clean it up. "I was just telling her we're trying to work things out."

Aaron's face took on a cold expression I'd never seen before, like he was shutting me out completely. That wench Tia had better watch out, because I was gonna get her ass for this. She had best believe it.

"Simone, didn't we just talk about this . . . us? Did I not just tell you that I think we should slow things down? With everything going on with the choir, the competitions and all, I don't have time for a serious relationship. Especially not one with drama," he said through gritted teeth. "I'm just learning this city, and I'm not ready to settle down with anyone at this point in time. Now, we have a good time together, but my only commitment is to the choir, and Tia's a big part of that. You got a problem with that, then take a hike."

"But, Aaron, I thought that after last night there's no question our relationship is progressing." I was trying to keep the tears from falling, to keep some shred of dignity. I'd never felt so humiliated in my life. Men tended to salivate at my feet. I wasn't used to getting played like this—and in front of Tia, no less.

"This is exactly what I was trying to tell you the other day." Aaron buried his forehead in his hands.

He'd told me on many occasions that he wasn't ready to get married, so I figured that's what he was referring to. I reached down and twisted the ring around on my finger to hide the diamond. "What are you talking about?"

"I told you I don't like drama. Why would you go to Tia with this mess? How could you embarrass me like this? She's my church liaison, the go-to person between me and the church. She's the one who's taken me around New York and helped me get settled in. Not that it's your business anyway, but Tia and I are just friends."

Aaron turned to Tia. "Tia, I'm sorry for Simone's behavior. She was totally out of line."

No, he didn't just apologize for me like I'm some little kid!

"You don't have to apologize for her," Tia said, but I saw that smug gleam in her eyes. I felt like scratching out her eyeballs. In my mind, I could see myself choking her to death.

"Oh, Aaron," I said, trying to play it off. "I was just messing with Tia." I turned to Tia. "Girl, I didn't mean anything by what I said." Inside, I was cringing. This whole thing was so embarrassing.

"Yeah, she was just playing," Tia said.

I didn't want that bitch covering up for me. I didn't want her sympathy.

"Simone, you need to back off," Aaron said. He looked back to Tia. "Tia, I needed to run something by you real quick, but I guess it can wait until choir practice."

Aaron exited Tia's office without so much as looking my way.

Aaron

35

I stomped out of the church, pissed off big-time after walking up on Simone acting like a fool. I couldn't believe she had the audacity to tell Tia she was my fiancée—not to mention the big-ass diamond she thought I hadn't noticed. I shook my head, wishing I could shake the entire situation from my mind. This was crazy. What I really didn't appreciate was Simone telling Tia to back off of me, like she owned me or something. Hell, Simone was the one who needed to back up off me. I couldn't deal with this type of thing, not now. I had way too many things on my mind with the growing choir, and having a crazy-ass, insecure woman chasing me around was only going to get in my way.

As much as I liked Simone, and I did have to admit she'd grown on me, sometimes she smothered me so bad I felt like I couldn't breathe. Even now, after the incident that had just occurred, she couldn't leave well enough alone. I had barely gotten out the church doors before she came running up out of nowhere and grabbed my arm.

"Aaron, hold up for a second. Let me explain."

I snatched my arm back. "There's nothing to explain. I don't want to hear any more lies. Everything out of your mouth is some kind of elaborate fabrication."

"That's not true," she huffed.

"Why, isn't it? You just lied in there about us being engaged. Do you know how embarrassing that is?" I tried to keep my voice down, because there were people walking by, but I was furious.

"Baby, I'm sorry. I didn't mean to embarrass you," Simone

whined, sounding all pitiful as she tried to keep pace with me. "But you don't need friends like her."

I stopped dead in my tracks and glared at her. "What did you say? You don't pick my friends! See, this is exactly what I mean. I can't deal with you."

"I'm not trying to pick your friends, but if we're dating, I'd like to be shown a little respect! You don't know Tia like I do. She's not as innocent as she pretends to be. I'm just trying to protect you."

I seriously doubted that what she said about Tia was true, but that was beside the point. What mattered was that Simone was trying to control me, and I wasn't having it. "I'm a big boy and I don't need protection. I can take care of myself. What you need to be concerned with is your own situation, instead of worrying about everything that's going on with me."

Suddenly her neediness turned into bitchiness. Guess I'd struck a nerve.

"What situation would that be?" she spat.

"The situation with your fath—I mean, Deacon Smith . . . dammit!" I shouted in frustration. "You know what I mean. The man is dead and you haven't shed a tear. That's not exactly healthy."

"Why do you keep bringing this up? The cops have dropped it, so why can't you? Deacon Smith was nothing more than a sperm donor, considering the circumstances," Simone protested. She held her hands up imploringly. "You met the man who raised me. That's my father."

"Yep, I sure did, and it just brings up more questions. Anyone ever tell you how much you look like Mr. Wilcox?"

"What are you trying to say, that I lied to the police?"

"I don't give a damn about the police. I think you lied to me."

"You know what? Fuck you, Aaron." She gave me the finger in the middle of the church parking lot. "I would do anything to have my daddy's blood pumping through my veins instead of Jonathan Smith's, that Judas to the church. So, if you don't believe me, you can kiss my ass." She started crying, and I actually felt bad.

"Look, I'm sorry. It's just some of the things you've said and done lately just don't add up."

"Well, if you were the bastard child of a suicidal church deacon, would you tell everyone the whole story?" she said as the tears streamed down her face.

"You're right, but I didn't think I was just anyone." I gently placed my arms around her shoulders.

"Dammit, Aaron, what do you want from me?"

"I want the truth. I wanna know why Deacon Smith was really in your driveway that night. I wanna know why he killed himself. I wanna know why you don't care for a man who gave you life, but you would take his money."

"Okay, we can talk about it all—later. I'll tell you everything you want to know tonight over dinner." She glanced at her watch, then spoke like everything was settled. "Look, I have a meeting inside the church. When I finish, I'll come back to your house. I'll make you dinner, give you a blow job, you can go down on me, and then I'll explain everything to you. How does that sound?"

She made it sound so simple. I knew it wasn't, but I'm a man and a sucker for a good blow job. "I don't know, Simone."

She rocked from side to side and batted her eyes at me flirtatiously. "Come on, baby. Don't you want me to suck it? I know I wanna suck it." She placed the tip of her thumb in her mouth. "I'll tell you everything you wanna know. Promise."

I felt myself weakening. "Okay, but I wanna know everything."

She nodded quickly with a grin. "Everything. I'll tell you everything. Just don't be mad at me anymore. I can't take it when you're mad at me."

Just as the two of us were reaching a truce and making plans for some hot makeup sex later that night, a car screeched to a halt next to us, totally ruining the mood. It was Andrew Gotti with that damn perpetual frown on his face. He got out of the car, and his sidekick exited the passenger side.

I sighed in resignation. "What do y'all want now?"

"Weren't you supposed to meet up with us yesterday?" Gotti

snapped, pointing at his watch. "I told you not to make me come looking for you."

I pounded my palm against my forehead. "Oh, no! It's Wednesday! Damn, I totally forgot!"

"Damn right. You ain't got that much time left. Why do you keep screwing around? Get in the car," the taller man barked.

The next thing I knew, Simone jumped up in the tall man's face. "Y'all can't do this. Who the hell do y'all think you are?" Her professional façade had dropped, and she was total sister-girl, hand on her hip, neck swiveling and finger pointing in the tall guy's face.

"Simone." I held out my hand to restrain her. "Let me handle this, okay? I'll meet you back at your house. We'll have dinner like you said. Everything will be fine."

I know she was trying to help, but this girl didn't have any idea what she was getting into. I hoped she didn't make matters worse for me.

"You sure?"

"Yeah, I'm cool. They're cool."

For a moment Simone looked uncertain, but finally she relented. She slid her door key off her key ring. "Here's the key. If you get there before me, make yourself at home. I'll be there later. The meeting's going to take awhile."

I nodded as I climbed into the backseat of the gray car. Looked like Simone wouldn't be the only one with some explaining to do tonight.

Monique

36

"Ah, can I help you, Mr. Mackie?"

I'd just walked into my office and found Aaron placing a Macy's bag on my desk. I wasn't at all surprised. I suspected all along that he was the culprit behind all those gifts. Lord have mercy, this boy was bold and disrespectful. Here he was trying to play secret lover, and my husband was right next door in his office.

I thought about how he'd copped a feel the first day we met, and I felt a little guilty. Maybe I'd led Aaron on in some way by not telling T. K. about his advances. But whether I did or didn't, he had no right to presume I was a loose woman who cheated on her husband. Well, as flattered as I might have been in the beginning, this nonsense was going to stop right here and now.

"Oh, hey, First Lady. I was just leaving you something," Aaron said nonchalantly. There was a good-natured chirp in his voice, as if he were doing me a favor. "I wanted to surprise you, but I guess giving it to you in person is just as good." He tried to hand me the Macy's bag, but I wouldn't take it.

"Surprise me?" I repeated incredulously. "Look, Aaron, this has got to stop."

He looked confused. "What has to stop?"

I took a breath and held it for a second before exhaling. "Look, have a seat."

He sat in the chair in front of my desk, the look of confusion still on his face. This younger guy was good. He sure knew how to lie and play the game. Now it was time for me to let him know that the game hadn't changed—and that I'd won a match or two in my day. I didn't catch the most eligible bachelor in the entire church for nothing.

"Aaron, you can't keep giving me gifts. They are totally inappropriate and out of line. I am a married woman."

"What does that have to do with anything?"

"It means you shouldn't give me such intimate gifts. Like I said, I'm married."

"You call this intimate?" He laughed this time, placing the bag on my desk.

"I don't see a damn thing funny, Aaron." He was really irritating me. This was a serious matter, and yet he was chuckling. "Every time I think about all the bishop has gone through for you, I get mad. And you've got the audacity to be flirting with his wife and sending her gifts." I paused because I was about to lose it on this man. "Not to mention that the first day I met you, you couldn't keep your damn hands to yourself. Don't you feel the least bit ashamed?"

"Shame about what, First Lady? You're the one who's tripping. Ain't nothing inappropriate about what I'm giving you," he pouted, acting like he was the victim here.

I calmed down enough to ask, "Okay, well, why don't we open the gift and see just how inappropriate it is?"

"Why don't we?" he challenged.

I reached into the bag and pulled out a long, rectangular box. I was sure it was a piece of jewelry, perhaps a bracelet or a watch. And he didn't call this inappropriate?

"I don't know where this is coming from, First Lady. No offense—you're a nice-looking woman and all, but you're a little old for me."

His comment hurt my ego, but he'd be eating his words when he had to explain to me and T. K. why he was spending his hard-earned money buying me expensive gifts. I ripped open the paper around the gift.

"I left a matching set for your husband too. I just wanted to show my appreciation for all your support of the choir."

I lifted the cover off the box and looked down at a black-and-gold pen set. I wanted to shrivel up and die. The darn thing couldn't have cost more than fifteen dollars.

"You gave one of these to T. K. too?"

"Yep. You, him, Deacon Frye, Tia, and all the members of the choir. Like I said, I just wanted to say thanks for the support."

I felt my face burning with embarrassment.

Tia walked into my office. "First Lady, I couldn't help but overhear your conversation. I have to tell you, I went to the mall with Aaron. In fact, I helped him pick out those pen sets for you, the bishop, and the others. He just wanted to show his appreciation. He didn't mean anything personal by it. I'm the one who suggested he do it. Sorry if you're offended."

"Oh my goodness," I said. "So, let me get this straight. You haven't been leaving me gifts before now?"

Aaron held his hands up innocently. "I'm sorry about you feeling like that, but no, I haven't been leaving you gifts. And I never tried to feel your behind. It was an accident. I really did fall. You may have misinterpreted, but I'm not that guy. There's a lot of things about me that I don't like, and with God's help I will one day change them, but I would never flirt with you or give you inappropriate gifts. I respect the bishop too much to do that."

Usually I go off and then feel embarrassed later, but this time I felt horrible right away. "Aaron, I'm sorry," I started, but he didn't give me time to finish. He held up a hand to stop me, then got up and stalked out of the office. He was upset, and understandably so.

"Darn, I guess I put my foot in my mouth this time, didn't I?" I sighed, looking at Tia.

"You sure did." Tia nodded. "Big-time."

I glared at her. "You know what, Tia?"

"What's that, First Lady?"

"You don't have to agree with me all the time."

She half laughed. "I know that, but this time you really are right."

"He probably hates me right now. You know I wouldn't have done that if I wasn't so paranoid about those gifts I keep getting."

Tia put her hand on my shoulder. "First Lady, I'm sure Aaron will understand if you explain it to him. He's just a little upset now. He'll get over it. He really is a sweet guy," Tia said as if she knew Aaron inside and out.

"Oh, how would you know?" I asked.

"You're the one who made me his babysitter, remember? Well, I've been babysitting him a lot lately. I've gotten to know him pretty well. Surprisingly, he's a decent guy, a good guy."

"A decent guy, huh? Sounds like someone's been doing a little more than babysitting." She shook her head to deny it. "Give it up, Tia. Are you hiding something from me?"

"No, we're just friends. He's cute and all, but I don't see him that way. I never looked at Aaron in a romantic kind of way. He's like a good friend or a cousin."

"Kissing cousins maybe?" I teased.

"Sorry, I'm not about to go down that road." Tia tossed her head and shrugged. "Mr. Mackie has enough female church members running behind him. I don't intend to join the harem."

Now that I thought about it, she was making sense. Simone had already proven that she was willing to do anything to eliminate her competition.

"You know what, Tia? You're absolutely right."

Tia

37

"Ladies, I know this session is coming to an end, but I really want to thank you all for coming out every week to share. And even for those of you who just come to listen, I pray that you hear something that helps you further along in your journey to survival. My prayer for you is that someday you feel so free amongst the group that you can openly release all the pain and fear you have bottled up inside. I know it's hard at first, but it was in this exact type of setting that I first talked about my own rape."

I believe in making eye contact with those I'm addressing, so I made an effort to look at every member in attendance as I spoke. I needed to make a connection with these women. Until my eyes landed on Aaron after I made my last statement, I'd forgotten that a man was, in fact, in the room. A man who, I might add, knew absolutely nothing about my story until now. That was evident in the expression that fluttered across his face.

Aaron and I had finished manning the phone lines, and I had a rape counseling session scheduled with five women immediately after. It was Aaron's idea that he sit in on the counseling session, to kind of see me in action. He felt that hearing from the actual rape victims and survivors, he'd be able to better assist some of the women on the hotline. When I explained Aaron's presence to the women, none of them had an issue with him being there.

"So, ladies, with that being said, I'd like to close out in prayer, and until next time, God bless you all." I said a prayer, the women and I all hugged, and then we bid our farewells until next time.

"So, Mr. Mackie, what did you think?" I asked Aaron, who hadn't said a word in the last few minutes. Something was sticking on his mind. Of course, I had my theory about what it might be, but I'd wait for him to speak on it. My wait wasn't long.

"Tia, why didn't you tell me? I had no idea."

"No idea of what?" I played along. Again, I thought it best for him to speak on it first.

"My God, that you were raped. I'm so sorry that happened to you."

I stared at him for a moment. "That's why I didn't tell you. That look right there."

"What? What are you talking about?"

"Pity. That look of pity you're giving me right now. I didn't want that. I don't want that. Not from you or anybody else." I began straightening up the room, taking the few chairs out of the circle we had put them in and putting them back into their usual horizontal rows.

"I'm sorry. I didn't realize that's the impression I'm giving."

"Well, it is." Anger was creeping in to some degree. I wasn't angry at Aaron, though. I was angry for letting it slip in front of him that I was once that woman on the other end of the hotline. Now he was going to see me as some weak, fragile girl.

"Hey, slow down." Aaron walked over to me and gently took my arm. "Listen, that look wasn't pity. It was awe. I'm in complete awe of you. I would have never known you've dealt with such horror. I mean, you are one of the strongest women I know, Tia. I've always thought the most of you, but now I think so highly of you that it's ridiculous. You are an awesome woman, Tia. You really are."

I was so moved by Aaron's words, and even more moved when he put his arms around me and embraced me. It caught me off guard—not Aaron's reaction, but my own. Usually whenever a man tried to get too close, an instant guard went up, kind of like the first time I ever met Aaron. But not this time. This time it felt different. This time it felt good.

Oh God, what was happening here?

The Bishop

38

I walked into the church's conference room a little anxious about the meeting I was about to attend. After conducting an internal audit, on my recommendation, Maxwell Frye had called a special finance meeting of the deacons' board and the board of trustees. Maxwell hadn't told me what the meeting was about, just that it had to do with the financial health of the church and that all members of both boards needed to be present. I did know he'd spent a lot of time with James the past few days going over numbers and figures.

After about fifteen minutes of pleasantries, I stood up, pounding my gavel on the podium. "Please take a seat. I'd like to get this meeting started so we can get out of here at a reasonable time. My wife made pork chops for dinner, and y'all know how much I love pork chops."

There was a burst of laughter, and then everyone settled down.

"As most of you know, since Deacon Smith's passing, Deacon Frye has been elected the new chairman of the deacons' board, and he asked me to call this meeting. So, I'm going to turn over the floor to him. Deacon Frye." I turned to my immediate right, where Maxwell was sitting next to me, shuffling through some papers. There was light applause, mostly from the members of the deacons' board.

Maxwell cleared his throat before he spoke. "Ladies and gentlemen, after visiting with our accountants, the finance committee, and the chairwoman of the board of trustees, I'm sorry to say I have bad news to report." Maxwell paused to let the impact of his words sink in. "Our church is bankrupt."

"Excuse me. What did you say?" one of the deacons asked.

"I said our church is bankrupt, and my recommendation is to file for Chapter 11 bankruptcy protection."

A hush fell over the room. To tell the truth, I was too shocked to speak. It felt like a nightmare. Just a year ago, our church was solvent. I knew we were in trouble, but not bankruptcy type of trouble. I would have to talk to Maxwell later about him not clueing me in to this problem before the meeting. I did not appreciate being blindsided like this.

Suddenly, everyone's eyes shifted suspiciously to Simone; then they looked back at Deacon Frye. Quiet whispers rippled among those in attendance.

"What?"

"How is that possible?"

"What's going on?"

"Where's all the money?"

"Well, needless to say, we have to make a lot of decisions," Deacon Frye continued. "We're in about five million dollars of debt, not including the mortgages on the church and on the school, which are somewhere in the neighborhood of two and a half million. But according to what Trustee Wilcox has told me, we've missed several mortgage payments, and it looks like the lien holder is about to call our note."

"Oh, no!" Voices rose up in consensus.

"Oh, yes," Maxwell said in a calm, even tone. "We're in financial trouble, and the only way out is bankruptcy."

Like a tornado of disbelief, voices began to rise to the ceiling, and now everyone was looking at me.

"How could you get us into this?" one deacon shouted.

"Bishop, this is your fault!" another added.

Deacon Frye stood up, raising his hand to regain control of the room. "Don't blame the bishop. He's not the one in charge of our finances."

Trustee Lisa Mae Watson stood up and pointed at Simone. "No, but she is."

Simone looked at Lisa Mae. "Look, you try to keep track of a school, one hundred employees, ten buildings that are in constant need of repair, and hold down a full-time job, okay, Lisa

Mae? No one should have to do all that for a measly five hundred dollars a week."

"James Black did, and he never cashed one check from the church." Lisa Mae folded her arms. "Can you say the same?"

Simone turned to me. "I don't have to put up with this. I bust my behind for this church every day, for peanuts."

Deacon Frye intervened on her behalf, though I was sure he must have laid into her when they met about this mess. "It's not the bishop's fault. It's not Trustee Wilcox's fault either. It's all of our faults. We are all leaders of this church."

"Here, here, Deacon Frye." I stood, speaking up for the first time.

Maxwell was talking confidently, but I know he didn't believe his own words. Just like everyone else, he blamed Simone for this fiasco, but it wasn't going to solve anything to rake her over the coals. We were going to need her to get past this.

"We need to find solutions." I turned to Maxwell. "Deacon Frye, what are we going to do?"

"Yeah, yeah. What about this great plan the bishop had about our choir making money?" Deacon Stevens piped up.

"You know the choir won one hundred thousand dollars in prize money last month," I reminded everyone.

Someone in the group countered with, "Yeah, and Aaron Mackie got to keep fifteen thousand of that, didn't he?"

I ignored the comment and soldiered on, hoping to instill some positive energy into this conversation. "They're on their way to the Eastern Regional Gospel Championship in the next week or so, where they could win another two hundred thousand and a shot at nationals."

Maxwell shook his head. "That's just a drop in the bucket. We need way more than two hundred thousand, and that's only if they win. What we need is time to rebuild the congregation and the offerings. The choir has started to prove it can help build attendance, but the only thing that will give us time is to file bankruptcy and sell some of our properties."

"What do you think, Trustee Wilcox? Do you have any solutions?" I asked.

"We have an offer on the property that the senior housing is on," Simone said. "It's for two million dollars. I say we sell it."

"Sell it?" I snapped. "You're the one who talked us into buying that property for three million dollars last year. Had us clean out the treasury and school fund to pay for it! We wouldn't have a construction loan if you hadn't insisted we needed the money to build that place. Those buildings are three-quarters of the way finished, and you want us to sell them for two million, along with the land?" If she weren't a woman, I think I would have hit her.

Deacon Frye spoke up. "As somebody in the construction business, I can tell you that what we could have gotten last year for the property is considerably less this year. Although, Trustee Wilcox, two million does seem kind of low. Let me see what I can get us. Once we file bankruptcy, the sharks will smell blood and we might not get that much. We may have to strike while the iron is hot."

I didn't want to agree, but I felt I had no choice because our situation was so dire. Perhaps if I had been better informed before the meeting, I would have had time to come prepared with suggestions. But because I wasn't, I had to trust Maxwell's expertise. "Do what you can, Deacon. I'd hate to sell that property for half of what we put into it."

Maxwell continued delivering more bad news. "I'm not finished. We've got a couple more orders of business. We need to repay our back debt. We owe a lot of people a lot of money, and they're breathing down our necks."

"What do you suggest?" I asked.

"We may need to sell the school to pay off some of this debt," Deacon Frye said. "We owe the city and state a considerable amount for back property taxes, sales tax in our stores . . . The list goes on and on."

"What exactly do you plan to do with the money from the sale of the housing property? Why can't we use that?"

"The construction company has a lien against the property. That's why they stopped working. Once we pay off that lien and pay the bank back for the construction loan, that money is spent."

I looked over at Simone. Had she paid any of our bills over the past year?

"We need to give it some time. We're moving kind of fast. First you're talking about selling the senior housing property. Now you're saying we may have to sell the school? That's too much."

The school was James's baby. He'd invested a lot of his personal time and money into that place. It was considered one of the best private schools in New York. Losing the school would be a terrible blow to our church's reputation—and mine.

"Well, let's see if we can work it out," Deacon Frye conceded. "But I make no promises. That school costs a lot of money to run, and the courts will probably make us sell it or the church. One or the other."

"Deacon Frye, how did this happen? And how can we prevent it from happening again?"

This time, Maxwell turned to Simone. "I'm not sure how it happened, Bishop, but from the internal audit my people did, I can see there are a lot of discrepancies. It looks like someone has been robbing the church blind. The only way to truly find out where the money went is to hire an independent auditing agency that specializes in nonprofit accounting and have them examine the books. We may also have to bring in the police."

"I don't think we need to spend that kind of money at this time," Simone objected. "Not when I can have my accountants do it for free."

I ignored her completely. From the way things were looking, Simone couldn't possibly expect us to give her any say in the matter. "All in favor of an outside audit say aye."

Everyone except Simone held up their hands.

"So, there it is. We'll hire an outside agency." This was one of the darkest moments of my tenure at First Jamaica Ministries. I needed to get out of there. Maxwell had laid out the facts about our shattered finances, and I needed some time to digest the bad news. "Deacon Fyre, thanks for making us aware of our dire situation. If there is no further business, I move to adjourn this meeting."

I felt totally drained. Maxwell had delivered terrible news, but we were still in the eye of the storm. Once word got out, we would have to brace ourselves for one hell of a hurricane.

Simone

39

I was pacing back and forth so relentlessly that I was probably wearing grooves in my living room floor as I waited for Aaron to pick me up. Everything seemed to put me on edge lately, ever since Maxwell Frye had laid the blame for all of the church's financial troubles at my feet. I hadn't talked to anyone about the meeting, so I was living in constant dread of word spreading to the general congregation. When Aaron found out, it would be embarrassing, but that was nothing compared to my father finding out. The prospect of his reaction had me petrified.

That's why I was such a wreck tonight. My father was in town, and he'd shown up at the dealership unannounced once again, this time with two white men nobody had seen before. I was at therapy at the time—well, okay, I was shopping, but that counted as retail therapy as far as I was concerned. Of course, you know those bastards who work for me didn't even pick up the phone to tell me he'd been there until after he left. Thank God I'd sent him his check so he wasn't in a bad mood when I talked to him. He said he wanted to meet me and Aaron for dinner.

The doorbell ringing was the only thing that halted my pacing.

"Hello, handsome," I greeted Aaron.

He walked in looking just as good as ever. I took in his manly scent. Some people had their own money, some people had their own zip code, but this man had his own scent, and I loved it. If we didn't have to go meet Daddy, I would have jumped him right then and there in my living room. Instead, I had to settle for a very passionate kiss that made my insides weak.

"Hello to you too," he replied happily when we ended our kiss.

Things were better between me and Aaron ever since our fight in the parking lot. When I went to his place later that night, I fully expected he would make me do as I'd promised and tell him all about Jonathan Smith being my father. As it turned out, though, he was not too interested in talking. I suspected that had to do with two things: one, he was happy to let me use my mouth for something other than talking, and, two, he seemed none too interested in spilling the details about the two thuggish-looking white guys who'd pulled up on us in the parking lot. So, I guess he understood that if he didn't want to answer questions, then he didn't get to ask any either. That seemed to be working for both of us pretty well ever since.

"You ready to get out of here and go meet Daddy?" I grabbed my purse.

"Of course. What exactly does he want to see me about?"

"I don't know. Maybe he wants to give you your own dealer-ship," I joked.

"Like you would ever let that happen," he joked back.

"No, that would be cool—as long as you remember that I'm the boss."

"You're just mad because your father likes me more than you."

"Will you cut it out?" I slapped at him playfully. "He's my fa-ther, not some girl you've got sprung."

"You mean like you?" He winked and squeezed my behind.

"Don't start nothing you can't finish," I dared him.

"Oh, if I start, I'm gonna finish. What time does that restau-rant close? Because your father just might have to sit around and wait for a while." He planted a hot kiss on my lips, and I wanted to melt. Why was this man teasing me? He knew I couldn't act upon the heated passion that rested between us.

"Come on, Mr. Mackie, you little devil. You know we can't stand my father up."

"Hey, why I gotta be a devil?" He acted offended.

"Because your horn is showing." I reached down and mas-saged his stiff package. "Now, let's go. Daddy's waiting." I let go of his stuff and headed for the door before it was too late.

When we arrived, my father stood up from his table in excite-ment before the host could even lead us all the way over to him.

"It's so good to see you," he greeted. Call me crazy, but I just

assumed he was talking to me until he said, "You, too, Simone."
He pulled Aaron in for a manly hug and a thump on the back.

"It's so good to see you, too, Mr. Wilcox."

When they finished their male-bonding session, I gave Daddy
a kiss and Aaron helped me to my seat before sitting beside me.
The waiter came over shortly after, and we ordered our meals,
then chatted like we hadn't just seen my father a few weeks ago.
Aaron had that kind of effect on people—not just women, but
people as a whole.

That was my man, and I was proud of him, as could be seen
by the grin that stayed plastered on my face as I watched him
converse with my father throughout our meal. I was feeling so
much better than I had earlier that evening—until Daddy said,
"So, uh, Aaron, I know you're all into that music thing, and my
people at the church tell me that you do a fine job at it, but have
you ever thought about going into the car business?"

I could tell Aaron was a little caught off guard by my father's
question. In fact, so was I.

"No, can't say that I have, Mr. Wilcox." Aaron sat back in his
chair.

Was he seriously interested in the idea? I sure hoped not. He
was my man and all, but it wouldn't do our relationship any
kind of good if we were both working in the car business.

"Well, a man with your gift of gab should give it some thought.
I could see you becoming the top salesman and moving on to
practically running the company."

What the hell was he talking about, running the company? *I*
ran the company!

Daddy continued on like I wasn't even at the table. "With
someone like you on the team, I could open up that chain I've always dreamed of."

And why hadn't he shared that dream with me before? I couldn't
hold my tongue any longer.

"Uh, Daddy, Aaron doesn't want to get into the car business."

"Hush, Simone. Let the man speak for himself."

Aaron glanced over at me. I'm sure he could see I wasn't
happy. He let out a chuckle. "I'm flattered, Mr. Wilcox, but
singing is my thing."

"For now, maybe, but I could see you helping me get this chain thing off the ground. I could train you. Teach you everything I know. I could come to New York for a while and work with you side by side. It would be like building my dream with the son I never had."

Finally my father turned to me like he'd decided to finally invite me into this conversation. "Then again, who's to say you won't end up being my son-in-law anyway?"

Aaron looked over at me, as if I had any control over the stuff that was coming out of my father's mouth. I wanted to sink down in my chair and crawl under the table. For the first time in a long time, I was completely innocent, but that didn't change the look Aaron gave me before he spoke to my father.

"Look, Mr. Wilcox, I like your daughter a lot. We have a lot of fun together, but I'm just getting used to the idea that she's my girlfr—"

"I know, I know. You've already told me. You and Simone aren't getting down like that." I was now officially more embarrassed than I'd ever been in my life, sitting there listening to my father attempt to use slang. "But it's just a seed I wanted to plant in your head, and hopefully the good Lord will water it in my favor. Amen?"

Aaron replied with a lackluster, "Amen."

I mean, what else could the poor guy say?

"Daddy, dinner was lovely, but it's time for Aaron and me to get out of here." I wiped my mouth with my napkin and raised my hand to signal for the waiter to hurry over with our check.

"Just one minute. I'm getting a call." Daddy reached for his cell phone.

About fifteen seconds into his conversation, his face became flushed and I could see the vein in his forehead throbbing.

"Daddy, what's the matter?" I asked when he hung up, although from the way he'd been staring at me during the call, I was terrified to hear his answer.

He expression only hardened further as he said, "I was just informed that First Jamaica Ministries is filing for bankruptcy."

Uh-oh. I glanced at Aaron out of my peripheral vision. From the look he was giving me, I was about to get it from both ends.

"Did you know that?" my father asked, but didn't wait for a

response. "Of course you knew it! You're the chairwoman of the board of trustees. I just don't understand how you could sit here and eat dinner with me for the past hour and not say a word about it."

No words came to my mind. I knew my usual baby-girl routine wouldn't work, so I just stared at him with no expression.

He turned to Aaron. "Did you know about this, young man?"

"No, sir, I can't say I did." He looked at me disapprovingly. I wanted to smack him. How dare he gang up on me like this with my own father!

My indignation allowed me to gather myself enough to finally speak up. "Look, Daddy, it's no big deal. We're just filing Chapter Eleven reorganization. I wasn't gonna ruin dinner over it. God, don't make a mountain out of a molehill."

"You don't think this is a big deal?" Aaron asked.

"No, I don't. Businesses go through Chapter Eleven all the time and come out fine. Look at General Motors."

"But the church doesn't have the government backing them," Daddy protested as I turned around to search for the waiter so he could hurry up and bring the check.

I heard Daddy let out a strange grunt behind me. I twisted around to look at him, and my heart skipped a beat. My father was slumped over, grabbing his chest.

"Oh my God! Aaron, help him, please! Help!" I yelled out. "Somebody call an ambulance. I think my father is having a heart attack."

Aaron

40

We'd been in the emergency room for almost an hour, waiting to find out about the condition of Simone's father. At the restaurant, I'd jumped out of my chair to catch him. If I hadn't been there, the poor man probably would have split his head wide open on that stone floor. Luckily that didn't happen, though it did look like he'd had a heart attack.

"Simone, try to relax," I coaxed as she paced the emergency room waiting area, her body trembling.

She cut her eyes in my direction. "I can't relax. That's my father in there. I need to know what's going on."

I got out of my seat and wrapped my arms around her shoulders. "I know, sweetheart, but the nurse said the doctor would be out to talk to you just as soon as he finished tending to your father. We gotta be patient, love." I was laying it on thick with *sweetheart* and *love,* terms of endearment I usually shied away from. In this situation, I felt it was called for to comfort Simone.

"I know, but it's been forever." Simone scooted out of my arms. "Where is that doctor?"

As if right on cue, the doctor, a short Indian man, came into the waiting room. "Simone Wilcox? The family of Brian Wilcox?"

"That's me! Over here." Simone ran over to the doctor, practically knocking him down. "How's my father? What happened to him? Is he going to be okay?" she questioned in quick succession.

"Your father is stable," the doctor replied. "From what we can tell, he's had an attack of angina."

"So, he didn't have a heart attack? But how could that be? He was grabbing his chest and left arm."

"Yes, but those are also symptoms of angina. Do you know when he's had his last checkup?" the doctor asked.

"Uh, not too long ago, actually. He got a clean bill of health. But didn't he tell you that?"

The doctor gave us an uncomfortable chuckle. "Um, your father doesn't seem to want to talk. He's a stubborn man, isn't he?"

She sighed. "Yes, he can be. I bet he's insisting he's fine and ready to go home, right?"

"Precisely. To be safe, though, we'd like to keep him overnight for observation and to run a few more tests. Angina is not terribly serious at this stage, but it can be a sign of heart disease."

"Okay, well, I'll go talk to him to see if I can convince him to stay," Simone said. Then she turned to me. "On second thought, maybe you should go talk to him, Aaron. I'm probably not his favorite person right about now."

I squeezed her hand. "How about we go together?"

She leaned in to give me an appreciative kiss.

The doctor cleared his throat when the kiss lasted longer than was probably appropriate for a hospital waiting room. "Well, that's wonderful. Now, in the meantime, we need to know a bit about his medical history, and again, he only wants to talk about leaving at this point. Do you know of any significant medical history we should be aware of?"

"Well, he's never really been sick before, but he does have sickle cell trait. That's the only thing I got from him, other than my looks."

Simone glanced over at me and winked, probably trying to assure me that her flirtatious comment to the doctor was harmless. That wasn't the part that had me ready to flip, though.

The doctor said, "That's good to know. Now, if you'll wait out here for just a little bit longer, we'll finish his exam and then you can come back and see him."

Simone visibly relaxed when she heard those words. I wanted to be grateful for the doctor's words, too, but it wasn't his words that kept repeating in my mind.

"Did you hear that?" Simone said ecstatically after the doctor walked away. "Daddy's going to be okay!" She threw her arms around my neck and embraced me.

"Yeah, I heard all right." I slipped from her embrace and went to sit down in the chair I'd been in for the past hour. What I actually wanted to do was walk my ass right on out of there and go home. As Simone came and sat next to me, looking all innocent, it took everything in me not to get up and do just that.

"I'm so glad you were there for Daddy. When I turned around and saw him clutching his chest after he made that god-awful noise, I panicked. But not you. You ran right over to Daddy to catch his fall. Thank you, Aaron. Thank you for being there for my father, and thank you for being there for me."

It all sounded good, but no longer did I believe a thing that came out of that woman's mouth. And no longer could I hold it back.

"Look, uh, I gotta go, Simone." I dug into my pocket, pulled out my wallet, and handed her fifty dollars. "Here's cab fare. I hope your father gets better soon."

I stood up, and Simone quickly followed suit, blocking my path.

"A cab? What are you talking about? Why are you leaving?"

I wasn't beating around the bush with her. "Because I'm sick of the lies. Why is there always so much drama with you?"

"What drama? Aaron, baby, what's really going on? Is this about the bankruptcy? If so, I can explain—"

"Oh, it's about that and a whole lot more. You know, Simone, I've never met anyone like you before. You're a habitual liar." I started walking out the door and she followed.

"Aaron, I have a sick father in there. He may not have had a heart attack, but he still needs me, so I don't have the time to be kissing your ass right now."

Obviously she needed me to spell it out for her. I guess she'd been telling so many lies she didn't even notice that she'd slipped up in front of me.

"And that right there is the problem, Simone. That sick man back there is your *father*. Not your stepfather or your adopted father, but your real, biological father! I mean, after all, you have the sickle cell trait that you inherited from him. Isn't that what you just said?"

She couldn't have looked more surprised if I'd thrown a pie in her face. I swear, if it wasn't so ghetto, I would have taken out my camera phone, snapped a couple pictures of Simone's face, and posted it on the church's Facebook page. She was so busted. It looked like all the blood had drained out of her face. I thought for a minute they were going to have to check her into the hospital right next to her father, but instead, I was checking myself out—out of her life.

"Good-bye, Simone. Oh, and tell your father I hope he gets better and he was right." I went to walk away, but she grabbed my arm.

"Right about what?"

"I am the one who ended up getting hurt in this relationship." I tried to step past her, but she held my arm tightly.

"So, is that it? You're going to walk right out of here without allowing me to explain?"

"Woman, do you know how many chances you've had to explain?" I hadn't meant to raise my voice, but Simone had a way of sparking my anger like few other people could. "I doubt you can even keep your lies straight, can you?"

"Please, Aaron. Let me just talk to you. This time I promise to—"

I shook her hand loose from my arm. "Good-bye, Simone. It's over. Now, go back in there and take care of your *father*." I stepped around her and headed for my truck.

Simone

41

I drove to Maxwell Frye's office on Queens Boulevard in Rego Park with a sense of trepidation. For some reason, Maxwell had insisted that we meet there at this late hour, instead of at the church. I went over our telephone conversation in my mind. He'd called me just as I was putting Daddy and my stepmother back on a plane to Florida. Lord knows I was glad to get rid of them once I was sure Daddy's health was stable.

"Meet me and the bishop at my Rego Park office at nine o'clock sharp. Leave the choir boy home. We've got some important church business to discuss."

His tone had been so short and cryptic I didn't know what to think. I didn't have a good feeling about this, and I didn't like the way he called my boo a choirboy, like he was less than a man or something. I knew one thing: Aaron could whip Maxwell's ass if it ever came down to a physical confrontation.

Speaking of being physical, I wished Aaron would answer my calls. I still couldn't believe he'd tried to break up with me. I say *tried* because I wasn't going to let him. He could say it all he wanted, but as far as I was concerned, he was still my man. I didn't care what he or anybody else said; I wasn't letting go. He just needed some time to miss me.

I slammed on my brakes, and my tires made the same sound on the pavement as fingernails going down a chalkboard. I'd almost run a red light worrying about my relationship troubles and thinking about this impromptu meeting with Maxwell. I had to get myself together and stop thinking the worst.

After narrowly avoiding an accident, I arrived at Maxwell's

office building in one piece. That didn't mean I felt any less nervous, though. My hands trembled and my stomach quivered as I approached his office on the fourth floor. I could not shake the feeling that had been plaguing me the last hour. Something was definitely wrong. But what was it?

As I stepped into the office, I felt like Daniel in the lion's den. Deacon Frye sat behind this huge mahogany desk, staring at the doorway as if he'd been waiting for my arrival ever since he hung up the phone with me. There were two other men in the office, one black and one white. I only knew the black man, and I wasn't happy to see him. Not at all. His name was D. L. Sherman. He was an accountant Frye had snooping around the church, but I hadn't paid him much mind until now as he sat staring at me. The tall white guy wearing a dark suit and a tie was someone I was unfamiliar with.

"Hello," I said, trying to will my heart to slow down. I took deep breaths and held my head up high as I walked over to a chair in front of Deacon Frye's desk. I slowly eased into the armchair, trying to maintain an air of composure even though I felt like running from the room. All three men nodded, but there was a grimness in their demeanor. No one spoke to me.

"Where's the bishop?"

Deacon Frye continued to stare me down. "He's not able to make it."

I tried not to squirm as I made eye contact with the men in the room. Each one maintained his laser-beam stare. I knew without them saying a word that I was on the hot seat for something.

Frye tortured me with a few moments of uncomfortable silence before he said anything. I was glad when he finally spoke, because rather than sitting there sweating in my seat, I needed him to hurry up and say whatever it was that he had to say so that we could deal with it.

"Do you have any idea why you're here?"

Oh, Deacon Frye was playing me. He was playing me good.

"No, I don't, but considering the people in the room, I'm gonna go out on a limb and say it has something to do with the church's bankruptcy."

"Let me just put it to you straight." He dropped his pen on

the desk and leaned forward dramatically. "Sherman here has found quite a few inconsistencies with the church's financial records. Interestingly, we went back a year or so and discovered these inconsistencies began when you became the chairwoman of the board of trustees."

It felt like my heart almost stopped beating, but I had to keep it together. I had to play this thing out until I knew exactly what they knew. You ever hear the expression "Give a person a rope long enough and they'll hang themselves with it"? Well, today was not the day I was going to commit suicide.

"What's that supposed to mean?" It came out as a whisper, but at least my voice didn't crack. I was still hanging on by a thread, though barely. My confidence was deflating rapidly.

Maxwell glanced at the two men, then shook his head. The room fell silent again. It was so quiet that I swear I could hear my own heart pounding.

Finally Deacon Frye stood up and walked around his desk. He stood in front of me and looked me directly in the eye. "What it means is you've been stealing. You've been robbing the church blind."

I jumped up from my seat and threw my hands in the air. "No, I haven't! What makes you think I'm stealing? This is preposterous! I don't have to stay here and listen to this!"

Maxwell slammed his hand on his desk.

"Look, Simone, save it, okay? The numbers don't lie. And neither does the paper trail." He turned to the accountant and nodded. "Go ahead, Sherman. Show her what you've got."

I turned to Sherman with weak knees, and he handed me a folder.

"We know you've been stealing," he said with conviction. "I know that's a strong allegation to make, but one that doesn't go without merit. Trust me. I'd never make that type of accusation without proof to back it up."

I flipped through the ledger. Sherman was good, better than I could have ever expected. He'd caught me dead to rights. Usually I could talk my way out of anything, but not this time. Not only was I frozen numb, but so was my tongue.

Maxwell spoke up again. "Now, I'd like to introduce you to a good friend of mine, Detective Sergeant Hart from the One Hundred Thirteenth Precinct."

My heart jumped into my throat. Everything in me wanted to split and catch the first flight to Mexico, but there was no running, not now, not with a policeman in front of me. So instead, I tried to play it cool.

"I didn't steal anything. I'm offended that you would accuse me, Deacon Frye. You've known me since I was a little girl."

"Look, cut the crap," Detective Sergeant Hart snapped. "We have enough proof to send you off for the next twenty years. I can slap the cuffs on you right now if you don't start cooperating."

I felt like a cornered rat. I was too pretty to go to jail.

"You've taken a lot of money," Deacon Frye said in a somber voice, his expression full of disgust.

That's when I broke down crying. I was caught red-handed. I'd really fucked up now. "I'm going to pay it all back," I blubbered. "I didn't steal it. I was just borrowing the money. I always had plans on putting it back."

Deacon Frye asked, "Before or after you got caught?"

"I was having problems making ends meet at the dealership, but things are looking up now. I swear I'll pay back every dime."

"Oh, we know you will," Deacon Frye insisted. "But paying back the church isn't the only thing you're going to do if you wanna stay out of a jail cell."

I didn't know exactly what he meant, but I wasn't in any position to negotiate. "Tell me what it is and I'll do it. I just don't want to go to jail."

Aaron

42

"Ladies and gentlemen, the winner of the 2011 Eastern Regional Gospel Choir Championship is . . ." The announcer hesitated in that dramatic, after-the-commercial-break-type pause, as if he was purposely trying to torture me. Still, I had no doubt he was going to be calling out the name of First Jamaica Ministries. None of the judges had responded to the other choirs the way they had when we finished our last song. I mean, once we hit that last note, holding it like our lives depended on it, the audience and the judges' table erupted in cheers. One judge caught herself standing up and then abruptly sat down. Another quickly wiped away an escaping tear. I almost felt sorry for the other choir directors because they didn't have a chance. I'm not saying that this year's competitors weren't good, because they were, but we were just a whole lot better. I just needed that damn announcer to make it official.

"First Jamaica Ministries of Queens, New York!"

All I heard was the word *First* before I jumped up in the air, pumping my fists, signifying to everyone in Boston's TD Garden that First Jamaica Ministries had won the Eastern Regional Gospel Choir Championship, and even more importantly that I, Aaron Mackie, had led them to that victory. I swear I think it was the happiest moment of my life.

I have to admit that I really didn't think we had what it took to be a winning choir when I first started at the church and there were only ten people in the choir. The group I met the first time I walked into the choir rehearsal room was nothing in comparison to what we were today. We were now a bona fide choir of forty-three, with at least two kick-ass soloists in every section, and when we finished singing, you knew you'd seen a show.

Now with the audience cheering wildly, I was basking in their praise. I couldn't remember the last time I felt this good.

Actually, I'd been feeling this good ever since I rid myself of all that stressful weight I'd been carrying around that went by the name of Simone Wilcox. She was one hell of a good piece of ass but definitely not one to get involved in a relationship with—if that was what you could call what we'd had. At least that was what she called it. I'd messed with women three times as long as I'd kicked it with her and never once had to deal with half the drama she dragged me through. She had a lot of baggage, though she would deny it in a heartbeat. I had way too much going on—and too much going for me right now—to deal with that.

"You really pulled it off, Aaron. We're going to nationals! We're going to nationals!" one of my choir members screamed. We cheered, hollered, jumped up and down, and some of us even cried. It was so overwhelming, because this meant that we were now qualified for the National Gospel Choir Championship and its brand-new first prize: a recording contract with Sony Records.

Backstage after the hoopla had died down, I felt someone approach me and slip her hand into mine.

"I'm very proud of you, Mr. Mackie. Very proud. You did the impossible."

When I turned around and saw Tia's smiling face, I felt my heart jump in a way that surprised me. I realized that this was the only place I wanted to be right now and that I was looking into the eyes of the only woman I wanted to share it with.

She gave my hand a squeeze, and I swear she meant it to send me a message. Wow! Where were these feelings coming from all of a sudden?

Turning toward her and grabbing her other hand, I said, "No, Tia, *we* did it. You have been here for me since day one. I would have never gotten as far as I have with this choir had it not been for you. You sacrificed your time for me while at the same time being pulled in a million other directions with everything else you have going. No woman, no person, has ever given up so much for me. Thank you, Tia. Thank you."

She lowered her head modestly. "Aaron, please. I can't take credit for this. I was just doing what—"

"What you were called to do." I finished her sentence. "Tia, you did this because you wanted to. You didn't have to. Since when is babysitting a grown man a calling?" I joked, though I was half serious.

She laughed. "Well, you're right about that, because you did need some babysitting. Between Porsche, Simone, and—"

My vibrating cell phone put a halt to our conversation. I hated to do it, but I had to release her hands in order to check the call. I sighed when I pulled out my cell phone and looked down at the caller ID.

"It's her again, isn't it?" Tia asked, then mumbled under her breath, "Speak of the devil."

"Yeah, it's her."

Simone wasn't even here and she was messing up the mood. She had been blowing up my phone all day, as if she didn't know I was taking care of some very important business. She didn't care about anything that I had going on. Like always, she was trying to make everything about her.

"Just turn your phone off. She'll take the hint when your phone sends her butt straight to voice mail." Tia rolled her eyes.

"That ain't the only place I want to send her."

Thankfully, Tia laughed. My comment had pulled her out of the attitude she was developing. I'd never noticed how cute, how contagious her laughter was. It wasn't a cover-up for something lurking beneath. It was real, genuine, and strangely enough, my feelings for her were becoming just as real.

"What? Why are you looking at me like that?" she asked when she noticed me staring at her.

"I . . . I don't know. I just . . ." I don't know what got into me, but I lowered my head and planted my lips against Tia's. I was absolutely amazed when she kissed me back.

When the kiss ended, I looked down at her and asked, "Did we just, um . . ."

She placed her finger on my lips. "Yeah, we did. Now do it again before I change my mind."

Monique

43

Other than our choir's recent popularity and winning streak, things hadn't been so good the past few weeks at our church—and thus, in my life. According to T. K., bankruptcy was all but a certainty for First Jamaica Ministries, along with the fire sale of our half-built senior housing complex and possibly the school. Fortunately, the bankruptcy would protect us from losing the church, but we were still poised to lose millions.

What I couldn't understand was why no one seemed to know where the money went, including Simone, the woman I'd helped get elected as chairwoman of the board of trustees. I hated to admit it, but maybe James was right when he called her incompetent, because from the conversation I had with her, she didn't seem to have a clue. The next time we went to visit James, I'd have to tell him I was starting to see his side of things.

My mind was so preoccupied with the church's financial troubles that I could only imagine how much worse it must be for my husband. I was sure he needed some stress relief even more than I did right about now, and I couldn't wait for him to get home. Typically I'd join him when he traveled to see the choir compete, but with everything going on at the church, we thought it best if one of us stayed close to home.

Until T. K. returned, I was glad for the distraction of an evening out. I'd received an e-mail that the deacons' board was meeting at Kabuki, one of my favorite sushi restaurants over in Forest Hills. I barely ever got offers from them to attend their meetings, so I e-mailed back my acceptance right away.

I walked into Kabuki and was greeted by a very pretty Asian

woman and an Asian man. They were both smiling and bowing like I was the Queen of England coming to visit their restaurant.

"You must be Monique," the woman said, bowing again. I was more than a little freaked out. I visited the restaurant about once or twice a month, but how the heck did she know my name? "You are the first to arrive. Please follow me."

First to arrive? I thought, glancing at my watch. I was ten minutes late. *These Negroes are really on CP time.*

She guided me to one of those private rooms where you have to take your shoes off and sit on pillows. A woman wearing a beautiful kimono came in carrying a tray of steaming towels.

"Am I early?" I asked the woman, thinking that I might have gotten the time wrong.

"No, you're on time," she replied. "The rest of your party will be right with you."

She walked away and closed the bamboo doors behind her, only to return a few minutes later with another tray containing a small gift box. When I saw it, I almost fainted.

"This is for you," she said, placing the tray in front of me.

"Who gave this to you?"

She gave me a coy smile and shook her head. "I cannot tell you. It would ruin the big surprise. Open your present."

I wanted to snatch her by her skinny little neck and choke the answer out of her, but I held back. It looked like I was finally going to meet my secret admirer.

With trepidation, I opened the box and found a stunning diamond brooch. Since it wasn't Aaron leaving the gifts, I assumed there was still the possibility that T. K. had been playing games with me for the past few months. Appraising the gift, I smiled. If it was my husband, he sure had gone all out this time.

"So, I see you got my gift." A familiar voice interrupted my contemplation. "Do you like it?"

I looked up, surprised to see Deacon Maxwell Frye.

"Okay, where's T. K.?" I asked, prepared to laugh at the practical joke he and my husband were playing on me. "You know this isn't funny, right, Maxwell?"

"I'm not laughing." He gestured to the diamonds in my hand. "Do you like it?"

The smile vanished from my face. *Oh, shit! This man is serious.*

"What?" I looked down at the marvelous piece of jewelry and dropped it, because all of a sudden it all made sense. "It was you, wasn't it? It was you all along sending me these gifts."

Maxwell shrugged. "Who else would it be? It's not like your husband even attempts to shower you with such fine gifts."

I wasn't going to allow him to talk about T. K. that way. "What my husband can or cannot afford is not your business. We do just fine." I picked up the package and extended it toward Maxwell. "Here, take this shit back."

Instead of taking it, he started pacing back and forth. "Why are you acting like I'm the one who's wrong? Truth is, I think you owe me some answers."

"Answers for what?" As far as I was concerned, this entire situation came out of left field, and Maxwell had lost his mind.

"How could you marry one of my best friends?" He shook his head. "I just don't get it."

I was struggling to understand this whole bizarre scenario, and then it hit me: Maxwell was still pining for me after all these years! My relationship with him seemed like a lifetime ago. We had dated for two years, though no one at the church knew it because he insisted we be discreet. Then he left the country without so much as a kiss good-bye, and I assumed that I must not have meant that much to him in the first place. I'd never even bothered to tell T. K. about it.

When Maxwell had come back to the country, he seemed genuinely happy for me and T. K. Now I was starting to think that had all been an act. It was definitely time to get the hell out of Kabuki and far away from Maxwell. I laid my palms on the table and eased myself to my feet. After his earlier dig at T. K., I couldn't resist shooting a little dagger in Maxwell's heart.

"It's simple. I fell in love with T. K. It wasn't like you put a ring on my finger, Maxwell."

He went on as if he hadn't even heard me. "But we were in love." Typical Maxwell. He always heard only what he wanted to, whether or not it was the truth.

"Love? Is that what it was? You don't leave someone you love and go to Iraq for five years without saying a word."

He tried to protest, but I cut him off.

"Once upon a time, I might have gone down the aisle with you, Maxwell, but you wouldn't even acknowledge we were dating. You didn't want anyone to know you spent every night with the church whore, remember?"

A look of guilt crossed Maxwell's face, and he lowered his head. "It wasn't like that," he offered weakly.

"Oh, no? Then how was it? All you had to do was let folks know we were dating, and that rain cloud over my head would have disappeared. You knew I wasn't sleeping with anyone but you, but you still let people think I was some whore sleeping with every swinging dick in the church. And why? Because you had your own reputation to look out for. Well, I've got news for you, Maxwell. Love is putting the ones you claim to love first! That's what T. K. does for me."

"Okay, I was selfish. I admit it. But you knew how I felt about you."

"Did I? Maxwell, you left me without a word. I didn't know you were gone until I read it in the church bulletin."

"That's because I wasn't supposed to be gone that long."

"You ever heard of an invention called the telephone? What about pen and paper? That usually works pretty good too. You didn't write, you didn't call, but you kept in touch with both James and T. K., didn't you? You couldn't keep in touch with the woman you supposedly loved. What is wrong with that picture?"

"Don't you understand what I was trying to do? I went away to make money so I could be with you. So you could have all the things those other women had. I knew that's what you really wanted. I could see it in the way you looked at them with their fine jewelry and fancy clothes."

"Oh, bull! I wasn't jealous of those women because of their clothes and material things. I was jealous because they could all walk into church with their heads held high, holding their man's hand. All I wanted was a man of my own. You didn't even think to take me with you."

"Oh yeah, those tight shirts and short skirts would have really gone over well in Iraq."

"See, that's what I mean. You're so concerned with what everyone else has to say that you didn't give a damn about me."

He slowed down long enough to get his anger in check. "Monique, I never stopped loving you," he said, sounding like he was desperate for me to believe him.

"I'm not a mind reader, you know. You never told me you loved me. Not once."

"Well, I'm telling you now."

I had to let out a laugh. Was he deaf *and* crazy? Did he not hear a word I'd said? "Maxwell, have you forgotten I'm married?"

"How could I forget? I think about it every fucking day," he cursed. "It should have been me."

"That doesn't change the fact that what we had is over." My voice was firm, and final.

"It doesn't have to be." Maxwell leaned closer.

"I'm married," I said, taking a step back. "And I love my husband."

"You don't love him. You're just settling. One night with me and all your dreams will come true. I promise."

"My dreams have already come true. I have all I need in Bishop T. K. Wilson."

"You have got to be kidding me. T. K. couldn't hold my condom in the bedroom."

I wanted to smack him for being so disrespectful. Instead, I hit him where I knew it would hurt most. "He doesn't have to hold a condom. He's my husband—*we don't use them*. In spite of what you think about T. K. and my marriage to him, he is my husband and I love him. I'd never leave him for any man—including you, Maxwell Frye."

"You don't mean that."

I could not believe the state of denial this man was in.

"Yes, I do. He didn't care what people thought. He fell in love with me and married me despite what people had to say. T. K. loves me unconditionally. That's real love, baby!" I said it as if I were throwing down the ace of spades in a card game.

Maxwell thought about what I said for a moment. I went to pick up my purse and leave, but he placed a hand on my arm to stop me. "Let me prove to you that we should be together," he said in a low, seductive voice. "T. K.'s out of town. Spend the night with me. Just one night. He will never have to know."

I shook my head at his audacity. "It doesn't matter if he would never know. *I* would know. How many times do I have to tell you? That's my husband and I love him. What don't you understand about that? Besides, he's your friend. How could you do this to him?"

"He stopped being my friend the day he betrayed me by marrying you. I'm just playing him close in order to be near you."

Before I knew what was happening, he grabbed my shoulders and tried to kiss me.

"Stop it!" I pulled away from his touch.

"You used to love it when I kissed you."

"You don't get it. Get away from me. It's over!" I pushed Maxwell out of my way and headed toward the exit.

"I'm not going to let you go, Monique."

"You don't have a choice, because I will be telling my husband about this little stunt you pulled."

"You can tell him whatever you want, but you'll be telling him from his jail cell."

"Whatever, Maxwell." I slid open the bamboo door and almost ran into a stocky white man who was standing there.

Maxwell came up beside me. He was so close that I could feel his breath on my neck. "Monique Wilson, meet Detective Sergeant Hart. He's the man who's going to lock your husband up for twenty years for stealing the church's money—that is, if you don't bring your ass back in here."

I stared at the white man, who pulled back his suit jacket, revealing a gold police badge hooked to his belt. I glanced at Maxwell, who was smiling like he'd won the lottery.

He's lying, Monique. Don't fall for it, girl. Just tell this fake cop to step aside and go home.

"My husband would never steal money from the church," I said confidently. "That church is his life."

"I wouldn't have thought so either, but his five accounts in the Cayman Islands say different. By the way, don't y'all own a condo down there in the Caymans?"

I wondered how the hell he knew about the condo. This was getting scary.

"Did you ever think about how T. K. has all this money and property and all of a sudden the church is broke? The church only pays him about two hundred grand a year. How much was that new house y'all just bought?"

"He writes books, does lecture series. The church isn't his only source of income," I replied in T. K.'s defense.

"Do you know how much they're paying for book deals these days? You spend that in a weekend at the mall." I got a lump in my throat. "Has he ever shown you your finances?"

I turned away from him, afraid to admit that I had never even bothered to check our account balances. I'd always been more than happy to let T. K. handle all of that.

"Let her take a look at the folder, Detective Sergeant."

The cop handed me a folder. I opened it, flipping through the pages of bank statements, wire transfers, and copies of canceled checks. When I got to the last page, I closed my eyes and whispered, "No, T. K. Dear God, no."

"You're in love with a crook, Monique. I guess I wasn't the only one willing to do whatever it took to keep you happy."

When I opened my eyes, I saw the cop had slid the door closed and Maxwell's hands were on my shoulders, massaging me. I didn't fight him this time because I was too numb trying to digest what I had read.

"So, do you still love this man?"

"You don't just stop loving someone, Maxwell." Tears were welling up in my eyes.

"Believe me, I understand. I feel the same way about you. I guess the only question now is, are you going to be a ride-or-die chick for your man? 'Cause if you really love him, you might want to hear what I have to say. Right now I'm the only thing standing between Bishop T. K. Wilson and a jail cell."

Simone

44

"Aaron, baby, please call me back. Please, baby." I clicked my phone shut angrily.

It had been two weeks since Aaron and I last spoke, and I had to admit to myself that we were actually broken up. I was absolutely miserable. I could barely eat or sleep because I was so worried about our relationship, or what was left of it anyway. I'd been calling his cell phone, home phone, and the phone in the choir rehearsal room nonstop trying to get him to talk to me, but he wouldn't answer. I even blocked my number a few times so that he wouldn't know it was me calling, but when I finally got through, he hung up as soon as he recognized my voice. I was getting sick of him dodging me, and if I didn't speak to him soon, I would have to do something real fucking drastic.

On the real, I was starting to feel like Glenn Close in *Fatal Attraction*. The first time I saw that movie, I just viewed her as some crazy, desperate bitch, but now I could feel her. There's nothing like wanting someone so bad and not being able to have them. It was not something I'd ever experienced—except, of course, with James Black. Back then I'd promised myself it would never happen again, and I meant it.

Trying my best to push Aaron to the back of my mind, I got off the Long Island Expressway at exit 39 and then headed east to deal with Maxwell Frye, the other man who was constantly on my mind these days. He had asked—well, more like insisted—that I come see him, because as he put it, we had unfinished business.

I checked out my surroundings as I followed the directions of my GPS through Old Westbury, Long Island. It seemed like each house I passed was bigger than the last until they were all mansions. My eyes almost bugged out of my head and my stomach fluttered as I drove through the winding streets with football field–length driveways. There was no doubt about it: Every house I saw had to run at least five million dollars. I didn't even know they allowed black folks to work in these communities, let alone live in them. Hell, I barely knew these neighborhoods existed so close to the city.

I pulled up to the guardhouse in front of Maxwell's gated community and had to wait for the guard to call Maxwell before I was allowed in. On the way over, I had seen so many beautiful, impressive houses, but nothing prepared me for the stately home where Maxwell lived. I gasped in awe as I pulled up into his long circular driveway. His house was a humongous two-story Tudor. I knew Maxwell was doing okay for himself, but I had no idea he was living like this. If I had, a whole lot of things would have been different back in the day, that was for sure.

If you thought I was shocked at the sight of Maxwell's home, you should have seen my face when I turned into his driveway and saw who was walking out the front door. Talk about doing a double take! It was none other than First Lady Monique Wilson.

The sight was so unexpected that I actually rubbed my eyes to make sure I wasn't seeing things. Now, I didn't want to jump to any conclusions, but what choice did I have? If this were late afternoon, or even six or seven o'clock in the evening, I'd just shrug it off because it could have been church business. However, it was eight o'clock in the morning, and her hair was all over her head. To top that off, I knew for a fact that the bishop was up in Boston at a gospel competition with Aaron and the choir.

Even if I wanted to believe there was a legitimate church reason for her to be at Maxwell's house this time of the morning, what happened next dispelled all doubt as to what Monique was doing there. Maxwell came out behind her wearing his robe like he was Hugh Hefner. He leaned in, and—if I can get ghetto for a moment—tongued her ass down.

I wasn't driving that fast, but the shock caused me to slam on my brakes, screeching to a halt right in front of the house and bringing their full attention to me. Monique made eye contact with me, then looked away, holding her head down. Now, that's what I call busted. Not only was I embarrassed for her, but I felt shame for her too. This was probably the end of our friendship as we knew it. Things would never be the same.

I waited in my car until after Monique pulled off in her Mercedes. Maxwell looked over at me with a smug grin. That's when I knew he'd wanted me to see the two of them kissing. For him, my arrival was nothing short of perfect timing. That son of a bitch wanted a witness. What a bastard. The last thing I needed on top of all my own drama was to be caught up in the drama that was sure to pop off between the bishop and Monique.

Maxwell met me near his front door. "What you just saw is between you, me, her, and the wood. Got that?"

I shrugged, but I couldn't hold my opinion, even if he did have me by the you-know-what. "You two are going to hell! Ain't no doubt about it! Ain't no asking for forgiveness for this. Don't you have any shame? Bishop Wilson is one of your best friends, and here you are screwing his wife!" I sneered at him. "You ain't shit, Maxwell."

Maxwell laughed. "Well, you know what they say: All's fair in love and war. Bishop Wilson's just losing the war."

I followed him into a foyer so large I could fit my whole house inside.

"Have a seat." It sounded more like a command than an invitation, and I had no choice but to obey because of the tight spot Maxwell had me in. I parked myself on a sofa made of leather so soft I could have made it my bed.

"Let me ask you something, Maxwell. Why do you hate Bishop Wilson? I thought he was your friend, but you act like he's the enemy."

"He's been the enemy for the past three years. He just doesn't know it."

"Really?" Maybe it was time for me to shut up, because I was confused.

"I genuinely loved the man like a brother," Maxwell started, "until I came back from Iraq to find out he was married to the woman I loved."

Okay, now this was getting crazy.

"Confused, right? Well, most people didn't know that before I left for Iraq, Monique and I were seeing each other."

"You and the first lady?"

Damn, Monique never told me about that. Guess we all have our secrets.

"She wasn't the first lady then. Back then she was just Monique."

I was surprised by the look of sincerity on his face as he explained, "She was the reason I went to Iraq in the first place—so I could afford a woman like her. And then I come back to visit, and she's married to my best friend." He looked around his opulent home. "Now I have all of this, and I can't even share it with her."

For a second I almost told him he could share it with me, because this brother was clearly rolling in dough. But the image of him tonguing down Monique in the driveway came to mind, and I realized he truly only had eyes for one woman. As crazy as it was, Maxwell Frye was in love with the bishop's wife.

I decided to test the waters, see how much information he would share. "So, I guess now the two of you are back together?"

"Sort of." He hesitated, rubbing his chin as if he knew what I was thinking and wasn't sure how much he should say. "We're trying to figure out how we're going to get the bishop out of the picture."

Call me a selfish bitch, but that gave me a glimmer of hope. Nothing like a good sex scandal in the church to take the focus off of me and our financial concerns. Then he broke the bad news to me: "And you're going to help us—that is, unless you'd rather spend the next twenty years in jail."

"Me?" Damn! I was going to be right up in the middle of this shit whether or not I wanted to be. "What do you mean, get him out of the picture? If you're talking about killing him, then I'll take my chances with the financial stuff and pray for a good lawyer and a sympathetic jury."

Maxwell laughed. "No, killing him would be too easy. There

are far worse things than death. A man's dignity and pride are very fragile things. Look at your partner in crime, Smitty."

"What are you talking about? What about him? Do you know why he killed himself?"

Again, that evil laugh escaped his mouth. "He was so ashamed of being on Jackie's list that when I called his wife and told her he was gay, he ended up killing himself."

"Jackie's list? Smitty was on Jackie's list?" You could have knocked me over with a wet noodle.

"He didn't make the actual list, but he was without question one of Jackie's lovers."

Oh my God! Smitty gay? No wonder he never looked at me in that way. Boy, had I been wrong about the reason for his suicide. My secret theory had always been that it had to do with me.

Yeah, that's right. Smitty and I were in cahoots. At first I was stealing because I needed to pay my father his share of the profits from the dealership, which I'd already spent. I continued because it was just too damn easy not to. Jonathan's motives for stealing were a mystery to me, mainly because I never bothered to ask. It was a partnership of convenience, not mutual affection. As the heads of the two most powerful boards at the church, we were able to cover up for each other so that our scam went undetected for quite a while.

Smitty came to me and told me he was done, that he didn't want to steal anymore, but I refused to stop dipping into the church funds. I'm sorry, but I just wasn't ready to give up my free-spending lifestyle. We finally came to an agreement: He was going to give me his half of our last job together, and then we would go our separate ways, each of us promising to carry the secret to our graves. I truly believed that he killed himself because the secret was eating him up, and he just wanted to get to his grave that much sooner. Maxwell's news was truly a bombshell.

"I can't believe Smitty was gay."

"Oh, he was gay, all right. One time about eight years ago when James and I were down in Atlantic City bar-hopping with a couple of fine-ass Spanish chicks—"

"Eight years ago?" I frowned.

"Oh, that's right. You and James were seeing each other about eight years ago, weren't you? Oops, my bad."

It was his bad, all right. He loved the fact that he could keep damn near spitting in my face. He wasn't the least bit sorry that he'd let that slip out—no more sorry than he was for me stumbling upon him and Monique.

"Just finish your story, Maxwell."

"Yeah, right. Well, we happened to go into this one bar. Now, it only takes about five seconds for us to realize this was a gay bar. James and I, we were ready to hightail it the hell out of there, but the two Spanish chicks think it's cute and wanna stay and have a drink. Like I said, they're fine, so we stayed." Maxwell chuckled. "Next thing you know, we're looking at the dance floor, and there's Jackie and Smitty bumping and grinding. Now, you know James. He thinks he's a professional photographer, and he's always got a digital camera, so he starts taking pictures of these two on the DL. They never even saw us. And no one was the wiser until I started blackmailing Smitty with information and James gave T. K. the file with pictures."

"Don't you feel any guilt behind his death?" I realized what a stupid question that was as soon as I asked it. Maxwell wouldn't feel bad about running over his neighbor's dog.

"Smitty was a means to an end. He could have made a lot of money, and I would have never told his wife if he had kept his mouth shut and did what he was told. He was stupid. My question for you is, do you wanna make a lot of money and stay out of jail, or are you stupid too?"

"Yeah, I wanna make a lot of money, and no, I'm not stupid. But what I still don't understand is where all the money went. I know Smitty and I took some, but for the church to be in such bad shape, someone had to have taken a lot more."

"Let's just say there is someone else taking money, too, and when he's exposed, the church will come tumbling down."

I was astounded by the depth of Maxwell's hatred for Bishop Wilson. "Are you serious? You're trying to destroy the church and ruin the bishop all in the name of love?"

"Yep, and I'm going to do it too. You, of all people, should understand, with the way things are going with you and Aaron."

He had some nerve bringing up my relationship with Aaron. But then again, he had a point. Maxwell was going through a great deal to be with the woman he loved. It made me wonder, was I doing enough when it came to being with Aaron? I needed to hurry up and finish this meeting with Maxwell so I could get back to work on winning over the man I loved.

Tia

45

Even though Aaron and I were sitting together, we didn't say too much during the first few minutes of the bus ride back home. That was because the choir members couldn't stop giving him praise. He was taking it all in for everything it was worth, but as he tired of it, he began to let on by saying, "To God be the glory, to God be the glory." Finally everyone let him be and talked amongst themselves.

"You know, eventually you are going to have to take some type of credit for how far this choir has come," I told him.

He gave me a nod. "A real leader doesn't have to tell people he's doing great things. The people who follow and believe in him can see it."

"I think you've been spending too much time with the bishop. You're starting to become quite the philosopher. Let me find out you gonna be a preacher one day," I teased.

"It crossed my mind a time or two," Aaron said with a chuckle. "I guess that would make you my first lady."

I took hold of his hand. "In order to be a first lady, you have to be married. I'm not even sure if I'm your girlfriend."

He stared at me, momentarily speechless. "Um, Tia, I thought we were just kidding around here. Aren't we getting ahead of ourselves?"

I lifted our hands, which were still clasped together. "Maybe for you, but I don't operate in the world of casual sex and emotions."

"Tia, I know I like you . . . but I just broke up with Simone."

Aaron and I had shared something far greater than just the winning of a competition. We'd shared a moment, our own private moment. Although I'd spent a great deal of time with him before, that kiss moved our friendship into a whole different realm—at least as far as I was concerned. But if he wasn't ready to turn in his player card, then I needed to give him an out now, before things went any further and I got myself hurt.

"Look, Aaron, I understand." I turned my body toward his. "I am not mad about that kiss. As if you couldn't tell, I welcomed it." I felt the heat of embarrassment flush my cheeks and hoped he didn't notice. "If it was something you did just because you were caught up in the moment, I'll take it as just that and move on." I paused and then decided to just go for it. "But if it was more . . . if it was the beginning of something real, then I'd love to see where we could take things."

"Oh, Tia, it was real," he admitted. "I must admit, though, I shocked myself. I don't know where it came from. It must have come from a feeling I had buried deep down inside up until now. But I guarantee you, those feelings were real."

I could hear his words, and they sounded sincere, but that wasn't enough. There was something else I needed to get straight.

"Simone, Porsche . . . I'm not them. I don't play those kinds of games. I don't do one-night stands and I don't—"

"Shhh." He gently pressed his index finger over my lips. "I know you are not Simone or Porsche, and that's why I'm so drawn to you."

"But women like them are what you're used to. And I'm so different from them, Aaron, in so many ways."

"Good, because if I wanted a woman like that, I'd have one. But I want you, Tia. The more I think about it, the more I realize I've wanted you since the day I met you on the stairs of the church."

Okay, I was blushing again, hard, and there was no way he didn't notice this time. But I had to pull myself together. There was still another ground rule to discuss, and when it came to a man like Aaron, I worried it could be the deal breaker.

"I've been living a celibate lifestyle, Aaron, and if you and I were to take this thing between us to another level, you need to know that I've made a vow that I'm going to remain celibate until marriage."

"Hmmm, is that so?" He leaned back, studying my face.

"That's so," I confirmed.

That's when I expected him to turn around, slump down in his seat, and act like I wasn't there anymore. He did turn around, but he wasn't pouting. He looked like he was deep in thought. My heart palpitated. Before anything had even really happened between us, it was about to be over.

"Well, then . . ." He sighed. "I guess that makes me celibate too." He leaned in and kissed me—and I swear I heard a few choir members around us offering quiet applause.

Monique

46

I stood trembling as I scrubbed my body ferociously, salty tears streaming down my face and mixing with the shower spray. I was trying to get Maxwell's revolting scent off me. This was my fourth shower in the past three hours. I felt used, disgusting, inside and out. How can you wash away sin? I'd been called a whore, a slut, a jezebel, and a hundred other derogatory names in my life, but none of them ever bothered me because I knew they weren't true. Now I couldn't say that about being called an adulteress, because I was one. I'd broken my vow to God, to T. K., and to myself to be faithful. I honestly didn't think I could go any lower.

Now I understood how Jonathan Smith must have felt when he committed suicide. He just wanted the pain of life to go away, to feel free again. I felt the same way, like nothing short of death was ever going to make me whole again.

T. K. would never forgive me if he found out what I'd done, what I'd allowed Maxwell to do. My reason for doing it wouldn't matter. I'd done it so that he wouldn't go to jail for crimes he'd committed, but T. K. would still never be able to stay married to an adulteress.

Regardless of the consequences to my marriage, though, I had no choice but to sleep with Maxwell. There was no doubt that he would have gone through with sending T. K. to jail if I hadn't complied, and I loved my husband enough to do anything for him. Yes, T. K. was wrong for stealing from the church, but I just couldn't let him go to jail. All the good he'd done by preaching the Word every week far outweighed this one lapse in judgment.

As disgusting as it was, I looked at sleeping with Maxwell as the only way to allow T. K. to continue to do good works. Maybe one day I would find a way to bring up the subject and convince him to stop stealing.

I didn't think I'd ever get the memory of Maxwell crawling on top of me out of my mind. I could still feel his rough hands moving from one section of my body to the other and his chapped lips kissing me in places they had no business being. I know technically it wasn't rape, but it sure felt like it. I felt violated and ashamed. What made it even worse was that I had to pretend that I was enjoying it, because when I didn't, he'd remind me of my husband's future if his police officer friend made one call to the district attorney's office.

God, if I could have just found a way to talk him out of it. I had hoped that by the time we got to his house I could reason with Maxwell's compassionate side, but I soon found out that he didn't have one. All he cared about was fulfilling his fantasy of getting me naked in his bedroom so that he could do his business. For a man with a heart condition, he sure didn't act like it. He had this warped recollection of the different things we used to do in the bedroom, like he'd fantasized about them so often that he truly believed we'd done those nasty things, and I swear he wanted to relive every one of them.

As if being intimate with him wasn't bad enough, the way he kissed me, making me trade saliva with him in front of Simone, had to be the low point of my life. I will never forget the look on Simone's face when we made eye contact. As scandalous as Simone had been lately, I could tell even she looked down on me for what I had done. I didn't think I would ever be able to look her in the face again.

I let out an anguished scream in the shower. I wished God would strike down Maxwell for putting me in this position, but I had no faith that God would bring me justice. For the first time in my life, I felt angry at God. He was supposed to look out for His servants, so how could He put me in this position?

I collapsed into an exhausted heap on the shower floor. Once again, suicide came to mind. I didn't think I could do it with a gun like Jonathan had, but there was a whole bottle of sleeping pills in the medicine cabinet that would do the trick. I lay there in the shower until the water ran cold, trying to gather the courage to get the sleeping pills and swallow them all.

"Hey, hon, I'm home."

I almost jumped out of my skin when I heard T. K.'s voice. I was in such a daze I hadn't even heard him open the bathroom door. What was he doing home anyway? He wasn't supposed to be here for at least another six hours.

"We won! We won the regional championship. Can you believe it? We're going to nationals. Boy, that Aaron is something else."

"That's great," I mumbled halfheartedly, hoping he'd go away so I could get myself together.

"Hey, why don't we celebrate our choir's victory in a spontaneous, romantic way?" Through the beveled shower glass, I could see him slipping out of his clothes, and suddenly my heart was in my mouth. "It's been a while since we've taken a shower together."

No, no, no, please, Lord. Haven't I had to deal with enough today?

"T. K., honey, I'm just about to get out."

"Well, stay in. I missed my wife so much. Trust me. I'll make it worth your while." I watched as T. K. slipped off his boxers.

"I missed you, too, but . . ." My heart hammered in my chest.

I'm not going to have sex with him, I vowed. *I don't even know if I can look him in the face right now. Dear God, please do something.*

I was prepared to lie to avoid him, tell him it was that time of the month or something, when his phone went off.

Thank you, Jesus! I thought I was literally being saved by the bell, until I realized he planned on ignoring it. He was about to step into the shower with me.

I turned my back in case my eyes were swollen from crying. "Honey, get your phone."

"I'm not going to answer that." He chuckled as he pressed up against me from behind, shivering when he felt the cold water. "I've got other things on my mind."

"That never stopped you before. Baby, please answer the phone," I pleaded. "You never know who it could be."

Finally, he relented, stepping out of the shower to retrieve his phone.

"Hello . . . Yes, this is Bishop Wilson. . . . What? . . . Oh, Lord."

I cut off the water and stepped out of the shower as fast as I could. He was standing there almost in a daze.

"What happened?" I asked, wrapping a large bath towel around myself.

"It's James. He's taken a turn for the worse. His left lung collapsed."

"Oh my goodness. That's horrible."

T. K. sighed. "Go ahead and get dressed. We need to get to the hospital. I'm gonna call Maxwell. I'm sure he's going to want to meet us over there."

The Bishop

47

I got up from behind my desk and walked over to the mini refrigerator in my office. I pulled out two Snapple iced teas, glancing over at Maxwell, who was sitting in his usual chair to the left of my desk. Simone Wilcox had just left my office with an offer from Pelican Trading Company to purchase the senior housing property. The offer was for three million dollars, one million more than the previous offer we'd received, but nothing close to what we had invested in the property or owed to creditors.

I held up a bottle. "You want one of these?"

"Yeah, I'll take one."

I tossed Maxwell a Snapple and headed back behind my desk.

"So, what do you think? Should we sell for the three million?"

He opened his drink and took a long swig. "I'm not sure, but the clock is ticking. We need to have that property sold before we appear in front of the bankruptcy court judge."

"I know, Maxwell, but for three million dollars? James told me the property is worth at least five, maybe more." I tried to open the Snapple, but for the life of me I couldn't get the plastic ring off the top of the bottle. My nerves were shot, and it wasn't because of the bankruptcy. My wife and I were having problems in the bedroom, and it was starting to get to me.

"Well, why doesn't James get us a better deal, then? I mean, with all due respect, the guy's been out of the real estate business for almost three years. I've got as much respect for James as anybody—you know that—but the man's lung just collapsed and he's on his deathbed. It's not like he's out there trying to find us a better deal."

"I understand what you're saying, Maxwell. I just don't want us to get shortchanged." No matter how hard I tried, I couldn't open the bottle. I flexed my fingers in frustration. I hoped I wasn't getting arthritis. "Doggone it!"

"Hey, Bishop, let me get that off for you."

Maxwell gestured for me to give him the bottle. I sighed and handed the bottle to him. Maxwell opened it in a mere flick of the wrist. I was too melancholy to even feel jealousy at his better physical strength. I was about five years older than Maxwell, and for the first time, I was beginning to feel my age.

"Listen, Bishop, about this property. I'll hold Simone off for the next week or two so we can listen to any new offers, but after that I'm gonna have to let her pull the trigger on this deal. Fair enough?"

I took a sip of my Snapple. "Fair enough." I guess I was looking downhearted, because Maxwell sat and studied me for a while.

"What seems to be the problem? You've been in the dumps the last couple of days. Is everything all right?" He spoke like a true friend. I'm sure he knew without me saying that something was on my mind.

"I don't know . . ." I hesitated.

"What's wrong with you? This whole thing with the bankruptcy got you down?"

"No, I can deal with that. My problem is more personal." I glanced at a picture of my wife. She was so beautiful.

"Oh, so now we don't talk about personal things anymore?"

"It's not just about me. It has something to do with my wife too."

Maxwell leaned forward, an interested look on his face. "T. K., what's going on? You guys having problems or something?"

I shrugged. "I'm not sure. All I know is my wife won't be intimate with me. It's been two weeks since we've had relations."

"Relations? Who are you, Bill Clinton?" Maxwell chuckled.

"We haven't had sex, made love, okay? Is that what you want to hear? My goodness, Maxwell, this is my marriage we're talking about here."

"It sure is, isn't it?" Maxwell tried to lighten the mood by teasing, "You know, you are getting a little older now. Maybe you're not ringing her bell the way you used to."

He laughed, making me feel much better—not!

"That's not funny." I frowned, scrunching up my brow. "I ring her bell just fine when she lets me."

"Hey, she's a young woman. She needs a stallion to ride, not a pony." His eyes sparkled with mischief. "Is the elevator still going to the top floor?"

"Of course it is!" I was not amused by his insinuation.

I'd always taken care of myself, and I hadn't slept around a lot when I was young. As a result, impotence had never been a problem for me, and I was still virile. I shook my head. "It's not a problem with me getting it up. It's a problem with my wife not wanting me anymore."

Maxwell's face became serious for a moment. "You don't believe that, do you? That Monique doesn't want you anymore?"

"I don't know what I believe, Maxwell."

"Well, maybe you should do some of the things you used to do when you first started dating."

"Man, I made a candlelight dinner and the whole nine the other night. When she finished eating, I thought she was going upstairs to put on a sexy nightgown or something, but when I got up there, she was asleep. The sad thing is, I don't think she was really asleep. I think she was trying to avoid making love to me. She never even touches me anymore. I can't stand this, Maxwell. I'm a very physical man."

Maxwell leaned in, looking me directly in the eye. "You think she might be fooling around? Maybe that secret admirer of hers finally won her over."

"My wife would never fool around," I snapped. I felt insulted that he would even suggest the possibility. We had a good marriage, a good sex life—that is, up until now. It was probably something stupid. Maybe she was going through the change or something, but no way was she cheating.

Maxwell held up his hands and leaned back. "Excuse me, Bishop. I didn't mean no harm. Hey, maybe you need to hit the gym. Maybe she doesn't see you as appealing as when you first got married."

"I probably could hit the gym," I conceded. I glanced down at the paunch around my middle. I was the same weight as when we met, though, so I didn't think that was the issue either.

"I would go to the gym with you, but I've got a heart condition. Plus, I'm getting my exercise other ways." He smoothed his mustache and flashed a sly grin.

"Yeah, I'm sure with all those young girls you're always messing with. Maxwell, when you gonna settle down anyway?"

"I've got a prospect waiting for me at the Marriott as we speak. You might even say she's the girl of my dreams."

"Well, good luck. Finding the girl of your dreams isn't easy. Women like that are worth fighting over."

"Who you telling? Believe me, I feel the same way." Maxwell stood up, shook the creases back into his pants, then came over to pat me on the back. "Well, Bishop, I'm outta here. Don't want to keep the little lady waiting."

I turned to Maxwell and nodded. "So, when am I going to meet this mystery woman?"

"If I have my way, sooner than you think, Bishop. Much sooner than you think."

Simone

48

I walked out of the bathroom an emotional wreck with tears and mascara running down my face. Ever since I heard the rumor that Aaron and Tia were together, I couldn't stop crying, and the fact that I'd just started my period didn't help things one bit. I'd been praying to God that somehow I might be pregnant with Aaron's child. We'd had a little slipup the last time we made love, and the condom broke. I told Aaron I was going to the pharmacy to get the morning-after pill, but I never did. Then Daddy had his stint in the hospital, and I slipped up, causing Aaron to break up with me—which, I might add, was totally unfair. Okay, so I lied to him, but I was going to tell him the truth after everything got settled.

All of this was plain ridiculous. I couldn't believe Aaron was really holding one little lie against me. He and I were made for each other. I was born to be not only his woman, but also his baby's momma, dammit!

All right, so if I wasn't pregnant with Aaron's baby, then it was time to decide my next plan of action, because crying all day wasn't going to get me anywhere. I wiped my tears away and gave the whole situation some serious thought. And of course, because I had plenty of practice at "storytelling," I came up with something in no time: Just because I wasn't pregnant didn't mean I couldn't say I was pregnant. A man of God like Aaron, who was on his way to stardom, couldn't afford not to marry me. He'd lose all credibility. Once we were back together, I'd just have to get pregnant in a hurry. Heck, I was young enough, and my friend Mary worked in a fertility clinic. She could get me some of those fertility drugs to speed up the process.

Shit, if I played this thing right, I wouldn't even have to go to Aaron; he'd end up crawling back to me. All I had to do was whisper in the right ears that I was pregnant with his child and that I planned on having the baby without his help, since he didn't want anything to do with us. That would make him come running quick.

I thought about picking up the phone and calling Monique in order to start the gossip chain with her. I knew Monique. She'd be the first to pull Aaron aside and read him the riot act for his actions. Then again, after busting her over at Maxwell's place last week, I'd been avoiding her like the plague. I mean, what do you say to a woman after catching her cheating on her preacher husband with his best friend? Now, that was some drama worthy of a Lifetime movie!

So instead, I picked up the phone and called Sister Judith Hampton, one of the elders in the choir. Sister Judith loved her some Aaron. In fact, she was always telling people he was her godson. She'd put him in his place, and if he didn't do the right thing by me and the baby, she'd talk about him like a dog. She would be the first of four phone calls I'd make that day, and if I didn't get a response from Aaron, I'd make another four calls the next night. Mr. Mackie was going to live up to his responsibility as an expectant father—and even if he wasn't an expectant father yet, it wouldn't take long before I had him by the balls.

"Praise God," Sister Judith answered jubilantly.

"Hey, Sister Judith, this is Trustee Wilcox."

"Hey there, Trustee. Did you hear about the regional gospel championship we won last week?" Sister Judith always sounded so happy.

"I did. Congratulations."

"That Aaron Mackie sure is something, isn't he?"

"He sure is, Sister. As a matter of fact, I wanted you to pray with me for him."

"Sure. Is everything all right with him?" Her voice wasn't so upbeat anymore.

"Well, Sister, we're all human, and we all have faults. I don't want to tell his business or mine, but I just want you to pray for us both and hope he decides to—"

I was interrupted by a knock at my door. I thought about ignoring it but decided not to, on the off chance that it was Aaron.

"Sister, I'll call you back in a minute. I might not need that prayer after all."

I jumped up off the sofa and dried my eyes, ran my hands through my hair, and then got a glimpse of myself in the hall mirror. My eyes looked all red and bleary, and I had dark bags under them. I pinched my cheeks to bring back some color but decided not to worry too much about my looks. If it was Aaron at the door, I wanted him to see how I'd suffered. He'd take me in his arms and ask for my forgiveness. Unfortunately, with my period being here and all, we wouldn't be able to have that bomb makeup sex, but I'd give him the blow job of a lifetime. I was getting hot just thinking about it.

I flung the door open in anticipation of my fantasy coming true but got a rude awakening. Standing there with scowls on their faces were the two thugs who'd pulled up on me and Aaron in the parking lot.

"Can I help you?" I held the doorknob tightly, hoping I could shut the door fast enough if they tried something.

"We're looking for Aaron Mackie," the tall one said brusquely.

"He doesn't live here." I tried to close the door, but the shorter one put his hand out.

"Well, is he here?"

"No, he's not here. I thought you were him." Come to think of it, these guys had just fucked up my fantasy. I felt myself becoming irate. "Who are you, anyway?"

"Don't worry about who we are," the tall guy snarled. "You expecting him anytime soon?"

"Why? What do you want with him?"

The short one took out a card and wrote something on the back, then pushed it into my hand. "Just give him this when you see him."

I watched the men walk back to their car before I glanced down at what the shorter one had written on the card. All it said was *Call me.*

I flipped the card over, and what I saw made my stomach lurch.

"Oh, shit! Talk about having someone by the balls. If I were you, Aaron Mackie, I'd be very nice to Simone Wilcox. Very nice."

Monique

49

Until I sat down at the bar and ordered a drink, I couldn't believe I had actually come inside this place. At least the last time, Maxwell had given me a room number so I could wait for him without the risk of being seen. I'd sat in my car for ten minutes before finally getting the courage to get out and make the trek to the door. Of all the times to be prompt in my life, it was under these circumstances. But here I sat at the bar of the Brooklyn Marriott, working on my second dirty martini. That was the only appropriate drink for this occasion, something dirty, because that's just how I felt—like a dirty whore.

When Maxwell sent me a text demanding I meet him at this hotel, everything in me just wanted to text him back "go fuck yourself," but I didn't. I couldn't, because I knew what he would do. He'd have T. K. arrested and sent to prison, and because I loved T. K.'s dirty drawers, I would never be able to deal with that.

"Another drink, miss?" the bartender asked.

I looked down at my almost empty martini glass. "Just one more," I replied as I picked the olive out of the glass. "Make it a double, if you don't mind."

The bartender turned to fix my drink. He couldn't fix it strong enough to suit me, though, because all I wanted was to be numb. I looked down at my watch. Maxwell was going on fifteen minutes late. Why did he have me sitting there for just anybody to spot me? Then again, that's probably exactly what he wanted. In his sick mind, he probably thought that if everything was out in the open, T. K. would leave me and I'd come running to him. Not in this lifetime. Not after what he was putting me through. I didn't give a damn how much money he had.

"Here you are."

This time I jumped at the sound of the bartender's voice. I was paranoid. Maxwell needed to hurry his ass up. If he wasn't there in fifteen minutes, I was outta there. I was not sticking around for the happy-hour crowd.

"Thank you." I picked up my drink and took a sip.

"And could you please bring me back a shot of 1800? I need something to chase my little blue pill," Maxwell asked the bartender. I was in such a daze that he'd snuck up right behind me. "Sorry I'm late, sweetness." When he bent down and kissed me on the neck with his chapped lips, I thought I was going to puke.

I gulped down my martini. I needed a buzz and quick.

"You're looking quite lovely," he complimented.

I hadn't yet spoken a word to him. There were no words. I just wanted to get him up in that room, let him do his business, and get the hell outta there.

The bartender brought Maxwell's drink.

"Thank you," Maxwell said, shoving a pill in his mouth before picking up the shot glass and swallowing it down in one gulp. I jumped when he slammed it back on the bar. He pulled out his billfold and peeled off a hundred-dollar bill and said to the bartender, "That's for me and the lady. Keep the change."

I could feel him staring at me as if I should be impressed by his little act, but I wasn't. I was repulsed by his presence in all ways.

"So, you ready?"

Now I spoke as I turned on the stool and faced him. "Ready for what?"

He shook his head and half smiled. "Do you really have to ask? We're in a hotel bar. What do you think?" He pulled a key card out of his pocket. "Let's go. I've already checked us in." He went to walk away, but I stayed right where I was sitting. "Come on, let's go. There's a king-size bed in a suite with our names all over it. I figured this could be our new thing, Thursday evening at the Marriott." He leaned in and I could feel his lips brushing against my ear. "It beats that stupid step class you're supposed to be at, and you get your exercise too."

He led me to the elevator and our room. I kept my head down

and my eyes on the floor. If someone from the church just happened to be in the lobby, I couldn't bear to see the look of disgust on their faces when they spotted us together.

Once we entered our room, Maxwell began kissing my neck. I didn't respond, but that didn't make him stop—until he announced, "I think my little blue pill is starting to take effect. God, it's amazing what you can buy off the Internet, isn't it?" He cupped his penis like I was supposed to admire it or something. "I'm going to the bathroom. When I come back, the old Monique better be here, undressed and waiting for me on the bed, ready, willing, and able."

I knew that wasn't a request, but an order. Maxwell went into the bathroom, and I sat down on the bed and began to remove my clothing. All the alcohol in the world couldn't erase the horror of what was going on. I was T. K.'s wife and Maxwell's whore. What a combination.

I reached into my bag and pulled out the Percocet that T. K. had been prescribed when he broke his arm last year. As tears fell from my eyes, I took two pills dry, swallowing them whole. The thought of just downing the entire bottle came to mind, but the last place I wanted to be found was in a hotel room Maxwell had paid for. I knew he'd make sure to rub that in T. K.'s face before he sent him to jail.

"I can't do this anymore." I stood up as Maxwell exited the bathroom wearing nothing but his briefs. As much as I didn't want T. K. going to jail, something had to give, because I was thinking about suicide too frequently. "I love my husband. I don't want him to go to jail, but I don't want to hurt him by sleeping with a man who pretends to be his friend either."

Maxwell didn't seem moved one way or the other. "If you don't go through with this, Monique, you know what I'm going to do. Or maybe I should just call him and tell him where his dear wife is?"

"Don't bother. I'll tell him myself," I said, and I meant it. I meant it all the way up until Maxwell took out his cell phone and extended it to me.

"Here, call him, then. Tell him everything." He opened his phone and pressed a number. "I have him on speed dial. Matter of fact, let me make it easier for you." He pressed speaker, and I could hear the phone ringing.

T. K.'s voice came on the line. I could have died right then and there. "What's up, Maxwell? Thought you had a hot date."

Maxwell smiled. "I do, and she's right here. She wanted to talk to you, so I was going to put her on the phone." He looked at me, daring me with his eyes. "Here, honey, say hello to my best friend, Bishop T. K. Wilson. T. K., she's a big fan. Matter of fact, she might like you more than she likes me."

As Maxwell came closer, I shook my head and gestured for him to shut off his phone. My eyes flooded with tears.

"You know, T. K., she's feeling a little shy all of a sudden. Maybe next time. I'll talk to you later."

"Talk to you later, Maxwell. Don't do anything I wouldn't do."

"Au contraire. I plan on doing everything you would do and a whole lot more," Maxwell said with a laugh, and then shut the phone. His mouth formed into a smile as he stared at me. "I take it you're about to take your clothes off, because my little blue pill has me ready to get this party started."

With no other options, I did as I was told. I just hoped the Percocet kicked in as quickly as his Viagra had, because I didn't want to feel a thing.

The Bishop

50

I entered James's hospital room to find him flanked by two white men I'd never seen before. James had summoned me there for a meeting about something that he felt could save the church. I sure hoped he had something good, because we had run out of other options. At Maxwell's urging, we had decided to go forward with the three-million-dollar offer on the senior housing property. I'd recently signed papers agreeing to go into negotiations with Pelican Trading Company, so the clock was ticking. Unless some sort of miracle happened, we would be selling that property at a huge loss.

"James, I'd like you to meet Aaron Mackie," I introduced.

I'd brought along Monique, Tia, and Aaron to visit with James. He had wanted to meet our new choir director for quite some time, and the way he looked now, I was glad I hadn't waited any longer to bring Aaron by. James barely had the strength to lift his arm and shake Aaron's hand. He was now wearing an oxygen mask instead of the tubes in his nose. I didn't need a doctor to tell me that my old friend didn't have much longer.

James lifted the mask with his free hand. "It's a pleasure to meet you, young man. I've heard a lot of good things about you."

Aaron's face lit up. "Likewise, sir. Bishop and First Lady Wilson have told me so much about you. I feel like I'm meeting a legend."

It was evident from James's smile that this made him feel good, though he said humbly, "Legends aren't always good, young man, but I appreciate the sentiment."

James said hello to Monique and Tia, and then turned back to me, pointing at the two white men. It was now time for him to make introductions. "T. K., this is Mr. Robert Cohn and Mr. Michael Goldberg. They're from Forest Hills Property Management, and they have a proposal to make you on the senior housing property."

I shook both men's hands. "Well, I'm willing to listen to anything you gentlemen have to say."

"Thank you, Bishop Wilson," Mr. Cohn replied. "We've put in calls to Ms. Simone Wilcox several times to find out if our offer to buy the senior housing property was approved, but we got no response. From what James has told us, he doesn't think the offer was ever presented to you. He told us that time was of the essence, so at his request, he set up this meeting and we're contacting you directly."

My eyes went from James to Monique. "Yes, time is of the essence. We only have a week before our follow-up meeting with the bankruptcy lawyers. And James is correct—Simone hasn't told us of any offer from you."

Goldberg handed me a folder as Cohn continued to speak. "We made her a ten-million-dollar offer for the property, with a five-day turnaround for payment. We can have a cashier's check in your hands Tuesday morning."

I couldn't believe my ears. I looked at James and said, "With ten million dollars, we wouldn't have to go through bankruptcy."

He nodded his head as if to say "I told you so." James had always told me the property was worth at least five million, and as usual, he was right.

Cohn continued his pitch. "Bishop Wilson, we think that's a fair price. The buildings are almost done, and we plan to make them into condos. From what we're hearing, our offer is only slightly better than our competitors', but our turnover time is much quicker."

"Competitors?"

"From what I'm hearing, there were quite a few bids. I've been in real estate for most of my life. Recession or not, that price for one hundred units on Merrick Boulevard is a good deal for us all."

I couldn't begin to comprehend why Simone hadn't informed us of this bid, not to mention all the others that were supposedly made, but I knew James. If he had brought these men here, then it was his way of telling me that this was the best deal for the church. We could sort out the mess with Simone later. In the meantime, I was not about to let these men out of the room without securing this deal.

"Mr. Cohn, Mr. Goldberg, if you can really turn things over by Tuesday, you've got yourself a deal. I'll call an emergency meeting of the joint boards and get this done tonight."

"Well, in that case, I'll have our attorneys prepare the paperwork and have it over to your office in the morning."

We shook hands, a gentlemen's agreement that we had a deal. "Thank you, gentlemen. Thank you very much."

"Don't thank us. Thank your friend over there."

I turned to James and he winked at me. Once again, my good friend had pulled off what others couldn't, and from his deathbed, no less.

After Cohn and Goldberg left, we made so much noise whooping and hollering that a nurse had to come down and threaten to kick us out.

When we finally calmed ourselves, I turned to James. "Thank you, friend."

James lifted the oxygen mask. "You're welcome. Now, call that bitch Simone and find out why she didn't tell you about those other offers."

I pulled out my cell phone. "Doing it right now."

I dialed her number and she answered. "This is Simone."

"Good afternoon, Simone. This is Bishop Wilson. I'm calling an emergency meeting of the joint boards. I've found a ten-million-dollar buyer for the senior housing property."

There was a muffled hesitation on the line, almost as if she had covered up the phone and was speaking to someone else. "Bishop, I'm sorry to say it, but we just closed on that property ten minutes ago."

I almost dropped the phone. "Excuse me, you did what?" I shouted. "To whom and for how much?" Oh my God, this couldn't be happening. This woman had to be the most incompetent businessperson in the country.

"We sold the property to Pelican Trading Company for three million dollars. You signed the papers yourself, remember?"

"I did no such thing! I signed papers agreeing to negotiate with them."

"Bishop, I'm not sure what you think you signed, but I have the papers right here in front of me. Didn't you read them before you put your signature on them?"

The truth was I hadn't read them carefully. Maxwell had brought the papers to me when I was rushing off to officiate a wedding, and I'd signed them without giving it much thought. Just like James, I trusted Maxwell to have the church's best interest in mind. Even after I'd signed them, he'd agreed to hold on to them for at least another week before moving forward. I had no idea how we'd gone from that point to now, with Simone insisting that the property was already sold.

"Simone, listen to me very carefully. You have to undo that closing. Tell them we will pay a million dollars to negate the deal. They can't say no to a profit like that."

"Bishop, they're not going to do it. The buyer already has plans to make them into condos. Besides, the funds have already been allocated to our creditors."

As I paced back and forth, I could feel James's eyes on me. I really wished this conversation was happening elsewhere. I wasn't sure James would be strong enough to handle this type of stress.

"Simone, why didn't you tell me you were closing today?" There was something she wasn't telling me. I could tell by the shakiness of her voice.

"The buyer called me this morning and said we had to make this happen today or the deal was off. I was busy getting everything together. I'm sorry. I'm just one person. I thought Maxwell would tell you."

"Maxwell knew?" Now I was both angry and confused.

"Yes, of course he knew. The closing was at his office. He's sitting right across from me."

"What? Put him on the phone!"

Again there was a muffled conversation on the other end, and then Simone said, "I'm sorry but he's busy right now. He says he'll talk to you later."

I flipped my phone closed, fighting the urge to throw it against the wall. "Fuck!"

The profanity that escaped my lips took everyone off guard.

James pulled down his mask and struggled to sit up in the bed. "Calm down and tell me what's going on, T. K."

"They sold the property to Pelican Trading Company for three million dollars."

"Oh, no," Aaron and Tia said in unison.

Monique said, "How is that possible? Can Simone even do that without you present?"

I started to explain what Simone had told me about the papers that I'd supposedly signed, but James stopped me.

"Hold on a minute. What was the name of the company that bought the property?"

"Pelican Trading Company."

"That son of a bitch." James shook his head.

"Who?"

"Back in the nineties, I used to do a lot of business with Pelican Trading Company. I helped the owner start the business and sold him a lot of property as his exclusive Realtor. I didn't even know he still did any business under that company name."

"Well, apparently he does, and he just bought our property. You think you can talk him into selling it back to us for a small profit?"

James shook his head. "I doubt it. The owner of that company is a pretty shrewd dude. He wouldn't sell unless he was going to make a huge profit. Knowing this guy, he may end up selling it to Cohn and Goldberg for fifteen million."

Just when I thought I'd heard enough to make my knees buckle, James threw the knockout punch.

"T. K., you're never gonna believe who the owner of that company is."

"Who?" Nothing could have prepared me for James's answer.

"Maxwell Frye."

Monique

51

"Maxwell Frye. Maxwell Frye . . ." T. K. kept mumbling under his breath as we sped down the Grand Central Parkway, weaving in and out of traffic toward Queens Boulevard and Maxwell's Rego Park office. We were headed there to confront Maxwell about the scam he had pulled with the senior housing property.

I glanced over at the speedometer. T. K. was doing eighty, and if traffic had allowed, I'm sure he would have pushed one hundred miles an hour. Tia and Aaron were sitting in the backseat. From the look on Tia's face, she was horrified by my husband's driving.

Thank God no one could see the look on my face. It probably looked like I had an upset stomach. That's just what I felt like inside, like I'd eaten something rotten and it was just sitting there covered with maggots. I know that sounds nauseating, but it was the truth. How else was I supposed to feel? I hadn't been in the same room with both T. K. and Maxwell since he started blackmailing me and our bi-weekly rendezvous started. I didn't know how to act.

"Slow down, T. K.," I pleaded, gripping the door handle. I was scared to death, not so much because of the speed we were going, but because of the collision that was about to happen when he and Maxwell bumped heads at his office. I'd never seen him this mad.

I was about to be in the same room with my husband and the man I'd been sleeping with, and it was under the worst of circumstances. T. K. was ready for war. He was so fired up that it appeared as though he'd use every gun he had to shoot Maxwell down. My only worry was that Maxwell had all the ammunition. If T. K. pissed Maxwell off too much, no telling what Maxwell would say to get back at him.

"I'm sorry. I'm just trying to get there before that bastard leaves." He eased his foot off the gas pedal, but I could see the anger and frustration written all over his face. Part of me was afraid he was going to kill Maxwell, while the other part of me wished he would—as long as he didn't get caught.

"I know that, but what good is it going to do if we don't get there in one piece?"

He shifted his eyes in my direction and I shut up quickly.

When we arrived at Maxwell's office, T. K. screeched to a halt at the bus stop in front of the building and parked it there without a second thought. He jumped out of the car and headed straight for the elevator with me, Aaron, and Tia on his heels.

"Hey, wait a minute," Maxwell's receptionist protested as we stepped off the elevator and walked right past her.

"I'm here to see Maxwell," T. K. said as he continued down the hallway.

"But you need an appointment. Besides, he already has someone in his office."

By this time, T. K. had already flung open the door and stepped into Maxwell's spacious private office. I watched as he appraised the situation with a cool eye. I hung back, letting Tia and Aaron go into the office before me, because I was scared to death of what might happen when Maxwell saw my face.

"Well, Bishop, looks like I lose this one," Maxwell said sarcastically. He reached into his pocket, pulling out his billfold. He peeled off a hundred-dollar bill and handed it to none other than Simone, who was sitting next to him. "You know, I bet Simone a hundred dollars that you wouldn't come over here."

T. K. went straight to the point. "Do you own Pelican Trading Company?"

"Now, where would you get something like that?" Maxwell smirked and glanced over at Simone, who had the nerve to smirk too. I wanted to smack that bitch, but like Maxwell, she had information that could destroy my marriage, so I held back.

He reached into his pocket and stripped off another hundred-dollar bill from his billfold and handed that to Simone too. "James, right?"

"Yes, James told me. Now, answer my question. Do you own Pelican?"

Maxwell had a smug gleam in his eye. "Yes, Bishop, I own Pelican."

They stared each other down for the next few seconds. "Good, then this is going to be easier than I thought since I'm *friends* with the owner." T. K. took a deep breath. "Maxwell, I need you to sell the properties back to us so we can save the church."

I was proud of him. He'd put the deal on the table in the calmest way he knew how, considering the circumstances. I could anticipate Maxwell's answer, though, so I knew that it really didn't matter how T. K. carried himself.

Maxwell cleared his throat. "I'm sorry, but I can't do that."

"What do you mean you can't do that?"

I could see every muscle in T. K.'s body tense up.

"Because I'm turning that property into condos."

I saw my husband do a double take, as if he couldn't believe the man standing before him had been one of his closest friends, his confidant. If Maxwell got to running his mouth, T. K. would have more he couldn't believe.

Up until this point, Maxwell hadn't made eye contact with me. I'd stayed strategically positioned behind my husband, Tia, and Aaron.

"Buying that place for three million was a steal. I thought it was gonna cost me at least four or five million." Maxwell shook his head and smiled like the whole situation amused him.

"You mean to tell me that you would let the church go down just so you can make some money?"

Oh, no. T. K.'s veins were starting to pop. I imagined his blood boiling inside. I didn't need a monitor to tell that his blood pressure was rising. Hell, I didn't need one to tell that my own blood pressure was going up too.

"Yeah, I'd do it to the church."

Looking at the expressions of everyone in the room, I could tell that they were shocked by this arrogant bastard—everyone but me, and possibly Simone. I'd seen this side of Maxwell recently. Unfortunately, I'd seen more sides of him than I could stomach right now.

"But more importantly, T. K., I'd do it to you."

"Why, Maxwell? Why are you trying to destroy our church family?" T. K. was beside himself, throwing his hands up in exasperation. "You know what? Forget it. I don't even want to know." T. K. took a step toward the door, and I think I was the happiest person in the entire borough of Queens at that moment—that is, until Maxwell spoke up.

"Are you sure about that?" Maxwell was playing my husband like a cat toying with a cornered mouse.

It pained me so much to stand by and watch it all go down, but then again, wasn't I complicit in some way? After all, I could have warned T. K. a while ago that Maxwell wasn't who he thought he was, but after weighing my options and counting the cost, I felt keeping T. K. out of jail was more important. Now that I saw the depths of Maxwell's hatred, I wondered if his story about T. K. stealing money from the church was even true. Had he doctored the papers I saw in order to get me into his bed?

For the first time since we'd arrived, Maxwell's eyes found mine. I tried to reposition myself to avoid his gaze, but it was no good.

"T. K., don't you want to know why?" Maxwell looked at T. K. briefly, then right back at me, taunting me. I felt like I might pass out.

"No, I don't want to know."

I felt my breath catch in my throat. I had to resist the urge to grab T. K.'s arm and drag him out of there before Maxwell said any more. But it was too late anyway. Maxwell was hell-bent on dropping that bomb.

"Well, allow me to share with you anyway," Maxwell insisted. "The real reason is love. You know that old cliché all's fair in love and war? Well, this is about love, and me and you, we're at war."

T. K. turned back to him. "What are you talking about, Maxwell? Have you completely lost your mind?"

"Maybe I have lost it, but only because of the woman standing next to you." All heads turned in my direction. "Or should I say the woman standing behind you? Way behind you, I might add."

Suddenly, my protective instincts kicked in. How could I stand back here, practically hiding, as this animal, who had stabbed my husband in the back, prepared to drive the knife deeper? I boldly walked and stood next to my husband, almost daring Maxwell to confess my sins. At the same time, though, I was praying to God that he didn't call my bluff.

"What the heck are you talking about?" T. K. demanded.

"You took the only woman I've ever loved," Maxwell said, looking directly at me. "So, I'm taking your church, the only thing you've ever really loved."

"Huh?" T. K. looked dumbfounded. "Will somebody tell me what the hell he's talking about?" T. K. turned to me.

T. K. knew that before we got together, I'd been around the block a time or two, and he loved me nonetheless. Even so, he never knew that his friend had sat behind the wheel of the car.

"I'll tell you what I'm talking about." Maxwell decided to explain further while I stood there wishing I could disappear. "Before I went to Iraq, I fell in love with Monique. I went to Iraq to make money so I could marry her."

He pointed at me, and everyone's eyes followed his finger to look at me with puzzled expressions. Well, with the exception of Simone, who just shook her head. "When I came home to visit three years ago, you were married to her."

My husband turned to face me. Just like I couldn't bear to let him touch me in these past couple of weeks, I didn't want him to look at me right now. I felt too ashamed.

"Is this true?" T. K. asked me. I couldn't speak.

"Oh, it's true all right," Maxwell said, his face hardening.

All I could do was drop my head by way of admission.

"Why didn't you tell me?"

"Look, T. K., there was nothing to tell. We were through." I lifted my head to explain. My husband at least deserved that much respect from me.

"But my best friend?"

In a panic, I threw my hands in the air. I wanted nothing more than to escape. "I'm not going to discuss this right now. We have bigger issues to deal with. I'm going to the car."

And I did just that. I exited the office, but I didn't go far. I didn't think my legs would carry me. I stood right outside the door with my back against the wall, trying to steady my breathing and slow my heart rate. I'd felt so suffocated in that room. I had to get out, but I also needed to hear just how much more Maxwell was going to tell my husband about us.

While I was still within earshot, I heard Tia say to my husband, "Don't worry about her, Bishop. I can go see about her if you'd like."

I didn't hear a response from T. K., and Tia never came out. There was silence, too much silence, so I leaned in and peeked, just to see what was going on in there. What I saw was a staring contest between Maxwell and T. K. Simone sat at the desk, looking almost too afraid to speak.

Finally T. K. spoke, breaking the silence. "I don't ever want to see either of you in my church again."

"What do you mean, your church?" Maxwell scoffed. "Oh, that's right. You don't know yet, do you?"

"Know what?" T. K. demanded.

"You know, I was going to save this and let you get the notification by messenger, but I just can't resist. I want to see the expression on your face when you get the news."

"Get what news?"

I watched the scene with morbid fascination, kind of like when you drive by an accident and can't resist looking.

"Not only did I buy the property, but I bought the church's mortgage note from the bank too. By the way, you're three months behind on your mortgage, and I'm calling the entire note. Expect to get our documents in the morning. You have exactly thirty days to come up with the three million dollars you owe, or I'm going to close your ass down and have the sheriff lock you out."

"You wouldn't." There was almost a pleading quality to T. K.'s tone.

"Oh, yes, I would." Maxwell stood up and walked over to a scale model of some buildings he had on a table. "I've been planning this for quite some time. I've already got the plans drawn up for a shopping center to be built on the site. Take a look." He started pointing at various buildings.

For a moment, I thought lightning had struck T. K., the way his body shook with anger. That's when he lost it and lunged for Maxwell's throat. He missed, but in the process, he smashed that model to smithereens.

"I'll kill you, you son of a bitch! I'll kill you!"

Maxwell scampered away behind his desk.

Aaron jumped in and grabbed T. K.'s arms, holding him back to keep him from reaching Maxwell with a right hook. "Bishop! Bishop! He's not worth it. You don't want to go to jail. Not for him."

Damn right he didn't want to go to jail. Not after I'd been screwing Maxwell to keep him out of jail. My heart was still thundering in my chest, and I'd never been so filled with rage. I wanted to go in there and kick Maxwell's ass myself instead of peeking around the corner. I just couldn't believe that he was the same person I'd once cared for. The person in there now was a monster. Had I ever really known the man named Maxwell Frye?

"Bishop," Aaron pleaded. "Calm down. Calm down, Bishop. I got this."

Aaron pointed at Maxwell, his lips curled in disgust. "You ain't shit, Deacon Frye, and neither is that yellow bitch sitting next to you. You two deserve each other, you know that?" He turned back to T. K. "Don't worry about it, Bishop. When you hired me, you hired me to save the church," Aaron explained. "Well, I'll be damned if I'm not gonna do just that."

"What are you going to do, sing on the subway platform with a tin cup and take donations? Or do you have some rich uncle down there in those sticks you came from, choirboy? Give me a break." Maxwell laughed. "That church is mine, and so is the school."

"You keep underestimating me if you want to. There's a million-dollar first prize at the National Gospel Choir Competition this year, and the recording contract alone has a three-million-dollar signing bonus. I plan on winning that contract and donating my share to the church."

Maxwell glanced at Simone, looking annoyed.

"Don't look at that bitch. She can't help you. Look at a man when he's talking to you, 'cause thirty days from now, the bishop and I will be back here to shove a three-million-dollar check down your throat." On that note, Aaron wrapped his arm around T. K.'s shoulder and led him toward the door. "Come on, Bishop. Let's get out of here. The stink seems to be getting worse."

Simone

52

I sat in Maxwell's office in shock, still trying to digest the last ten minutes of my life. Had my ears just heard correctly? Had Aaron just called me out of my name? Had he just done the ultimate no-no and called a black woman the B word? Not just any black woman, but me? He wasn't calling me a bitch when I was sucking his . . . never mind. To top that off, he had the nerve to bring that heifer Tia up in my face again. As much as I hated to admit it, Aaron was slowly but surely becoming the enemy, and he had no idea what I did to my enemies.

"Wow, I guess you two won't be getting back together any time soon, huh?" Maxwell chuckled as he picked up the pieces to his model. "I know that had to hurt when he called you a bitch. I've never met a black woman who took that well. But I will say this much: He and Tia do make a cute couple, don't they?"

I shot him an evil glare. Leave it to Maxwell to pour salt into my wounds. You would think he'd have some loyalty to me. I'd just helped him destroy the church I practically grew up in. I didn't even want to think about what my father would say when he found out.

"Earth to Simone." Maxwell's antagonistic voice brought me out of my thoughts. "Don't let him get to you when you could be doing something else."

The underlying sinister tone in Maxwell's voice let me know that he had some suggestions for just what I could be doing. Right now, after being humiliated by Aaron yet again, I was open to any and all suggestions, even from Maxwell. But I didn't want to appear too eager. I already needed him more than he needed me. Needy wasn't my thing, though, so I had to do my best not to show it.

"Who says he got to me?" I replied with a shrug.

"That look on your face says it all, my dear," Maxwell stated. "Besides, you never were that great at hiding your true colors. Like most people, he eventually saw the true you." Once again, Maxwell chuckled. He was getting a real kick out of this. It was almost as if he wished he'd been the one to call me a bitch.

"I guess compared to you, being a bitch isn't so bad," I shot back. I couldn't let Maxwell be the only one throwing out insults in this conversation.

"Touché." He smiled, and then a serious look immediately cast over his face. "Look, I couldn't care less about you and that little punk's business between the sheets, but what I do care about is his business—his private business."

Okay, now Maxwell had me confused, and it showed on my face.

"What I'm trying to say is, like I said a minute ago, don't let him get to you. You just make sure you get the last laugh."

"And how do you expect me to do that?"

"Think, Simone. What's more important to him right now, more than anything?"

I thought for a couple of seconds. I almost thought he was referring to Tia, but then I realized what it was. "That national choir competition, of course."

"Right, and whatever happens, he cannot win that competition. If Aaron wins, T. K. gets to keep that church, Aaron looks like a hero, and I don't get my shopping center. None of which are acceptable outcomes."

"So, what exactly do you want me to do?"

"Surely you two weren't screwing twenty-four seven. Surely you two must have talked a little. Shared some intimate secrets, maybe? Secrets of his private affairs, things that not even Bishop knows about." Maxwell walked in close to me and rubbed his hand up and down my cheek. "Things that a man reveals only after he's been between the legs of a sexy woman like yourself."

"Hmmm, are you trying to say I'm sexy?" I teased.

"I've never said you weren't a fine woman, Simone," Maxwell said. "As a matter of fact, if my heart didn't already belong to Monique, I might give the choirboy a run for his money. But I've got my mind set on making a certain first lady my lady."

"You wouldn't even make it to first base with me, Deacon." I shut him down before he got any ideas about including me in whatever it was that he and Monique had going on. "Let's just cut to the chase. What exactly is it you want me to do?"

"I want you to do all that you can to keep him from winning that competition."

"Are you serious?" Now it was me who chuckled. "You've seen them perform. They're good. They're damn good. They could actually win."

"Then keep him from even showing up at the competition to perform. The choir is good, but not without him. He's the backbone." He said it as if it were that easy. "I want you to take any information you have that could hinder him from even being in that competition."

"Okay, let's say I do have something on Aaron and I do make sure he loses nationals. What's in it for me?"

Maxwell's smirk returned once again. "You mean aside from the satisfaction of ruining the man who just called you a bitch? Well, if you can pull it off, it's worth three hundred thousand dollars cash. That should be enough to pay back the money you stole from the church and your old man's business, with a little something for your trouble. Think of it as a get-out-of-jail-free card. They can't prosecute you for something that's been returned and explained as an accounting oversight on your behalf."

A mischievous grin crossed my lips.

"You like the thought of that, don't you? So, think long and hard, Simone. There's got to be something." Maxwell grabbed me by the arm and applied pressure. "I need this to be a done deal. That means if he comes crawling back to you on bended knee, you better not let dick get in the way of this." He pointed a finger in my face. "Because I swear to God, if you screw me on this . . ."

That much money at stake really got my brain churning. I

thought about the business card those two goons had left with me not too long ago. I knew it would come in handy, but I had no idea just what a gift it had really been. "I think I have just the thing to keep lover boy and his little whore from winning that competition." I licked my lips. I could already taste the sweetness of revenge. Aaron had humiliated me for the last time. It was now my turn to humiliate him and be free of Maxwell at the same time. "Don't worry. By the time all is said and done, Aaron is the only one who's going to be screwed."

The Bishop

53

I stormed out of Maxwell's office only to find that Monique had not left but was standing in the doorway. I thought she might have gone to the car. When she saw me exit Maxwell's office, she just stood there like a fat kid on a diet whose hand was caught in the cookie jar. How could she not have told me she'd had a relationship with Maxwell, of all people?

I halted and stood there looking at her. I opened my mouth, but no words came out. Thank God, because no telling what they might have been.

"Come on, Bishop, let's go." Aaron grabbed me by the elbow to move me on. Both Tia and Monique followed.

"Are you okay?" I heard Tia asking my wife.

Is she okay? I know I sure as hell wasn't. What I did know was that I'd been betrayed, and Maxwell wasn't the only one who was guilty.

As we headed for the car, I was glad to see that it hadn't been towed, considering I hadn't noticed when we got there that I'd parked at a bus stop.

"Bishop, I can drive if you'd like," Aaron stated as we approached the car.

"Thanks, son, but I've got it." I went to the front passenger door and opened it for Monique. Although right about now I thought her to be less than a lady, I still wasn't going to be anything less than a gentleman to her—at least not in front of these young people.

"Thank—" was all Monique got out before I slammed the door closed. Okay, so a little less than a gentleman, but considering what I'd just learned about my wife, could you blame me?

Once everyone else was in the car, I got in and sped away from the curb.

"Bishop, you can just drop Tia and me off at the church. We'll get home from there." Aaron was trying his best to be accommodating. At least somebody was considerate of me. My wife sure hadn't been.

"Thanks, son. You sure you don't mind?" I responded.

"Not at all. My truck is there, and I'll drive Tia home."

The drive to the church was a blur. I couldn't even tell you how many stop signs or traffic lights there were. I don't remember stopping. I don't remember anything. That's just how fogged my mind was.

I could feel Monique looking at me every now and then while I drove. She wanted to say something. Hell, I wanted to say plenty, but we both knew this wasn't the time. Not with company in the backseat.

Pulling up in front of the church, I put the car in park. Aaron got out first so that he could walk around and open the door on Tia's side and let her out. I decided to get out and have a word with him.

"Aaron, I just want to thank you for what you said back there. You know, about using your share of the winnings to help save the church."

"It's no big deal, Bishop," he said nonchalantly. "And I mean every word."

"I know you do, son. But this is a lot for one man to rest on his shoulders. I don't want you to think you have to win to save the church. This is not your problem."

"That's where you're wrong, Bishop. This is my church just as much as it is yours. I worship here and I make my living here. Anything that affects this church affects me." He placed his hand on my shoulder. "So, don't worry. I'm not going to let you or the church down. We're going to win that competition and the money."

"Thanks, Mackie, for everything." I returned to the driver's seat while he and Tia went on their way.

I pulled off, and it wasn't five seconds before I spoke. "So, am I the only one in the congregation who didn't know about you and Maxwell?"

Monique instantly burst into tears. I didn't say a word to comfort her. I just waited for her to calm down. A few minutes later, she wiped her tears. Just as she fixed her lips to speak, my cell phone rang.

"Aren't you going to get that?" I could tell she was stalling.

"No." I always answered my phone, but I just didn't feel like talking to anyone.

"Okay, then," she said with a sigh when the phone stopped ringing. "Well—"

My phone started up again. I wanted to hear everything she had to say without interruption, but whoever it was must have felt it was urgent.

"Hold on a second. Let me just get this person off the phone."

"Hello."

"Is this Bishop T. K. Wilson?"

"This is," I confirmed.

"Bishop, this is Dr. Whitehead from Columbia Presbyterian Hospital. I was told to give you a call if there was any change in Mr. Black's condition."

I did not like where this was going. This was the same man who'd called when James's lung had collapsed.

"Is James okay?" Given how agitated James was when we left him, I braced myself for bad news.

"Bishop Wilson, I'm sorry to say, Mr. Black—"

"No, no, no," I began repeating before the doctor could even finish his sentence. I was not ready for what this man was about to say.

"Mr. Black passed away about fifteen minutes ago."

I struggled to focus on the road as my eyes filled with tears.

"T. K., baby, what is it? What's wrong?" Monique sensed something was wrong, but I ignored her.

"Doctor, I'll be right there," I said before hanging up the phone.

"T. K., what is it? Is James okay?"

I wiped my eyes, trying to collect my thoughts, but it didn't work. I was an emotional wreck. I loved James Black like a brother. Now that Maxwell was exposed, James was the only real friend I had left, and now he was gone. I hadn't felt that alone since my first wife passed away.

"No," I told her. "James passed away."

"Oh my God. Are you okay?"

She reached out for me and I pulled away. "Don't touch me. Just don't touch me, okay? Not now."

Aaron

54

It was late, probably sometime after midnight. I was seated at the piano in the choir practice room, diligently practicing "Blessings," a song I'd written for the choir to sing for nationals. I'd never worked so hard on anything in my entire life. I just had to win, because, as the bishop put it the other night, the fate of the church rested squarely on my shoulders. I'd told him confidently that we would win this thing. I'd meant it at the time, but as each day passed, I could feel the pressure increasing every time a church member wished me well or told me how much they were counting on me. I wasn't about to let anyone down, and I was not going to be defeated. Especially not by that bitch Simone.

Speaking of Simone, that wench continued to blow up my phone on not only a daily basis, but on an hourly one as well. Can you believe the nerve? Simone was like an apple with a worm in it. She looked good on the outside, and was pretty sweet as long as you didn't get too deep into her, but she was purely rotten on the inside. I just wished she would leave me the hell alone. You'd think that after everything that had happened between us, she'd get the hint, but she didn't.

Tia, on the other hand, was everything that Simone was not. Hearing from her always brightened my mood, which was why I was happy to hear her ringtone. "Hey there, beautiful," I answered.

"Hey, babe. I just wanted to say good night."

"You're so sweet, you know that?" I pressed a couple of keys on the piano.

"You still at the church?"

"Yeah, I'm trying to get it together."

"You already have it together, Mr. Mackie. Don't stay up too late, okay?"

"I won't. Good night."

" 'Night, babe." She kissed into the phone, and I did it back before hanging up.

"Well, isn't that cute? You're all kissy face with that black bitch on the phone, but you won't even answer my calls."

My back was to the door, but I'd know that voice anywhere. I turned to look at Simone, and the hairs stood up on the back of my neck—not just because I didn't want her there, breathing the same air as me, but because of what she was wearing, which was practically nothing. Say whatever you want about her, but you could never take away the fact that Simone was one of the sexiest women on the planet.

"What do you want?" I snapped. "I really don't have anything to say to you."

She had a smug look on her face as she sashayed over to me. "What do I want? I want my man back. That's what I want." She stood looking down at me. I watched as she ran her hand across the top of the piano, continuing to speak before I could shut her down. "I want to lie on top of this piano with your head buried between my legs as you play me a song. I want—"

"Well, that's not happening. And watch what you say. We are in a church." I stood up just to get the image she'd described out of my head. Simone knew that was one of my fantasies. And well, to be honest, I'd been with Tia only a couple of weeks, but this celibacy thing was starting to get to me. I think I was officially the king of cold showers.

"That never stopped you from suggesting it in the past."

"Well, that was fantasy and role-playing. This is reality, and we're in a real church. A church you've been kicked out of, I might add. What are you doing here anyway? Haven't you caused enough trouble?"

"I came here to see you. I want you back, Aaron. I know I made some mistakes, but I wanna make it work this time. I swear."

"Have you totally lost your mind? Get the hell outta here, Simone." I pointed at the door.

"You're gonna have to drag me out." She put her hands on her hips and shot me a daring look.

"I will if I have to. I'd prefer it if you left on your own. It's late and I have work to do." I walked to the door, opening it. Believe it or not, that arrogant wench sat down on my piano bench.

"Well, I'm not going anywhere. We need to talk." She crossed her legs defiantly, like she had the final word on the matter.

"I don't have anything to say to you, Simone. Now, get out!" I was struggling to keep my temper in check.

"Aaron, I'm trying to be nice here. This could go in an entirely different direction. I still haven't forgotten you called me a bitch when we were in Maxwell's office."

"Well, if the shoe fits . . . ," I said, unable to believe her audacity. She wanted to focus on one word I'd used, like she hadn't just helped pull off the biggest scheme ever against the church. Didn't she realize that this church was my bread and butter, my livelihood? If she was messing with the church, then ultimately, she was messing with me.

"Don't push it!" She pointed a finger. "Now, why don't you come over here and let me unzip those pants so I can suck that dick like I used to? I know Tia's prudish ass ain't sucking it for you, and I know how much you love a good blow job."

I took a deep breath and tried to regain my composure, although my Johnson was not cooperating at all. Just the thought of having her mouth around my stuff had me fully erect, and there was no hiding it from Simone with the thin pants I was wearing.

"My, my, my. What do we have here? Somebody missed Momma, didn't he?" She was almost singing. She gestured for me to come to her, and I took a couple of steps closer.

The thought of walking over and letting her do what she'd suggested came to mind. Simone did have some impeccable oral skills. I watched her lick her lips as she waved for me to come closer. Again, even though it had been only a couple of weeks, it felt like a lifetime since I'd done anything to relieve my sexual tension, and I was so backed up. All that kissing and touching I did with Tia hadn't helped any either. One time wouldn't hurt, would it? I mean, even if Simone decided to tell Tia, I could always deny it. She'd never believe Simone over me. Tia trusted me.

I stopped in my tracks. When it came down to it, that was the point: My girlfriend trusted me. I looked down at my penis and shook my head. *Sorry, dude. For once it's time for me to start thinking with the big head and not the little one.*

I looked up at Simone. "I asked you to leave nicely. I'm not gonna ask again." I pulled out my cell phone. "I still don't understand why you would do what you did to this church. Then again, I'm still trying to figure out why you lied about your father to the police and me. Or why you lie about anything, for that matter. I guess now I know why your father wanted me to run his company instead of you."

"Don't you judge me, Aaron Mackie." I guess I finally hit a nerve. "You don't know what I've been through. What it's like being me."

"Poor little spoiled rich girl. Thinks she can do whatever she wants. Well, here's a news flash: One day you're going to die a very lonely, bitter woman. 'Cause from what I can see, there's only one thing you're good at other than being miserable, and a brother can find that on any street corner in Queens for a bag of weed and a forty ounce. Now, get out of the church before I call the cops."

She crossed her arms and jutted out her chin defiantly. "Make the call. But then I'm just going to call your friend Andrew Gotti."

I froze with the phone halfway to my ear. Just the mention of Gotti caused panic to spread throughout my body. I'm sure Simone could see it all over my face.

"That's right. I know all about Andrew Gotti."

"So, what about him? What's there to know? Just another white man, as far as I'm concerned." I tried to pull myself together and act cool, like I wasn't pressed, but I don't think she bought it for one second.

Simone started walking her fingers across my piano in a taunting manner. I wanted to grab her hand and break each finger. "I'm sure the bishop would love to know about him. Oh, and Tia would just lose her mind if she found out Gotti was your parole officer."

My back went straight as a board and I swallowed hard.

"So, you were in jail?" she questioned. She might not have been sure, for all I knew, but I had pretty much just told on myself with my body language.

"Yeah, I was incarcerated." I glared at her defiantly. "What about it?"

"You got the nerve to get mad for telling a little white lie about my father, and you're an ex-con on parole?"

I hated the way that sounded.

"I didn't lie to you, Simone, or anyone else for that matter."

Simone came closer and stuck her finger in my face. "But you didn't tell the truth either."

"It just never came up," I said, though I knew my point was weak.

"Omitting the truth is just as bad as a lie. Maybe worse, because you're intentionally being deceitful. I believe it's what the saints refer to as *lying by omission*." She put her finger to her chin and looked upward as if she were deep in thought. "Do you really think you would have passed that vote if the church boards knew you were on parole?"

I didn't answer, so she continued. "Hmmm, I wonder who else you've omitted the truth from? The bishop, or maybe Tia?"

I could see the wheels churning in her evil little head. "Look, you can't tell anybody about this." I was no longer trying to play it cool. This was serious. She had to know that I needed her to keep her mouth shut about all this.

"I won't tell a single soul—as long as you take me back to your place and make passionate love to me." Simone had a coy, coquettish lilt in her voice.

I was tempted to take her up on it. I really did not need this to get out, at least not until I could win the national championship I was brought here to win. I stared at her as I contemplated my options, and for the first time, I felt like I understood how scandalous Simone really was. She would stop at nothing to get what she wanted. I wondered if she had something to do with the church's missing money the bishop had been talking about. I sure wouldn't put it past her. I decided right then and there that she wouldn't hold me hostage to her little games and drag me down to hell with her.

"Look, I'm not going to play this little game with you, Simone. The last thing I'm gonna do is sit here and allow you to blackmail me. I don't care who you tell."

Simone gasped as if I had slapped her. It's like I took all the wind out of her sails by taking away her power over me. "This is not over, Aaron. Trust me, this is not over by a long shot."

With that, Simone spun on her heels and stomped out of the choir room, slamming the door in her wake.

God, I hoped she didn't call my bluff. If she did, how in the world was I going to explain this, especially to Tia?

Monique

55

We were lying in bed next to each other, but T. K. wasn't touching me, and I wasn't touching him. We had our backs to each other. This was unusual, because we'd slept in the spoon position for most of our marriage. Things had been like this since James's death—or, as you may recall, the day Maxwell told T. K. about our past relationship. I never knew there could be such a distance between two people in a king-size bed.

I could hear T. K.'s breathing, and I could tell he was awake because he wasn't snoring.

"You could have told me." Suddenly, his voice pierced the silence.

"What?" I lifted my head. I wasn't sure what he was saying; I was just grateful that he was talking to me. Right about now, even if he had said "Go to hell," that would be better than the silent treatment he'd been giving me every day in our home.

"You could have told me about Maxwell."

I took a breath, knowing that no matter how much I wanted to, there was no escaping this conversation. "He was the last thing on my mind when you and I started courting. You told me that you didn't want to know about my past. You said you didn't care who I'd been with, what people thought or said. You said all you cared about was me and you. So, I followed suit. From that moment on, it was always about me and Bishop T. K. Wilson. Everything else that had happened in my past, any other man I'd been with, I erased them from my mind—and that goes for Maxwell."

I rolled over, facing T. K.'s back. Finally, he faced me. My heart was pounding against my rib cage. I knew he might start asking more questions about Maxwell and me, questions from our past that could eventually lead up to the present. If he did, should I tell him? Should I admit to sleeping with Maxwell?

"You did know Maxwell and I were friends." His tone was more accusatory than questioning.

"Yes, but that was way before I fell in love with you."

"Why would you date me if you knew this?"

"I was through with him. I love you. I will do anything in the world for you. You just don't know." I stopped myself before I went too far.

T. K. let out a deep breath but didn't respond. It was my turn to turn the tables now.

"Can I ask you a question?" I said. "Have you ever taken money from the church?"

"What?"

"You don't have to lie to me. Did you?"

"No! Absolutely not!" T. K. shot straight up in the bed.

"Would you put your hand to God?"

He was appalled, but I was serious.

"Yes, I would. But why do you think I would steal? That's preposterous." He lay back down in the bed, but I could still feel the tension.

"Someone told me that you were stealing from the church."

"Who said that? I've never stolen from the church. I've only given to it. You know that. You know me."

"I know. It's just that—"

"Who told you that?"

"You've got to promise me that you won't say anything."

T. K. shot me a look, reminding me that I wasn't in any position to be calling any shots. "Maxwell. Maxwell's the one who told me."

"And you believed him?"

"He showed me papers, told me he would have you sent to jail. I didn't know what to believe. All I knew was I loved you."

"That son of a—" T. K. knew he was about to hit the roof, so he stopped himself.

I waited quietly. I wanted to reach out and comfort him but knew it wasn't the right time.

He said, "Maxwell's been doing a lot of talking lately, especially when it comes to me and you. He really does hate me, doesn't he?"

"Yes, because he knows he can't have me and that I will never love him."

T. K. looked me directly in the eye for the first time in days. "Do you have any feelings for that man?"

"No. I've got no feelings for him at all. I love you, T. K., and only you."

"Then Maxwell Frye will have to get over it, because our love is here to stay."

I let out a sigh of relief. Finally, we were both on the same page.

"I think he's trying to ruin both of our lives," I said.

"Don't worry. As soon as this competition is over, I've got something for Maxwell Frye."

Now all of T. K.'s anger was directed at Maxwell and not at me. I was glad for that, as long as he didn't find out what I'd been doing recently.

"You don't hate me, do you?" I asked.

"I can never hate you. I love you." There was a pause. "Is that why you haven't been sleeping with me? Because you were ashamed of me?"

I didn't answer.

"Wow, okay. You don't have to answer that."

"Baby, I love you," I said.

"I love you too. I've missed you."

For the first time in weeks, T. K. took me into his arms and held me tight. We began to kiss, first slowly, tentatively; then we intertwined our arms, our legs, our hearts and made love for the first time in a long time and became one again.

Simone

56

There was only one day before Aaron and the choir left for Washington, D.C., to compete in the National Gospel Choir Championship. Maxwell had been on my ass constantly about making sure they ended up on the losing end. He was very clear about not wanting them to get the money they needed to pay off the mortgage on the church and the school. He kept emphasizing that if he didn't get what he wanted, I wouldn't get the three hundred thousand dollars he'd promised me, and I'd wind up in jail.

He had no idea that I already had a plan in place to take care of the situation but I can't lie—I found Maxwell's threats to be quite motivating. My original plan was to make sure Aaron was so shaken up by my threat to expose his criminal past that he'd come running back to me with his tail between his legs. Either that or he'd pack up and leave town to save himself from the humiliation of being exposed in front of the church.

He'd tried to play all hard the night I showed up at the church, but he was afraid I was going to tell. I could see it in his eyes. His pride wouldn't let him give in, but he was definitely concerned. The only reason I hadn't exposed his ass right away was because I didn't want to play all my cards at once. I also didn't want to give him or the church enough time to recover from the bomb I was about to drop on their heads.

There was also the little fact that despite everything that was going on, I still loved Aaron and I knew that once I revealed his little secret, there was no turning back. I'd probably lose him forever. That was not something I wanted, but unfortunately it was either him or me, and, well, self-preservation is key. Things were down to the wire now, and it was time for me to accept that Aaron and I were through and it was time to bring down his egotistical ass.

I walked into the school building around 6:30 p.m. with a small folder under my arm. I found what I was looking for when I heard Tia's voice coming out of a classroom. I peeked in the small window and saw her sitting in a circle with about ten other women. When I pushed open the door, everyone in the room turned to look at me. Tia's eyes seemed to bug out of her head with surprise.

"Can I help you?" Tia asked.

"Pardon me. This *is* the rape counseling group, isn't it?" I continued to speak before anyone could answer. "I know I'm late, but it's okay for me to come in, isn't it? I don't have to register or anything, do I? Is everyone welcome? I just have so much I need to get off my chest." I patted my eyes with a tissue.

The expression on Tia's face said exactly how she felt: *Hell no, you're not welcome.*

But before she could say a word, the other women were welcoming in the timid, shy-acting woman I portrayed. Tia watched as one woman pulled a chair into the circle so that I could take a seat.

"Thank you for having me. I'm sorry again for being late," I stated.

"Oh, don't worry about it," Tia lied. "We welcome you." She was gonna have some heavy repenting to do afterward. I know she hated me as much as I hated her, but she had no idea how much she would hate me when it was all said and done.

"Thank you, Sister Tia." I smiled.

Sister Tia. Now, that was a good one. I wanted to laugh, but I kept my composure, and believe it or not, so did Tia. She ignored me as best she could and got right back to her meeting.

"So, anyway, ladies, like I was saying, tonight we're going to talk about something we haven't touched upon yet, and that's forgiveness: forgiving ourselves and the person or persons who hurt us."

There were several sighs, and some of the women shifted uncomfortably in their seats. I could tell they weren't anywhere near the point of forgiveness. Good for them. Tia was spewing a bunch of feel-good crap anyway.

"I know, I know, ladies. Forgiveness is easier said than done. But remember, I've been in your shoes before, and I've forgiven the men who raped me."

"But how do you forget?" a woman asked. "I can't even look in the mirror without replaying the whole scenario in my mind."

"You will never forget, but you can move on. That, however, is for another night, or maybe a one-on-one session. Let's deal with forgiveness tonight."

Tia had her mouth poised to continue speaking when I interrupted. She had better be ready for a lot of interruptions tonight, because I was planning on making a habit of it.

"Pardon me, uh, Sister Tia, but, uh, I have something specific that I was hoping to discuss tonight."

I know she wanted to smack me for taking over her meeting. You should have seen the look the bitch gave me when I said, "I promise it won't take long, and then you can get back to the matter of forgiveness. It's just that it's so heavy on my heart right now."

I gave each woman in the group a sad puppy-dog face. Then I put my hand over my chest as if something was ailing me, something I just had to get out.

The woman sitting next to me put her hand on my shoulder. "It's okay, baby. Let God use you up in here."

I glanced over at Tia, who was clenching her fists at her side all the while nodding with false concern. "Please, Simone, what is it that's on your mind?"

"Well . . ." I leveled my gaze on Tia. "I was just wondering what do you do when someone you know is dating a rapist?"

There were gasps around the room, just as I'd hoped. This was going to work out perfectly. I couldn't have gotten a better response if they were all on my payroll.

"You tell the person," one woman said, and several quickly agreed.

"Simone, the ladies are right," Tia cosigned. "You have to tell this woman. Imagine how you would feel if something happened to her, if she became one of the rapist's victims."

This was intense. From the look on these women's faces, they would have taken up arms and followed me to kill the son of a bitch—which might not have been such a bad idea if I didn't love him.

I paused for dramatic effect, before I looked at Tia and said, "You're right. I should tell her." I turned my head, making eye contact with every woman in the circle. I wanted to be sure I had everyone's undivided attention before I announced, "Tia, you're dating a convicted rapist. Aaron Mackie is a convicted rapist. And those two goons you always see coming around are his parole officers. If I were you, I'd be careful." I leaned back and folded my arms, watching the drama unfold.

"Huh?" Tia sat there, absolutely stunned. She couldn't say a word, but the other women did.

"Oh my God! Isn't he the man who sat in on one of our meetings?" a woman asked.

It was kind of obvious from the way she spoke about Aaron that she wasn't from our church, and neither were the other women, for that matter. I didn't recognize any of them, now that I thought about it. Then again, I guess if I'd been raped, I wouldn't go to a support group in a place where everyone knew me. I don't care what type of agreements they have to keep things confidential—women talk! Besides, who knows who you might run into?

"Yes. He could have been here trying to pick up information on how not to get caught next time," another woman replied.

"Or even worse, what if he came here to find another victim?" The woman who said this shuddered, genuine fear evident on her face.

I almost felt bad for putting them through this—not completely, but almost.

"What if he's got his mind set on one of us?"

I felt the energy in the room shift. My announcement had just the effect I'd been looking for.

"Jesus, Tia, not only are you dating a convicted rapist, but you brought him into our lives too. We were supposed to be able to trust you."

I could almost see Tia's heart breaking into a thousand pieces just thinking that she could have betrayed these women. Now, that's what I call dropping a bomb on someone's head!

Tia swallowed hard, standing up. "Excuse me, ladies. I'd like to speak to Simone outside for a second. Certainly there has to be some mistake. I'll be right back."

"Sure, no problem, Tia. I'd be happy to."

She gestured for me to go to the door and I obliged. As happy as I was about the success of this mission, I was careful to walk solemnly so as not to blow my cover in front of these women.

We stepped out into the hallway ready for war. If she thought what I just dropped on her head was something, she hadn't seen anything yet.

"Yes, Tia?" I turned to face her as if it were just another day. As if I hadn't just come in there and made statements that turned her world upside down.

"How could you make up such lies about Aaron? I know you hate me, but I thought you actually loved him. How could you throw him under the bus like that?"

"I wouldn't, Tia. After all, who in their right mind would publicly make such strong allegations if they didn't have proof?"

"I . . . I just can' t believe it."

"Then believe this." I handed her the folder, then watched as she opened it and began reading.

"See, I told you. It's all right there in black and white. He's a registered sex offender, Tia."

"Oh my God." Before I realized it, the papers she was reading had slipped through her hands.

"I'll get it." I bent over and picked them up, then handed them back to her. "Here, you can keep this. I have plenty more copies. We may be enemies, but I just thought you should know."

She stood there frozen.

"Look, I know you don't want to believe this coming from me, but like my father always said, the best way to find out the truth is to go to the source. So, why don't you just go ask Aaron for yourself? And make sure you tell him I'm the one who told you."

Monique

57

It had been a long, emotional day for everyone. Per James's request, his body had been cremated and there was no funeral, but we still held a memorial service for him at the church. Although many people over the past year or so had written him off because he went to jail, we were all pleasantly surprised by the turnout at the memorial. The pews were packed like it was Sunday service, and you wouldn't believe how many women were crying. I didn't know half those sobbing women even knew James that well, but from the tears they were shedding, it looked like they knew him a hell of a lot better than the rest of us.

I don't know if anyone shed more tears than my husband, though. T. K. had taken James's death extremely hard. He'd held himself together long enough to put together the service just the way his friend wanted, but once we stepped foot in the church and saw the urn holding his ashes and James's portrait beside it, T. K. lost it. He had to struggle to keep his composure during the rest of the service. I gave him a sleeping pill at home to calm his nerves and help him sleep through the night.

I was sad that James's kids didn't show up, but I wasn't surprised. They hadn't been around at all during his incarceration or his illness. However, I was amazed that Simone hadn't shown up, despite the fact that I had texted her the time and place. Yes, she was banished from the church and I personally couldn't stand her right now, but I did know how she felt about James. I thought she might have wanted to be there. Believe it or not, that bastard Maxwell was there with two large guys who looked like bodyguards. Luckily he knew enough not to start anything at such a solemn occasion.

Even though Maxwell behaved himself in public, having him there made the day even more difficult for me. It was painful to see my husband's true friend reduced to ashes in an urn and his worst enemy sitting in the pews. For much of the service, I couldn't even pay attention. I was too busy thinking about what, if anything, I could do to stop Maxwell's attempted takeover of the church. Unfortunately, he pretty much had my back up against the wall, because as soon as I tried anything, he'd tell T. K. what I'd been doing lately. Short of killing Maxwell, there wasn't much I could do.

I had to try, though, which was what brought me to the church at two in the morning, letting myself into the book-keeper's office. I had a strong suspicion that the papers Maxwell had shown me were forged. If I could locate the originals, I would have proof of T. K.'s innocence, and Maxwell would no longer be able to threaten to send my husband to jail. Hell, if I was lucky, I'd find proof that Maxwell was the one who stole all the money. At that point, Maxwell could put an announcement in the church bulletin that I'd slept with him, and not a soul would believe him.

I guess I could have turned on an office light, but just in case someone drove by the church, I didn't want to bring any unnecessary attention to myself. So, I pulled my flashlight out of my purse and headed for the file drawers. Unsure of what I was looking for, I started by going through the church's records of accounts receivable and accounts payable.

My heart was pounding. I had no idea what I was going to find in these files, and regardless of what it was, I knew that the outcome would be painful for me. What if, by some million-to-one chance, I was wrong about the forgery and the files confirmed that T. K. actually had been stealing?

I shook off that thought as quickly as it had come to mind. My gut told me that I would only find papers that proved T. K.'s innocence. But then I would have to deal with the overwhelming guilt and shame for ever having doubted him—and for allowing Maxwell to trick me into dishonoring my marriage the way I had.

After awhile, I was able to find what I was looking for—statements from the same dates that Maxwell had shown me, along with images of checks in the amounts Maxwell claimed T. K. had stolen. These, however, were the originals, and they showed something quite different from the ones in Maxwell's file. None of the check images had T. K.'s name on them. Maxwell had probably copied the files, covered the real names on the checks with Wite-Out, put T. K.'s name in their place, then copied the doctored version to conceal the Wite-Out.

"Oh, praise God! He was telling the truth!" I said jubilantly. "My husband was telling the truth, and here's the proof that Maxwell's ass was lying all along."

Once I got myself together, I had to take a closer look at the statements to see if I could discern where the money had actually gone. I was hoping to find a way to pin it all on Maxwell, but the trail of debits and credits to the account, as well as the checks that were written revealed something even more shocking than I could have imagined: Jonathan Smith and Simone Wilcox were the true thieves!

Now some things were starting to make sense. This must have been why Smitty killed himself. Maxwell must have known he was stealing and threatened to expose him. I knew from experience how effective Maxwell's threats could be. That was probably also why Simone was at his house that morning. He must have been holding the embezzlement over her head too.

"That son of a bitch," I said aloud. He'd been blackmailing everyone, including me. I could kill him for what he'd made me do. And rest assured, I would never do it again.

All of a sudden, the lights blazed on, temporarily blinding me. I let out a scream, squeezing my eyes shut.

"What are you doing here?" a man shouted.

I raised the hand holding the flashlight to protect myself. "I'm the first lady of the church. Please don't hurt me." I opened my eyes and tried to adjust to the light.

"It's all right, First Lady. It's me, Aaron." When my eyes finally focused, I saw Aaron standing in the doorway, wielding a large bat. His brow was furrowed in concern.

"What are you doing here?" I said. I slowly closed the file drawer, though I'm sure Aaron saw. I was also still holding the flashlight and the file that proved T. K.'s innocence.

"I've gotta win this competition. We're leaving tomorrow night, so I'm working day and night on the songs. I was here practicing when I thought I heard a noise coming from this end of the building." He looked around the office suspiciously. "My question is what are you doing in the bookkeeper's office at two in the morning with a flashlight?" He flicked the light on and off, finally leaving it on. "The light seems to work just fine."

Seeing how loyal Aaron had been to the bishop, I decided to take a chance. I needed an ally, and other than T. K., he seemed to be the only one who cared about anything around here. "Aaron, can you keep a secret?"

He nodded. "Sure, First Lady. As long as you're not involving me in any felony or robbery of the church, I'll take it to the grave."

"No, nothing like that." I swallowed a lump in my throat before I continued. "I had heard some rumors about my husband stealing money from the church, and I was trying to prove they weren't true."

Aaron finally relaxed and put the bat down by his side. "Well, did you find what you were looking for?" I could see his concern. He really looked up to the bishop.

"Yes, thank God. They're not true." I raised the file that was still in my hands.

"Who would say such a ridiculous thing about the bishop?"

I suddenly felt so ashamed of myself I wanted to cry. Here was Aaron, who'd known the bishop for only a few months, and he had not even a moment's doubt that the rumors were false. I, on the other hand, was his wife and had allowed myself to be duped. How had I ever let myself believe that T. K. could steal from his beloved church?

"Believe it or not, it was Maxwell who was whispering in my ear, telling me that the bishop was stealing from the church."

"Man, that dude's going straight to hell. I ain't never seen anyone as devious as him."

"Yeah, well, I might be going there with him," I mumbled under my breath.

"Excuse me. What did you say, First Lady?"

"Nothing." He was staring at me funny, so I think he might have heard part of what I said. Still, I wasn't about to repeat it.

"So, if it wasn't the bishop stealing, who was it? Maxwell?"

"I don't see any proof of it, but Maxwell's too smart for that anyway. He'd never be stupid enough to put his name on something that was illegal. But Jonathan Smith and your girl Simone weren't." I handed him the file and he thumbed through it briefly.

"First Lady, I have no idea what I'm looking at."

"Okay, let me explain. Simone and Smitty were stealing from the church. Because they were the chair of the deacons' board and board of trustees, they would write each other checks, and wire transfer money to each other—Simone would even write checks to Wilcox Motors."

"Now, that's bold."

"Sure was, but with James gone to prison, they could do whatever they wanted. Nobody was going to miss ten or fifteen thousand dollars a month, especially since they were in charge of the money."

"What about the bookkeeper? Didn't he notice anything?"

"I doubt it. You've seen Mr. Wright. He's darn near eighty years old, and he only comes in three times a week. Simone pretty much has him intimidated. So, up until Jackie got busted and the weekly offerings dropped off drastically, they were good to go. First Jamaica Ministries was a cash machine. T. K. and the boards trusted them."

"Oh my God, that's where that thirty thousand dollars came from!" Aaron shook his head in disgust.

"What thirty thousand dollars?"

"The thirty thousand dollars Simone was supposed to get from Deacon Smith before he died. That woman is scandalous."

"Not as scandalous as Maxwell. He's been pulling puppet strings around here for quite some time. Simone's a little fish compared to him. And Smitty was right when he told Bishop this thing was bigger than it seemed."

We were both quiet for a moment. I was trying to wrap my head around the depth of the deception that had been happening right under our noses.

"So, what are you going to do? Are you going to tell your husband? I'm sure Bishop will know what to do. He always does."

If only it were that easy. "No, I don't think so. At least not until nationals is over."

"I don't understand. Why?"

"Because Smitty and Simone aren't the only ones Maxwell has something on."

Aaron tilted his head and studied my face as if he were trying to read my mind. "They're blackmailing you, too, aren't they?"

I answered with a nod.

"With what? What could they possibly have on you?"

"My husband. I was trying to save T. K. from going to jail," was all I said. Tears welled up in my eyes.

I think he knew what my mouth couldn't say, because he reached out and touched my hand. "It's all right. You don't have to tell me. Some things are better left unsaid." Aaron looked down at the file and then back up at me. "Now that you've shared something with me"—he hesitated for a few seconds— "I'd like to share something with you."

Aaron

58

Choir rehearsal was under way, and with the exception of Tia not being there, everything was perfect. It was our last practice. The bus would be leaving for D.C. in about three hours. The sopranos were hitting high notes without effort, the tenors were riffing to perfection, and the basses would have given the late, great Barry White a run for his money. Nothing could disturb our groove. We were tuned to perfection, and a win at the National Gospel Choir Championship was within our grasp.

The choir wasn't distracted from their practice, even when the doors to the choir room flung open and Tia rushed in. She ran up on me like she couldn't wait to kiss me. It had been two days since we'd seen each other, so I was happy to see her, too, but it would have to wait until we at least finished our song. It was her index finger stabbing my shoulder that pulled me from my choir directing. Even then, the choir didn't stop. They just kept on singing like they were performing for the Lord Himself.

"I need to talk to you." That's what it sounded like Tia was saying, though it was hard to tell.

"Huh?" I leaned my ear in closer to her mouth while my eyes stayed focused on the singers. I thought I'd be able to hear her more clearly, but she kept rambling about something.

"I said I need to talk to you!" she screamed at the top of her lungs. Her voice was so loud that the choir stopped singing to appease her attempt to communicate with me.

"What's up?" I asked.

"I need to talk to you. Right now. Alone."

Though I could tell she was trying to maintain her usual professional demeanor in front of the choir, I thought I detected something like disgust in her tone, and behind her eyes was outright anger.

"Uh, choir, can you all excuse me for a moment? Keep practicing while I talk with Sister Tia here. Sister Judith, do you mind taking over for a moment, please?"

As Tia and I headed out of the choir room, they started singing again.

"Hey, everything okay?" I asked Tia once we were outside the choir room. "I was worried about you. It's not like you to be MIA for a whole day. I figured it might have something to do with the hotline or something, though."

She rolled her eyes, so I playfully wagged my finger in her face, hoping to lighten the mood. "So, I guess I'll give you a pass for being late. You ready to go to D.C.? The buses will be here in a couple of hours."

She responded with tears falling from her eyes. "I'm not going to D.C. I'm not going anywhere with you ever again."

"Tia, what's wrong? It's not your brother, is it?"

"If I were you, I'd leave Kareem out of this. You're lucky he doesn't kick your ass."

"For what? Tia, what did I do?" I pleaded. I was now officially frustrated as hell.

She glared at me. "I spoke to Simone. She told me you've been to prison."

I stood there stunned, as if once again I couldn't hear a word she was saying. But I'd heard her all right, loud and clear. Believe it or not, I'd almost forgotten about Simone's threats. I'd been so frantic preparing for the competition that I hadn't spent much time worrying about it, and after awhile I figured that if she hadn't said anything by now, she wouldn't say anything at all.

"Have you, Aaron? Have you been to prison?" she demanded.

I couldn't bring myself to answer her, because I was afraid of what she would ask next.

"I'll take your silence as a yes." She looked horrified, like she was my victim, or my victim's family.

"Listen, Tia, I wanted to tell you. I should have told you, but—"

"But what?" I tried to reach out and hold her, but she backed away. "Don't touch me. Don't you ever touch me again," she said angrily. "If I wasn't a Christian woman, I'd spit in your face right now."

Inside, I was berating myself: *I should have told her. I should have told her.* But outwardly, I placed my anger elsewhere.

"That damn Simone! That whoring bitch!" I started pacing in front of her.

"Don't blame this on Simone. This is all you." She pointed a finger at me. "I can't stand you, Aaron Mackie."

"But what about forgiveness? You always preach forgiveness."

"Are you serious? Don't even talk to me about forgiveness. I hate you!"

Whoa. This was not the Tia I knew. She used to look at me with such admiration, but this look she was giving me now . . . it was pure hate. I'd seen that look before. From strangers, it was bearable. From Tia, a woman I was falling in love with, it hurt. It hurt really bad.

"I'm sorry, Tia, but it all happened so long ago that I—"

"That you thought I wouldn't find out?" she finished my sentence.

"I know how this might look, but if you'd let me explain, perhaps—"

"Perhaps you should just go to hell!" Tia spat as a fresh wave of tears fell from her eyes. It pained me to know that I was the cause of her anguish. It was never my intention to hurt this sweet, wonderful woman.

"Tia, please. Let me explain."

"No, Aaron. No need to explain. Nothing you say could possibly change the way I feel right now. I trusted you. I let you in, let you into my group, and you betrayed me. How could I have been so stupid?"

"You're not stupid. And you can trust me," I said in my own defense. "I lied to you, but it will never happen again. I promise."

"My God, you're a fraud and a menace to society, and I'm sure everyone else will agree." She balled up her fist and hit a wall. "You know what bothers me the most is that for all the years I've known Bishop Wilson, he's never been wrong about much. But it looks like you fooled even him. Looks like he picked the wrong person to represent this church, and I'm sure he'll agree when I tell him. I swear if we didn't need to win that competition to keep this church, I'd tell him about you right now. When you get back, win or lose, if you don't tell him, I sure as hell will."

Tia turned away, leaving me standing there with a million things racing through my head. I wanted to go after her, but my head wasn't on right, and with her being angry, it wouldn't do any good.

"Cut! Cut!" I yelled repeatedly as I reentered the choir room. I was frustrated and not in any mood to continue working. What I needed was a drink. "Choir rehearsal is over."

The confused singers stared at me as if I'd just walked into the room naked.

"I'm sorry. You guys have done great, but something has come up. I need to go for a little while. I'll see everyone on the bus in three hours." I looked to Sister Judith, my adoptive godmother. "Sister Judith, can you make sure all the equipment is shut down and the room is locked up?"

I didn't even wait for her to reply before I rushed out the door, hoping to find Tia. I had to try to explain one more time.

Monique

59

I was down on my knees in the front pew at the church. I don't think there were many people in the building other than myself and the janitor. Most of the church leaders, including my husband, were down in D.C. for the national choir championship. T. K. had practically begged me to come, but I decided to stay behind because I had a lot of praying, repenting, and thinking to do. I knew Aaron would do what was necessary to win the competition and save the church. Unfortunately, that wasn't going to solve any of my problems. I would still have this sick, disgusting feeling of adultery hovering over me. When I left the church, I was planning on confronting Maxwell with the fact that I knew he'd doctored those papers. There was no better time than when my husband was out of town.

I lowered my head and began to pray.

"Lord, I come before you with a humble heart. Please forgive me for the mess I've made of my life. If only I had known Maxwell was lying on my husband. I should have known T. K. would never steal from the church, but those files Maxwell gave me looked so real. I was just trying to do right by my husband."

Suddenly, I felt a presence as someone slid into the pew behind me. I unfolded my fingers from my praying, pushed myself up from my knees, and turned around to look behind me. There sat Tia, with a lost expression on her face.

"Hey there, Tia. What are you doing here? Aren't you supposed to be in D.C. with the choir?" Her eyes were red, and there was no doubt in my mind that she'd been crying.

"I had a change of plans. Why aren't you at the competition?" Tia got up from her pew and came to sit next to me.

"Well, I thought somebody needed to stick around the church just in case Maxwell and his goons came snooping around," I replied, and then shot her a puzzled look. "But I'm not in the choir and you are. Why didn't you go to the competition? Is everything all right?"

Tia sighed, a pained expression on her face. "I guess you'd find out sooner or later."

"Find out what?"

"I'm not in the choir anymore."

I gave her a surprised look. "But you're the choir administrator. Even if you don't sing, shouldn't you have gone with them?"

"I'm not the administrator anymore. I quit."

"You quit?" *Oh, Lord, she done caught the man cheating already.* "I hope you didn't let some little lovers' quarrel get in the way of your professionalism."

"First Lady, I wish this was only a lovers' quarrel. That I could deal with."

"Tia, what did he do?" I stopped beating around the bush, and she didn't hesitate to give an answer.

"He's a rapist, plain and simple. And I don't deal with rapists."

She might as well have hit me in the head with a hammer because I was floored. A shameless flirt he was, but a rapist? That was almost laughable considering all the women lined up to give it away to him. Then again, maybe Tia wasn't one to give it up.

"Tia, honey, he didn't rape you, did he?" I tried to be as sympathetic as possible, but I still couldn't wrap my head around the idea of Aaron being a rapist.

"No, some woman in Virginia."

Now I was becoming concerned. Tia was a rape expert. If Aaron was really a rapist, she'd be the one to find out. Forget Maxwell and all his schemes, scandal like this could bring down First Jamaica Ministries once and for all.

"How'd you find this out? Were you checking up on him on the Internet?" I did not want to have to explain all this to T. K. I'd already kept enough from him to start with.

"No, someone told me."

"Someone told you? Who told you?"

Tia lowered her head. "I'd rather not say."

"What do you mean, you'd rather not say? If he's a rapist, it should be public knowledge. How do you know it isn't a lie?"

She looked at me with eyes wet with tears. "Because he admitted it, First Lady. He admitted it to me."

"Admitted what?"

"That he went to prison."

I was skeptical now. "He admitted he was a rapist?"

Tia hesitated a bit, then said, "Yes. He admitted it when he said he went to prison."

"Tia, he admitted he was a rapist? He said those words, that he raped someone?"

She hesitated again. "I read the report that Simone gave me, all about what he'd done and that he was on the registered sex offenders list for Queens."

My mouth flew open. "A report that *Simone* gave you? Girl, how could you be so stupid to believe anything that woman has to say without checking it out? You know how she is."

"But he admitted it."

I kept shaking my head. It sounded like Simone had taken a page from Maxwell's playbook, handing out files of "information" on people they wanted to destroy.

"Look, Aaron is not a rapist," I said confidently.

"How do you know?"

"Because I know that Aaron went to prison, but it wasn't for rape. He went to jail for three years when he was twenty-two, and he's been on probation for eight years. He just happened to get one of the worst parole officers imaginable since he relocated to New York."

She gave me this puzzled look. "How do you know all of this?"

I paused. "To be totally up front, the other day Aaron and I kind of swapped secrets. Everyone has their demons, Tia. Aaron's had his since he was twenty-two years old."

"But he went to prison. That still makes him a criminal. What did he go to jail for?"

"What Aaron told me was that back when he graduated from college, he and some friends ended up drunk at some party. He did the irresponsible thing and drove. Unfortunately, he got into a car accident and killed a man. He's spent most of the past eight years in church and working to take care of the man's family. He sends his wife a check every week."

"Is that why he goes to get those money orders every Friday?"

"Maybe, I don't really know."

"Do you think he was telling the truth?" Tia looked hopeful.

"I don't have to think. I know." I leaned over and hugged Tia.

"So, why are those men harassing him so much if he's doing the right thing?"

"Even though he served time in prison and is doing everything correctly, that parole officer won't give him a break. It turns out that the parole officer had a child who was killed by a drunk driver. He reminds Aaron that he's a piece of crap just like the lady who killed his child."

"Oh my God." Tia put a hand to her mouth. "The guilt Aaron must be carrying around—that is, if what he told you is really true."

I could see that Tia was going to be a hard person to convince. She had a wall up so high that I didn't know if God Himself had the strength to tear it down.

"Come with me." I took Tia by the hand and led her to my office. I logged onto my computer while she stood over me.

"What are you doing, First Lady?"

"Just hold on for a second. You'll see." I began putting in keyword search terms into Google. Ten minutes later, I had pulled up Aaron's case record and the sex offender list, on which his name did not appear. His case records confirmed the story he'd told me, and more so, they convinced Tia that she hadn't been falling in love with a rapist.

"How could I have been so stupid?" Tia said. "How could I let Simone play me like that? I should have checked this out before I went on a rampage."

"It happens to the best of us. Believe me," I told her. "Now, what you need to do is get up there to the competition and be with your man."

"And I think you need to do the same," Tia said with a smile. She looked like a huge burden had been lifted from her heart.

I grabbed my purse, feeling one hundred percent better too. "Who's driving? Me or you?"

Aaron

60

I squeezed Tia's hand nervously as we waited onstage for the awards ceremony to begin at the National Gospel Choir Championship. It meant the world to me that she had raced to D.C. at the last minute to tell me she knew the truth about my prison sentence. Before she arrived, I was an emotional wreck, and I'm sure it would have affected my performance. I would have to remember to send some flowers to the first lady to thank her for convincing Tia that the papers she saw were forged. And as for Simone, well, I was too blessed to stress about her right now, but I had faith that one day she would get what she deserved.

By the time our choir took to the stage, I was in the right frame of mind, and First Jamaica Ministries gave their best performance ever. "Blessings" was off the chain, if I do say so myself. Of the other two choirs standing onstage with us now, I only considered one to be our competitors for first place. First Baptist Our Savior out of Atlanta had been darn good—much better than I expected, actually. The third choir onstage was South Baptist from Houston. They put on a good performance, but they were not in the same league with us and First Baptist Our Savior. That's why it was no surprise when the first announcement was made.

"Ladies and gentlemen, in third place in our National Gospel Choir Championship, from the great state of Texas and the fine city of Houston, the South Baptist choir."

It took everything in me not to jump up in the air and scream, "Thank you, Jesus!" We were one step closer to winning that prize.

I glanced over at Bishop Wilson, who was standing next to

the first lady with his arm around her. He gave me a thumbs-up. I knew he was nervous, too, but the one thing I had to say about that man is he never let anyone see him sweat. He was such a nice man, too, a good man, and he had so much riding on this. I really wanted to win it more for him than myself.

I watched as South Baptist went up and received their trophy. They seemed happy, almost as if they hadn't expected to place at all. It must have been a good feeling for them, because if we had come in second or third, I know I wouldn't be smiling the way their director was.

"Ladies and gentlemen, we are now at the point of the competition that you've all been waiting for, when we announce the winner of the 2011 National Gospel Championship."

Well, this is it, I told myself. I couldn't wait to go up there and collect that prize money for First Jamaica Ministries.

"Now, we have two great choirs who have battled it out since day one of our competition." He pointed at us. "First Jamaica Ministries from Queens, New York, directed by Aaron Mackie and pastored by Bishop T. K. Wilson."

I don't know if it was our close proximity to New York or just because they loved us, but the crowd went crazy.

It took a good three or four minutes for the applause to die down so that the announcer could acknowledge our competitors, First Baptist Our Savior out of Atlanta. They received enthusiastic applause, too, but to me, the audience's reaction didn't seem as intense.

When the crowd quieted again, the announcer kept going on and on about nothing. I wanted to scream at him, "Can you shut up and announce the winner?" He must have felt my vibe, because he finally stopped babbling about nonsense and got to the point.

It was tense when he announced the third-place winners, but I almost couldn't bear the anticipation as I waited for him to announce the second place, and ultimately the winner. "And second place goes to . . ."

Second place was good, but it wasn't number one. I wanted number one. I needed number one. The church needed number one.

"The outstanding choir from . . ."

This guy was prolonging the drama as much as he could, and it was killing me. I wanted him to just spit it out. Just say "Atlanta, Georgia," so we could get to the business of collecting our first-place prize. But it never came. What came was, "Queens, New York, First Jamaica Ministries!"

I heard what he'd said, but it didn't register in my mind right away, because there was no way we were supposed to come in second. Yes, I knew there was the possibility that we could lose, but deep down, I never thought it would happen. I thought it was our destiny, that God wanted us to win to save the church. The announcer had to be reading the card wrong. We did not just lose this competition.

I turned and looked at Tia, who had tears streaming down her face, then over at First Baptist Our Savior, whose members were jumping up and down like they just witnessed the Second Coming. My legs got weak, and I dropped to my knees. I felt Tia's arms wrap around me.

"I'm sorry," I cried. "I'm so sorry. I don't know how we didn't win."

"It's okay, baby. You did the best you could. Nobody blames you." Tia attempted to console me, but nothing could comfort me now—nothing but that first-place trophy, and more importantly, the check that came along with it.

"But my best wasn't good enough. We're going to lose the church." I looked over at Bishop Wilson, who was holding his wife. Just like Tia, she was in tears. Bishop looked up and caught my gaze.

"It's okay, son," he mouthed.

But I knew it wasn't okay. Things were far from okay.

Simone

61

I pulled up to Wilcox Motors looking good and feeling good. I'd just taken a huge weight off my shoulders by depositing a cashier's check for two hundred twenty thousand dollars in the church's account. I'd taken only two hundred thousand, but Maxwell explained that if I paid back the amount with ten percent interest and wrote that it was for a repayment of a loan, there wasn't a court in the land that would convict me. As Maxwell put it, this was my way of covering my ass. I'd also put another fifty thousand in our company account to cover some of the money I'd been taking and to cover Daddy's monthly check. Wouldn't he be surprised when I sent him this month's and next month's payments? I was left with only a measly thirty grand, but it would be good enough for a few months of shopping, and maybe even a few weeks down in the Bahamas.

I walked into the dealership, and a hush fell over the showroom. I noticed a few of the salesmen glance at me and then avert their gazes.

That's right, dammit! The boss is here. Get your asses to work.

When I made it to the administrative area, my secretary said, "Your father—"

"What is it?" I grabbed my heart, which felt like it almost leaped out of my chest. Something about the strange look on her face made me fear the worst. "Is he all right? Do I need to go to Florida?"

"No, he's in your office." Anita looked like she was hiding a smirk as she turned her head and went back to work. I wondered what that was all about. Was this bitch looking to get fired?

I rushed into my office, where I could feel the tension as soon as I walked in. There sat Daddy at my desk, and next to him were two very familiar people, both of whom I'd fired in the past six or seven months: Michael Nixon, the salesman I used to date and fired for getting married, and Lisa Blackwell, the accountant with the big mouth.

"Daddy, what the hell are they doing here?" Obviously he wasn't sick. I didn't know what was going on, but it definitely wasn't good. "And what are you doing here, for that matter? Aren't you supposed to be in Florida regaining your strength?"

"Sit down, Simone." He spoke in an even tone, but I knew from experience that sometimes he used that tone when he was about to unleash his fury.

Daddy stood up, towering over me. I'd forgotten what a tall man he was. I noticed a muscle twitching in his jaw, like it did whenever he was angry. "I'm here to take back my company."

"Excuse me? You're doing what?" I stood there, a vein throbbing in my temple. "What are you talking about? Have you been taking your meds? You should be home resting."

"Don't patronize me, child. When I left you in charge of this dealership, we were making a considerable amount of money in profits." He picked up a sales journal. "Since you've been in charge, we've been declining in sales every month, and losing money the past six months."

"You don't understand," I protested, hands held out in an imploring manner.

"Oh, yes, I do understand. And these two kind people have explained it to me."

I cut my eyes at the two Judases.

"What can they tell you? They don't even work here anymore. They're both part of the reason that this company was doing so poorly."

"You're my daughter and I love you, Simone, but somehow I don't think so."

"Daddy, I can't believe you'd take their word over your own flesh and blood. I—"

"Well, believe it, Simone, because that's how it is. And effective today, Michael and Lisa will be co-running this dealership. I'm sure I'll get my check on time from them. Isn't that right, guys?"

They answered in unison, "Yes, sir."

This wasn't happening. It had to be some kind of crazy-ass dream. My father would never throw me under the bus. Not him, not me.

"Daddy, this isn't funny. You know, you almost got me." I started to laugh.

He handed the journal to Michael. "I'm serious, Simone. I'm sorry, but you're out, they're in."

I studied his face and my stomach knotted up. He was serious. He was firing me.

That's when I lost it. "You gotta be fucking kidding me! You can't do this to me!" I stomped my feet, throwing a temper tantrum like I used to when I was a little girl. When it didn't work, I dropped to my knees and started pleading. "Daddy, please. Please, Daddy, give me another chance. I was gonna write you this month and next month's checks. Please, Daddy."

"You can plead all you want, but it's already done." My father pointed to the recently rehired employees. "Listen, I want to talk to my daughter for a minute. We'll get back to what we were working on in a minute." He nodded at the two of them, and they left the room. I thought about jumping on their backs as they left the room, but I'd get them after I dealt with my father.

"Daddy, have you lost your mind? How could you do this to me? I'll have you put away in an asylum for the mentally ill. Can't you see how crazy this is?"

He nodded. "You know, Simone, I'm sure you would try to have me locked away if it would help you, but all that will do is get you totally disinherited."

That hurt more than a slap in the face.

"Daddy, please. You can't do this. Wilcox Motors is my life. I've worked here my entire life."

"It's already done. Listen, why don't you go back to school or find a new trade? I don't think the car business is for you."

"I hate you! I hate you!"

"Yeah, yeah, and I love you too," he said as if he wasn't the least bit moved by my emotional outburst. "Get over it, Simone. You're not fourteen anymore. You are a grown woman and I'm not going for it."

"What do you expect me to do now?"

"Same thing everyone else does when they get fired. How about look for a job, or go down to the unemployment office? You like shopping. I'm sure you'd be a great salesperson at Bloomingdale's."

"I can't do that. Do you know how embarrassing that would be?"

"Well, then, I hope you saved some of that money you stole from me and the church."

"What are you talking about?"

"You know exactly what I'm talking about. You're lucky you haven't been arrested." He looked at me with disappointment written all over his face. "I've given you the best of everything, Simone, but you never appreciated it. I spoiled you, trying to make you be as strong as a man. But you've gone too far. What you did was despicable. You wanna steal from a family business, fine, but from the church? I'm ashamed of you."

I couldn't say anything. I'd really hit rock bottom. First I was caught stealing from the church, Aaron dumped me, I was banned from the church, and now my own father was through with me. Tears began to roll down my face. Finally I reached into my bag and shoved copies of the cashier's checks into his hand.

"I didn't steal from the church, Daddy. It was a loan. I paid it back with interest. Look, see for yourself."

He looked down at the paper. "You really have a sense of entitlement, don't you? Maybe you found a way to keep your ass out of jail, Simone, but that still doesn't make this right."

"Daddy, I did the right thing when it was all said and done. Why can't you accept that?"

"You just don't get it, do you? I thought I raised you right, but I guess I didn't. I'm afraid for you, Simone. A woman like you needs a strong hand, from a good man." Daddy's voice turned a little more gentle. "Let me give you a little advice. That young man you were with, Aaron, he's the best thing that ever happened to you. I advise you to get married and have some babies with him."

"Well, that's not possible. We broke up because of you and your fake heart attack."

He shook his head, chuckling. "Somehow I doubt it was me that caused him to break up with you, but if I were you? I'd try to get him back."

"Daddy, why are you doing this to me? I'm your daughter, your only heir."

"Simone, if you were messing with the church's money, you didn't think I would realize you were probably screwing up mine too?" He sighed. "You've screwed up a lot of things here. Now, me and those two people out there have quite a job to do fixing it back up. Good-bye, Simone," my father said as he headed out the door. "I'll see you on Thanksgiving."

The Bishop

62

I was sitting in my office, taking one last look around. I'd closed my doors to keep from looking at all the unhappy faces as they moved boxes out to the waiting trucks in the parking lot. Hold on, let me stop lying to myself. I closed the door because I was starting to get emotional and didn't want anyone to see the tears welling up in my eyes. I'd spent most of my adult life preaching in this building. I just couldn't believe it was going to be gone in the blink of an eye.

First Jamaica Ministries' choir was good at last week's competition, but the judges didn't seem to think we were good enough to win. Personally, I thought that we'd won, but of course, I'm a little biased. We did receive a nice check for two hundred grand but that was nowhere near the three million dollars we needed to keep Maxwell from calling our note and closing our doors tomorrow morning. So, here we were, packing up to leave.

I'd shed quite a few tears over the past several weeks, more than I can remember shedding since my first wife passed away. Sadly enough, I'd buried my best friend of more than twenty years and found out my wife used to be intimate with my other best friend, who had basically lost his mind and was trying to destroy me by foreclosing on my church. I guess when you really looked at it, I had a few reasons to shed some tears. It was hard, but I was trying to stay optimistic.

We had our last Sunday service this morning. I preached a sermon on patience and understanding. I reminded the congregation that God won't give us more than we can bear. Perhaps it was His will that we move to a different location and start anew.

During the service, many of the women were crying. I saw tears in some of the men's eyes also. Heck, I shed a few myself. This was a dark moment in our church's fifty-year history. I had a lot of faith in the Lord, but this was the first time in years that I'd questioned His judgment. I mean, something had to give. I couldn't continue to be strong for everyone else without a glimmer of hope.

As I sorted through the papers from my file cabinets to pack them away, there was a knock on my office door. "Come in."

Mackie stuck his head in. I'd seen him only a few times since we'd returned from Washington, D.C. I was pretty sure he'd been avoiding me. From what my wife and Tia told me, he'd taken the second-place finish pretty hard. He was upset that he'd let me and the church down.

"Is there anything I can do for you?" he asked.

I glanced around the room. "No, I've got the rest of this, but thanks, Mackie."

"Okay. Hey, Bishop, can I talk to you for a moment?" He looked so downhearted.

I gestured for him to enter. "Sure. I've wanted to talk to you too."

Aaron stepped in and closed the door behind him. "I just wanted to say I'm really sorry, Bishop. I know I let you down, but if I have to spend the rest of my life doing it, I'll make it up to you."

"You didn't let me down. And you darn sure don't have anything to make up. You did your best, which was more than a lot of other people around here did. Besides, just because we don't have the church's building doesn't mean First Jamaica Ministries is gone. We'll rebuild. This isn't the first space we've ever been in."

Mackie looked more hopeful at my words. "I'm glad to hear that, Bishop. I've saved up a little money since I've been here. If I have to, I'll work for free. I'll do anything for the church."

"I know that, Aaron, but for right now, let's take everything one day at a time."

He nodded. "Okay, so what did you want to talk to me about?"

I sat back in my chair. "Well, I've got a little bit of good news for you."

"I could use some good news," he replied.

"So could we all. I spoke to a friend of mine down at the New York parole board." Aaron looked a little uncomfortable. "He's going to have your parole officer changed, effective today. You should be getting a call from your new PO this afternoon. You won't have to deal with that Andrew Gotti guy anymore."

A huge smile came across Aaron's face. "Wow, are you serious? Thank you, Bishop. Thank you so much. That man had it out for me. I couldn't do anything to keep him off my back."

"Well, you don't have to worry about him or his partner anymore." It felt good to do that for Aaron. I took it as a sign from God that even though we were going through some hard times, we would persevere—and I would continue my ministry. It was still my calling to look out for His flock, even in small ways such as this. God might present me with challenges, but He would also continue to present me with opportunities.

There was another knock at the door.

"Come in," I said.

Aaron made a move to get up and leave, but I told him to stay.

A strange white man walked through the door. He had *lawyer* written all over his face. I groaned inside. *Oh, my goodness. Not another one of Maxwell's lawyers.* We weren't supposed to be out until the next morning, but his people kept coming by to do inspections.

"Bishop Wilson?"

"Yes, how can I help you?" I leaned forward in my chair.

The man looked around and smiled. "From the looks of things around here, maybe I can help you."

"How's that?" Whatever he was selling, I sure wasn't in the mood to buy.

"My name is Byron Byrnes. I'm an attorney."

"No joke," I wanted to say, and from Aaron's demeanor, he seemed to agree with me.

"You were a friend of the late James Black, weren't you?" he asked.

"Yes, I was. What does this have to do with Mr. Black?"

"Well, I'm Mr. Black's attorney. I don't know if you knew this, but Mr. Black was a man of considerable assets." He set his briefcase down on my desk and took a seat next to Aaron.

I nodded. I didn't know how much he was worth, but I'd always known James was shrewd in his business dealings. He'd racked up a pretty penny or two, and a lot of property.

Mr. Byrnes continued. "His net worth was somewhere in the neighborhood of thirteen million. Unfortunately, with him being sick and incarcerated, he lost a little money during the stock market crash. But still, thirteen million isn't anything to sneeze at."

"Not at all!"

"Well, Mr. Black has a daughter and a son who are estranged from him, I understand."

"I don't know if I'd call it estranged, but they've been away for a while. I think his son is somewhere in Europe. I'm not sure where his daughter is."

"Well, with the absence of his children, he's made you administrator of his estate, the majority of which has been left to them to split equally if they should ever return or be located."

I smiled. "Good old James always made sure he provided for his kids."

"He also put money in a living trust for First Jamaica Ministries. The way he had it set up, you are the sole administrator and have decision-making power when it comes to all moneys in the trust."

"Wow, and he left some money to the church too." I looked at Aaron and said hopefully, "Hey, maybe we can pay off some of these debts and find a new home for the church after all."

Aaron looked skeptical. "Man, when my daddy died, it took forever for us to get that little bit of money he left."

"Yes, that's pretty common, but this trust is not like the items in Mr. Black's will, so we don't have to worry about probate." Mr. Byrnes pulled a folder out of his briefcase. "Now, I have some papers for you to sign, and then you gentlemen can go about your business."

"How much are we talking about here?" I asked.

He placed the papers in front of me and pointed to the color-ful tabs that marked the lines where I was supposed to sign. "Somewhere in the five-million-dollar range."

I stopped my hand mid-signature and looked up at him. "What did you say?"

"About five million." He started pulling out more papers from the briefcase. "Here are the bank papers and the check-book. I'll bring this signature card over to the bank so it's offi-cially the church's money."

I stared at this man for about fifteen seconds before the full impact of his words registered. Finally I turned to Aaron and let out a whoop of joy. "Praise God!"

Aaron joined me, hollering in elation and praise. He ran over and grabbed me, and we both started jumping up and down and carrying on.

"Hey, what's going on in here, T. K.? Why are you guys shouting?" I looked up and saw my wife.

Other members of the church came running in. When they saw Aaron and I hugging, one made a snide remark under his breath. "I knew this choir director couldn't stay straight but for so long."

I showed Monique the bank statement and the checkbook but never stopped jumping around with Aaron. "This is James's es-tate attorney. James has saved the church, Monique! He saved it!"

Monique looked at Mr. Byrnes for some clue as to what I was saying. He explained everything he'd told me and Aaron, and then she came over and threw her arms around me. "Oh, baby, this is wonderful!"

"Yes, God is always right on time, isn't He?"

Next thing you know, there were fifteen or sixteen people jumping around, dancing in my very empty office.

"What the hell is everybody so happy for? I told you to be out of the building by eight a.m. You haven't got half this crap out of here." Maxwell's gruff voice interrupted our celebration. He was accompanied by a small man who looked like another lawyer, as well as three goons. They were probably bodyguards, because he knew everyone at the church wanted to kill his behind.

I strode over close enough to Maxwell that the bodyguards moved in as if they were going to try something in this room full of witnesses.

I ignored them and asked, "How much do we owe you again?"

"Three million should cover it. What, you gonna write me a check?" Maxwell laughed hard, even slapping his lawyer on the back for dramatic effect.

I turned to Byrnes. "Can I write a check right now?"

Byrnes nodded. "As many as you want."

I took great pleasure in pulling out my pen and writing a check to Maxwell's traitorous behind. "Here's your three million dollars." I handed him the check. "Now, get the hell outta my church."

Maxwell looked down at it briefly, then threw the check back at me. "This is not even as good as the paper it's written on. You don't have that type of money."

"Yes, we do," I replied with relish. "This is Byron Byrnes, James's estate attorney. James left money in a trust for First Jamaica Ministries, and it's more than enough to pay the mortgage. There!" I threw the check back at him.

Maxwell turned to the sheisty-looking guy with him. "You're my lawyer. What can we do about this?"

The attorney shrugged as he studied the check. "As long as this check clears, it looks like there's nothing we can do."

"Oh, yes, there is something you can do," I said.

"What's that?" Maxwell asked.

"You can get the hell out of my building before I kick your ass out for trespassing!"

"This isn't over, T. K." He glared at me, then turned to my wife. "This isn't over by a long shot."

"Yes, it is, Maxwell." I placed my arm around my wife. "Now get out of my church."

Monique
Epilogue

It was sunset when I stepped out of my Mercedes and headed confidently toward the front door. I was on a mission, one that I hoped would finally put everything in my life into perspective. On the good side, we'd saved the church just in the nick of time and avoided bankruptcy, thanks to James Black's help from the grave. Yes, God had shown us favor. I just hoped He'd show me a little of that favor when I walked through Maxwell's door and then later, when I returned home to tell my husband all that had gone on between me and his ex-best friend. Yes, I was going to admit everything to T. K. If my husband was going to find out about this, then it was going to be on my terms, not Maxwell's.

I'd told T. K. I was going to visit some friends, although Maxwell was far from a friend. In fact, it was like I was going to face Lucifer himself. When T. K. kicked him out of the church the other night, I could see the desperation and anger in Maxwell's eyes. He had lost the battle for the church, so there was only one more way he thought he could defeat T. K., and that was by sleeping with me or telling on me. I'd been avoiding his calls, and he'd finally gotten bold enough to call my house today to demand that I come see him. I don't know what he would have said if T. K. had answered instead of me, but I wasn't willing to take that chance. It was time for me to put a stop to this.

He'd said "Get your ass over here" as if I were his personal slave. Maxwell was still under the impression that he had me by the curlies, and he could do and say whatever he wanted to me. He was never going to let this end peaceably, not as long as he thought he had T. K.'s supposed thievery over my head. Well, today I was going to bust his bubble and tell him which side of my ass he could kiss. He could no longer pose a threat to our marriage, and I wanted him to stop calling me or I'd have him arrested for harassment.

I took a deep breath, pulled my bag close on my shoulder, then rang the doorbell. I stared at Maxwell's lavish porch, feeling as if I were standing at the entrance to Sodom and Gomorrah.

Maxwell opened the door, and I noticed he was wearing the same smoking jacket he wore the morning he kissed me in front of Simone. The sash was loose, and his chest was revealed. I had no doubt he was completely naked underneath.

"Well, well, well, don't you look good?" he said, eyeing me up and down and smoothing his mustache in a suggestive manner.

I felt as if I was going to be sick just thinking about what he had on his mind.

"I've got some champagne by the Jacuzzi. Your favorite—chocolate-covered strawberries—too."

This man was blackmailing me, and he had the nerve to try to romance me, like I was going to have some sudden epiphany that he was the one for me. I gritted my teeth as I stepped inside. "I'm not here for champagne or strawberries."

"I know you're a woman who likes to get straight to the nitty-gritty, Monique, but the bedroom can wait a bit. I have about ten minutes until my little blue pill kicks in, so I thought we'd get started in the Jacuzzi." He didn't even give me a chance to speak. He just strutted back to his patio. Steam rose from the hot tub into the night air.

I followed him and watched as he slipped off his robe and eased into the hot tub. Like I expected, he was butt-ass naked.

"Come on in," he beckoned. "It's nice and hot, just the way I like it." He reached over and lifted a glass of champagne, as if seeing it would entice me to join him.

I shook my head. "Do you really think I'm going to get in the Jacuzzi with you? You must be crazy. I'm not getting into nothing with you."

"Come on, Monique. Don't be shy. I've given the entire staff the night off. We've got the place entirely to ourselves. Come on now, take off your clothes. It's going to be fun."

"I'm not taking off shit!" I folded my arms across my chest.

Maxwell laughed. "See, I hate to do things like this, but I think you've forgotten who has the upper hand here. You don't want me sending your precious T. K. to jail, do you?" He'd been telling that lie about T. K. for so long that it rolled off his tongue with ease, but it was my turn to laugh now.

"You know what, Maxwell? I've been waiting for weeks to tell you this."

"Tell me what?"

"That I know you were lying. That I know you forged those papers. That I know my husband is a good, honorable man, and you ain't never getting any of this ever again."

Maxwell's face was getting red. I wasn't sure if it was because of the hot tub or because he was so damn angry, but I was loving it. I decided it was time to twist the knife a little deeper.

"T. K. beat you, Maxwell. He won the woman, and he also won the battle for the church, which means he's won the war!" I laughed hard.

"He hasn't won a damn thing!" Maxwell splashed angrily. "I've got the senior housing property, and I'm going to make millions on it. So what, I didn't get the school or the church? I got to drag T. K. through the mud, and I'm still gonna be fucking his wife. Now, get your shit off!" he yelled.

"I ain't taking off nothing. What part of *we beat you* don't you understand?"

Maxwell flinched and an expression of pain crossed his face, but he pulled himself together and threatened, "If I were you, I would take my clothes off and get in this tub."

"Fuck you. Kiss my black ass." My voice was low, deadly. I was about to turn around and leave.

"If you don't get in this hot tub, Monique, I will call your husband and tell him everything." Maxwell motioned furiously. "I know him—he'll throw your ass out on the street."

"Go to hell, Maxwell. You can tell him whatever you want. He's not going to believe you. If he even agreed to talk to you, he would never believe a word that came out of your mouth. You've already proven yourself to be a liar."

"Maybe not, but I'm sure he'd believe the videos I took last time you were here. If I let those tapes out, it will make the Jackie scandal look like a walk in the park. Who wins then?" He gave me an evil grin. "As famous as T. K. is with all his books and DVDs we might even make the *National Enquirer* or TMZ. I always wanted to be a porn star. What about you?"

I felt shock ripple through my system. I had no idea he'd been taping us, but he did get up once and spend a bit of time in his walk-in closet, saying he was looking for some K-Y Jelly. At the time, I'd just been grateful to have a few minutes away from him, but now I realized he could have been fiddling with video equipment in there. Jesus Christ, what had I gotten myself into?

"Now, get your clothes off or go find a good divorce attorney, because you're gonna need one."

"You son of a bitch." I studied his face, realizing I had no choice once again. I reached for the top button on my blouse with tears streaming down my face. "Do you know how much I hate you?"

"You don't seem to hate me when I climb on top of you," he said with a smirk.

"I was faking to protect my husband."

Coldhearted bastard that he was, he completely ignored the distress in my voice and taunted me with, "Hey, why don't you do a little striptease as you undress?" I wanted to reach over and choke him.

I slowly undid a second button on my blouse, cursing my decision to come over here thinking I could end this whole thing. As my hand moved down to the third button, I considered begging Maxwell for mercy. To my surprise, he was the one who began begging.

He gasped loudly, and then his face tightened. He doubled over and moaned, "Oh, shit! Monique, help . . . me," he stammered.

I dropped my hands to my sides and looked at him with fascination. Clearly he was in pain, but I found myself having absolutely no feelings of sympathy for him. "Why? What's wrong with you?" I asked unemotionally.

He put his hands over his chest. "Call nine-one-one," he wheezed, slumping over again. "Please, I need to get out of this hot tub. I need a doctor. It's my heart."

I felt a brief impulse to reach over and help him out, but something inside me prevented my hand from touching his. I just stared at him. It did look like he was having a heart attack, but it was as if my feet were glued to the floor.

I was surprised by how calm I felt. If it were T. K., I'd be panicking and doing mouth-to-mouth resuscitation, because he was my life, but Maxwell . . .

"I need your help . . . please . . . ," Maxwell managed to say between short gasps for air.

"You know, Maxwell, you're not as smart as I thought you were." I clucked my tongue and shook my head. "Did you even read the health warnings about your favorite little blue pill?"

He reached his hand out to me. "Monique . . . help me! I don't . . . want to die!" he pleaded. I could tell he was struggling to catch his breath. His eyes looked haunted by some inner struggle, but strangely enough, they did nothing to move me.

"The warning says if you have a heart condition, you shouldn't use Viagra." I waved my finger at him. "And as for the hot tub, well, that is definitely a no-no for someone with a heart condition."

I watched Maxwell recoil in pain, but I didn't budge. It's a shame when you hate someone that much.

"You know, between the hot tub and that Viagra you've been taking, you probably are having a heart attack." I almost didn't recognize my own voice; it was so cold and flat.

"Go to hell, you . . . you bitch." Maxwell's voice was getting weaker.

"Yes, I am a bitch, and I'm probably going to hell for all that I've done and been through, but one thing's for sure: It looks like you'll be there before me. Tell Satan hello for me."

I stayed there and watched as Maxwell slumped over, his body locking into a fetal position and his head going underwater. I waited until the bubbles around his face stopped percolating. He was no longer breathing.

I fixed the buttons on my blouse, put my Coach bag over my shoulder, and headed for the front door, never looking back. I thought about returning to the house and looking for the tapes, but then it came to me. Like everything else, Maxwell was probably lying. He didn't have any cameras outside his house that I could see. What would make me think he had any inside the house? It was finally over. And the best thing about it was that with Maxwell gone, I didn't have to tell T. K. a thing.

Discussion Questions

1. Would you have left your church if you found out the male choir director was sleeping with men in the congregation?

2. Were you surprised when Aaron's first pastor returned to his house, and did you think he was going to shoot him?

3. Aaron was paid over seventy-five thousand dollars to come and work for First Jamaica Ministries. Do you think Bishop's offer was too high?

4. Were you shocked by Smitty's death? And did you think he was murdered?

5. Did you think Aaron was going to be gay when you first started reading?

6. There was a lot going on in Aaron's life. Did you think he was doing something criminal when Andrew Gotti kept showing up at the church?

7. Do you think Simone was really in love with Aaron?

8. What were your feelings about Tia?

9. Who was your favorite female character in the book?

10. Did you think Maxwell was going to end up being a villain?

11. Rank this book from one to ten, with ten being the best.

12. Were you shocked by Monique's actions? Could you sleep with a man to protect the one you love?

13. Did you think the bishop might have robbed the church?

14. If you were Tia, would you have believed Aaron was a rapist?

15. What did you think of James Black, and were you sad that he died?

16. Do you think Monique had anything to worry about when she walked out of that house without looking for the tape?

17. When it was all said and done, would you have told the bishop about sleeping with Maxwell if you were Monique?

18. Would you like to read another book with Aaron Mackie?